THE BLOOD PHOENIX

AMBER CHEN

PENGUIN BOOKS

PENGUIN BOOKS

UK | USA | Canada | Ireland | Australia
India | New Zealand | South Africa

Penguin Books is part of the Penguin Random House group of companies
whose addresses can be found at global.penguinrandomhouse.com.

www.penguin.co.uk
www.puffin.co.uk
www.ladybird.co.uk

First published in the USA by Viking, an imprint of Penguin Random House LLC, 2025
First published in Great Britain by Penguin Books, 2025

004

Printed and bound in Great Britain by Clays Ltd, Elcograf S.p.A.

The authorized representative in the EEA is Penguin Random House Ireland,
Morrison Chambers, 32 Nassau Street, Dublin D02 YH68

A CIP catalogue record for this book is available from the British Library

ISBN: 978–0–241–62439–5

All correspondence to:
Penguin Books
Penguin Random House Children's
One Embassy Gardens, 8 Viaduct Gardens, London SW11 7BW

To all the girls who dare to dream –
these seas can never trap those who are meant to fly

CHAPTER 1

WOULDN'T IT BE NICE TO SPEND FOREVER accompanied by the silence of the seas?

The thought floated through Aihui Ying's mind as she lounged inside her tiny vessel, a bubble-like capsule big enough for one, staring through the yun-mu glass window at the schools of fish swimming by.

Down here, there was no ruckus from playful children or irate market vendors, no whirring of airship propellers or horns from docking ships, not even the cry of a condor or the rushing of waves against the shore. Just peace. Silence.

She found herself yearning for such pockets of quiet these days, which was why she'd sped up work on her latest creation, affectionately nicknamed the Octopus. It was a submersible craft propelled by the mechanical undulations of bronze tentacles, fitted with a kaen-gas bag that functioned like a fish's swim bladder. From afar, it looked exactly like its namesake—a giant, golden octopus.

Ever since she helped old Eidu fix a retractable fishing net onto his rickety boat so he would no longer have to cast nets by hand, she had received daily visitors at her front door clamoring for assistance with trivial tasks, believing that engineering would be the solution to all their woes. For the most part Ying was happy to help, but the constant fuss that invaded her life also meant that she barely had space to think. Or to indulge in haw candy.

She took a large bite out of the candied fruit on its bamboo skewer, letting the sweet and sour flavors explode in her mouth.

"Mmm."

Best haw candy across the nine isles.

Unfortunately, such tranquility was destined to be short-lived.

Moments later, the very important guests that she had been waiting for showed up in a burst of whitish sea-foam, kicking up a cloud of bubbles with their graceful tails. A pod of bearded seals out on the hunt—not expecting that today, they would be the hunted.

Through the glass she saw someone waving at her from another Octopus, trying to catch her attention. He pointed down at the vessel's control board, signaling that it was time for them to conduct their test.

"I've barely made it halfway through my candy," Ying grumbled. Reluctantly, she tossed her skewer aside, focusing on the myriad buttons and levers in front of her. Maneuvering a wooden control shaft, Ying carefully repositioned her vessel so it was facing the approaching herd, then she pulled down the periscope and peered through the glass. Her index finger readied upon a button the size of a weiqi piece.

One, two—

"Damn."

A harpoon fired from the concealed hatch on the neighboring Octopus, its glinting silver tip completely missing its mark. The frightened seal herd scattered.

Glaring out through the yun-mu window, she pointed one accusatory finger at her incompetent companion, then reached for the lever that controlled the vessel's gas bladder, shoving it down to inflate the sack. The Octopus slowly rose, eventually bursting through the water's surface. She steered the golden orb toward the shore, popping open the exit hatch and hopping out once she hit land. Clutching a coarse rope, she dragged her Octopus over to a makeshift wooden shelter a little farther up the shore, where a neat row of three other orbs sat in wait.

"Ying, I'm sorry!"

A tall young man with a healthy bronze tan and nimble limbs clambered out of his own vessel. Dragging his Octopus along the sand, he jogged to catch up with her, the long braid on his half-shaven head bobbing as he went.

"It was an accident. I know I should have waited for your cue, but my finger slipped! I really didn't mean to mess things up," he apologized.

"I already said that you didn't have to come with me."

"It's safer that way. The seas are unpredictable." The boy wrangled the rope out of her hands, taking over the chore of parking both their vessels. "I promise I won't make the same mistake the next time."

"What makes you think there'll be a next time?" Ying muttered, rolling her eyes.

Jangmu Feng-kai was considerate to the point of being utterly exasperating, so she couldn't be angry with him even if she wanted to. She had tried to provoke him into losing his temper several times to no avail. Compared to the boys back on her home isle of Huarin, or those she had known in the Engineers Guild, Feng-kai was genuinely the most accommodating, thoughtful, and mild-mannered person she had ever met. She should consider herself lucky to be matched with such a fine specimen of a boy—at least that was what everyone deigned to remind her of on a daily basis.

Two years ago, after the debacle of her running off to Fei and enrolling in the prestigious Engineers Guild, her older brother, Wen, had been furious. He hadn't spoken to her for a full three months after she returned to Huarin, and he locked her in her ger to reflect on her mistakes. Then the Jangmu clan of Larut came knocking with an unexpected request—for Ying's hand in marriage.

If she had continued to stay on Huarin, she knew that Wen would force her to marry eventually, and she was certainly not entering into any political marriage like her brother wanted. If she had to leave, then she would leave on her own terms. So here she was on the isle of Larut, engaged to Feng-kai, her childhood acquaintance and the son of one of her father's closest friends.

Perhaps it was A-ma watching over her from above, helping her to spread her wings and fly once more. Or to run away. The memory of her father's loss still brought an ache to her heart. Time had slowly mended those wounds, but the scars would always remain.

Ying sat herself down on the soft sand and turned her gaze toward the open sea, glistening a brilliant azure blue under the sun's illumination. She had once stood beside another boy upon the city walls of Fei and admired these same seas, and he had promised her the world. Funny how she could still remember that moment as if it were yesterday.

Ye-yang used to write to her every now and then, but she had burned every letter without reading them. It hurt to see his familiar brushstrokes on each envelope, reminding her of his betrayal. The letters stopped after the announcement of her engagement to Feng-kai nine months back, as she'd thought they might.

Was he angry? she sometimes wondered.

In the initial days, she had feared that he would show up on Hua-rin and take her back to Fei, but her worries were unfounded. Even up till the day she set sail for Larut, Ye-yang didn't appear. Why would he? He was the High Commander of the Antaran isles now, and there were far more pressing issues that needed his attention.

"A-ma's getting impatient. He's been asking after the progress of the Octopus," Feng-kai said, walking over to join her. His sunny expression turned somber. "More and more fishermen are refusing to go out to sea because of the pirates."

The recent surge in pirate attacks on fishing vessels was causing great anxiety to Feng-kai's father—the clan chief. Piracy had always been a problem in the Dunzhu Straits, the strip of sea that lay between the nine isles and the Qirin empire, but the situation had worsened ever since the former High Commander, Aogiya Lianzhe, passed away two years back. The Jangmu clan relied largely on the trade of seafood to survive, so the livelihood of the people on Larut would become a serious problem if things continued to spiral in this trajectory.

"I've already told him many times that the Octopus isn't going to solve his problems," Ying replied, wrinkling her nose in disdain. "It can't even catch a seal, much less pirates."

"Could we not fit some sort of defensive weaponry onto them? Something that could help us buy time for our boats to escape if there's an attack?"

She could hear the hopefulness in Feng-kai's voice, optimistic as ever. He sat down beside her and began tossing stray seashells into the water.

"You think too highly of me," she said with a sigh. "We don't have the materials to build anything beyond a fishing harpoon. And even if I *did* have all the resources of the Engineers Guild at my disposal, I still wouldn't be able to build something that could make a dent on a Demon's Blade."

The Demon's Blades were rumored to belong to one of the most notorious pirate fleets that sailed the straits, known only as the Blood Phoenix. Ying had never actually seen a Blade before, but she had heard enough about those horrifying deep-sea monstrosities from the mouths of frightened sailors to be able to paint a decent picture in her mind. These were gargantuan vessels with streamlined bodies supposedly resembling a sharpened cleaver, and propellers large enough to rival the Cobra's Order's biggest airships. Unlike regular ships, the Blades were hidden beneath the water's surface, slicing through the depths of the ocean.

No one knew how the pirates came to control the Blades, but they were the reason the Cobra's Order was struggling to eradicate the pirate threat from the straits. It was difficult to fight an enemy you could not find.

It was also why the Jangmu chieftain had been so enamored with her idea of building a submersible when she had first pitched it to him. If the Antarans had eyes under the sea, then the pirates and their Blades would no longer be invisible—nor invincible. Unfortunately, the Octopus was only designed to catch seafood, not pirates.

Feng-kai shrugged. "If anyone can figure out a way to defeat the Blades, my bet's on you, Ying," he said, flashing her a bright smile.

Optimistic and annoying, as always, Ying thought.

Feng-kai's perpetual cheeriness often grated against her nerves, through no fault of his. Facing his upbeat and positive outlook on life was like looking in a mirror and seeing everything she was not, emphasizing the gloom and guilt that still haunted her dreams. When she closed her eyes each night, she still saw the blood that stained the curved blades of her flying guillotine, still saw the unblinking eyes of the former High Commander, judging her even in death.

"Well, A-ma only cares about the pirates, but E-niye . . . You told her that we'd postpone the wedding ceremony till after the construction of the Octopus." Feng-kai pointed toward the row of golden orbs. "Now we already have five."

Ying buried her face in her hands. "Feng-kai, you know that this entire engagement—"

"Is only an act. Yes, I know that. You never let me forget," her friend said. His smile faltered. "Are you really planning to leave, though? Where will you go?"

"I don't know. Explore the world," she replied, staring out at the horizon. From here, all she could see was the shimmering surface of the Dunzhu Straits. Somewhere across this patch of sea lay the shores of the Empire—and beyond that, who knew?

The Antaran isles were her home, yet it didn't feel like she belonged here anymore. No matter how hard she tried, she couldn't forget the time she had spent in Fei and at the Engineers Guild. As long as she remained here, there would always be something that would force those memories to resurface. Her friends' banter, the guild masters' lectures, his forlorn yet determined silhouette, and her own bloodstained hands—all these voices and images kept invading her mind when she least expected it, triggered by a nut, a bolt, or a lotus lantern set afloat by a hopeful child.

So she was choosing to escape. Like a coward.

She had made it clear to Feng-kai from the start that this engagement was only a temporary arrangement, an act that would allow them both to get what they wanted. For her, an escape from her brother's control; for him, a dowry large enough to help tide the Jangmu clan over after last year's crisis, when a freak hailstorm had destroyed more than half the village.

"But how are you even going to make it across the Dunzhu Straits? Hardly any trade ships ply the routes between the nine isles and the Empire anymore, and even if you find a ship willing to make the journey, it's still too dangerous!"

Ying smiled. "I'll find a way," she said.

Feng-kai didn't know that she had secretly started making adjustments to her Octopus, steadily increasing its speed and durability so that one day it might take her all the way across these straits. There was still quite some way to go before it would achieve what she needed it to do, but she was confident that she would get there soon.

"Is there nothing that might make you want to stay?" Feng-kai asked.

Ying knew that he was looking at her, but she kept her gaze pinned upon the sea. She was well aware that Feng-kai harbored certain hopes about their relationship, hopes that maybe time would change her mind about things, turn their charade into a reality, but she could not give him the answer he wanted.

She had given her heart away once—and she wasn't sure she ever got it back.

"I'm sorry, Feng-kai," she said softly.

He clapped her on the back and let out a jovial laugh, but she could detect the slight disappointment threaded within. "Don't apologize. Like you said, we agreed on this from the start. You delivered your half of the bargain, so I'll deliver mine," he said.

"Feng-kai! Come on, it's time to go!" a loud voice hollered at them from afar.

Some distance down the shore, a group of boys had gathered with fishing harpoons and nets in hand, waving at Feng-kai and Ying.

"You're still going out to sea? It'll be dark soon," Ying said.

Feng-kai picked himself off the sand, dusting the grains off the back of his black cotton trousers. "That's when the conger eels come out," he replied. "A large order came in from Muci. We'll have to work extra hard to make up the numbers, since some of the older fishermen are still unwilling to return to the seas."

"Pity. There's roast goose at the tavern tonight."

"Save me a goose leg. I'll be back in about two hours."

Ying scoffed. "What makes you think I'll do that, after you cost me my harpoon test and a seal? I'm going to eat the entire bird myself."

Feng-kai grinned, then waved and broke into a jog to catch up with the other boys. Ying watched as the group disappeared in the direction of the fishing wharf. Then she turned her gaze back toward the calming sea and the warm, amber glow of the setting sun.

Ru-er's tavern was arguably the most notable establishment on the isle of Larut, and for good reason. There was no cook across the nine isles, including the capital of Fei, who could rival Ru-er's skill in the culinary arts—because she simply was not Antaran.

Wei Ru-er was Qirin.

She had arrived on the isle of Larut last year after being rescued by one of the fishing boats, dehydrated and barely alive. They had found her floating on a piece of driftwood after a storm, because she had—quite foolishly—attempted to cross the entirety of the Dun-zhu Straits in a regular fishing sampan, in search of her husband who had gone missing at sea.

With the dwindling in civilian strait crossings following the rampant piracy and rising tensions between the nine isles and the Empire, Ru-er had no means of seeking passage back to her home-town, so she stayed. Initially, the villagers on Larut had been wary of her, but Ru-er quickly won them over—through their stomachs.

Ru-er's tavern was located upon the gently sloping plains with the twinkling night sky as its roof, bordering the mushroom-capped gers of the village. Ying settled down at her regular spot, warming her hands in front of a toasty fire while waiting for her goose to be served.

"One roast goose and one bowl of dumpling soup, on the house," a middle-aged woman with violet threads woven into her braids called out, smiling broadly as she walked over, balancing a wooden tray in one hand. In her other hand, she waved a clay jar. "And some milk wine. Freshly brewed!"

"I can't finish all that, Ru-er." Ying laughed.

The tavern owner set everything down on the grass, then wiped her oily palms against the cream-colored apron tied around her shapely waist. "Isn't that boy of yours coming to join you?" she asked.

Feng-kai was in no way "hers," but Ying didn't bother correcting Ru-er. There were appearances she needed to keep up, and as far as everyone on Larut was concerned, she was supposed to be getting married to Feng-kai soon.

"I don't know. They've gone out for the night catch," she replied, glancing down at the glistening, crispy skin of the goose. Since Ru-er had given her free food, she might be charitable enough to save Feng-kai the leg after all.

To Ying's surprise, Ru-er sat herself down instead of returning to the kitchen.

"Don't you have many orders to be getting back to? You don't have to keep me company. I'm fine on my own," she said, wondering if the tavern owner was doing this out of pity for her lonesome self.

Ru-er chuckled. "If they want to eat my food, then they can wait," she said, placing a hand on Ying's shoulder. "The chieftain's wife stopped by earlier, wanting to discuss the menu for your wedding banquet."

"W-w-wedding banquet?"

"Indeed. Twenty taels, she said, for a feast that will impress even the High Commander!"

The High Commander?

Ying spluttered on her mouthful of wine, the pungent beverage shooting right up her nose. Ru-er burst out in laughter, giving her a few kindly pats on the back.

After Ying had regained some composure, Ru-er continued, this time more solemnly. "You don't love him, do you?" she asked.

Ying bit down on her lip, fingers fidgeting with the wine jar in her hands.

Was it that obvious? So far, no one in the village had questioned the legitimacy of her relationship with Feng-kai, so she had always assumed that her ruse was foolproof. Ru-er was the first.

"I can tell, because I know what it's like to truly love someone. Friendship, yes, kinship, certainly, but love? You've never looked at that boy like you love him, although I can't say the same the other way around."

The tavern owner stared into the flickering flames with a distant look in her eyes, and Ying guessed that Ru-er was thinking about her husband again. She must have loved him very much, to have tried sailing the treacherous waters of the Dunzhu Straits just to get him back.

"I don't know what you're talking about," Ying denied, plucking at the grass by her feet. A tinge of sourness tickled her nose—partly from the wine, mostly from her guilt.

"Is there someone else? I can't think of a better reason why you might close yourself off to someone like Feng-kai."

The memories of Ye-yang that she had carefully locked away in the recesses of her mind came flooding back to the forefront. She remembered every chiseled angle of his face, the warmth of his embrace, the exact shade of gray in his stormy eyes—and the pain of his betrayal. Two years had helped to smooth over much of the turmoil within her—the grief from her father's death, the anxiety of infiltrating the guild, the nightmare of Aogiya Lianzhe's blood on her blades—but the wound left by Ye-yang was still tender and raw.

The anger had faded, but the hurt remained.

Sometimes she wondered if things could have been different between them if Ye-yang had been honest from the beginning, if he had told her the truth behind her father's death, if he hadn't made use of her to further his ambitions of becoming High Commander. But there was no what-if. No changing the past.

The thought made a lump rise up in her throat.

Ru-er swung an arm around her shoulder, giving her a comforting squeeze. "It's fine. You don't have to tell me about it if you don't want to," she said. "I just thought I'd offer some words of advice, as someone who's been through a little more. Don't settle. That's what a lot of people do. They settle—for someone they can get along with, or someone who can provide. If you ask me, it's far better to live alone than to subject yourself to a life with someone you do not love, because that would be unfair to you both. Now, shall we—"

A loud explosion rang out. The ground beneath their feet rumbled.

From the direction of the coast, a bright flare shot up into the night sky, erupting into a magnificent image of a soaring phoenix.

"What's that?" Ying wondered.

Ru-er let out a strangled cry. "The mark of the Blood Phoenix," she whispered, undisguised terror in her voice. The tavern owner muttered a prayer in the Qirin language as she scrambled to her feet. "Hurry, we must help, before it's too late."

"Help? Help who?"

There was no answer, because Ru-er had already taken off sprinting. As she ran, the tavern owner repeated the same cry for help to the other villagers, gesturing for them to follow her to the beach.

Ying tilted her head back toward the sky, where the phoenix still hung like a fiery harbinger, wings outstretched and beckoning. An inexplicable fear stirred within her gut.

She got up and ran.

CHAPTER 2

THE GARDENS OF QIANLEI PALACE WERE UNDENIABLY beautiful. Camellias were blooming in vibrant shades of vermilion and blush pink, contrasting with the warm golden tones of the chrysanthemums. Every now and then, a soft plop echoed from the gourd-shaped pond as a curious koi leapt out for a glimpse of the world above, almost colliding with the dragonflies trailing their rainbow wings against the water's surface.

As beautiful as a gilded cage could ever be.

The tip of a sword pierced through the air, forceful, perhaps overly so, but with the slightest hint of a tremble.

A nimble figure leapt up, back arched as she threw herself into a sideways rotation, in perfect synchrony with the dramatic rise and fall of the zither's melody. The flowy silk fabric of her periwinkle sleeves and long skirt spun gracefully as she moved, creating a harmonious tapestry with the floral blooms that surrounded her. The blade of her sword drew a perfect arc above her head, reaching the end of its trajectory just as the heel of her left qixie touched the stone floor.

To be a lone rock in the middle of a flowing river.

To be that sharpened blade in the face of a thousand enemies.

Her slender fingers tightened around the bronze hilt of her sword, tiny rubies glinting as they caught the sunlight. In her mind, she continued reciting the lines to her mother's favorite poem, trying to embody the essence of each word with the movements of her lithe limbs.

To be the calm amid a raging storm.

The rhythm of the strings began to pick up, and she struggled to keep pace. Pearls of sweat beaded across her forehead despite the chilly breeze. Her right heel wobbled with a tiny misstep, threatening to throw her off balance.

A strong arm caught her around her waist, stabilizing her for the briefest of moments, then spinning her out again. Her breath hitched. One round, two rounds, and with the third, she sprang up and took flight, sword pointing toward the stone statue of two intertwined cobras that sat by a twisting juniper. Beside her, a young man in black court robes unsheathed his own serpent-hilted sword and followed suit, matching her dance moves with even more confidence and precision.

Their eyes met. Their swords touched. Their palms struck, sending each other in elegant backward cartwheels through the cold air until their feet touched the ground once more. The wooden fingers of the mechanical zither player strummed the final note, its melancholy reverberating until only silence remained.

"Much better than before. You've been practicing." Aogiya Ye-kan, the fourteenth prince, smiled as he slid his blade back into its sheath.

"Not good enough," Aihui Nian replied. She walked over to the stone table by the pond and set her blade down. Had Ye-kan not shown up in time, she would have fallen and likely sprained her ankle. She considered herself a seasoned dancer, but sword dances had never been her forte. They required a conviction and composure that she had not yet mastered.

"Don't be too hard on yourself. Nobody's expecting you to be perfect."

What if they do? What if I *expect myself to be perfect?*

"*I trust you, Nian,*" her brother had said to her before she set sail for Fei. "*I trust that you'll know what's best for the clan.*"

Nian gazed down at her own reflection in the pond's glassy surface. A beautiful young girl stared back, with her face exquisitely powdered and lips dabbed with rouge, long hair pinned up with gold hairpins inlaid with opalescent kingfisher feathers.

She could barely recognize herself.

It had only been six months since she arrived at the capital, but already this awe-inspiring but frightfully grim environment had stripped her of who she used to be. Her laughter, her smiles, her hopes and dreams—all of it felt like a faraway memory, left behind on the Huarin grasslands.

A pebble hit the pond surface, skipping three times across the water. Her reflection rippled, then vanished.

"Isn't it a bit cold to be practicing outdoors today?" the prince quipped. He poured them cups of pu-er tea from the porcelain teapot sitting on its brazier. "And where are your servants? Skiving?"

Nian shook her head. "I sent them away. They were fussing too much." The palace attendants had a tendency to overreact to the littlest things. As if she were made of porcelain and could shatter at the barest touch.

It was better out here on her own, far less stuffy than her quarters. When the occasional breeze blew by, she could close her eyes and pretend that she was back home on Huarin.

"What brings *you* here? Did you have a meeting with"—she caught her tongue, swallowing the name that she had been about to say back down her throat—"the High Commander?"

Despite having been here for several months and knowing that she would eventually marry Ye-yang, the former fourth beile and incumbent High Commander of the Cobra's Order, there still existed a gulf between them that she couldn't bridge. The High Commander had been nothing but kind to her since she arrived, but that kindness was always tinted with a touch of brotherliness, making her unsure of how to navigate this relationship and her position in this palace.

Perhaps it was a good thing that their wedding ceremony had been postponed in light of the High Command's recent preoccupation with the pirate and Qirin refugee crises. It gave her more time to parse through her own feelings about being here, to figure out where exactly she was supposed to stand.

"More pirates, what else?" Ye-kan answered brusquely. "They're being a real hindrance. We were supposed to recommence the military campaign against the Empire last month, but that's all in shambles because our ships can't make it across the Dunzhu Straits. Our airships are useless without cover from below." He snorted. "You know what's even funnier? We actually received a message from the tenth isle this morning, with the Monggu clan offering to help us defeat the pirates. *Help?* From those traitorous bastards?" A flash of fury blazed across Ye-kan's dark irises.

Nian frowned, her eyes quickly surveying their vicinity. Thankfully there was no one else close by. "Don't talk about these things in the open. You never know who's listening," she warned.

"You worry too much. Even if someone tries to sell me out, do you think they'd succeed?" the prince scoffed.

Ye-kan had had his title raised to beile a few months ago, after he successfully led the bannermen in a raid of the Southern Rays, exterminating the pirate fleet there completely in a swift and ruthless attack. Although he had technically replaced Ye-yang as the fourth beile of the High Command, everyone still called him Number Fourteen out of habit—and he had since become known as the fourteenth beile. He had also been given command of the Plain White Banner, which had previously been under Ye-yang's control. With his star on the rise, it was no wonder the youngest prince of the Aogiya clan was walking around the palace these days with a wind in his step.

Still, it was better to be cautious.

Sipping her tea, she pondered the pirate situation and the tenth isle—Yokre. Before coming to Fei, she had diligently studied many records detailing the history of the High Command and the Aogiya clan. The conflict between the Monggu clan of Yokre and the Aogiya clan of Fei had reached a climax when she was only a young child—in the early days of the unification of the nine isles by the former High Commander, Aogiya Lianzhe. Refusing to submit to Aogiya command, the Monggu clan had sought an alliance with the Qirins instead. Tension between the two clans reached a deadlock, eventually leading to the exile of the tenth isle by Aogiya Lianzhe, its people branded as traitors.

What she found interesting though, was the relation that the Monggu clan actually had with the Aogiyas.

Ye-yang's mother had been from the Monggu clan, and the incumbent clan chief—Monggu Yutai—was Ye-yang's maternal uncle. With Ye-yang at the helm, Nian wondered if the strained ties between the tenth isle and the High Command would begin to ease.

"The cessation of trade must be affecting the tenth isle as well. Perhaps that's why they are offering to help," Nian suggested. "Maybe they're sincere about mending relations with the High Command?"

"Sincere? Monggu Yutai asked for control of two entire banners and the isle of Larut in exchange for his so-called help. *Two banners and a whole isle!* A-ma used to say that Monggu Yutai's greed knows no bounds, and he was right."

At the mention of the late Aogiya Lianzhe, the light in Ye-kan's eyes dimmed. Nian knew that he had been reminded of the loss of his parents once again. Although Ye-kan did not bring this up often, she knew that their unexpected passing two years ago continued to weigh heavily on the young prince's mind. It was the reason why he had given up what was once his greatest ambition, engineering, and thrown himself entirely into the war effort. He was trying to do his parents proud—as was she.

"A-jie wrote to me about a week ago," Nian said, swiftly changing the topic.

"What did she say?"

"That everything's fine on Larut. Jangmu Feng-kai is treating her well, and she's made some progress on her latest engineering project. Something about underwater exploration?"

Ying had spent most of the letter rambling about her latest creation, which Nian could hardly comprehend. Still, she was happy to know that things were going well in Ying's life, after the fiasco following their a-ma's death. She shuddered at the thought of how furious their brother Wen had been after Ying's return from the guild, and she had truly feared that he would have Ying thrown into a wicker basket and drowned.

"Doing so well that she can't even bother to reply to *my* letters?" Ye-kan mumbled, looking miffed.

"I'm sure it's only because she's incredibly busy. You know what she's like when she's working on something," Nian said comfortingly.

"Not too busy for you."

"I'm her sister!"

"Well, the next time you write to her, tell Aihui Ying that I'm renouncing our friendship if she continues to discriminate against me like this. I'm a beile now. Does she think that I have so much time on my hands to send letters to check on her? Throwing my good intentions to the wolves . . ."

Nian shook her head, amused at how the supposedly formidable beile had devolved into a petulant child.

Truthfully, she had not learned about her sister's friendship with the fourteenth prince until she arrived in Fei and Ye-kan showed up at her door unannounced, assuming the concerned older brother role of his own volition. Ying and Ye-kan had been apprentice candidates together at the Engineers Guild, but somehow Ying had never mentioned this before.

Many things about her sister seemed to have changed after her time in the capital. The Ying who returned was quieter and more withdrawn, like there was a dark cloud hovering above her, casting a shadow over her once-vibrant personality.

Her a-jie wouldn't tell her why, and when she tried to ask Ye-kan, the prince only hemmed and hawed, refusing to divulge anything either. Something had happened in Fei, something to do with their father's death, something that Ying and Ye-kan wanted to shield her from.

If only she were stronger. Wiser. Then maybe they would deem her worthy of sharing this burden.

"I'll be sure to carry your message to her," she replied, moving to refill their tea.

The prince blinked. "No! No, don't do that. I didn't actually mean any of it," he said hurriedly. Then he saw the half smile on her face and scowled. "You're just making fun of me. You Aihuis are all the same. I wonder why I even bother with the likes of you."

"Hurry up! If the High Commander's medicine gets cold, I'll have you whipped!" A shrill voice drifted to their ears. It belonged to one of the palace's chief stewards, the infamously crabby Nergui. He was at the far end of the gardens, heading toward Chongzheng Hall—the High Commander's study. Behind him trailed a timid attendant balancing a small porcelain bowl upon a wooden tray.

"You met with the High Commander earlier, didn't you?" she asked Ye-kan.

"If you're meaning to ask if he's unwell, then the answer is yes. I would have the world's worst migraine too if I hadn't slept for three nights in a row. Number Eight has always had a problem with recognizing his own limits. I swear he thinks he's invincible sometimes."

A migraine?

Her father used to get migraines every now and then, from staying up too late in his workshop toiling over his engineering projects.

Nian stood up.

"Ye-kan, I'm sorry, could you excuse me? I just remembered that there's something I need to do." Without waiting for the prince's reply, she quickly left the pavilion, heading back to her quarters.

What if he throws me out?

Nian stood outside the ornate latticed folding doors of Chongzheng Hall, clutching a circular silver container. Several times she raised her hand to knock, then let it slide back down again. She was about to beat a hasty retreat when the doors swung open, revealing the portly figure of the High Commander's other chief steward, Hitara Qorchi. He blinked in surprise, then quickly bowed.

"Lady Nian, what brings you here? Are you here to see the High Commander?" he asked.

Qorchi was far more pleasant than Nergui, which also made him the more popular of the two chief stewards. Nian's anxious heart settled a little.

"I know he's busy, but . . ." She bit down on her lower lip, holding out the silver case. "This is a balm for migraines, made from an old Huarin herbal recipe. Could you maybe pass it to him?"

"Qorchi, who is it?" a mellow voice echoed from inside.

The steward smiled at Nian. "Lady Nian, why don't you give it to His Excellency yourself?"

"Oh, that won't be necessary. I can just leave it and go—"

Still in mid-protest, Nian found herself nudged across the threshold and through the doorway.

The High Commander's study was a large, somber room with an oppressive aura, threatening to swallow her whole. Two rows of thick nanmu pillars lined each side, carved with the winding bodies of serpents that evolved into fearsome dragons soaring among the clouds. A long desk made from expensive huanghuali wood, its curvaceous legs carved into the image of fearsome cobras, sat at the far end. On it, a small rack of hanging brushes and other writing implements stood alongside a towering pile of unread scrolls.

The only item that felt strangely incongruent with the rest of the room was a small octagonal lamp that sat on the opposite corner of the desk, its wooden panels carved with images that Nian could not make out. It reminded her of the lamps that her father used to make—not something the High Commander should own.

A tall young man with broad shoulders stood behind the desk, with his back to the door. The braids of his hair were fastened around the back of his head with an intricate gold cuff, molded with the crests of waves. He was staring up at the huge tapestry hanging from the wall—a map of the nine isles, its surrounding seas, and the eastern border of the neighboring Great Jade Empire. On the map were numerous circular wooden pieces, kept fixed to their positions by the lodestones embedded within. She quickly located the piece labeled "Fei," a diamond-shaped slice of land with ink strokes outlining its layered cityscape and winding canals.

"Your Excellency, Lady Nian is here," Qorchi announced, promptly shutting the doors and leaving Nian alone with the High Commander.

A dozen spiders ran amok in the pit of her stomach as her nerves began to unravel, but it was too late to regret her decision to come here. She took a deep breath and walked closer.

"What do you make of our current situation, Nian?" the High Commander asked, still studying the map.

"E-e-excuse me?"

"The situation of the nine isles." Picking up a long bamboo stick, he casually flicked two black pieces off the map entirely, then shifted several others away from the center of the Dunzhu Straits and back to the western edge of Fei. "We've lost two of our airships during the last skirmish, and seven ships from the Bordered Yellow Banner's fleet have been recalled due to severe damage, but our enemies"—he tapped on the red pieces sitting at various positions along the straits—"have barely suffered a scratch. Tell me, has the Order become so weak?"

The High Commander turned to face her, left brow arched in wait. His silver-gray eyes pierced toward her, forcing an involuntary shiver down her spine. Although he was only a few years older than she was, he carried himself with a gravitas and solemnity that made him appear far beyond his actual age. It was to be expected, she reasoned. How else would he be able to command the Eight Banners of the Cobra's Order and rule over the nine isles?

Still, he intimidated her, his aura making her shrink in his presence.

She frantically shook her head. "Of course not, Your Excellency."

"Then why?"

Ah, it was time for another lesson.

In the early days of Nian's arrival to the palace, their meetings had been painfully brief, with barely more than two sentences passing between them, usually revolving around the weather and how she was settling in. Then, unexpectedly, she beat him in a game of weiqi, sweeping his final black seed off the board.

After that, each meeting became part lesson, part exchange of ideas. Their conversations evolved into discussions on strategy, with the High Commander mentoring her on a range of topics from history to politics to social dynamics within the nine isles. Sometimes Nian wondered if he viewed her more as his protégé than his prospective wife, but then she'd quickly dismiss the idea. Who was she to think that she was worthy of his tutelage?

This was, however, the first time he was engaging her in discussion on an actual problem plaguing the Cobra's Order, a discussion that she rightfully should not be allowed to partake in.

This was *trust* of the highest order.

The thought of that sent ripples of pride through the still waters of Nian's heart.

She looked past his shoulder and up at the hanging map, carefully studying the various counters in play. The black pieces representing the Cobra's Order outnumbered the scattered red pieces of the pirate fleets significantly.

Then why were they losing?

"Because the pirates have a hidden weapon that we cannot counter? Or perhaps there's someone within the Order who's working with them, helping them stay one step ahead." She clapped a hand over her mouth, appalled at how the words had simply spilled out. Just because Ye-yang had invited her to air her thoughts didn't mean that he would welcome the suggestion that they were harboring traitors within the High Command. She dropped to her knees. "I apologize, Your Excellency. I've said too much."

"Not at all. I asked the question, you merely answered," Ye-yang replied. He reached over and lifted her gently by the elbow, helping her to straighten back up. "You're very perceptive—and correct, on both counts. How then might we be able to turn the situation around?"

Nian instinctively backed away, staring down at the floor. Her heart leapt at his praise, yet at the same time she had the urge to flee.

Sucking in a breath, she said, "We weed out the enemy from the shadows."

"Very good. Much better than Number Fourteen. His preference is to use brute force to eliminate the remaining pirate fleets, by using our advantage in numbers against them." Ye-yang shifted almost all the remaining pieces representing the Order's fleet toward the middle of the straits, until the black overwhelmed the red.

It was very much aligned with Ye-kan's character, Nian thought. The fourteenth prince was brash and highly impatient, so it was unsurprising for him to opt for what seemed to be the quickest, most direct way to victory.

"What's your assessment of Number Fourteen's solution?"

Nian carefully studied the new formation on the map, then she ventured a hesitant reply.

"Even if we manage to defeat them using sheer numbers, the cost to the Order will be great. It'll also leave Fei and the other isles undefended. That's far too risky."

Ye-yang nodded in approval, then turned his attention back to the map. "Unfortunately, sometimes the threats from within are greater than those from without," he replied quietly.

Nian opened her mouth to ask him what he meant, but the doors to the study were abruptly flung open, cutting her off before she even began. A flustered Qorchi rushed in, sweat lining his forehead.

"Your Excellency," he cried, waving a missive in his hand, "we've received an urgent report from Larut!"

"Larut?"

Ye-yang immediately spun around, snatching the message from his steward's outstretched hand.

Isn't that where A-jie is?

Nian stepped aside, knowing that her audience with the High Commander was over. She kept a watchful eye upon Ye-yang, curious to know what the report said.

Ye-yang's expression darkened as he skimmed the page, fingers tightening around the parchment until it crumpled at the edges. In that moment, Nian noticed something different in him. There was anger in the way he locked his jaw—and a hint of fear in his stormy eyes.

For the first time, she saw emotion in him. For the first time, Aogiya Ye-yang felt *human*.

"Prepare an airship. I'm going to Larut," he ordered, marching straight for the doors.

"Right away, Your Excellency," Qorchi replied, jogging behind his master.

Left forgotten, Nian shifted her gaze back to the map on the wall, locating the isle of Larut, north of Fei. Ying described Larut as nothing more than a sleepy fishing port. What sort of an emergency could have arisen there? And more importantly, what could have possibly triggered those emotions in someone who she had believed was made from stone?

CHAPTER 3

THE SHORES OF LARUT HAD DESCENDED INTO chaos.

People were wading waist-deep into the sea to retrieve arriving sampans, hulls littered with holes and decks aflame. The wounded were being hauled to land on the backs of the able-bodied, blood staining their faces and clothes, leaving them unrecognizable. Shrill orders were screamed into the cold night air as the village's leaders tried to restore order amid the mayhem.

And still the boats kept streaming in.

It wasn't only Larut fishermen. There were bigger trade ships bearing flags of the other isles, even dozens of Qirin refugees, wearing coarse cotton robes with their long hair hanging disheveled around frightened faces.

"Shift the dead over there," Ying shouted to one of the chieftain's deputies, pointing at a grassy patch farther inland. Then, lowering her voice, she said, "We have to separate those who can be saved from those who can't. If they're not going to make it, move them to the space outside the boat repair sheds. Lay out some straw mats to make them comfortable. Everyone else can be taken to Ruer's tavern—the physicians are already there."

The deputy nodded, hurrying away to execute his orders.

An unconscious man with blood streaking down the sides of his face was rushed in the direction of the repair shed. This shed would become his final resting place, an entire ocean away from his hometown.

A pang of grief surged through her, bleak as the smoke-filled skies.

I hope at least you'll find some comfort in the blanket of stars. However little that might be, in one's dying moments.

Stemming her melancholia, Ying surveyed her surroundings. It had been over three hours since the mark of the phoenix burned in the sky. By now, even its final smoky vestiges had vanished with the sea breeze, yet the horrific aftermath had barely begun. Already the pile of corpses they had pulled from the burning boats and freezing seawater was enough to fill a sizable ger—and the number was set to grow.

"Where's Feng-kai?" she mumbled, searching through the crowd for any sign of her friend. He had been out at sea when the attack had taken place, but she held on to hope that he would escape unscathed. After all, he was Jangmu Feng-kai—the pride of the clan, as strong as he was resourceful, who never failed to look after everyone in times of need.

But now that she finally had a pause to breathe, threads of worry began to weave their way into Ying's mind.

Surely he should be back by now? Unless . . .

The more she let those thoughts sit, the deeper the sense of foreboding became. She pressed a hand across her heart, willing it to stop thrumming.

No, it can't be. Feng-kai's fine. Maybe he stayed behind to help.

That had to be it. He would never leave another in the lurch, even if it meant putting himself at risk. Feng-kai was foolish that way.

Not far from where she was, Feng-kai's father, the Jangmu

chieftain, was standing by the water's edge with the waves rushing over his leather boots. The burly man was stock-still, eyes glazed as he stared out at the carnage before him.

Ying quickly walked over.

"Shi-ye, are you all right? Do you need help with anything?" she asked, addressing the chieftain by what everyone on the isle called him—the tenth lord. He was famously known to be the tenth and youngest son of the family, who somehow managed to outlive all his older brothers to become clan chief. The lucky one, they said.

After a long bout of silence, the chieftain finally spoke.

"I was hoping I wouldn't live long enough to see a day like this," he said slowly, with a deep sorrow that hung upon every word like a winter's fog. "Did I do something wrong, Ying? Should I have invested more in the isle's defenses? Asked for more support from the High Command? Was it because I was complacent?"

"You did what you could, Shi-ye. It's not your fault," she said, even though she knew her words would bring scant comfort.

The injured, the dead, the brokenhearted survivors—every one of them was a familiar face to him. Family. Now he was being forced to watch his home, his family, crumble into ashes before his eyes.

Her own heart was aching, crying, despairing at the death and destruction that she had witnessed over this single night, much less his.

"Sometimes our best is simply not enough," the chieftain replied.

"Shi-ye! Shi-ye!" someone came shouting. It was Tabai, another of the chieftain's deputies. The gangly man wore an ashen expression on his sweat-covered face as he ran up to them.

"They salvaged a sampan farther up shore. The young master—he . . . he . . ." Tabai's voice trailed off, tears glistening in his eyes as they reflected the cold moonlight. The grief suffused in his voice, written on his face, was enough to spell out the rest of the message he had come to bear.

Feng-kai's father closed his eyes, the slight tremble of his shoulders betraying the pain within. As if the deaths of his clansmen were not enough, Abka Han had to punish him with the death of his only son.

Ying reeled, heart sinking like a stone to the bottom of the sea. Fear rattled within her chest.

"That's not possible."

There had to be some mistake.

She had to see for herself, else she would not believe such nonsense. Turning in the direction that Tabai had come from, Ying ran.

It's just a case of mistaken identity. There's too much chaos. Didn't Madam Birya wrongly identify a Qirin refugee as her own son?

There was no way it could be Feng-kai. He was Abka Han's blessed. He once sailed into the eye of a horrific storm to rescue a stranded merchant ship and returned with only two scratches. That was no less dangerous than a pirate attack. If he could survive that, then he could survive—

An anguished cry ripped through the air with the intense pain that could only come from a mother's broken heart. Feng-kai's mother was kneeling on the sand, cradling a fallen silhouette in her arms. Her tear-stricken face was raised to the skies, as if begging for a miracle.

The air was snatched out of Ying's lungs. Her steps slowed.

Feng-kai lay in his mother's arms, eyes still wide open and staring up at the inky darkness—except he wasn't the same Feng-kai that she had waved goodbye to mere hours ago. His right sleeve had been torn off and a section of his arm was missing, severed midway up his bicep to leave only a bleeding stump. His robes were drenched with blood and seawater, tattered in so many places to reveal mangled patches of flesh embedded with shrapnel.

Ying bit down hard on her lip to stop herself from screaming. Her fingers clenched, nails digging into her flesh until it bled.

"The young master went back to save more people, but they fired the cannons and, and . . ." The fisherman who had been recounting the tragedy broke down and wept, pressing his forehead against the sand, as if to beg for forgiveness. "Without him, we would not have survived."

His words would mean nothing to Feng-kai's distraught mother, whose tears continued to flow as she hugged her little boy close to her chest. Ying stepped forward and placed a hand on the woman's shoulder, if only to tell her that she was not alone. She swallowed her own tears, willing herself to stay strong.

"Do you know who did this?" Feng-kai's e-niye asked, her voice trembling and wreathed with sorrow.

"The Blood Phoenix," Ying replied. All she knew was that it was a notorious Qirin pirate fleet that had recently been sighted more frequently on the Antaran half of the straits. Everything else about the fleet was a mystery.

Feng-kai's mother turned and looked up at her, streaks of red lacing the whites of her eyes. Despair blossomed into anger, and anguish hardened into blades of steel.

"I want them dead. *Every last one of them.*"

Three days after the attack, they sent off the dead on pyres of fire that burned upon the bloodstained shores of Larut for an entire day and night. It went against tradition, but there were simply too many to bury. The final death count stood at sixty-seven, of which more than half were nameless souls who were not from this isle.

Ying stood before the charred remains of the funerary pyres in her white mourning robes, staring at the mounds of blackened soot that remained. A gust of wind blew, carrying a cloud of ash up into the air and out toward the open sea.

Feng-kai would be happy to be able to travel the world in this manner.

While he was alive, he had always been too duty-bound to stray far from home, dedicating much of his time and energy to serving his clansmen. He had told her many times about how envious he was that she'd had the chance to venture to Fei and witness its magnificence firsthand. He wanted to do the same, but there was always one reason or another that prevented him from going.

Go now and take a look at those towering pagodas and winding canals for yourself. Maybe then you'll believe me when I tell you it's really not so special after all.

Ying blinked back her tears.

What if she had held him back and not let him go out to sea that night? What if she had treated his suggestions about the Octopus more seriously? Could she have created the defensive tool that Shi-ye had wanted, that Feng-kai had believed she could?

But there were no what-ifs.

She hadn't stopped him from going. She hadn't turned her submersible into anything more than a glorified fishing boat. All she had done was think of herself, think of how she was going to run away.

"Ying!"

She quickly wiped away the dampness from her cheeks before she turned to face Tabai, who was striding over from the village's direction. The chieftain's deputy still wore dark circles around his eyes, his shoulders drooping with weariness as he walked.

"Is Shi-ye looking for me?" she asked.

While Feng-kai's mother had collapsed with grief and barely found the strength to emerge from her ger to attend the funeral rites, the Jangmu chieftain had pressed on with remarkable stoicism, continuing to attend to the myriad issues that needed his attention. Despite that, Ying knew that Feng-kai's loss, and that of so many of his fellow clansmen, weighed heavily upon his heart. Shi-ye was merely too responsible to let his own sorrow come before affairs of the clan.

Tabai nodded. "We have a visitor. Shi-ye wants you to join them at the chieftain's ger," he said, turning to lead the way back.

"Who is it?"

"Someone from the capital. Hopefully they're here to provide aid. Almost a quarter of our fishing boats didn't make it back, and those that did have been badly damaged. More refugees are also streaming in, but how are we going to feed them? We barely have enough supplies to keep our own clan afloat!"

Ying paused before she shook away the stray thought that had come to mind and continued keeping pace with Tabai.

It can't be him. There must be a thousand more important things for the High Commander to attend to than a pirate attack on a small isle.

Still, the thought of having to face someone who came from Fei left her unsettled. What if it was someone she knew? How was she supposed to behave then?

Those questions swirled in her mind till they arrived at the doorstep of Shi-ye's ger. The chieftain's gruff voice could be heard drifting from inside the white-walled tent, describing the refugee settlement situation with a tone of deference that was unfamiliar. Only someone of considerable standing could warrant such subservient behavior from the chieftain. The uncertainty and nervousness inside her continued to unspool.

Tabai knocked on the cinnabarine latticed door, pushing it open to announce their arrival.

"Ah, Ying, there you are." Shi-ye beckoned for her to come in. "I was just discussing the pirate threat with the High Commander, and mentioned your work on those deep-sea scouting vessels. His Excellency thinks there's great potential there."

Shi-ye's voice continued buzzing in the background, but Ying could register none of it. The moment she stepped in, her gaze landed upon the all-too-familiar silhouette of a young man seated at the front of the tent beside the Jangmu chieftain. A regal black fur cloak was draped upon his square shoulders, braids bound back in a high ponytail that highlighted the sharp angles of his jaw and the gold cuffs around his ears. He looked up from his cup of tea and toward her, the liquid silver of his eyes bringing back a flood of memories she thought she had locked away for good.

"It's been a while, Ying," Ye-yang said, the barest of smiles hanging upon his lips.

"Ying," Tabai hissed, tapping her at the elbow.

Snapping out of her stupor, Ying moved forward and bowed, fist to chest in formal greeting. "Your Excellency," she said, the words spilling stiffly from her tongue.

"I'm happy to hear that you haven't left your engineering skills to rust," Ye-yang continued, seemingly unperturbed by the frosty reception. "The guild's loss has been the Jangmu clan's gain. When are you planning on returning to Fei?"

"*Returning* to Fei? The guild?" Shi-ye looked momentarily confused, then his graying brows dipped in a frown. "Why did you not mention this sooner, Ying?" he asked, sounding miffed at having been caught unawares.

When her engagement to Feng-kai had been negotiated, Wen had intentionally left out all mention of her transgressions in Fei and the Engineers Guild, because "no clan would dare take you in otherwise," he declared. Ying had no quibble with that. She was more than willing to lock that chapter of her life away and pretend it never happened.

"I'm not—"

"Shi-ye, could you step outside for a moment? There are some things I wish to discuss with Ying—in private," Ye-yang interrupted, not giving Ying a chance to finish. His tone remained cordial, yet there was a pointedness to his words that made it clear that this was not a question. It was an order.

Shi-ye obediently stood up from his chair and gestured for Tabai to follow him out. As he brushed past Ying, he gave her a light nudge with his elbow. A reminder of the numerous requests that the clan needed the High Commander to grant in order for them to tide over this crisis. The ger's door swung shut, leaving Ying alone with Ye-yang.

Silence steeped between them, thick and uncomfortable, and two years of distance suddenly felt like not very much at all. He looked much the same as the last time they bade farewell—same angular jawline, same stern brows, same aquiline nose—yet there was also something different. The gravitas in his aura had intensified—resembling his father, the late High Commander, far more than she liked. In these two years, he had come into his own as leader of the Cobra's Order, earning the respect and loyalty of those under his command and becoming a formidable presence that the Antaran people turned toward in these difficult times. Looking at him now, she could see why.

Yet he also looked . . . tired.

There was a weariness etched into every line on his face, more creases lining his forehead than she remembered. Frowning had always been a bad habit of his, whenever he was deep in thought, or whenever nightmares plagued his mind. His broad shoulders also sagged a little more, as if the invisible burdens he carried upon them had grown heavier with time.

Looking directly into those clear gray eyes, she wondered what he saw in return. Had *she* changed? Or was she still the same Ying who had turned and walked away from him two years ago?

"How are you?" Ye-yang asked.

Ying flushed, looking away. She suddenly wished that Shi-ye and Tabai hadn't been so quick to leave. At least with them around, she could continue pretending that she was only Aihui Ying, the girl who had been widowed before she was even married, instead of the Ying who once foolishly tried to conquer the apprenticeship trial of the Engineers Guild while seeking justice for her father's death—the Ying who got her heart shattered in the process.

"I'm sorry for what happened. It must have been terrifying," he continued.

A pause.

Ying continued to stare at her feet, waiting. Waiting for what he had to say next. Waiting for herself to come up with an acceptable response.

The answer was not what she expected.

Strong fingers grasped her by the left arm, pulling her into a warm embrace. His arms wrapped themselves around her shoulders, pressing her cheek against his chest. The faint, steady rhythm of his beating heart echoed in her ear. Then there was the familiar fragrance of tie guan yin that enveloped her, the autumn notes and floral scent she had come to associate with him.

A light gasp escaped her lips.

"Do you know how worried I was?" he said, resting his chin against the top of her head. "Thank Abka Han that you're safe." His voice was soft, tender, without the authoritative edge that she had heard earlier. Each word was like a gentle caress upon her heart, trying to convince her to let him back in.

A tinge of sourness tickled the tip of Ying's nose. Had he truly come here because of her? That fleeting thought had crossed her mind when she first stepped into the chieftain's ger, but she'd promptly rejected it. It was too incredulous and self-important. She was nobody in the grand scheme of things.

And he should allow her to continue thinking that way.

Pressing her palms against his shoulders, she slowly pushed him away and took a step back.

"I'm fine, Your Excellency. I'm sorry to have caused you any inconvenience," she said, trying hard to pull back the tears that had begun to pool in her eyes. When he moved forward, she moved back, refusing to let him bridge the gap between them. His jaw clenched, exasperation showing.

"Ying, must it be this way? It's been *two years*. Surely that's enough time for us to put all the unhappiness behind us? To move on?"

"I thought I already made it very clear back then." That there was no turning back time. He had lost that chance from the moment he chose to lie to her about her father's death. She had given up that chance when she flung a blade into his father's heart.

"And I thought *I* had made it equally clear that I was going to come back for you, Ying," he replied. "Come home with me. You've been away long enough."

"I'm not going anywhere. *This* is my home now."

Frustration sparked in Ye-yang's eyes. Jealousy rearing its ugly head. "Jangmu Feng-kai is dead. Whatever engagement that existed between you is void. Even if he was still alive, did you think that I would actually let you marry him?"

"It's not up to you to decide," Ying retorted, anger boiling up inside her. How dare he speak of Feng-kai in this callous manner? Belittle her choices like this?

"I know you, Ying. This is not the sort of life that you want nor deserve. You wouldn't be content trapped in this fishing village, becoming the wife of an ordinary man . . ." He hesitated, a hint of suspicion resting on his lips. "Or maybe you weren't intending to marry him at all. Where were you planning to go, Ying, with those underwater vessels of yours?"

Ying swallowed hard. How had he seen through her plan so easily? She had told no one about it, not even Feng-kai, yet Ye-yang had read her like an open book. She hated that feeling of vulnerability—how she couldn't keep things a secret from him, even though he had kept plenty of secrets from her.

"I don't know what you're talking about," she replied tersely. "Stop presuming you know everything, Ye-yang. You don't know what I want. You've *never known*." If he did, he wouldn't have used her the way he did, wouldn't have lied to her and betrayed her trust. If he hadn't done any of that, then she wouldn't have left him in the first place.

He stared at her, shoulders stiffening and fingers balling into tense fists by his sides.

"Fine, then you won't mind if I requisition all your prototypes and have them brought back to Fei so that the guild masters can study them further."

"You can't do that!" Ying exclaimed, eyes flaring with indignance. She had poured months of sweat and tears into creating the Octopus, yet he could rob her of it with the snap of his fingers.

A curve of a dimple appeared on Ye-yang's face, as if he was pleased with her reaction. "Come back to Fei, Ying," he repeated. "The Engineers Guild is where you belong, where your ideas can truly take flight. I can give you all the resources you need—as long as you don't use them to run away."

"No." Ying swiveled on her heel and headed for the door. It was impossible trying to argue with Ye-yang when he clearly wasn't going to take no for an answer. It was a waste of time to keep trying.

"What about if I throw in the approval to all the requests that Shi-ye has asked for? Additional food supplies to help them cope with the low fishing yields; manpower to repair their damaged ships, and to help settle the refugees; increasing the sea patrols around Larut's waters so that their fishermen and traders are better protected. Everything they need to overcome this crisis, I can give to them. My only request is that—"

"I go back with you."

Ying closed her eyes and took a deep breath before slowly exhaling. This was a bargain, and also a threat. Her powerlessness in the face of his authority was a blow to her pride, a reminder that she had never truly escaped his control. Might *never* be able to escape, as long as she remained within the nine isles.

She pushed the door open and walked right out.

"I'll give you some time to think it through. My airship will leave Larut tomorrow." Ye-yang's voice echoed after her.

She didn't look back.

CHAPTER 4

LATER THAT NIGHT, THE ROARING FLAMES OF bonfires lit up the grassy plains. The first strains of chatter rang out in the air as the people of Larut began to pick up the pieces of their broken lives. The dead had moved on—and so must the living.

Ru-er's tavern was open for business again, and she was tirelessly serving up hefty portions of roast meats and dumplings to her hungry guests. Ying was one of them, sitting alone as usual, away from the noisy crowd.

Tonight, there was another reason why she was reluctant to join in. Ye-yang was there, partaking in the welcome feast that Shi-ye had generously thrown in his honor. He was seated beside the chieftain, engaging in polite conversation with a congenial expression on his face. Everyone seemed quite taken by the High Commander, particularly some of the unmarried girls of the clan, who were hovering in the vicinity like flies.

Ying ripped off a goose leg and placed it on a plate.

"Here's the roast goose I owe you," she murmured to the skies before pouring a small cup of wine across the grass. A farewell gift to a good friend.

Someone placed a comforting hand on her shoulder. "He'll get your well wishes. Your gods will carry your words to him."

Ying looked up to find Ru-er standing behind her, an

encouraging smile on her flushed face. "I hope so," she replied, although deep down she didn't really believe that. Her faith had never been strong, and witnessing so much bloodshed could well have destroyed the last remnants of it.

When she turned back, her gaze met Ye-yang's, and her lips puckered into a scowl. Could he not give her a moment of peace? Was it not enough that he was forcing her to make such a big decision overnight, that he needed to continue behaving like a thorn in her side?

Anger coursed through her veins. The gall that he had to be making use of the entire isle of Larut as leverage to coerce her into returning to Fei.

I don't have to go back, she thought.

There was a merchant ship heading to Noyanju at daybreak, and she could easily stow away without anyone noticing. But Noyanju was still within Antaran territory, and all of the nine isles belonged to him. What if he found her again? Also, her conscience wouldn't let her abandon Shi-ye and the people of Larut, not after all the kindness she had received from them.

"It's him, isn't it?" Ru-er suddenly asked, knocking her out of her daze.

"Huh?"

The tavern owner had settled down beside Ying and was helping herself to some wine from the jar. "Him"—she pointed toward Ye-yang with her free hand—"the one you can't let go of."

Ying balked at the incisiveness of Ru-er's remark.

"No!"

"No need to deny it. It's written all over your face. Now I know why Feng-kai never stood a chance. He was a good kid, but when you put him next to a boy like that"—Ru-er tipped her head in Ye-yang's direction—"then there's no competition to speak of."

"It's not like that," Ying argued. "Do you even know who that is? He's the High Commander! The equivalent to your emperor." She clapped her hands over her cheeks, trying to hide the flush of embarrassment.

Ru-er shrugged. "Shi-ye told me when he gave me a hundred and one instructions about what to prepare for tonight's feast," she replied. "But High Commander or not, he's still only a boy, and a boy who is quite infatuated with you, from the looks of it. He's turned this way at least a dozen times already."

Ying groaned, taking a swig of wine from her cup. Had he? She wasn't keeping count because she was too busy trying to be invisible.

"I don't know what happened between the two of you, and how you ended up here, engaged to someone else, but maybe this is heaven's way of giving you a second chance," Ru-er continued, giving her a squeeze on the shoulder. "Life is too short for regrets, Ying. Don't wait until you've lost someone before you realize how much they mattered. Don't make the same mistake I did."

"Sometimes there are no second chances," she whispered.

Just like how Feng-kai would never get a second chance at living life.

She sighed, letting the alcohol burn down her throat, hoping that it would burn away the guilt that was crawling up her spine. Guilt at being the one sitting here. The one who survived.

If Ru-er knew what had transpired between her and Ye-yang, maybe she would not be giving the same advice. It was too difficult to forget the past, not with their fathers' ghosts lying between them.

Ye-yang stood up and made his way over to her.

"What does he want now?" she muttered.

Ru-er stood back up. "Looks like you have company," she declared. The tavern owner swiftly excused herself with a knowing smile, retreating back to her kitchen.

"Your Excellency," Ying greeted, bringing her fist stiffly across her chest.

To her surprise, he said nothing in return. Instead, he sat himself down and picked up *her* wine jar, taking a big swig. His cheeks were flushed and his gaze unfocused as he stared into the bonfire. Somehow, this version of Ye-yang felt painfully familiar.

"You've been drinking too much again," she complained. Surely by now he should have learned what his own limit was.

"It would be rude to turn down their generosity," he replied, gesturing at the festivities on the plain. One could easily forget that this isle had experienced great tragedy mere days ago, given the level of fanfare they were according to the High Commander's visit.

"Yet you would deny them the aid they require and use them as pawns to get what you want."

Ye-yang leaned back on the grass, slipping his hands casually behind his head. Ying stared at him, aghast. She quickly surveyed their surroundings to check if they had caught anyone's attention.

"What are you doing!" she hissed.

"Don't worry. They think I went to relieve myself, and they're too drunk to notice otherwise."

Ying was not convinced, keeping a wary eye on the revelers. Shi-ye certainly looked inebriated. Red-faced and wobbly on his feet, he had begun enacting one of his usual tall tales in front of the riotous crowd. The chieftain was using the wine to numb his pain—and it hurt her to see that.

No one else was looking their way. Hopefully the cover of the shadows from the nearby bushes would be enough to hide them from view. The last thing she wanted was for a scandal to erupt. Even though her engagement to Feng-kai had only been a farce, she did not want to disrespect his memory by being caught up in a rumored tryst with the High Commander.

"If you want to make yourself less conspicuous, then maybe—" Ye-yang grabbed her by the arm and pulled her down. Ying landed hard on her back, and a myriad of stars greeted her from the darkened skies. She tried to sit back up, but the tight grip of his fingers prevented her from doing so.

"Aogiya Ye-yang, let me go!"

A mirthful laugh escaped his throat. His fingers relaxed, leaving only a light, tingling touch upon her skin. "Thank you, for still being the only one willing to use my name," he said.

Ying fell silent. Since his mother's death, Ye-yang had always been alone. He had subordinates and rivals, but no true family nor friends. Things could only have gotten worse after he took on the mantle of High Commander. How had he spent these past two years? He must have tried to tell her, in those many letters that he wrote, but she had fed them all to the flames.

You did the right thing, she told herself. She didn't need to know. How Ye-yang lived his life was none of her concern. He had lost the right to her sympathy a long time ago, when he chose to trade in her trust for secrets and lies.

"I know I was a little heavy-handed when I spoke to you earlier," Ye-yang said. "I'll accede to Shi-ye's requests and provide the aid that Larut requires, regardless of your decision, although I may not be able to grant as much as he's hoping for. As High Commander, I have a duty to the people—to *all* the people of the nine isles."

Ying turned to look at him, blinking back her surprise. He wasn't going to use this against her anymore?

"Remember I once told you that war with the Empire is a necessity?" he continued, tone somber. "That if we don't fight, we'll die?"

Ying remembered, but she still believed that there had to be another way. That was what her a-ma had taught her, that there would always be a peaceful resolution to any problem. She had already strayed from her father's wisdom once, in the name of revenge, and it had left her with scars she could never erase. She vowed never to do that again.

The Antarans had coexisted with the Qirins for centuries, albeit uneasily. Although border clashes happened from time to time, tensions between them had never escalated to the point of a full-fledged war before.

"We cannot afford to wait any longer, Ying. Piracy across the

Dunzhu Straits has spiraled out of control. Someone is supporting these pirate fleets, giving them supplies, weapons, intelligence, everything they need to prevent our warships and trade ships from crossing these waters."

"The Qirin court?"

"That is one possibility, yes."

"But surely rampant piracy also harms their own interests? Look at the number of Qirin refugees that have been flooding our shores!"

"Perhaps they view it as a necessary sacrifice. There are Qirin interests, and then there are Qirin interests. What the royal court cares about can be vastly different from the cares of an ordinary fisherman."

A shadow cast itself upon Ying's mind. She had heard stories from Ru-er and the other refugees, about how pirates had mercilessly raided and fired upon any ship that came into sight, how they had been forced to abandon the bodies of their brethren to the depths of the ocean and had floated to the nine isles on the backs of driftwood and debris. To think that their suffering could be at the behest of their own emperor and court officials was horrific.

"Whatever their plan is—it's working," Ye-yang continued. "Our land is already reaching its limits, and our harvests are dwindling every year, yet the refugee situation keeps bringing more people to us. If we cannot find a way to rid ourselves of the pirates and open up the straits once more, then there is no future for our people. They are suffocating us, Ying." He turned toward her, gaze earnest, flecks of silver dancing in the gray. "That is why I need your help."

Ying could feel his warm breath against her cheek and the giddy scent of the wine tickling her nose, but she pretended not to notice, keeping her eyes leveled at the stars. "What could I possibly help with? You have the entire Cobra's Order at your command, and the resources of the Engineers Guild. If they can't give you the answers you need, then neither can I."

"The guild masters have been trying their best, but they've been working on this for too long. They are far too mired in their own circles of thought that they cannot see beyond. They need a new perspective, a new idea. Something like your 'Octopus'—I believe that's what you call it?"

Hearing Ye-yang bring up the Octopus time and again left an inexplicable twinge of bitterness at the back of her throat. Would he even have come for her if he hadn't been aware of her invention? Maybe not. He was here because she was of use to him again.

"It's only good for fish-watching," Ying mumbled.

"With the guild's resources at your disposal, it can become far more than that, and you know it." Ye-yang sat up, pointing at the boisterous party going on. The drums had been brought out, and villagers were dancing around the bonfires. "I know you won't do this for me, Ying, but I'm hoping you will do it for them. Not just Larut, but all the nine isles."

Ying folded her arms squarely across her chest, her mind sieving through all the reasons to turn him down. She was but one inconsequential engineer. There was no way she could succeed where so many other guild masters had failed. No one in the guild would be happy to see her return, anyway, not after she had deceived them by entering their trial in the guise of a boy, then rebuffed their offer of acceptance when they extended it to her.

Besides, why would she want to go back to Fei, a place that harbored so many painful memories?

Then she remembered how Feng-kai had smiled and waved goodbye before he left for that final fishing trip, the setting sun drawing a close to his brief but well-spent life. She remembered the anguish on his mother's face as she held his body close and swore vengeance upon the Blood Phoenix. She remembered the blood and tears that had flooded the beaches of Larut that night, and the flames with which they had sent their dead off with the wind.

Tonight, the people of Larut danced and sang, yet there was a trace of sorrow that lingered in the gaiety. Grief that they would carry with them for the rest of their lives.

What if Ye-yang was right, and she *could* make a difference? Wasn't this what her a-ma had been preparing her for—to use her skills to help those in need?

Maybe if she had returned to the guild earlier, if she had put more effort into refining her submersible design, then Feng-kai would not have died. Maybe she could have helped to defeat the pirates, helped save all those innocent souls who were now damned to an eternity upon the seas.

Maybe this was all hubris, and it would amount to nothing.

Still, she had to try. She had to do something to atone for everything she hadn't done, to assuage the guilt at being the one who survived.

She picked herself off the grass and stood up, turning to head back to her ger.

"Where're you going?" Ye-yang called after her.

"If we're leaving in the morning, then I have to pack, don't I?"

A shrill cry rang out from a lone condor circling the skies above. A blessing—or perhaps a warning.

Wish me luck, Feng-kai.

Only time would tell if this was the right choice.

CHAPTER 5

FEI WAS EVERYTHING SHE REMEMBERED—AND YET it was different.

Ying sat in a steam-powered carriage with expensive silver trim around its polished black façade, gazing out through the sheer curtains draped across the windows. They trundled across one of the towering arched bridges of the capital, with numerous waterways crisscrossing several stories below. Passersby jostled shoulder to shoulder as they went about their daily business—traders hawking colorful earthenware and skewers of golden-brown spun sugar, students rushing to class with bamboo carryalls stuffed with scrolls, servants balancing baskets of meats and vegetables. There were even a few chimeras striding beside exquisite palanquins—a white tiger with silver legs, a stag with bladelike antlers—guarding their wealthy owners with their fearsome half-beast, half-mechanical bodies.

Everything about Fei felt familiar, with one glaring exception.

"I didn't expect to see so many refugees here," she murmured.

Ten, twenty, fifty—so many that she lost count.

They were almost invisible, blending in to the background with their coarse threads and weary faces, drifting along the cobbled streets like mere shadows to Fei's affluent residents.

"Like I said, the situation has been worsening. Fei has not been spared. Already there are many who have petitioned the High

Command to close our gates to these refugees," Ye-yang replied, his lips set in a grim line.

"Close the gates? And leave them to *die*?" If Fei were to shut its doors, then the refugees hoping to seek shelter would be relegated back to the violent oceans, where they would be at the mercy of either pirates or the harsh elements of nature. Ying could hardly believe the cruelty and selfishness of those who dared suggest such a thing.

Even Larut, with what little they had, had never broached the possibility of turning these people away.

Ye-yang nodded. "I've managed to fend off their demands so far, but this isn't a long-term solution. If this continues, then I may eventually have to shut the gates, for the sake of our own people." He looked across at her and smiled. "It's only your first day back. No need to be overly burdened by such matters. How about paying a visit to Nian? There must be many things you'd want to catch up on."

Nian.

Ying quickly shook her head, keeping her gaze leveled toward the passing cityscape. "No," she replied, trying to ignore the churning in her gut. "Don't tell Nian that I'm here."

Nian was one of the biggest reasons why she was reluctant to return to Fei.

She missed her sister dearly, yet there was a certain guilt that continued to gnaw away at the back of her mind. Guilt for the many secrets that she was keeping. Even being here in the same carriage as Ye-yang felt like she was betraying Nian in some way.

She could not risk Nian finding out about her past relationship with Ye-yang. She couldn't bear to break Nian's heart.

If things went smoothly, then she would be away from Fei as soon as she could, before the ghosts of her past caught up with her. There was no need to complicate things by alerting Nian to her presence.

Ye-yang sighed. "You know that I prefer for you to stay within the palace. Things are a little unstable in Fei right now. The palace would be far safer than the guild."

"Is that an order?" she snapped. He had already tried to convince her multiple times on their journey from Larut to Fei, and obviously wasn't taking no for an answer.

"I would never order you to do anything against your will."

"Yet here I am."

The carriage turned a corner, and the imposing stone walls of the Engineers Guild came into view. Heavy wooden gates swung open to let them through, and the unsmiling guards flanking both sides raised their fists across their chests in respectful salute.

When they pulled to a stop, Ying slowly alighted, eyes fixed upon the long flight of steps that led up to the fortresslike compound looming above. Once upon a time she had scaled those steps, bright-eyed and eager to prove herself. To belong.

Now, staring at those same stairs, there was none of the excitement and trepidation from before. Dread wormed its way through the cracks in her mind, anxiety turning her palms clammy.

She never expected to be standing here again.

To be facing the demons she had left behind. The people she had let down.

She instinctively stepped back, coming up against Ye-yang's chest. He placed a hand on her shoulder.

"If you're not ready, we don't have to do this. Everything has already been prepared for you inside the palace—workshop, materials, tools—and if you need anything else, we can always have it brought in. You don't have to see anyone from the guild if you don't want to."

"No." Ying moved away, putting some distance between them once again. "It's much easier for me to work in the guild. Besides, I don't belong in the palace—you know that."

Their gazes locked—one accusing, the other regretful.

The air stilled between them, and the invisible wall that had existed ever since their falling-out two years ago felt more tangible than ever. He was the High Commander, and she—a wisp of a passing cloud.

She looked away, pretending she didn't see the hurt in his eyes.

He was the one who made that decision for them, back when he accepted the engagement to her sister. This was the consequence that they would have to live with.

A cold wind blew across the vast expanse of the gray stone courtyard, sending fallen leaves swirling about their ankles. A lone figure descended the stairs, familiar maroon guild robes draped over his bony frame. As he approached, the man glowered and let out a loud harrumph.

Ying's stomach did a backflip.

"Master Gerel," she greeted, legs trembling beneath her.

Already she was regretting her decision to return.

Ying tugged at the front of her robes, adjusting the waistband for the umpteenth time as she stood next to Master Gerel outside the doors of the grand master's quarters. She had been given the maroon of an official guild member—something she had once yearned for—yet it felt like she was wearing someone else's skin.

This doesn't belong to you, she thought. She had given up the right to wear these robes when she tore apart her guild acceptance letter and scattered it to the wind. She had been so determined then, so adamant in her decision never to return to this place.

Yet fate had other plans in store.

Turning her head, she stared down the long, musty corridor, at the murals depicting the most illustrious inventions of the guild carved into the stone walls. Chimeric beasts, majestic warships, cranes and intricate machinery used to construct the most fantastical buildings—paintings of a dream she once had. A dream she *still* had.

She hadn't given up on engineering. Nor had she given up on her desire to follow in her father's footsteps.

She just wasn't sure that the guild was the right place for that anymore.

Doesn't matter. You're only here as a guest. A passerby.

Once she had completed the task that Ye-yang required of her, she would leave, setting things back the way they were. The world was limitless. There had to be a place where she belonged.

She shifted her weight uncomfortably from left to right, turning her attention back to the latticework panels of the grand master's doors.

"Send her in," a raspy voice croaked from inside.

Gerel pushed the doors open and nudged her in with the sharpest bit of his elbow.

The interior of the room was dimly lit, with all the windows tightly shuttered. As if someone was afraid of the slightest ounce of sunlight sneaking in. A musky odor of medicinal herbs filled the space, mixed with a subtle hint of sandalwood incense.

Ying took a few hesitant steps forward, making her way over to the daybed where the grand master was seated.

"Grand Master," she greeted, bowing deeply.

The sight of the elderly man left her shaken. The guild's grand master had already looked ancient before, with his snowy white hair and wispy beard, but now his wrinkled complexion was ash gray and his thin lips pale and cracked, like a withered husk of what he used to be. Ye-yang had mentioned that the grand master was ill, but she had not expected that it would be so serious.

So this was why Ye-yang was concerned.

If Grand Master Quorin passed on, then the leadership of the Engineers Guild would come into question. The guild masters would end up spending more time fighting over the position than working on tackling the pirate problem.

"I didn't expect to see you back so soon, young Aihui," the grand master said. He paused to cough. Flecks of blood stained the white of his handkerchief. "You've broken one of the guild's most sacred rules, by entering our trial under a false identity. Someone like you was never meant to join our ranks."

"I apologize for what I did, Grand Master. I know that—"

The old man raised one emaciated hand. "I am well aware of your reasons, and even though I don't agree with your methods, I can understand why you chose to do what you did. But that is water under the bridge now." He coughed again, more violently than before. "Do not misunderstand, I'm glad that you have returned. The guild needs young talent like yourself, now more than ever. If you have anywhere near half of your father's gifts, then perhaps you might be able to deliver the miracle that we so desperately need." His eyes glazed over with worry, and the creases across his forehead deepened.

"I'm not sure I'll be able to live up to those expectations," Ying replied quietly.

When she had first entered the guild for the apprenticeship trial, she had believed that anything was possible. That she could do anything she set her mind to. That she could convince everyone she was worthy of the guild, despite being a girl. Yet when she finally won their begrudging acceptance, when the grand master himself acknowledged her talent and placed his hopes in her hands, she wanted nothing more than to burrow into a shell.

Why? If this wasn't what she wanted, then what *did* she want?

Quorin shook his head. "You underestimate your own capabilities. I watched your father grow up within these halls. What made him stand out was not his skill, but his heart." Ying looked up at the grand master, confused by his words. "Everything that Shan-jin did was firmly guided by his own principles—the desire and determination to use engineering to serve the people. *All* the people. From your earlier performance in the apprenticeship trial, I saw your father's shadow in you." He sighed. Resting his elbow against the mahogany table, he leaned his head against the back of his hand and closed his eyes. "Always let your heart guide your mind."

Always let my heart guide my mind.

Ying raised a hand to her chest, feeling the steady rhythm of her own heartbeat beneath her maroon guild robes.

But what if I don't know what my heart wants to say?

"Go now. Gerel will let you know what needs to be done." The grand master lifted his hand and gave her a tired wave, dismissing her from the room.

The grouchy mien of Master Gerel greeted her once she stepped out from the grand master's quarters. "Follow me," he barked, immediately swiveling on his heel and marching down the corridor.

"The grand master has briefed us on the purpose of your return," Gerel continued as they walked, his thin brows pinched with annoyance. Ying did not begrudge him that. Gerel had never liked her from the first day she entered the guild, if only because of his longstanding, albeit one-sided, feud with her father in their younger days, so her reappearance must irk him tremendously. "So far, most of the guild's efforts toward the neutralization of the pirate threat lie with the Black Ops division, which is led by Master Lianshu. You shall be working with them."

"Black Ops?"

Even as a trial candidate, Ying had never imagined that she would one day enter the guild's most secretive division, responsible for producing some of the most useful—and abhorrent—creations of guild history. Mechanical prosthetic limbs, such as the metallic arm worn by the guild master in charge of the Order's airship yard, Kyzo, had come out of the Black Ops division. But so had the half-beast, half-machine chimeras, monstrosities that guarded the homes of

Antaran nobility and readily tore trespassers into pieces. Her mind buzzed with trepidation.

"Only for the duration of your *temporary* stay in the guild," Gerel emphasized. Abka Han forbid that he would formally place her in any guild division. "I don't think you need me to remind you of the confidential and critical nature of the work that the Black Ops division does. If you dare leak any of their research beyond these walls—well then, the consequence of that shall be far more severe than that of *lying* your way into the guild."

"I understand, Master Gerel," Ying replied.

They continued walking in silence.

The atmosphere in the guild was worlds apart from what she remembered. A hushed silence filled the corridors, apprentices hurrying to and fro with anxious footsteps as if time was worth its weight in gold. There was no laughter, no jokes, only solemn discussions and stern instructions echoing from every workshop and classroom they passed. A heaviness weighed upon Ying's heart, the strings in her mind pulled taut.

The circumstances in Fei had changed, and the guild was no exception.

They arrived at the guild archives, a small three-story pagoda at the eastern edge of the sprawling compound that housed not only the dusty records of Antaran engineering history but also Master Lianshu's personal workshop. Ying paused outside the doors, exhaling slowly.

Lianshu was unlike Gerel, or Grand Master Quorin. Lianshu

had been her father's closest friend. She was the sister of the former High Commander, Ye-yang's aunt, her teacher. There were too many threads that bound them together, that tied them back to the ghosts of the past. If she had a choice, she would not want to step through these doors again.

To her surprise, instead of climbing to the top floor where Lian-shu's workshop was located, Gerel walked over to one of the many shelves on the ground floor of the pagoda, shifting a stack of scrolls aside to reveal a circular stone cogwheel that was embedded into the wall.

The cog had twelve teeth, each one inscribed with the character representing the twelve different time segments in a day.

Mao, Chen, Wei, Zi.

Ying watched as Gerel rotated the wheel to four specific positions. As the final character clicked in place, the walls rumbled and a hidden trapdoor in the pagoda's stone floor slid open, revealing a long flight of descending stairs.

"This way."

Gerel led her down the steps until they passed a doorway and emerged into an expansive cavern, excavated deep within the very hill that the guild compound sat on. Ying gawked, stunned by this unexpected revelation. In all the time that she had spent in the guild, she had never known that such a place even existed.

The cavern was even larger than four hangars in Master Kyzo's airship yard—and there was an actual full-sized airship sitting in it right now. A mosaic of a dozen other vehicles, contraptions, and bizarre creations also occupied the space, with a handful of apprentices bustling around with their tools.

Ying walked up to a familiar creature—a golden, mechanical dragon—suspended from leather harnesses in all its frightening majesty.

Seemed like only yesterday she had destroyed Master Lianshu's mechanical pet during the final test of the guild's apprenticeship trial. What improvements had the guild master built into the serpentine beast since?

"Ah, there you are. What took so long?" someone called out. A head popped up from behind the tail of the dragon automaton.

Even if everyone had changed, Aogiya Lianshu had not.

Her frizzy hair still looked like it was about to burst free of her braids, and she wore the same bronze goggles as the first time they met. Energy still hummed from her bright, marble-like eyes. It was as if the events from two years ago hadn't left a single blemish on her.

As if her best friend—Ying's father—had not been killed.

As if her brother—the former High Commander—had not died.

As if she had absolutely *nothing* to do with any of that.

Ying had once believed that Lianshu was a kindred spirit, someone who shared the same dreams, who understood the struggles of trying to succeed as a female engineer. She didn't think that anymore. She was not in any way like Aogiya Lianshu, nor did she aspire to be. No matter how much she loved engineering, she could not prioritize it above everything else—especially not family.

Seeing Lianshu stand in front of her as if nothing had ever happened left a bitter taste at the back of Ying's mouth.

"I'll hand her over to you. Remember to submit your division's weekly progress report—it's overdue," Master Gerel replied with a scowl. He turned to Ying. "Don't create any trouble while you're here, is that clear?" The guild master spun around and stalked away, disappearing through the doorway from which they came.

"So." Master Lianshu clambered across the dragon's back and hopped off, landing nimbly in front of Ying. "How does it feel to be seeing an old friend again? Almost had to decommission him after you melted a hole through his stomach, but thankfully this fellow pulled through." She stroked the gleaming metal scales of her creation, almost affectionately. "You can hardly see where he's been patched up."

"It's . . . the same one?"

The guild master folded her arms across her chest, beaming like a proud mother. "Of course. The first child is always the most precious," she quipped. "I'm going to miss him when he finally flies the coop." Turning around, she craned her neck and squinted her eyes, as if trying to locate something within the cavern. "Are Tongiya and Niohuru still not back?" she shouted to no one in particular.

Tongiya? Niohuru?

Ying's heart lurched at the mention of the clan names belonging to her two friends in the guild, Tongiya Chang-en and Niohuru An-xi. Were they also part of Lianshu's Black Ops division? It couldn't be. She was certain they had aspired toward other divisions before. Chang-en had wanted to join Weaponry, while An-xi's ambition was to build grand palaces in Architecture.

It had to be a coincidence.

Right on cue, the stone walls at the far side of the cavern began to slide open, revealing a door made for giants—the alternate entrance that the engineers must have used to bring in all the large vehicles and equipment that filled the den. Sunlight came streaming in, bathing the colossal space in a magical glow. Several steam-powered wagons were driven in, each carrying a single spherical object hidden beneath thick sheets of oiled cloth.

Her submersibles.

"Sorry we're late, Master Lianshu," a buoyant voice called out. "The streets were packed because of the solstice festival!"

Against the glare from the sun, Ying saw two cloaked silhouettes alighting from the wagons—one tall, the other short, both equally wiry. They stopped. Even though their faces were masked in shadows, she knew that they were looking right at her.

A nervous slab wedged itself at the base of her throat.

"Well, well, if it isn't Aihui *Min*."

CHAPTER 6

THERE WAS SOMETHING AMISS in the High Command. Ye-yang had only returned to Qianlei Palace earlier this morning, and already the threshold to his study had been crossed by a never-ending stream of officials and stewards. Tense expressions hung on their haggard faces, the bags under their eyes exposing their lack of sleep.

Hiding behind one of the vermilion pillars of the sheltered walkway beneath the serpentine figures of emerald and indigo painted on the beams above, Nian watched as yet another soldier came running toward the imperial study. His black brigandine armor was stained with splashes of dirt, and sweat trickled down the sides of his face from the exertion of his journey. In one of his hands, he clutched a rolled-up scroll.

"Urgent message from the front line," he reported to Nergui, who was on duty at the High Commander's door.

Front line.

The words rolled uncomfortably inside her head. She had paid enough attention to the idle chatter of the servants to know that the war against the pirates of the Dunzhu Straits had intensified in recent days.

She yearned to find out more about the situation—how severe things were, what the Cobra's Order was doing to tackle the threat, whether her siblings were safe—but that would be overstepping her bounds. Wen had warned her against that many times before she left Huarin. *"Know your limits, Nian. Don't go poking your nose into things that are none of your business, and know what boundaries you need to keep. This clan doesn't need a second Aihui Ying,"* her brother had said.

Is it so bad to be like A-jie? she often wondered.

But she was Nian. Loyal, obedient Nian, who would never dare create any trouble for her family. Everyone had their roles to play, and this was hers.

"Lady Nian, why are you still here? The High Commander has been waiting for you."

She startled, spinning on the heel of her qixie. Qorchi was standing behind her, beaming as always.

"Of course," she stammered. She didn't know why Ye-yang had summoned her, and the uncertainty left butterflies fluttering in her stomach. Should she really be here, taking his time away from more pertinent matters?

Sucking in a breath, she stepped out from her hiding place and headed for the study.

Inside, Ye-yang was standing behind his desk, perusing one of the many petitions that had been submitted. The wooden pieces on the map of the nine isles that hung behind him had moved since the last time she was here, evidence that this game of weiqi they were playing with the pirates was still in motion.

When her arrival was announced, he glanced up and smiled.

Smiled.

When was the last time she had ever seen him smile? Had she even seen him smile at all?

The corners of his lips tilted upward, and his eyes creased into half-moons. A dimple she never knew he had deepened upon his left cheek. All of a sudden he seemed years younger than the stoic, commanding figure he always portrayed—like the young prince she had first seen at the royal banquet, the one that made her heart leap when he looked her way.

She lowered her head, hiding a rush of pink to her cheeks.

"Your Excellency," she greeted.

"Ah, Nian, just the person I wanted to see." Her blush deepened. "There's something I need your help with."

"*My* help?"

Ye-yang nodded, handing her a scroll backed with shimmering gold silk. "The biannual hunt will be held shortly after the summer solstice. We've postponed it by a year because of the former High Commander's passing, but there's no excuse to delay it any further," he explained.

Nian skimmed through the contents of the scroll, which contained the proposed details for the upcoming solstice hunt. According to the astrologers, the most auspicious time to conduct the hunt was in four weeks' time, and a set of prayer rites were recommended to ensure bountiful blessings from Abka Han in the year ahead. She looked up, perplexed.

"Traditionally, preparations for the solstice hunt are overseen by the High Commander's principal wife, but since that position is vacant for now, I'm afraid I'll have to burden you with this responsibility."

Nian blinked, her heart skipping a beat. A part of her was overjoyed that he thought her capable of shouldering such an important task, yet another part was unsure over his tone and choice of words.

But that position is vacant for now . . . *Does that mean it won't be vacant for long?*

Their wedding ceremony had already been postponed once, but it couldn't be postponed indefinitely. Perhaps after the solstice hunt . . .

"Nian, are you all right? Do you have concerns?" Ye-yang asked, watching her expectantly.

She quickly shook her head. "No, Your Excellency. I'm not sure I'll be able to perform up to expectations, but I will try my best," she said.

"Good. I understand this might sound daunting, but rest assured that Nergui and Qorchi will support you with whatever you need."

There he was, smiling even more vibrantly than before, sending ripples skimming across the surface of her mind. Then his gaze slid down toward the octagonal lamp sitting on his desk, the flickering candlelight illuminating each carved panel with an amber glow. A glimmer of warmth threaded through his cool gray irises.

That was when Nian realized that his smile wasn't for her.

He was looking *through* her—and seeing someone else. Someone else who he had reserved all his affection and emotions for.

"If there's nothing else, then I'll take my leave," she said, dropping into a curtsy.

"Wait, there's one more thing . . ." Ye-yang hesitated, then he shook his head. "Never mind. I suppose this can wait, until everyone's ready." He waved his hand, dismissing her from his study.

What does he mean? What can wait? Until who is ready?

Questions continued to circle within Nian's mind after she left the High Commander's study. Something was off about Ye-yang's behavior today, and it bothered her that she didn't know what. It was a stark reminder, if anything, that she was only an outsider here—in the palace, and in Ye-yang's heart.

She had been more hopeful before, when she'd first arrived in Fei. She'd imagined that marriage would be what her parents' relationship had been—mutual respect, growing trust, two people gradually drawing closer together until their hearts could touch. Until they could understand each other even when they weren't speaking.

That vision had quickly unraveled.

Ye-yang was a mentor, a guardian, a brother—but it never felt like anything more. He was like a piece of jade. Beautiful. Awe-inspiring. Cold.

The glare coming from the reflection of the setting sun's rays distracted her from her thoughts, forcing her to shield her eyes.

She tilted her head toward its source, admiring the glittering coat of fresh gold paint that had been given to the hall's gabled roofs, a row of tiny stone animal guardians standing watch over each gracefully curving eave. This palace residence used to belong to Lady

Xana, the former High Commander's favorite consort, and was situated closest to the High Commander's own resting quarters, Qingning Hall. A month ago, renovation work had begun at the residence, creating quite a stir within the palace. Although the chief stewards insisted that it was simply part of general restoration works, the rumors spreading among the servants was that Qianlei Palace would soon be welcoming a new mistress.

Nian had never spared much thought for such gossip before, but after today's meeting with Ye-yang, she wondered if there was perhaps a shred of truth in there.

The pale pink petals of the plum blossom trees planted in the hall's front garden peeked out from above its perimeter walls, a gust of wind sending a flurry of blush pink scattering in mesmerizing swirls. The garden was certainly more splendid than her own, which only had a few bonsai and camellia bushes that she cared for.

A tap came at her shoulder. She startled.

"I was looking all over for you. What're you doing here?"

Ye-kan was standing behind her, tracing the direction of her gaze toward the half-constructed palace hall. A smile rose upon her lips.

"I was just heading back to my quarters. The High Commander wanted to see me, about the solstice hunt," she replied, shoving all the messy thoughts to the back of her head. "Haven't seen you in the palace for a while. Have things been busy?"

Ye-kan typically appeared in front of her every other day, either to scrounge green bean cakes or to complain about politics between the banners, but he had been glaringly absent for the past week. Every morning, she found herself staring at the moon gate leading to her quarters, wondering if Ye-kan would show up—but he didn't. It had become a bad habit, a habit born out of her own pathetic loneliness.

"*Very* busy. The streets are teeming with refugees now, and there's been a few pirate attacks off the shores of the other isles." His brows furrowed. "Apparently there's also been one near Larut. Has Ying said anything?"

Nian shook her head in alarm. "I haven't heard from A-jie in weeks," she said. "How bad was it? It can't have been that serious, right?" If it was, surely Ye-yang would have said something earlier.

"I'll have to try to get my hands on the situation report to find out . . ." Ye-kan tilted his head thoughtfully, taking in her anxious expression. Then he reached over and flicked her across the forehead with his index finger, an impish grin stretching across his face.

"What was that for!" she yelped, rubbing the sore spot from the unprovoked attack.

"Enough gloom and doom. All that frowning will ruin a pretty face," the prince said. A rush of heat flared across Nian's cheeks—although Ye-kan didn't seem to notice. Taking her by the wrist, he started dragging her in the direction of her residence. "Let's go, there's no time to waste."

"Go where?" Nian looked around, hoping that there was no one in the vicinity to witness this. Even though Ye-kan was used to doing whatever he wanted in the palace and no one dared say a word against it, it didn't mean she had the same entitlement. The last thing she wanted was to become the focus of attention upon the tongues of the prolific palace gossips.

"How does the summer solstice festival sound? It starts tonight."

"You must be joking."

"Do I look like I'm joking? I even prepared your disguise!" Ye-kan held up the gray cloth bundle he had been carrying in one hand, his dark irises twinkling with glee.

"You're going to sneak me out of the palace?" she exclaimed. "No! That's completely against protocol."

"It's only against protocol if someone finds out, and no one will." Letting go of her hand, Ye-kan took her by the shoulders and steered her onward, leaving no room for negotiation. "Hurry up and change. There's going to be a fireworks display, and I don't intend to miss it."

Rule-breaking and daredevil stunts had always been Ying's cup of tea, never Nian's. *There has to be at least one level head in the family,* their father used to say. Leaving the palace disguised as a male steward was about the boldest thing she had ever done.

Anxiety gripped Nian's heart from the moment she stepped out of her quarters, hair braided backward in a single plait and face hidden beneath a broad-brimmed straw hat. When the guards at the palace's quietest western gate had stopped her and Ye-kan for the regular exit inspection, she had been this close to fleeing back to the safety of her quarters. Ye-kan's firm grip of her sleeve stopped her from escaping.

As it turned out, her fears were unfounded, because the

fourteenth beile easily scared the guards back with one ferocious glare. No one even dared question him about what he was doing inside the palace after hours, or come close enough to detect that the frail attendant trailing beside him was actually a girl. They waved him through with obsequious smiles, spouting meaningless words of flattery until the duo were out of earshot. The heavy palace gates heaved shut behind them, and Nian finally found it in herself to breathe.

She stayed close to Ye-kan as he led them down a twisting path of arch bridges and narrow alleyways, until they emerged on the main commercial street of Fei that ran from the east to the west of the city. Along the broad pavement, gas lamps burned bright as day and rainbow-colored paper lanterns dangled from bunting that zigzagged above their heads. The street thronged with festivalgoers, accosting her with riotous cacophony and a sudden rush of life—a far cry from the quiet, peaceful surroundings of the palace. The final vestiges of trepidation dissipated, swept away by the novelty of her circumstances.

Ye-kan reached out and gently pushed her gaping jaw shut. "Welcome to Fei—the better part of it," he joked. "Now, where shall we start?"

If she could, Nian wanted to be everywhere at once. This was a side of Fei that she had never seen before—magical, scintillating, and also a little dangerous—the Fei that she remembered Ying speaking of with plentiful love and longing in her eyes. She had always wondered why her sister had chosen to go to Larut instead of returning to Fei. It wasn't as if there weren't suitors from clans based in the capital seeking her sister's hand in marriage. Ying probably thought she hid it well, intentionally skirting around any mention of Fei, but Nian had easily seen through her sister's act. Ying had obviously left a part of her heart here—and now Nian was beginning to understand why.

Ye-kan bought them each a bag of the most heavenly smelling roasted chestnuts, tossed in a wok larger than any that Nian had ever seen, and they continued meandering along, basking in the vibrancy of the festival.

"I'd have brought you out sooner if I'd known how easily entertained you were," Ye-kan remarked.

"Don't speak as if it's as simple as taking a walk in the palace gardens," she said, a hint of mournfulness woven into her voice. Mourning the life that she had left behind.

Tonight was the exception, not the rule. That reality remained crystal clear inside her mind. But if this was to be the one and only time she could freely roam the city's streets, then she was determined to savor every sight and sound. To make it count.

"Oh, look, there's a fishing game!" she squealed, rushing over to a stall where two large makeshift bamboo tubs had been set up for people to catch tiny, colorful fish with paper nets. She picked up a net and a wooden bowl, then squatted by one of the pools. Ye-kan handed two coins to the beaming stall owner.

"You do realize that this is a scam, right?" the prince said, just as Nian's first attempt at scooping some fish ended with a torn net.

Nian picked up another net and tried again, but the moment she tried lifting a fish out of the water, the weight of the little creature made the rice paper rip. She was not alone in this struggle. Everyone else who was attempting the game seemed to be facing the same challenge, and a tidy pile of broken nets lay in the straw basket by the gleeful stall owner's feet.

It was very much a scam—but she was not about to admit defeat. She flexed her fingers and reached for a third net. "Pay the man," she told Ye-kan. "I'll make sure you get your money's worth of fish in return."

Ye-kan reluctantly handed the coins over, still looking skeptical.

Nian carefully dipped the net into the water at an angle, until the entirety of its circular paper surface was submerged. Concentrating on a golden molly with tiny black flecks on its tail that was swimming close to the wall of the tub, she steadied her hand, then swiftly lifted the net—and the fish—out of the water. There was a soft plop as the little gold fellow slipped into her wooden bowl.

Her eyes lit up.

"Well done!" the stall owner said, wanting to reach for her bowl. "I'll have that bottled up for you right away."

"Wait." Nian held out her hand to stop him. She pointed at the wooden sign sitting in front of the stall. "I'm allowed to catch as many fish as I like, as long as my net holds." She held up her net by its bamboo handle. "It's not broken yet."

Three nets and almost thirty fish later, Nian and Ye-kan finally called it a day, leaving the distraught stall owner to weep over his near-empty tubs. The small crowd that had gathered cheered as the duo walked away, with Ye-kan carrying two large glass jars of rainbow-colored fish, one tucked beneath each arm.

"I didn't think you were being serious when you said I'd get back my money's worth," the fourteenth beile said, chuckling merrily. "Our Lady Nian certainly taught that swindler a lesson!" They turned into a quieter alley, seeking some respite from the noisy crowd. "How did you manage to do it? Those nets were so flimsy. They were obviously made to break."

"It's about technique," Nian explained, still giddy with success. She took off her straw hat, sweeping back the loose strands of hair that had fallen across her face. "Most people just rush into it without giving any proper thought about *how* they should be using their nets. You have to slide it into the water at a slight incline"—she angled the brim of her hat in the correct way—"so that the pressure doesn't tear the paper straightaway. Also, the entire net needs to go in before you try moving it to catch a fish. If only half the net is submerged, then the wet half is going to weigh down the dry half—ripping it down the middle."

Ye-kan stopped.

"What's the matter?" Nian asked, turning to face him.

"I used to wonder if you and Ying were truly sisters, because you seem completely different, but tonight I'll admit I was wrong. The same Aihui blood definitely runs in your veins, and the same Aihui brain is hiding in here," he said, leaning forward to knock her forehead lightly with his own.

Nian blinked. Heat seared up her neck and across her cheeks, painting it crimson.

"What nonsense—of course we're really sisters," she muttered. She quickly spun around and continued marching toward the other end of the alley, eager to put some distance between them.

"Why're you going so fast? Wait for me," Ye-kan called out, his footsteps echoing behind her.

Nian didn't slow down. Instead, she picked up the pace, veering left once she stepped out of the passageway and onto a larger street. They had left the chaos of the solstice festival behind them and entered a quieter part of town, although the loud music and chatter could still be heard drifting above the rooftops. Most of the doors flanking both sides of the street had been shuttered, with only a handful of people rushing by, all headed toward the festivities.

She patted her cheeks, willing the flush to go away.

Stop overreacting, she scolded herself. *He was only teasing. He's always teasing.*

This was all Ye-kan's fault. Why couldn't he be serious and—

Nian stopped. A familiar silhouette was standing in front of an open doorway a short distance ahead, faintly illuminated by the yellowish glow of the lanterns above.

It can't be . . .

CHAPTER 7

YING SAT ON HER HANDS, AWKWARDLY SHIFTING her weight from side to side to ease her own fraying nerves. She had rehearsed this in her mind over a dozen times—what it would be like when she returned to the guild, and how she would behave—but now that the day had finally arrived, it was far worse than she imagined.

On the opposite side of the circular table sat Chang-en and An-xi, arms stiffly folded, both with stern, unsmiling expressions on their faces. They were in the Silver Spoon, sitting in the middle of a boisterous crowd of festival revelers, yet the silence was suffocating. Neither of them had said a word to her since they left the guild.

Were they angry? They must be, after finding out she had deceived them by masquerading as a boy in the guild's trial, and then vanishing without a trace. Two years ago, she had fled from Fei racked by fear and guilt, and in her haste she had not left so much as a farewell note for her old friends. In hindsight, that was a terrible mistake.

"Chang-en, An-xi, I'm sorry, I—"

Chang-en's eyes narrowed, razor-thin, as if he was going to skin her alive.

Ying's voice trailed off. Perhaps bridges burned could not be so easily mended. She was naive to think that her feeble attempt at an apology would do any good.

"You're *sorry*? Do you think that a simple 'sorry' will erase all the pain that you've caused?" Chang-en stood up, pressing his palms against the table. "Will 'sorry' make fifty taels reappear in An-xi's pouch?" he demanded, nostrils flaring dramatically. Maybe a little too dramatically.

Ying blinked in confusion. "Fifty taels? What fifty taels?"

"That's enough," An-xi snapped. "How many times do you need to rub it in?"

"More times." Chang-en suddenly dashed around the table, throwing his arms around Ying and lifting her up in a bone-crushing hug. "How dare you leave without a word and not even write *a single letter* to us all this while?" the boy shrieked, spinning her in dizzy circles. "Ha! I knew you'd come back!" He set her down, revealing a broad, cheeky grin that stretched from ear to ear. "I bet fifty taels that it would be you, but An-xi refused to believe me. Insisted it was going to be some retired guild master."

Ying gripped the table edge to stabilize herself, still reeling from the unexpected turn of events. Was that what the fifty taels was about? A bet?

"You knew I was coming?"

"Gerel told everyone there would be a newcomer joining the guild, personally nominated by the High Commander to support the ongoing piracy war effort." Chang-en clapped his hands in delight. "I guessed it was you right away."

"About that . . ." Ying rubbed the nape of her neck, trying to recall the lines of apology she had rehearsed.

Chang-en slung his arm around her shoulder and sat her back

down. Like old times. "No need to worry about it. Can't say the same for An-xi, but as far as I'm concerned, no hard feelings whatsoever! I completely understand why you had to pretend to be your brother. The guild is far too outdated with their rusty rules and protocols. Why should guild membership be restricted only to boys? Look at Master Lianshu, and look at you! Unanimously voted best engineer of our year!"

Ying shifted her gaze toward An-xi, now sitting sullenly on his own. Even though Chang-en seemed willing to let bygones be bygones, she dared not assume the same about An-xi. The mousy boy from the capital's esteemed Niohuru clan had always viewed her as equal parts rival and friend, and had every reason to be upset with her for having the gall to return after all she had done.

She opened her mouth to speak, but he abruptly cut her off.

"Why bother coming back if you'd already decided to abandon the guild?"

Ying hung her head in shame. Perhaps An-xi would give her the tongue-lashing she deserved. Even now she couldn't reveal the entire truth behind her sudden departure. There was too much darkness in that encounter that could not be erased.

"Excuse me, who was it who moped about for a full month after Ying left? As if someone in your family died?" Chang-en said, wagging a finger in An-xi's direction. "And remember that one time when you got drunk at the Red Tower and you said—"

An-xi leapt up, stretching his entire body across the table to clap one hand over the other boy's mouth. The rest of Chang-en's remark was relegated to unintelligible gurgles. "Shut up," he hissed. "I did no such thing." He glanced sideways at Ying, glowering with annoyance. "Don't listen to him. He's always making things up."

Chang-en pried An-xi's fingers off his mouth. "That's not true. I clearly remember you saying—" The rest of it was smothered by An-xi once again, this time accompanied by a sharp pinch to the forearm. Chang-en howled in pain, tears welling up in his eyes.

A mechanical serving cart running along the crisscrossing network of tracks that lined the restaurant floor stopped beside their table, bearing all the dishes they had ordered. A welcome distraction from the little squabble. Ying quickly moved to unload the cart, arranging each plate on the table.

She placed one roasted chicken leg on Chang-en's plate and the other on An-xi's.

"That's all for a peace offering?" An-xi asked, arching a skinny brow. He picked up his chopsticks, and for a moment Ying thought he was going to take the drumstick and throw it back at her. But he didn't. Instead, he reached for another plate and picked up some wood-ear mushrooms tossed in vinegar—Ying's favorite dish—and casually dumped it on her empty plate.

Ying stared down at the tangle of fragrant black fungus mixed with shredded carrots lying on her dish, then across the table at An-xi, who was nonchalantly chewing on his drumstick. A warm glow filled her heart, and a tiny smile crept onto her face.

A peace offering.

～♾～

The streets of Fei thrummed with life as the month-long celebrations for the summer solstice carried on in full swing.

Against a backdrop of the sparkling night sky, street vendors lined both sides of the broad cobbled path to hawk their festive offerings—lucky charms and dainty dough figurines, skewers of sugared fruit and piping hot bowls of sesame tangyuan. Traveling performance troupes had set up stages at intersections, juggling plates and spitting fire, delighting the hordes of Fei residents that had gathered.

If one did not look carefully, they might forget that this was a time of crisis for the Antaran isles.

Chang-en and An-xi had gone on ahead, arm in arm as they raised their horrendously off-tune voices in song. From the way the inebriated duo was zigzagging down the street, it was questionable as to whether or not they would eventually make it back to the guild—or end up in a canal.

Ying lingered behind, pausing to take in the enchanting night scenery of the capital, lanterns flickering like dozens of fireflies in the darkness. Strangely enough, being back in Fei gave her the feeling of . . . *home*. It was unlike Huarin, which held her fondest childhood memories and to which she would always be tied by blood; instead, it was like reuniting with a close confidant, someone who shared her hopes and dreams.

Letting go is easier said than done.

"Hey, what—"

Her money pouch was swiped from her waist, and the thief was sprinting down the steps of the bridge, soon to vanish into the crowd that thronged the busy street.

Ying gave chase, squeezing through the swarm of festivalgoers while keeping her focus trained on the culprit's mop of messy hair, the turquoise fabric of her pouch still visible in his clenched fist. He sidestepped into a small alley leading off from the main street. She followed.

"Stop! Come back here!" she yelled, dodging and hitting away the bamboo sieves that were being flung her way. She leapt over several crates and boxes that cluttered the narrow alley, the strength in her legs ebbing. The gap between her and the thief was growing. Once he reached the other end of the alleyway, she would likely lose him.

Just then, the boy stopped running.

A tall figure shrouded in shadows stood at the mouth of the alley, blocking his escape.

"Stealing?" a familiar voice said. A sword was unsheathed, its tip pointing down at the thief's jugular.

"Ye-yang?" Ying exclaimed. What was he doing here? "Wait, stop!" She ran over and grabbed hold of Ye-yang's hand to stop him from moving his blade. "Don't," she said. "He's only a child."

The cowering boy was staring up at them with wide-eyed fear, his cracked lips trembling. He looked barely ten, the topknot on his head and the tattered clothes he wore identifying him as a Qirin refugee. He moved a trembling arm and held out Ying's pouch.

"Please, let me go. I'll return this to you. Please."

"The punishment for theft in Fei is fifty lashings," Ye-yang replied.

The sight of the gleaming blade in Ye-yang's hand brought back the horrific memory of how he had so effortlessly slit the throat of

Ye-kan's mother, Lady Odval—a memory so laden with guilt she could not bear to confront it. Her heart clenched, the insides of her gut twisting into knots.

It was a sharp reminder of the ugly side of Fei, the one that she had been eager to leave behind. Mired in fraught political tensions and thin family ties, it was a place that would always be contaminated by the stench of blood and lingering ghosts.

The bright lights and effervescence of the city had almost made her forget that.

Ye-yang slid his sword back into its scabbard, much to Ying's relief.

"Let him go," Ying insisted. "Look at him, he's barely surviving as it is."

Her eyes fixed upon the pinprick of blood leaking from the boy's neck, where Ye-yang's sword had been. She swallowed, fear from the past and present intertwining like thick vines around her heart.

Steadying herself, she took the pouch from the child and took out two silver taels, pressing them into the boy's hand. "Here, take this and buy yourself some food. If you need shelter, there's a temple in the eastern quarter of the city."

"Wait," Ye-yang intervened. He pointed to the left, saying, "There's a medicinal hall a few doors down that way—Shan-yi Hall. You can seek shelter there, and get those bruises sorted out. Shan-yi Hall doesn't charge any fees."

It was then that Ying noticed how the boy's arms were laced with purplish welts that looked like they had been left by a violent thrashing. Some were almost healed; others were still raw and oozing with pus. A pang of sympathy struck her.

The kid nodded vigorously, then dashed off before Ye-yang could change his mind about filleting him with that blade.

Ying followed Ye-yang out of the alley. She shoved her own ghosts out of her mind, keeping her thoughts trained upon the Qirin boy they had encountered instead. What had this child been through to end up this way? And how did he deserve any of this suffering?

She let out a deep sigh. Turning toward her companion, she asked, "What are you doing here?" Surely the High Commander had better things to do than lurk around alleyways.

"What if I said I was looking for you?" he replied, a mischievous twinkle in his eyes.

Ying balked, suddenly regretting ever asking the question.

"I'm only teasing," he continued, the smile on his face broadening. "Coincidentally, I was paying a visit to Shan-yi Hall—the shelter that I sent the boy to."

"What is that place? I've never heard of it before," Ying remarked, although it was not surprising given her limited exposure to the city. Much of her time in Fei had been spent cooped up within the Engineers Guild. Still, she knew enough about the mercenary culture and exorbitant prices in Fei to be pleasantly surprised at its existence. A medicinal hall that didn't charge its patients? Almost impossible to comprehend.

"Interested in taking a look?"

They meandered down the street, coming to a stop in front of an open doorway with a large vermilion signboard hanging overhead. The characters "Shan-yi Hall" flew across the wood in bold brush-strokes that looked awfully like Ye-yang's own handwriting.

"When I first brought up the idea of starting these safehouses, it caused quite the uproar. Almost every official and commander, including Number Fourteen, didn't approve of it," Ye-yang explained.

"*You* started Shan-yi Hall?" Ying tilted her head to the side and gave Ye-yang a quizzical stare. "But why?"

It was no wonder the court was against it, given how the increasing presence of refugees was already straining the city's resources.

She took a step forward, peering curiously through the doorway.

The entrance opened to a squarish courtyard, leading off to three small rooms. Several of the compound's occupants milled about, most of them women and children, dressed in threadbare cotton robes that were far too inadequate for the chilly Antaran weather. Warm ginger soup and tangyuans were being doled out in small clay bowls, and Ying spotted the thief they had encountered, joining the queue with a delighted grin on his little face.

"Because it is more detrimental to our interests if we're saddled with corpses instead," Ye-yang replied. "These refugees are not going anywhere. It's either we assimilate them into Antaran society, or we leave them to the mercy of the seas. There is no in-between. Taking them in while leaving them to self-destruct will cause many problems for Fei that will only take a further toll on us—increasing crime, spread of disease, festering squalor. Since I have committed to opening our gates to these people, then I must find a way to keep them alive, so that hopefully they may one day be of service to the nine isles."

"You wish to take them in *for good*?" She had always assumed that one day, when the pirates were no longer a problem and the Dunzhu Straits were safe for passage once more, all these Qirin refugees would return to their homes on the mainland. It was inconceivable that Ye-yang should intend to *keep* them. "Are you not worried about insurgents? Qirin spies?" she asked.

Ye-yang stopped, cocking his head to the side and regarding her with a bemused glimmer in his eyes. "Naturally," he said, as a matter of fact. "But if we're going to take over the Empire, then it only makes sense that we view all Antarans and Qirins as equals—as one family."

"One family. Someone's getting ahead of himself," Ying muttered. As much as she thought that the idea of treating the Qirins fairly was an admirable one, it was overly idealistic.

It seemed that Ye-yang had not given up on his lofty goal of conquering the Empire, a goal that she still could not agree with. There was too much sacrifice required for that, sacrifice that Ye-yang deemed necessary, but she did not. One life, then two; one lie, then another. When would it ever stop?

Warm fingers suddenly interlaced themselves with hers. Ye-yang took a step closer, until there was barely a finger's width of space between them. He tipped his chin down, looking right into her eyes, the misty swirls of his breath tickling her cheeks.

"Ying, I said I'd come back for you," he said quietly.

"But I never said I'd return." She tilted her head to the side, avoiding the burning intensity of his gaze.

"Yet here you are."

He placed one hand against her cheek, gently running the pad of his thumb against her skin. A tremble ran up Ying's spine, her heart racing inside her chest.

"Remember when I asked you if you would be willing to stand by my side, if ever I wanted to conquer the world?" he continued. "You're the only one I want standing beside me, Ying. Think about it—think about the incredible things that we could do together. The future we could build. For us. For *everyone*."

She remembered. She had never given him a reply, because by the time she thought she was certain of what her answer was—everything fell apart.

Ye-yang leaned forward, his lips coming ever closer to her own. She could taste the fragrance of tie guan yin that lingered on his skin, and a part of her wanted nothing more than to close the gap between them.

She wanted to say yes. She wanted to throw away all the nightmares of the past, to pretend that they did not exist.

But she couldn't.

You made up your mind, Ying. You chose to leave.

She slowly pushed him away, taking two steps back. His warmth around her disappeared, replaced by a miserable whistling of cold air against her face and neck.

"No," she said. "We can't go back, Ye-yang."

They could only keep going forward as time continued to plod on with its steady, unforgiving pace. Their paths would continue to diverge, until someday he would finally realize that he no longer needed her as an emotional crutch, until she became a mere speck of dust in his memories.

Bang!

A riot of colors exploded in the sky, painting the darkness with vibrant strokes of orange and gold. It was beautiful, yet through the bursts of rainbow-colored fireworks, Ying could see the shadow of a fiery phoenix stretching across the night, wingtips dripping with the blood of her friends from Larut.

Her fingers clenched tightly by her sides, nails digging into her palms.

Then a silvery voice cut through the noise, parting the fog that clouded her mind.

"A-jie?"

CHAPTER 8

YING HAD NOT HEARD NIAN'S VOICE IN months, and the heavens knew that she missed her sister dearly, but when those words drifted into her ears, her entire being froze over. The simple address that she had always taken for granted—A-jie—now hung above her like an executioner's blade. She turned slowly, readying herself to face the inevitable.

"Nian," she called, her gaze settling upon the familiar lithe figure standing down the street.

"A-jie, it's really you!" her sister exclaimed, rushing forward and throwing her arms around Ying. "Why didn't you tell me you were here? What's going on?" Nian took a step back, then quickly bowed her head when she realized that Ye-yang was also there. "Your Excellency," she said, surprise lancing through her greeting.

Ying's heart leapt up her throat.

Nian had always been incredibly observant, so there was no telling whether or not she would be able to unmask the secrets that Ying had been trying to hide.

She returned her sister's questions with a nervous smile.

A dozen words filtered through her mind, slipping in and out of her grasp. Her tongue ran dry. Guilt—that ugly beast that she had tried so hard to relegate to the shadows—began extending its righteous tendrils within her.

"I . . ."

"I was here for a meeting with Official Niohuru, and I happened to intercept a thief who had stolen your sister's pouch," Ye-yang said, rescuing her from her predicament.

It was the truth, yet it felt no better than a lie. Ying's stomach did a backflip.

"A thief?" Nian reached out and took her by the hands. "Are you all right? Did you get hurt?"

"I'm fine," she said. Thankfully, Ye-yang's explanation did not seem to have raised any suspicions. Mustering a weak smile, she patted the silk pouch hanging from her waistband. "Got my money back too. What are *you* doing here? And dressed like that?"

She studied the gray men's robes that Nian had on, recognizing it as the same uniform that Nergui's palace underlings wore.

Nian startled, suddenly dropping to her knees.

"I'm sorry, Your Excellency. I know I shouldn't have—"

"It's my fault," a commanding voice interjected. A tall figure stepped out from the alley and hurried over, lugging two jars of fish under his armpits. "I was the one who brought her out. It's festival night, so I thought . . ." Ye-kan's voice trailed off when his gaze landed upon Ying. His eyes bulged. "When did you come back?!" he exclaimed.

Ying scratched the nape of her neck. The stars must be terribly misaligned, for her night to have ended up in this tangled mess. First Nian, then Ye-kan, the very two people who she was not yet prepared to face.

In two years, the fourteenth prince—that bratty little boy she had first met in the Engineers Guild—seemed to have grown up, and he now towered almost a whole head above her. Time had broadened his shoulders and sharpened the once baby-smooth angles of his face, making him shed the last vestiges of his childhood. Now he carried the stern, authoritative aura of a beile.

The aura of an Aogiya.

"It's a long story," she said, trying to figure out where to begin.

"Why don't we head back to the palace first? There must be plenty that you want to catch up on, and this is not the best place for such a conversation," Ye-yang suggested. He bent over and took Nian gently by the elbow, helping her back up to her feet. Nian glanced up at Ye-yang, a shy smile hanging from her lips—a smile that pricked at Ying's heart like a dozen needles.

Tonight had been a close shave, one that she vowed never to allow again. The deep-rooted fear of Nian discovering the truth behind her and Ye-yang's past was a thorn that dug into her flesh, overshadowing the joy of their reunion.

Their paths had already been mapped out, and it was Nian who was destined to walk beside Ye-yang, not her. She had to steel her heart, sever the invisible threads that still connected her to him, that kept nudging her in his direction.

Nian trusted her. She couldn't betray that trust.

She turned away from them, only to find Ye-kan staring her down with a dark, almost disapproving look in his eyes. It wasn't hard to guess what was in his mind, because the same thought was running through hers.

You're the outsider here. Don't you dare forget that.

◯ഌ

"A-jie, I'm sorry."

The sisters sat around a circular rosewood table in the middle of a small pavilion in the gardens of Nian's palace quarters, two porcelain cups and a glass teapot on its bronze burner laid before them. A clear, golden liquid bubbled within the pot, filling the air with the subtle fragrance of jasmine.

Tea—not the comforting goat's milk that they liked to boil over the hearth in their shared ger.

"Don't be silly. What's there to be sorry about?" Ying replied.

After returning to the palace, Ye-yang and Ye-kan had left to give them the time they needed for themselves. She'd briefly recounted the circumstances that had led to her return to Fei—the attack off the coast of Larut, Feng-kai's death, the crisis faced by the Jangmu clan, and the invitation for her to return to the guild. She was here because she wanted to help. *As an engineer.* Nothing more.

"For everything that you went through. Feng-kai . . ."

"Is in a better place now. Just like A-ma and E-niye." Ying picked up her cup and gave it a light swirl, watching the tea leaves dance in the eddying current. The tea tasted bitter, tainted by the sorrow of each loss. "He lived his life without any regrets." Which was far better than what she could say for herself. "You don't have to worry about me, Nian. I can look after myself."

"Still, you should have written to me sooner," Nian replied, wrinkling up her nose. "How long will you be staying in the capital? Are you going to be here for good?"

The way Nian's eyes lit up made Ying's throat constrict with guilt.

I'll be gone as soon as I can.

But instead, she shrugged and said, "Who knows?" She turned her gaze toward the clear night sky, admiring the peaceful shimmer of the stars. "Enough about me. How have you been? Has Ye—" She caught her tongue. "Has the High Commander been treating you well?"

She would have to be more careful when speaking about Ye-yang in front of Nian, in case the casual manner that she was used to accidentally exposed the secrets she was trying to hide.

Nian puckered her lips together. "I suppose he has," she replied. "His Excellency has been very hospitable."

His Excellency? Hospitable?

Ying knew about the delay in the wedding ceremony because of the period of mourning following the former High Commander's death, but she had never doubted that it would happen eventually. Everyone in the nine isles knew that. There was no way that Ye-yang could renege on a promise that his father made in front of all the Antaran officials and clan chieftains—or could he?

Why else would he have repeated the exact same thing tonight that he had told her two years ago? That she was the one he wanted standing by his side?

She bit down hard on her lower lip, suddenly fearful that Ye-yang might actually mean what he said. That he would not marry Nian, because of her.

Nian had her teacup pinched between her thumb and index finger, the picture of elegance against the cool glow of the kaen-gas lamps hanging from the corners of the pavilion. She had changed out of her attendant's attire and put on a set of plum-colored silk robes befitting a palace lady. Her hair was done in a tasteful swallowtail updo, pinned in place with a pair of kingfisher feather hairpins.

This version of Nian stirred up a memory in Ying's mind—a memory of the first time she had seen Lady Odval, Aogiya Lianzhe's principal wife, back when the lady had entered the grand hall for the High Command's victory banquet. She remembered how the breath had left her at the sight of Odval's grace and beauty, and most of all, her composure. As the only woman granted the right to attend the banquet, she walked with her head held high, as if she were floating on a bed of clouds.

Nian reminded her of a younger version of Odval. As dignified, as refined, as fitting for this palace.

Pride swelled inside her at the sight of how her little sister had blossomed, but worry also seeped through the crevices of her mind. Qianlei Palace was built from dreams—but filled with nightmares. Lady Odval's anguished cries still whispered in the wind, haunting these walls.

She quickly shook away the chill that had crept up the back of her neck.

"What of Ye-kan, then?" she asked with a smile. "That harebrained idea of sneaking out of the palace was his, wasn't it?" The fourteenth prince was no stranger to running around in disguise and flouting rules, but she was admittedly surprised that Nian had agreed to play along.

In all the years they had spent growing up together on Huarin,

Ying had never managed to get Nian to step a single toe out of line. Ask anyone from their hometown and they would say that the Aihui daughter leaping off cliffs and climbing through dirty tunnels was Ying—never Nian. Yet tonight, the better daughter of the Aihui clan had escaped the palace dressed like a male attendant, despite knowing that it was against the rules.

Not that she thought it was a bad thing. She had always thought that Nian could afford to take a leaf out of her book from time to time. Loosen up. Be free.

Nian was incredibly intelligent, possibly even smarter than she was. The only thing that was limiting her younger sister was her irrational respect for propriety and protocol.

"I told him I didn't want to go, but he insisted! You know how stubborn he can be. He threatened to carry me out in a sack if I didn't walk with my own two feet."

"Mmm, that does sound like Ye-kan. Does he bother you a lot? Should I tell him to stop?"

"No!" Nian straightened up. "I mean, there's no need for that. It doesn't bother me." Despite the dim lighting, Ying spied the hint of a suspicious blush spreading across her sister's cheeks. "I appreciate his company. It's rather quiet in the palace most of the time." Nian took her hand, eyes shining. "You don't know how happy I am that you're here, A-jie."

Again, the sense of guilt started gnawing at the back of her mind. Were it not for her, perhaps Ye-yang might treat Nian a little better, a little more warmly. Perhaps this gilded palace might feel more like a home.

I must find a way to leave Fei as soon as I can. She glanced over at Nian, who had shifted her gaze to the golden koi darting within the crescent-shaped pond beside the pavilion. *I'm the one who's sorry, Nian. I only want you to be happy. I hope you know that.*

❧

In the cavern of the Black Ops division, Master Lianshu circled the Octopus again and again, carefully studying the shiny bronze vessel that Ying had built. She ran her fingertips over the smooth, cold surface of the metal, let out a circumspect hum, then continued with her inspection. Ying, Chang-en, An-xi, and a handful of other guild apprentices hung around, waiting for her verdict.

"Quite incredible," Lianshu murmured. Through the translucent yun-mu lenses of her goggles, Ying could see the glint of excitement in the guild master's magnified eyes, like she was a magpie that had spied a shiny new toy. "Can this really allow a person to traverse underwater? To what depth? And for how long? What exactly is it made of?"

"Only to about forty ren, and the amount of air it can carry is enough to last a person two sticks of incense. The body and tentacles are made from bronze, the window is yun-mu, and the airbag is woven from cows' stomachs," Ying recited. Her tone was detached, mechanical, placing as much imaginary distance between herself and Lianshu as she possibly could.

A part of her wished she didn't have to work with her father's old friend—a "friend" who had a hand in causing his death—but she had no choice in the matter.

"Cows' stomachs?" The guild master blanched, her gaze

dropping toward the beige-colored sack that lay deflated at the base of the vessel. A few apprentices made loud retching noises. Lianshu stepped back. "Well, whatever works, I guess. Although there has to be a better substitute for that," she said. "Forty ren and two sticks of incense isn't anywhere near good enough to challenge the Blades. The enemy will be gone before we even catch a whiff of them."

Lianshu walked over to the nearby cavern wall, reaching to untie a string that unfurled a large, rolled-up map that was hanging from silver hooks. The yellow parchment extended from ceiling to floor, stretching across the length of a regular carriage. Ying marveled at the intricacy with which the geography of the Antaran territories and its neighboring Dunzhu Straits was depicted. She found her home of Huarin, a tiny bean-shaped landmass farthest from the straits, and Fei, a brilliant diamond with tiny buildings painted on its western coast, surrounded by sturdy city walls.

Even the tenth exiled isle, Yokre, with its mountainous landscape, was drawn to scale near the map's northern edge. Yokre was similar in size to Fei, but arched gracefully like a crescent moon. It also lay closer to the Empire than any of the other isles, almost midway across the Dunzhu Straits.

Picking up a long strip of bamboo, Lianshu used its tip as a pointer and drew an imaginary line bisecting the waters of the straits. "This area is where the pirates are most active. It's almost like they are intentionally forming a barrier between us and the Empire," she said. Then she pointed at three specific spots, all within close range of Larut. "Here's where the Blood Phoenix has been sighted with high frequency. They're not the only pirate fleet to roam the straits, but they're by far the most notorious."

"And the Blades?"

"We would assume that where the fleet goes, the Blades will be close by. However, because they spend most of their time underwater, they're near impossible to detect until it's too late, so there are few survivors who are able to provide information about these machines. If we want your little Octopuses to be of any use, they must minimally be able to travel across this distance undetected"—she drew the bamboo tip across a distance that spanned almost a quarter of the straits' width—"and depending on how fast we can get them to move, I'd say we'll need to make the air supply last at least . . ." She set down her pointer and raised all ten fingers on her hands.

Ten sticks of incense.

That was five times the capacity of her current design.

While Ying pondered over the sheer magnitude of her challenge, Lianshu popped open the hatch to the Octopus prototype and clambered in, knocking around a few times before she climbed back out again.

"Very fascinating indeed," the master declared. "I'll have to take it out for a drive sometime." She picked up a tall stack of books that had already been sitting on the workbench, offloading the entire pile into Ying's arms. Ying staggered under the weight. "These journals contain everything we know about the Blood Phoenix fleet and its Blades, so make sure you read them all. Know yourself, know your enemy, and there is no battle that cannot be won," Lianshu said, ironically quoting an old Qirin adage. She turned to the rest of the apprentices. "Done wasting time? Get back to work! We've still got a test run to prepare for."

The crowd scattered.

Ying peered down at the stack of unlabeled journals she was cradling, then at the dull sheen of her submersible. It was only ever supposed to be an escape tool, yet somehow it had unwittingly come to shoulder the hopes of an entire people.

Know yourself, know your enemy, and there is no battle that cannot be won.

Setting the books down on the table, she took a deep breath and began to read.

CHAPTER 9

READING TURNED OUT TO BE A FRUSTRATING affair. By the time she finished the entire stack of a dozen, Ying concluded that the High Command knew very little about what mattered when it came to the Blood Phoenix.

There were inconsistent records of the number of ships in the fleet, ranging from five to a whopping twenty; the descriptions of who its leader was varied wildly—some said it was a giant of man, with conjoined brows and a mouth full of silver teeth, while others claimed it was a wraithlike woman, with a yin-yang face that allowed her to see and command a legion of ghosts; and then there was barely any information on the elusive Blades whatsoever, merely sketchy rumors of walls of steel that rose from the waters.

"How am I supposed to know my enemy when there's so little to go on?" she grumbled, tapping the tip of her brush impatiently against her workbench. It was no wonder the guild had yet to make a breakthrough. Considering the number of assumptions that were being made about the Blood Phoenix fleet and its Blades, it would be a miracle if Master Lianshu's plans actually worked. Not that she was even aware of what those plans were.

She could simply follow Lianshu's instructions and modify her submersibles accordingly, but would it be enough? Did it even matter whether or not it was enough? As long as she could deliver what was expected of her, then she could just pack up and leave. Whether or not the Order eventually won the war was none of her concern.

The thought left her conscience prickling against her, reprimanding her for her callousness. It was easy for her to run away, but there were plenty of others who didn't have that luxury. Villagers whose roots sank deep into Antaran soil. Refugees stranded an entire ocean away from their homes.

"Why so grouchy?" Chang-en teased, peering over her shoulder.

"Because she's accomplished, let me see . . ." An-xi walked up to join them, rubbing his narrow chin mockingly. "Absolutely *nothing*?"

Ying scowled. She picked up one of her crumpled parchments and flung it at An-xi, ignoring the squeaks of displeasure coming from her friend. He deserved it.

She hadn't accomplished nothing. She had already adjusted the body shape of her submersible, switching it from its original orb shape to a more streamlined oblong, similar to the ballonet of an airship. She'd also toyed with the idea of giving it a pointed head so that it could slice through water. Like a shark. Or like a *blade*.

Trouble was, she wasn't sure if any of that would be any good. The haziness of her understanding of the Blood Phoenix and its Blades kept needling her, even as she was making steady progress toward completing her assignment.

"If you have nothing better to say, then shut up," Chang-en said to An-xi. Slinging his skinny arm across her shoulders, he asked, "How about some stewed dumplings? That'll cheer you up!" It was almost dinnertime, and most of the other apprentices had already streamed out of the cavern to head for the dining hall.

"Not now," she replied. "I'm almost done with my revised sketch. If I finish it tonight, then I can submit it to Master Lianshu first thing in the morning."

"You shouldn't skip meals, A-jie."

Ying turned, bewildered to see her younger sister emerge from the entrance archway, the elevated heels of her qixie clipping against the stone floor. "Nian? Why are you here?" she asked.

"To make sure you're looking after yourself—which you clearly aren't," Nian replied, clucking her tongue in reproach. "Don't worry. I didn't sneak out this time. His Excellency gave me permission to come visit." She held up the three-layer bamboo basket she was carrying. "I made your favorites. Pickled cabbage with shredded pork, roast pigeon, and braised tofu."

Once the basket lid was lifted, the rich aroma of spices and herbs wafted into their noses. Ying's nose tingled with a little sourness as she watched her sister slowly lay out the homemade dishes on the table.

Smells like home.

Or at least what home used to be.

"You always forget to eat once you get busy," Nian said. She picked up a pair of chopsticks and pressed them into Ying's hand. "Help yourselves. There's plenty to go around," she added, smiling at Chang-en and An-xi. The former could barely keep the drool from leaking out of his mouth, while the latter was simply standing stock-still, shell-shocked by Nian's presence.

Ying picked up a piece of tofu and shoved it into her mouth, savoring the familiar flavors of Nian's cooking that she had missed.

Since their mother's passing, Nian had diligently taken up the responsibility of tending to the family's daily needs, including feeding her siblings thrice a day. It was a role that rightfully should have fallen to Ying, as the eldest daughter of the household, but Nian was willing, and Ying had simply taken that willingness for granted. She had been so selfish before.

She wrinkled up her nose, trying to hold back the tears.

She already owed Nian too much, and each day she spent in Fei meant that her debt to her little sister would continue to grow.

"What's the matter? Does it taste bad?" Nian asked, peering worriedly at Ying.

"No, of course not. It's just . . . I thought I'd never get the chance to taste your cooking again," Ying replied, her words a garbled mess because there was too much tofu stuffed in her mouth and too many emotions stuffed in her mind.

Nian beamed. "Then I shall have to feed you every day while you're here."

"Make sure you bring extra portions," Chang-en quipped. He pointed at the pickled cabbage. "This is especially good! The spice has just the right amount of kick."

"You can't treat Lady Nian like your personal cook," An-xi hissed. "She is to be the High Commander's principal wife!"

"She's not his wife yet, is she?"

An-xi immediately clobbered their gormless friend across the head, but it was too late. There was no retracting the words that had spilled from his greasy mouth. Ying noticed her sister's smile stiffen slightly in response to Chang-en's careless remark.

Even though Ye-yang had used the former High Commander's untimely passing and the ongoing battle against the pirates as reasons to delay the wedding ceremony, those excuses had almost run their course. Pirates or not, surely the High Commander could not keep postponing the inevitable—unless it was *not* so inevitable?

Ying sighed, self-reproach clawing deep in her gut. As much as she didn't wish to hurt Nian, her presence would end up doing that all the same. She had to leave Fei as soon as she could, maybe leave the nine isles altogether. If Ye-yang couldn't find her, he would eventually be forced to forget her. Maybe then he would be able to treat Nian the way she deserved.

The awkward silence between them was interrupted by a low rumble. The stone doors to the cave rolled open, allowing a small entourage of supply wagons to enter. A bulky figure wearing the black brigandine armor of the Order led the way atop a fierce brown stallion, the numerous gold cuffs lining both his ears gleaming ostentatiously under the lamplight. A look of mild surprise crossed his face when he saw them, then a familiar sneer appeared.

"Well, if it isn't the three good-for-nothings reunited," he said.

"Is that right? How come I only see one, then?" Ying replied drily. Evidently someone was still bitter about having failed the guild's apprenticeship trial. She had not thought about Fucha Arban ever since she left Fei, and probably would have left him forgotten if he hadn't appeared. Judging from how Arban had been relegated to delivering guild supplies, it seemed like he hadn't been doing too well for himself.

Arban scowled. He signaled to his men to begin unloading their cargo, then he leapt off his horse and marched up to her. His squarish, muscular jaw tensed with hostility. "You've always been a brazen one. How dare you show your face here after what you did, Aihui *Ying*?"

"You should ask the High Commander that question, seeing as he was the one who invited me back. As for you, I see they've assigned you the job that you're most suited for," she said, gesturing at the supply carts.

"You little rat," Arban spat. "I'll split you from nose to navel, and we'll see if you can still be so smart-mouthed then." His sword flew out of its sheath, its tip piercing toward Ying's nose.

Chang-en and An-xi let out a shared squeak of terror.

A shadow darted in front of Ying, sending a jolt of alarm rushing through her veins.

"Nian! No!"

Arban's sword stopped, mere inches away from Nian's face. Ying quickly pulled her sister back to her side.

"Why did you do that?!" she scolded. Her heart was still racing in her chest, fearful of what might have happened if Arban hadn't held back.

Nian's face had gone white as a sheet, her petite frame trembling visibly. "I . . . I saw the sword coming at you and I just . . ."

She'd just stepped in. Shielded Ying. Protected her.

That was how Nian had always been. Always thinking of others first, placing their well-being above her own. It was something that was ingrained in her bones, something that had become second nature to her, so much so that she didn't think twice about putting herself between Ying and a blade.

Shame washed over Ying, drenching her like a crushing wave. How could she let Nian step in to protect her when she had done nothing for Nian in return? Why couldn't she be the one protecting Nian for a change?

She glared at Arban, eyes spitting fire.

"Now, now, no need to be so serious, everyone," Chang-en interrupted, his smile hanging stiffly upon his face. "We're all old acquaintances here. Can't we take a joke?"

Instead of lowering his blade, Arban shifted it in Chang-en's direction. "Shut up, Tongiya Chang-en, or I'll skewer you as well."

A silver folding fan slipped out from Ying's right sleeve and into her palm, its metallic leaves unfolding in smooth clicks. Flipping it horizontal, Ying took brief aim at Arban's sword-bearing arm, where his thick biceps strained against the fabric of his uniform. She undid the locking mechanism, then gently tapped at the rivet. Instead of the needles that she'd previously used, a tiny projectile barely the size of a mung bean came shooting out from the fan's hollowed-out ribs.

So tiny that no one even noticed.

"Argh!" Arban roared. His sword fell to the ground with a resounding clang that reverberated throughout the cavern. He clutched at his arm, staring down at the small rip in the cloth. "What did you do!" he screeched, pointing an accusing finger at Ying.

The few soldiers he had brought with him rushed over.

Ying shrugged. "I didn't do anything. Did you see me do

something?" she asked, having already slipped her fan safely back into its hiding place.

Arban pushed up his sleeve, eyes bulging with horror when he saw what was happening to his skin. His tanned face ran a gamut of colors, from a ripe shade of red, to purplish-blue, and finally a frightened ash gray. Ying arched her neck, peering curiously across at her handiwork.

The miniature projectile had left a small, clean puncture wound in Arban's arm, but what was most alarming about it was that the hole was *growing*. Blink, and it had already expanded from the size of a goji berry to that of a red date, carving a shallow, bloodied crater in the flesh.

"What's happening to him, A-jie?" Nian whispered into her ear.

"He'll be fine," she answered quietly. "It should stop soon."

It being the minuscule drop of ming-roen ore that she had injected into each of those projectiles, the devilish substance capable of corroding anything and everything it came into contact with. Taking inspiration from the ore-filled cannonballs that she had created for the final test of the guild's apprenticeship trial, Ying had spent hours staring painstakingly through her magnifying lens in order to scale down the cannonball design to such a miniature level. The impact from the projectile hitting its mark would force its brittle yet corrosion-resistant metal casing to shatter, allowing the liquid ore to leak from within—giving it free rein to eat away at its victim's flesh.

Still, it was only a teensy droplet, enough to disfigure but unlikely to kill unless it struck someone straight in the heart. Arban might be traumatized for a while, but he would certainly survive.

"Sir, we should get you to a physician," one of Arban's men said, urging him to leave.

Arban hesitated for a moment, as if contemplating whether or not he should stay and make good his threat to dice Ying into pieces. He glanced down at his raw, bubbling wound, then bent over and picked up his fallen sword, sliding it back into its scabbard.

"Just you wait," he snarled, eyes spitting venom as he glared at Ying. "You think you can do whatever you want because you have the High Commander's protection? Very soon he won't even be able to protect himself." Still clutching on to his injured arm, Arban turned and left, taking his posse with him.

Once the heavy cavern doors slammed shut, Chang-en and An-xi collapsed like limp beansprouts—one against the workbench and the other onto a stool.

"Gods be damned, Ying. Why did you do that?!" An-xi yelled.

"Because Arban was pointing a sword at my face? Because he almost stabbed Nian?"

"This is guild territory. You're under the protection of the guild and the High Commander. He wasn't actually going to do anything to you!"

Ying arched a brow. "Are you seriously defending Arban right now? You know what he's like. He deserves to be taught a lesson," she retorted.

"It's exactly because I know what Arban is like, that's why you shouldn't have done that!" An-xi scolded, the tips of his large ears reddening with frustration. "*Two years* have passed. Things are not the same as they used to be. Do you know what happened to Arban after he got axed from the guild's trial? His father had him *flogged* in front of his entire family because he 'brought shame to the clan's name,' then he kicked him out and told him not to come back until he got himself a decent position in the Order. Arban had to *clean spit* off the second beile's boots in order to worm his way back into the Bordered Blue Banner as a measly supplies guard. Do you know what happens to a person after going through such humiliation? Do you know what happens when you *break* someone that way?

"Things changed, Ying. People changed." An-xi pointed at himself. "You remember that I wanted to join the Architecture division?" Then at Chang-en. "And he wanted to try Weaponry? How did the both of us end up here, huh? Do you even know? Do you even *care*?" He threw his hands up in the air. "You ran away, and the world moved on. You can't just come back expecting everything to be as you left it."

"Don't make it sound like it's my fault! I didn't *choose* to come back. Coming back was a mistake." Frustration flared up inside her, exasperation at how they would never be able to understand what she'd been through, how helpless she had been.

"No. Leaving was."

Ying fumbled for the right counter, but the finality and resoluteness in An-xi's words left no room for argument. An excruciating silence hung thick in the air. Then An-xi stormed away, disappearing through the exit.

"O-kay," Chang-en said, rubbing the nape of his neck. "I'll go and check on him. Don't worry too much about what he said. You

know how hypersensitive he can be. It'll all blow over by morning."
He stuffed another piece of tofu into his mouth before hurrying away.

Ying sank down onto an empty stool, An-xi's tirade still raging
inside her mind.

Was I really wrong to leave? And was I wrong to return?

"A-jie, are you all right?" Nian asked, giving her shoulder a light
squeeze. "I know it seemed harsh, but I think he was only worried for
you, else he wouldn't have reacted so strongly."

"I know." She closed her eyes, sighing deeply. But knowing that
didn't make her feel any better—in fact, it made her feel even worse.

CHAPTER 10

THREE WEEKS LATER, YING STOOD ON BOARD one of the Order's ships—a black-sailed colossus named the *North Wind*—as it bobbed upon the rough waters. She could hardly see the shores of Fei anymore, its majestic arch bridges and emerald rooftops a mere pinprick in the distance. The skies had been clear when they set sail, but now dour gray clouds hung overhead, the occasional rumble hinting at the imminent arrival of a storm. Staring out at the expanse of dark, tempestuous ocean that lay before her, Ying marveled at its vastness. Perhaps she had been too full of herself, believing that she could cross the Dunzhu Straits in the tiny golden vessel that she had built.

"*But there are no limits to dreaming,*" her father had once told her, "*and every great invention begins from the littlest of dreams.*"

She closed her eyes, letting the sea breeze run its invisible fingers through her hair. Unfortunately, the crisp, briny air did little to ease her throbbing headache.

Ever since her little blow-up with An-xi, Ying had not had a good night's sleep. The accusations he had flung at her plagued her mind, making it difficult to concentrate on anything. It was a miracle she'd even managed to finish work on her new prototype of the Octopus.

Today, they would judge whether or not it could achieve what it was supposed to.

"You don't look well," Ye-yang's voice echoed from beside her.

"We can turn back and reschedule the prototype test." He was watching her with his brows dipped in a frown, clearly disapproving of her insistence on being here.

"I'm fine. It shouldn't be much longer," she replied. She could sense Ye-yang's bristling frustration, but she chose to ignore it. To Ye-yang and the High Command, a delay of a single day might not be much, but to her, every passing day was one too many. The argument with An-xi only served to solidify that conviction.

An-xi had barely spoken to her since, the two of them brushing by each other awkwardly every time they crossed paths in the guild. They had traveled to the docks on board the same squeezy wagon this morning, without exchanging a single word. Several times she contemplated apologizing to him, but eventually stopped short because she didn't know what to say that would matter. She could not bring back two years of lost time.

In An-xi's words, things had changed. Even if she regretted her decisions, she still had to face the consequences, no matter how much it hurt.

A flash of gold broke through the water on the starboard side of the ship, its curved, shiny surface swaying with the ebb and flow of the waves. The hatch at the top popped open, and a head of frizzy hair appeared.

When she heard that the new prototype was ready for testing, Master Lianshu had jumped at the opportunity to helm its maiden voyage. Ying didn't stop her, because she knew she couldn't. When it came to matters of engineering, absolutely nothing could stand in the way of Aogiya Lianshu and what she wanted to do.

"Well, that was incredible!" the guild master declared, voice vibrating with exhilaration. She arched her neck toward the bronze tripod sitting on deck, where several sticks of incense had been left smoldering. "How long was I gone?" she asked.

"Five sticks of incense, Master Lianshu," the apprentice who had been manning the incense counter shouted in reply.

Five sticks. That was still only half the amount of time that they required.

Ying had already tried her best to increase the air capacity on board and streamline the vehicle, yet this was the best she could do.

"How far did you manage to go?" she asked.

Lianshu held up the open palms of both hands, a smug grin tugging at her lips. "Great job, kid!" she said. "That completely surpassed my expectations."

Ten fingers. Ten buoys. Ying squinted into the distance, trying to spot that tenth buoy from her vantage point. She could barely get past the third one before the increasingly tumultuous waves made it impossible to continue counting.

To assess the total distance that the Octopus could cover before the stored air ran out, they had carefully positioned floating buoys at fixed distances from the starting point. According to rough estimates and extrapolations made by the guild masters and the generals of the Cobra's Order, any underwater vessel would have to be released approximately ten buoys away from the Blood Phoenix's fleet, because that was the closest that the Order's ships could get before they would invariably alert the enemy, giving them time to redirect their Blades.

I did it.

Ying blinked, still trying to reconcile the implications of Lian-shu's report.

Her new prototype had made it ten buoys *and back*, which meant that not only could it carry someone to the pirate fleet, it could also bring the person back to safety. That had been one of her greatest concerns as she tinkered with the design of the vessel. If the Octopus could only manage a one-way trip, then so would its driver. The idea of sending someone away—knowing they would never return—was not one that she liked to entertain. Too many lives had already been lost without volunteering even more.

"The speed generated by the newly streamlined body and the water propulsion mechanism was impressive," Lianshu remarked, having steered the Octopus alongside the ship. She clambered up a rope ladder and onto the deck. "I didn't expect us to overcome that challenge so quickly, but now that we have, we can move on to the *actual* test. Unfortunately, the explosive force still isn't quite up to expectations, but I think if we tweak the gunpowder formula a little more, we should be able to—"

"Wait," Ying said. "What are you talking about? What actual test? What gunpowder formula?"

"Gunpowder for the explosives that we're going to fit to these vessels, of course," Lianshu replied, clucking her tongue in admonishment. "How else did you think we're going to destroy those pesky Blades? I'm not absolutely certain the Firecrackers will work yet—officially they're called the Bladebreakers, but I much prefer Fire-crackers, don't you?—anyway, hopefully the force will be sufficient to crack open the hull of these things"—she gestured at the Octopus prototype that was being hauled back up on deck by the other apprentices—"so that we can shred those Blades into pieces."

Ying's blood ran cold.

They were going to fit explosives to the vessels. Explosives so devastating they would rip the entire metal body of the vehicle apart, turning the Octopus into an erupting ball of deadly projectiles—into a Bladebreaker.

"But if you do that, then the driver . . ."

The Octopus was not designed to be a driverless vehicle. It required someone to steer and operate the various mechanisms on board, which was why air storage had been such a critical issue. The jubilation from moments ago quickly faded away, replaced instead by an existential dread.

"How many of these are you intending to deploy?" she whispered.

"Fifty to a hundred?" Master Lianshu replied. The chirpiness of the guild master's tone was harshly dissonant with the implications of those numbers. A hundred vessels meant a hundred explosives; a hundred explosives meant a hundred dead.

Even if the Octopus was capable of a return journey—this journey was never meant to happen.

"Ying, you don't have to be a part of this if you don't want to," Ye-yang said softly, placing a reassuring hand on her shoulder. "You've already done enough."

Ying briefly shut her eyes, letting out a long, slow breath. An icy wind blew across the back of her neck, sending a shiver down her spine.

I should do that, she thought.

Leave.

Her job here was complete and her end of the bargain fulfilled. She had given them her prototype and made it work exactly as they required. Whatever they did to it now, whatever deformed, mutated monster they created, was out of her hands.

Arms folded across her chest, Lianshu regarded Ying with disdain. "Bloodshed and sacrifice are part and parcel of war. I truly don't get it. Shan-jin was exactly the same, always waxing lyrical about how we should try to reduce casualties to zero, how we should find ways to avoid death. It's naive!" she said. The guild master stalked away, belting out instructions in preparation for the next stage of testing.

"Why didn't you tell me?" Ying asked quietly. "You already knew, didn't you? Even before coming to Larut."

"If I had told you, would you have come back?"

"Of course not." Ying looked up at Ye-yang, disappointment and disgust reflected in her eyes. An-xi said that time had changed everyone—everyone but Aogiya Ye-yang. With him, it was still lies and secrets and half-truths, never trust and honesty.

"We've already tried everything, Ying. Every single one of our airships—all six of them—were shot down by projectiles that came from underwater, before we even so much as glimpsed a shadow of those Blades." Ye-yang sighed. "We need eyes beneath the surface, and once we find the Blades, we need to destroy them swiftly, decisively, before they even see us coming. What we have now is not good enough. Our weapons were not designed to combat these enemies."

"And how do we know that these Bladebreakers are going to work any better? We don't even know what a Demon's Blade actually

looks like, or what they're made from. To be sending so many men—
boys—to their deaths for the sake of a mission that is hardly guaran-
teed success is absurd!"

If her a-ma were around, he would have a solution. He would find
a way to overcome this crisis facing the Antaran isles without having
to resort to pointless sacrifice.

"I don't take uncalculated risks, Ying." Ye-yang hesitated for a
moment, then he pulled out an unlabeled journal from between the
cross-folds of his robes and handed it to her.

Ying skimmed through its contents. Each page had a scrap of
parchment attached, written in messy, unintelligible code, followed
by a translation of the actual message that it contained. There were
only six such fragments in total, yet it was alarming enough.

"This . . ."

The information was patchy, but it still formed the most cohesive
and plausible account of the Blades that she had come across. Key details
about the vessel's overall structure and form, brief notes on its operating
mechanisms—enough for her to paint a hazy image in her mind.

A ship reminiscent of a blue whale, with a skeleton of metal and
walls of glass.

That's why they know the explosives will work.

"You have a *spy* in the Blood Phoenix?"

There was no other explanation for this. The source had to come
from within.

"I *had* a spy in the Blood Phoenix. We've received no updates for
over a year."

Ying's fingers clenched around the journal. Once again, she was the fool. Ye-yang had it all figured out, each step carefully calculated and planned from the beginning. She was merely one of the many pieces on his weiqi board, as she had always been.

A bolt of lightning crashed from the skies—and into her heart.

What more was he keeping from her? How else was he planning to manipulate her to achieve what he wanted?

Every betrayal, every lie, still bled fresh inside her mind, the scab ripped off before old wounds could heal. Tears burned in her eyes, tears that he didn't deserve.

"Master Lianshu, we're almost ready," an apprentice hollered over the roar of thunder.

Ying turned to see Chang-en hand An-xi a bundle of innocuous copper cylinders, each one no longer than the width of a scroll. An-xi disappeared through the hatch of the prototype vessel to fit the cylinders within, then hopped out a moment later.

The explosives.

Dread pooled in the pit of her stomach, acid churning as she watched them slam the hatch shut and roll the prototype over to the catapult mechanism sitting near the bow of the ship. Once everything had been prepared, the Bladebreaker would be flung into the distance, where it could detonate out of range from the *North Wind*. There would be no casualties today, yet the success of this test would foretell the deaths of dozens.

"Hurry up! Let's get this going before the storm arrives," Lianshu shouted at the apprentices who were loading the Bladebreaker onto the catapult harness. She shoved one of them aside and began adjusting the straps herself. "Okay, everyone stand by!"

A single raindrop landed on Ying's cheek.

"Launch!"

At the guild master's command, the giant catapult was fired, sending the bronze vehicle hurtling through the air. Ying watched with bated breath as her prototype, with its deadly cargo, plunged into the ocean with a resounding splash. She imagined it sinking slowly into the murky depths, closer and closer to the trenches below.

One, two, three, four, five—

The sea rumbled, as if a monster were stirring from the deep. The *North Wind* shuddered. Ye-yang's arm immediately went around Ying's shoulders, stabilizing her from the ship's sudden sway.

Master Lianshu stared unblinking at the circular gauge in her hand, linked to an underwater detector suspended beneath the *North Wind* that would measure the amount of force released by the explosion. If there was an explosion.

The pointer on the gauge remained perfectly still.

Ying almost let go of the breath she had been holding—but then the silver needle swung violently across the face of the meter, straining to fly entirely off its pivot.

Her heart sank.

Master Lianshu's explosives had worked.

"Aha!" The guild master held up the gauge, a victorious smile stretching across her face. Cheers erupted from the other apprentices.

"Ying, it worked!" Chang-en cried, running over to her. "I can't believe—"

Suddenly, the ship lurched sideways, knocking everyone off

balance. Chang-en crashed into An-xi, who had been minding his own business nearby, and the two of them went rolling toward Ying. The ominous gray skies cast a grim shadow upon them. Rain pelted down relentlessly, and lightning zigzagged in flashes of glaring white.

Ying leaned forward, clinging on to the wooden taffrail. Her eyes widened.

"Ye-yang, look." She pointed one trembling finger straight ahead, where a yawning hole had appeared in the middle of the black waters. It was growing by the second, waves lashing violently as water emptied into the gaping maw.

Had the explosion triggered this? Or was this Abka Han's way of showing his displeasure at what they planned to do?

"It's a maelstrom," Ye-yang replied. Turning toward the ship's captain, he shouted, "Collapse the sails and veer hard left! We have to get out of the vortex radius before we're dragged down!" Already the ship's hull was tipping farther and farther left. Men were struggling to keep their footing, and Lianshu was hugging the thick wooden trunk of the ship's catapult tightly.

The captain spun the wheel with steady hands, and the deckhands quickly took in the sails, as befit trained members of the High Commander's personal guard. With their swift actions, the *North Wind* began to right itself, inching away from the eye of danger. Ying's heart raced inside her chest as she held on for dear life, with the wind and rain sending her hair whipping in all directions. The only thing that was keeping her moored was the warmth of Ye-yang's chest against her back, like a protective shield around her.

She turned to look at him, and the calm gray pools of his eyes seemed to say that everything would be all right.

"We're going to die!" An-xi shrieked through the thunderous roar of the winds. He was still tangled with Chang-en not far from Ying's feet, his skinny arms hugging a baluster.

The ship seemed to stabilize as it sailed farther away from the walls of the vortex. Relief was palpable on the faces of everyone on board. But just as they thought they had made a narrow escape, the hull of the *North Wind* struck against the side of a craggy rock that had been concealed by the turbulent waves. The entire vessel keeled left.

There was a loud, forbidding crack—and the taffrail that Ying, An-xi, and Chang-en had been leaning their weight on snapped. They fell.

"Ying!" she heard Ye-yang shout.

He grabbed her by the right arm, barely in time to stop her from plunging into the lapping waters below. Ying dangled precariously in midair, with Chang-en hanging on to her left leg and An-xi clinging to his waist.

She glanced down. Chang-en's fingers were now sliding dangerously down her ankle—then they slipped away altogether.

"No!" she screamed, watching helplessly as her two friends plummeted into the unforgiving waters, terror the only thing she could see in their eyes. "Chang-en! An-xi!" She searched the dark, crashing waves for any sign of them, but there was none. They had disappeared, swallowed up by the merciless seas.

"Ying, hold on. I'm going to try to swing you back up," Ye-yang said, with only one arm still circled around a baluster and the other holding on to her. His arms strained, the muscles along his neck pulling taut.

"Let go!" she cried.

If he didn't let go, then he would die with her. The rain continued to batter down, sea spray thrashing violently at her feet. She was not going to make it out of this storm—but Ye-yang still had a chance.

Reaching up with all the might she could muster, she pried his fingers away from her.

"Stop! What're you doing?" Ye-yang stared down in alarm, fear flashing across his eyes. "Don't you dare!"

Ying let her gaze linger upon his face one last time, tracing the slope of his thick brows and the familiar sharp angles of his cheeks down to his jawline. It was unfair that he was still this handsome, even with his braids tangled by the wind and his robes ripped by splintered wood. She wondered if she looked a wreck and that would be the last memory he had of her.

Forcing out a smile, she said, "Goodbye, Ye-yang," just as she managed to free herself completely from his grip. She hurtled downward, the distance between them growing wider.

"Ying!"

And then, as her back struck the surface of the angry waters, she saw him let go—and leap in after her.

CHAPTER 11

PLANNING FOR THE HIGH COMMAND'S SOLSTICE HUNT turned out to be a lot more enjoyable and less intimidating than Nian had imagined. The days in the lead-up were filled with never-ending meetings with the various supervisors, overseeing preparations for invitations and scheduling and food choices, and even ensuring that there would be an adequate supply of arrows and other hunting implements for the participants. Nian had never been busier—and never happier.

"Most of the clan chieftains have already arrived yesterday. We're expecting the stragglers to reach Fei within the next few days, in time for the banquet," Qorchi reported, skimming down his long list of illustrious attendees.

The solstice hunt had always been a significant event for the High Command, a chance for the chieftains of the many Antaran clans to gather and renew their pledges of allegiance. This year was particularly important, because it was the first time that they would be swearing fealty to a new High Commander, one who had yet to prove his mettle in the eyes of many.

Soon, all these distinguished guests, including the other beiles, would descend upon the hunting grounds located at Wu Lin, the mist-filled woods at the northeastern section of the isle that was usually used for military training exercises. Clean, white gers had been set up to form a temporary campsite that the hunt's participants would use over the three-day period, surrounding an extensive area of freshly hewn grass that would be the hunt's main rallying point.

"And preparations for the banquet?" Nian asked.

"Everything is in order, Lady Nian."

"I would not expect anything less from you." With the graceful flick of her wrist and a gracious smile, Nian dismissed Qorchi to carry on with his duties. Dense clouds rolled across the sun from the direction of the coast, casting a bleak shadow across the camp. The low rumble of thunder echoed overhead.

She would have to quicken her inspection of the site, before the rain began. Hopefully the storm would pass quickly, and Abka Han would bless them with good weather for the coming days.

The soft clipping of horseshoes made her take pause. She turned, finding Ye-kan riding toward her upon his black stallion. He was wearing a set of emerald-green riding robes that complemented the slight tan of his skin, black leather boots pulled halfway up his calves. His braids were neatly fastened with a polished silver cuff, accentuating the hollows of his cheeks.

"What brings you here? I thought you might have gone along for Ying's prototype test," Nian asked, trying to shift her focus away from the pounding of her own heart.

She had learned about today's excursion from Ye-yang, who mentioned it in passing when she had delivered her update about the solstice hunt preparations last evening. After that rather unexpected turn to her guild visit three weeks back, Nian had been meaning to check in on her sister, find out if things had been resolved with

Niohuru An-xi, but the hectic schedule made it impossible for her to step away. It was just as well, since Ying would also have been busy building her new prototype. She would have to wait until after the hunt to seek permission for another trip down to the guild.

Ye-kan beamed, sliding off his steed and striding to her side. "I was going to, but I thought a certain someone might miss me," he said. It was only a joke, but it made the butterflies flitter in Nian's stomach. "How are the preparations going? Need any help?"

She shook her head. "We're almost done. I was going to head back to the palace after doing a final inspection of the campsite."

Ye-kan raised his eyebrows, seeming impressed. "Already?" He glanced down at her mud-stained boots and the blades of grass clinging to the hem of her robes. "You could have let the servants do all this, you know. When E-niye organized the solstice hunts, she never even stepped foot out of her parlor. She'd have a fit if a single drop of mud got onto her shoes."

"I can't possibly hold a candle to your e-niye, can I?" Nian smiled. She had only seen the woman once, but it was enough to leave a lasting impression.

She still remembered the moment when Lady Odval had walked into Qinzheng Hall for the Fu-li victory banquet, trailing a careful step behind the former High Commander. She was resplendent in silk the shade of brilliant turquoise, silver embroidery of lotus flowers trellising up the fabric of her skirt. There was a proud tilt to her chin, and her swallowtail updo was decorated with a dozen pins with gold filigree bearing the likeness of peonies and phoenixes in flight.

Compared to Lady Odval, she was an ugly duckling. Out of her depth.

"Don't belittle yourself," Ye-kan replied, briefly surveying the campsite. "You've done good! Better than anything *I* could have done. Don't compare yourself to my e-niye. She was an absolute terror—that's how she got everyone to fall in line. Whenever she was mad, she'd tap on the table with that murderous silver nail guard of hers, like this"—he placed an index finger on her arm, tapping painfully slowly—"and that's when you'd know you were in serious trouble." He placed two fingers above his head, like curved horns. "My e-niye was a qilin reincarnate."

She smacked him on the arm. "Can't you be serious for once?" she complained, stifling a laugh. "If you have so much time on your hands, go to Yuanxi Hall to help entertain the clan chiefs. Don't get in my way."

"Why would I do that? I'll only be an eyesore, as always." Ye-kan snorted. "Don't worry. My older brothers will gladly fill those shoes for you. Who knows what they're plotting at this very moment?"

Hopefully nothing mutinous, she thought. Before coming to Fei, she had overheard Wen and the clan elders discuss the fraught political situation within the High Command several times, enough to know that Ye-yang's position was still unstable. They had to ensure that the solstice hunt went off without a hitch—so that those other factions had no excuse to siphon power away.

"Beile-ye! Lady Nian!" An anxious Nergui appeared out of nowhere, running up to them with a black silk bundle clutched to his chest. He was drenched from head to toe, loose strands of hair hanging disheveled across his ashen face.

"Something terrible has happened," Nergui cried. His beady eyes took an anxious skim of their surroundings, then he hurriedly ushered them both inside one of the tents. Once the door was shut, he said, "The High Commander is *missing*."

"What do you mean?" Ye-kan asked cautiously.

Nergui fell to his knees, pressing his forehead to the ground. "It's all my fault, Beile-ye," the steward cried. He lifted his tearstained face. "A storm struck while we were out at sea, and our ship was caught in a maelstrom. In the chaos, the High Commander fell overboard, together with . . . together with . . ." His gaze shifted toward Nian, and all at once she knew. "With Aihui Ying."

"What did you say?" she whispered.

Ye-yang had gone overboard . . . with Ying?

Dread and alarm intertwined inside her, forming a suffocating web around her heart.

"I should have been faster! I should have caught him!" Nergui burst out, slamming his forehead against the floorboards.

Ye-kan sank down onto an empty chair, staring blankly ahead. "Have we sent out a search party?" he asked.

"The High Commander's personal guard has been deployed, but it will be difficult for them to make much progress until the storm subsides." Nergui carefully unwrapped the bundle he had been carrying, bringing out a nanmu box, intricately carved with the same cobra emblem that was emblazoned on all the formal court robes of officials in the High Command. He placed it gingerly in front of the fourteenth beile and opened it to reveal a large jade seal the shade of vibrant green, with a curled, slumbering serpent sitting silently on top.

Nian's eyes widened. Was this—the imperial seal of the High Command?

"Why are you showing me this?" Ye-kan asked, forehead creasing into a frown.

Nergui picked up a brocade scroll, the only other item that had been wrapped in his bundle, unfurling it carefully. Clearing his throat, he began reading. "'By order of His Excellency, the High Commander, it is decreed that should any misfortune befall him, rendering him unable to wield command over the Cobra's Order, this responsibility should pass to the fourteenth beile, Aogiya Ye-kan, until the time when the High Commander is able to resume his duties. If that day does not come within three cycles of the moon, then the position of High Commander shall formally be passed to the fourteenth beile on the first day of the fourth lunar month.'"

Time momentarily stood still as the chief steward's words reverberated in the air. A crash of thunder boomed overhead as the first foreboding drops of rain struck the roof of the ger.

This was almost . . . a succession decree. The weight of what was written on that scroll had far-reaching implications beyond anything Nian could have ever anticipated. There were three other beiles in the wings, all of whom were far more senior than Ye-kan. It was absurd for them to be sidelined in favor of the young fourteenth prince.

"This is a secret decree that the High Commander drafted

specifically for you," Nergui explained. "There is another that is meant to be announced to the entire court, placing you in charge of the High Commander's seal in his temporary absence."

"That's impossible," Ye-kan snapped when he finally came back to his senses. He grabbed the decree out of Nergui's hands, reading each line carefully for himself. His face drained of its color. He stared at the chief steward, then at Nian. "It's impossible," he repeated. "Why would he do that?"

"It is not our place to question the High Commander's orders, Beile-ye," Nergui replied. "Please, we need you to abide by the decree and assume command—immediately. The first and second beile have already heard rumors of the incident and have sent their stewards to inquire after the situation. If they discover the truth, if they realize that the High Commander could be . . . could be—"

Dead. If they realize that the High Commander could be dead.

"Don't say it!" Ye-kan barked, his eyes flashing with a deadly glare. "Nothing will happen to the High Commander. He's survived worse before." His gaze darted toward Nian, and his tone softened. "And Ying too. Nothing will happen to either of them. They'll return soon, I'm sure of it."

Nian lowered her eyelids, briefly regulating her own unraveling state of mind. Her heart bled at the thought that she might never see her beloved sister again, worry taking a stranglehold over her heart. But there was no time to indulge in sorrow. The solstice hunt was in a few days, and the High Commander's absence would certainly be called into question.

When she opened her eyes once more, resolve shone in her dark irises. She turned to Ye-kan and said, "Nergui is right. You have to take command. You know what will happen if any of the other beiles are given this authority. They will not wait a single day before they burn this decree and declare themselves the new High Commander. When that happens, there'll be a bloodbath in the palace and within the Order, because they will not allow any of Ye-yang's supporters to live."

And that included them.

Upon further thought, Nian could understand why Ye-yang had prepared this edict as a fail-safe, in the unlikely event that he met with any accidents. If his absence was only temporary, then Ye-kan would be the only Aogiya who could likely be trusted to hold command—and return it when the time came—if only because Ye-kan had never shown any ambition for this seat of ultimate power.

"But I'm not prepared for this!" Ye-kan protested. He ran his fingers through his hair in frustration. "The only thing I'm good for is wielding a sword and crossbow! Send me to fight a war, sure—but you cannot put me in front of that pack of scheming wolves and expect me to play their political games."

"It won't be for long," Nian replied, placing a reassuring hand on his shoulder. "Just like you said, the High Commander will return. And so will my a-jie. When they come back, everything will go back to the way it was." Maybe if she said it enough times, then she could also convince herself of this—that Ying and Ye-yang were not lost to the seas.

Ye-kan still looked bothered and uncertain, but he remained silent, swallowing five cups of water instead.

"How many made it back from the ship?" Nian asked the steward.

"Besides Lady Lianshu, there were three guild apprentices and four of the High Commander's personal guard who returned. They've all suffered minor injuries and have been temporarily sent to the palace," Nergui said.

Nian folded her arms across her chest, pondering the situation. She had never met Aogiya Lianshu before, but she had heard bits and pieces about the eccentric guild master from Ye-kan. Although Lianshu technically had no stake in a succession battle, there was no guarantee that she would cooperate with them instead of revealing everything to the other beiles. The three other apprentices were also liabilities.

"Keep them locked in for now. At least until the solstice hunt is over and the other clan chiefs have left Fei. No one else must know about what really happened," she declared. "The banquet will proceed as planned."

CHAPTER 12

THE FIRST THING THAT YING SAW WHEN she regained consciousness was someone staring down at her, so close that all she could see was a pair of beady, buglike eyes. She instinctively shot right up, crashing against the stranger's forehead.

A piercing howl rang out.

"Heavens! Is this how you treat your savior?" the girl screeched, hopping around the room while clutching her head. "I knew we should have just left you to freeze in the ocean!"

Ying ignored the racket, quickly surveying her surroundings. She was in a small, sparsely furnished room, with only a single wooden bed, a square table, and two bamboo stools. "We're on a ship?" she asked, noting the slight sway of her body. Her nose tickled, and she burst into a loud sneeze. A slight chill crawled all over her skin.

"Where else do you think you'd be? I fished you out, and this is the thanks I get!"

Her self-proclaimed savior was a young girl who looked only about Nian's age, with rosy cheeks and greasy hair done up in two pigtails. She wore a drab blue aoqun, with brown patches at the elbows of her pipa sleeves. "You're Qirin," Ying said.

"From Wei Zhou," the girl admitted, sticking her chin proudly in the air. She flopped onto a stool, propping one leg up on the table. "Looks like the seawater hasn't addled your brain."

Ying searched her memory, putting together all the messy pieces that she could gather. They had been testing Lianshu's explosives with her submersible, and then a horrific storm had struck. Thunder and lightning flashed in her mind's eye, followed by the sight of the wooden taffrail cracking beneath her. Chang-en's and An-xi's terrified faces before they were swallowed by the lapping waves. She had been falling toward the choppy waters down below—and then the last thing she remembered before she was engulfed by the sea was Ye-yang, diving in after her.

"Was I alone when you found me? Was there anyone else with me?" she asked anxiously.

The girl smirked. "Thought you'd never ask." She grabbed a handful of roasted melon seeds from a bowl on the table and popped a couple into her mouth. "Tall young man? Angular jaw, ridiculously high nose bridge, and eyes that look like storm clouds?"

Ying nodded.

"He's dead."

Her heart stopped, overwhelmed by a sudden, numbing sense of disbelief. He was . . . dead? How was that possible? He was Aogiya Ye-yang, High Commander of the Antaran isles. He had single-handedly engineered his own rise to power, outwitting all his competitors—and his own father—to win the final victory. He was supposed to rescue the Antaran people from the crisis they were facing, to sweep across the Empire to fulfill his ambitions.

He was supposed to atone for how he'd treated her, so that maybe one day she might be able to finally forgive him for what he had done.

How could he be *dead*? And for what? Because he had jumped in to save *her*.

Her throat constricted, making it hard to breathe.

Ye-yang is dead. Chang-en and An-xi are dead. Everyone is dead, and I'm—

The Qirin girl suddenly burst out in a roar of laughter, clapping her hands in delight. "You believed me! You *actually* fell for it!" she said.

Ying stared, confused.

"I'm only joking. Gods, you're a gullible one." The girl wiped the tears from her eyes. "Those three are fine." She paused, puckering her lips. "Well, not exactly *fine* fine, but alive."

"Three?" Hope sprang up inside her. They were alive. All of them. "Where are they? Are they badly hurt?" Ying moved to get off the bed, but the moment she shifted her body, a piercing shot of pain gripped her left arm. She winced, glancing down at the thick bandage wrapped around her forearm.

The girl clucked her tongue in disapproval. "There's no hurry. I already said they're alive, didn't I?" She picked up a small clay bowl and held it in front of Ying. "Ginger soup. I'm sure you don't want to catch pneumonia and actually die. You're lucky there was a warm current passing through the straits, else you'd have frozen to death."

Ying took the bowl warily, studying the golden liquid swirling within.

"If I was going to poison you, then I wouldn't have rescued you," the girl said.

Raising the bowl to her lips, Ying let the spicy liquid slide down her throat, warming her from the core.

"What's your name?" she asked.

"Jiang Yunshang."

"Yunshang . . . That's pretty. I'm Ying."

"I know. He already told me," Yunshang quipped. "Bunch of clueless guild novices caught in an unfortunate storm, right?"

Ying supposed she could consider herself a novice, and perhaps Chang-en and An-xi too, but Ye-yang? The half-truth had likely come from him, knowing his knack for lying.

She nodded slowly, playing along.

If they were on board a Qirin ship, it would be best if Ye-yang's identity was not exposed in case that brought danger upon all of them.

"Truth be told, I'm not sure which is more unfortunate"—the sly grin on Yunshang's face widened—"the storm, or escaping it."

"What do you mean?"

Yunshang plucked the empty bowl out of her hands, then stalked toward the cabin door, flipping the latch aside. She beckoned for Ying to follow along.

The door opened to a narrow corridor with more cabins flanking either side, ending in a short flight of stairs. Ying made her way up, trailing behind the Qirin girl, eventually emerging out on the main deck. Sunlight streamed down from the cloudless skies above, forcing her to shield her eyes from the sudden glare. It was almost as if the nightmarish storm from earlier had merely been a figment of her imagination.

When her vision finally acclimatized, the first thing that caught her attention was a large black flag billowing from one of the ship's masts, with the stylized image of a phoenix spreading her wings emblazoned in vermilion.

A memory was called back to the forefront of her mind—of the same phoenix looming high in the midnight sky, coldly watching on as a harbinger of death.

Her blood ran cold.

Yunshang spun around, sticking her hands on her hips, chin tipping proudly toward the flag.

"Welcome to the Blood Phoenix."

Before she could even close her gaping jaw, Ying was herded across the deck by Yunshang, who had a surprising amount of strength in those spindly arms.

Keep calm, she told herself.

It was easier said than done.

How could she possibly when they were on board one of the ships of the most notorious pirate fleet that roamed the Dunzhu Straits? In her mind's eye, she could still see the flames that consumed the horizon on the night of the Larut attack, see Feng-kai's lifeless body lying in his mother's arms.

This fleet—these *murderers* were the ones responsible for that.

Fear intertwined with anger as Ying's eyes roamed around the main deck and beyond. As she and Yunshang made their way down portside, she carefully took in the details of her precarious surroundings. There were two slightly smaller ships flanking the one that they were on, each with the same gigantic bamboo-battened sails that extended toward the skies. At least six more ships trailed behind. The hulls of each ship were painted deep maroon, matching the color of the flying phoenix—and fresh blood.

"Where are you taking me?" she asked, trying to disguise the tremble in her voice.

"I thought you wanted to see your friends?"

Along the way, they passed by several other ship hands, all of whom greeted Yunshang with a merry smile but narrowed their eyes at Ying with grave suspicion. The curious thing about it was that every single crew member was female—and when they reached the ship's bow, where the captain stood with her back to them, her slender fingers resting upon the wooden wheel, it finally struck Ying that the Blood Phoenix was in fact a fleet manned entirely by women.

Muffled cries drifted into Ying's ears.

"An-xi! Chang-en!" Ying rushed over to her friends, equal parts relieved and worried to see them there. Then her gaze met a pair of concerned gray eyes. She opened her mouth to call his name, before swallowing it back down again. She didn't know what Ye-yang had told Yunshang, so it was best to say nothing instead of the wrong thing.

The trio had been lashed to a wooden mast with coarse ropes binding their arms and legs, dirty rags shoved into their mouths. Thankfully, besides tattered robes and a few scratches here and there, they were, as Yunshang had said, very much alive.

"Er-dangjia," Yunshang greeted.

Er-dangjia? So this woman wasn't Li-na, the infamous captain of the Blood Phoenix.

The fleet's second-in-command turned, her feline gaze coming to rest upon Ying. Ying's breath hitched in her throat.

With sun-kissed skin a glorious shade of bronze and high cheekbones that accentuated the elegant tilt of her eyes, the woman was a stunning beauty. Even the late Lady Odval, who famously carried the title of "peony of the nine isles," would pale in comparison.

She was also considerably younger than Ying expected, possibly only a few years older than she was. Yet she was a pirate, and a leader among them, no less.

Ying lowered her head, raising her fist across her chest in an Antaran bow. "Thank you for saving our lives," she said quietly, trying her best to hide her unease.

The woman smiled, yet Ying could detect no warmth in her manner, only danger. "Don't thank me, thank Abka Han," she said, pointing up at the sky. "I only save those he refuses to take. If you managed to survive a storm of that magnitude, then I daresay you're not meant to die yet."

"You're Antaran?" Ying exclaimed. She had assumed that the entire crew was Qirin like Yunshang, judging from the knee-length tunics they wore and the loose-fitting black trousers tucked into sturdy leather boots. Even the captain herself wore maroon robes with a Qirin-style circular collar and had her long hair bound in a topknot, secured by a plain silver hairpin, and yet she had invoked the name of the Antaran god of the sky.

"I was born in Noyanju, to an Antaran father and a Qirin mother," the captain replied, "but my home is here now, upon the seas."

This woman was half Antaran, and yet she had joined this band of renegades who were acting in direct opposition to the interests of the nine isles, whose cannons and crossbows had claimed so many innocent Antaran lives. Ying's gaze flickered down toward the small silver crossbow that hung from the captain's waistband, cold fury flowing through her blood.

At the side, Yunshang picked up a feather duster and proceeded to amuse herself by tickling An-xi's ribs. He writhed and squirmed, face reddening as he struggled hopelessly against his restraints. The rag in his mouth, however, managed to come free.

"Stop it! Let me go, you vile, depraved sea slugs, or I'll—"

Yunshang stuffed the cloth back in. "Er-dangjia, can I feed this one to the sharks first? His breath stinks," she said.

Ying blanched, unsure if the girl was joking or being serious.

Before the captain could respond, a rumble shook the entire ship, followed by the sonorous sounding of a bullhorn. Ying instinctively reached out and clutched on to Yunshang's arm, just in time to prevent herself from being knocked over by the violent vibrations of the deck.

What was that? Another whirlpool? Or an earthquake?

Shrugging away Ying's hand, Yunshang strolled over to the starboard side and glanced out, completely unperturbed. "Prepare for docking!" she hollered, and a chorus of acknowledgment echoed back from the rest of the crew.

Ying followed the girl to the side of the ship, curiosity getting the better of her. A gasp left her lips when she peered over the taffrail.

The sea was parting, and through the crevice that formed, a monstrous creature—machine—was rising from the depths. Its length stretched almost two times that of the ship, with a smooth, silver back that gleamed under the sun's illumination. Its curvature almost reminded Ying of the back of a whale, but no whale would bear a tattoo of a bloody phoenix upon it. It was both frightening and magical, watching the vessel continue to rise above the surface. First a metallic top, then a body that was made entirely of glass, reinforced by a crisscrossing lattice of steel—a ship that was all window and no wall. Giant propellers brought up its rear, fanning out like a majestic tail that rose with a dramatic splash.

From afar, it would look like a shard of glass slicing through the sea.

A *blade* of glass.

CHAPTER 13

THIS WAS ONE OF THE INFAMOUS Demon's Blades of the Blood Phoenix fleet that everyone had heard of but no one knew anything about, sitting right before her in all its glory, sparkling like a jewel born from the ocean.

A true sight to behold.

Through the vessel's translucent glass walls, Ying could see the silhouettes of people moving to and fro, and a part of her burned to know what it was like on the inside. Her little Octopus was only large enough for one pilot, but a Blade was even larger than the largest ship she had seen sitting within Fei's harbor.

"Extending the bridges," someone bellowed.

Glass panels swung open from the side of the parked Blade, and a series of wide metal plates began to unfold one after the other, forming long gangways that extended toward the ship's deck.

There were three bridges in total, each one wide enough for two men to cross shoulder to shoulder.

A shadow appeared on the other end of the middle bridge as the first person emerged from the Blade and onto the sturdy gangway. A middle-aged woman with two shocking streaks of silver in her hair, extending from her temples toward the tight bun at the back of her head. She was seated upon a wooden wheelchair, operated by the small steam-driven engine fixed behind the backrest. A gray woolen blanket covered her from the waist down, shielding her legs from view.

"Da-dangjia," the crew greeted in unison once the woman arrived on the main deck.

Li-na.

This was the commander of the Blood Phoenix, rumored to be one of the most formidable pirates who sailed the straits. This was the woman responsible for the massacre off the coast of Larut.

Feng-kai's blood was on her hands.

Ying's fingers curled into tight fists by her sides, the sight of Li-na stoking a rising anger inside her.

The scant accounts of Li-na and her fleet in the High Command's record books had all been wrong. Not a single entry had painted a picture of Li-na that was anywhere close to the person she was staring at now.

"Da-dangjia"—Li-na's second-in-command stepped forward, her tone respectful—"did something happen? We weren't expecting the *Diamond* to surface for another couple of days."

The *Diamond*—an apt name. A diamond could remain untouched by fire, so what better home could there be for a phoenix reborn in flames? There were no diamond mines in the nine isles, but Ying had seen a diamond once, brought to Huarin by a merchant who had returned from the Empire. The many facets of the tiny stone had twinkled beneath the sunlight, reflecting the rays in the same dazzling way each glass panel of the Blade did.

"There's been a slight hiccup with the air pumps," Li-na replied.

Her voice was deep and mellifluous, carrying itself well across the deck even though her lips barely seemed to be moving. In her hand she held a small, circular bronze device, flipping it open to reveal a series of interlocking gears and springs connected to two pointed silver hands.

Ying had seen something similar before. Her father had brought one home—a gift from a traveling merchant—and claimed that it was supposed to tell time. A pocket watch, he said. She never figured out how exactly it was meant to do that, but she'd spent hours staring at the ticking hands, mesmerized by its rhythmic motion.

"We might have to remain docked for a while, depending on how quickly Wenjun can fix the pumps." Li-na's gaze fell on Ying, and then shifted toward the three young men still bound and gagged. "We have stowaways on board?"

"Not exactly. A couple of apprentices from the Engineers Guild that we rescued from yesterday's storm," her deputy replied. "I thought to wait for your arrival before deciding what to do with them, since their identities are slightly unusual."

Li-na studied them some more, her expression inscrutable. Then she turned to her second-in-command and said, "You're becoming soft, Keyan. Throw them overboard."

"What? No! You can't do that!" Ying burst out.

The crew members sprang into action, some moving to untie the boys while two others came behind Ying and took her by the shoulders. Long, dirt-lined fingernails dug into her flesh.

"No?" Li-na lifted her gaze, regarding Ying with a supercilious tilt of her chin. "Give me one good reason why I shouldn't feed you to the sharks, and maybe I'll reconsider. But let me tell you something, child—I rarely reconsider."

Ying fumbled for the right things to say, but panic left her mind a blank.

Li-na only waited for a brief moment, then she snapped her fingers, and Ying was pushed toward one of the gangways. Chang-en and An-xi were hauled behind her, both screeching through their gags.

Ying turned to Ye-yang, shooting him a look of distress. Didn't he always have a plan? Surely he wasn't going to let them be thrown back into the sea? Something about the calmness in his eyes told her that he had something up his sleeve, but it was disconcerting not knowing what it was.

Her feet were forced onto the silver metal bridge, and one glance at the lapping waves down below made her knees go weak.

Bang!

A sudden explosion sent her entire body ricocheting backward and tumbling onto the deck. An uproar went up among the crew. Everyone dashed toward the starboard side, craning their necks to get a better look at the source of the blast.

Thick plumes of white smoke were issuing from a hole—a fairly large one—that had been blown out of the glass near the *Diamond*'s rear.

"Wenjun a-jie!" Yunshang cried, her small face ashen with fear as she leaned out over the taffrail.

A string of fitful coughs came through the hole. As the smoke began to clear, a face covered in white powder appeared, spluttering and spitting as she tried to expunge the foul fumes from her lungs. The girl was keeled over, attire disheveled and long, straight hair hanging loosely about her shoulders and across her face. If it were night, she might pass for a ghost.

"Wenjun a-jie, are you all right?" Yunshang called, clearly delighted to find the other girl still alive.

"Caught a damned faceful of kaen gas!" the girl named Wenjun complained. "Shit tastes vile, let me tell you that." She cleared her throat loudly, then spat out a large glob of phlegm into the waters below. Then, still unsatisfied, she stuck out her tongue and wiped it furiously against the palm of her hand.

"Wenjun, what happened?" Keyan asked, her gracefully arched brows tipping into a frown. Beside her, Li-na remained impassive, as if the hole in the side of her submersible didn't concern her.

"I was trying to fix the air pumps, then *boom!* and here we are," Wenjun replied. Her shoulders sagged miserably. "The good news is that nothing flammable was involved, so there's no fire to put out. We also have enough spare glass panels to repair this—" She gestured at the gaping hole. "The bad news is the pumps are in a far worse state than before, and I don't know if I can fix it by myself. We might need to send for Master Cixin."

"But Master Cixin's gone on another one of her soul-searching retreats. She won't come back for at least another cycle of the moon." Keyan turned to Li-na. "Da-dangjia, we can't let the *Diamond* remain exposed for so long."

Something clicked in Ying's mind. A lifeline that might save them from having to walk the plank.

Her hand shot into the air. "I can help," she said.

All eyes turned toward her, some curious, mostly mocking. On the *Diamond*, Wenjun stood up and went on tiptoes to try to see who was speaking.

"You?" Li-na asked, a tinge of iciness in her tone.

"We," Ying said, correcting herself. "We can help. We're from the Engineers Guild, remember?"

Li-na scoffed and waved her hand. "Get rid of them."

"What? Didn't you hear what I said? We're from the guild. We can help to repair the ship! Why are you doing this?"

"*Because* you're from the guild."

Ying was pushed back toward the gangway, each unwilling step leading her closer to death.

"Wait, wait, wait!" Wenjun suddenly shouted. She disappeared from the hole in the *Diamond*, hazy silhouette sprinting along the length of the vessel until she appeared on the bridge. Coming right up to Ying, she drew apart the long curtain of hair that had blown across her face, revealing a pale, almost ghoulish complexion with large, walnut-like eyes. She stared.

Then she swiveled to face the captains, a certain cunning flashing in those lively eyes. "Da-dangjia, Er-dangjia, the tournament!" she said. She ran over and whispered something into their ears.

Li-na pursed her lips together thoughtfully. An agonizing moment of silence passed.

"Fine," the captain finally said. "We'll do as you suggest. Take them away and lock them in the stores for now."

~~~

They were all shoved down a hatch and sent tumbling belowdecks into the ship's food store, a cramped space that reeked of salted fish and brine-soaked vegetables. Their wrists and ankles were bound with rope, although one of the crew's matrons had kindly helped to remove the rags from the boys' mouths.

"Ying, are you all right?" Ye-yang asked. He quickly set himself upright in a sitting position, inching over to where she was. "You're hurt," he said, staring down at the blood that had stained her cream-colored sleeve.

"It's from the storm. Nothing serious," she replied. The wound must have reopened when she was struggling to free herself from the viselike grips of those deckhands, but it was the least of her worries. Every fiber of her body remained tense with fear, every muscle on high alert. "What about the rest of you?"

An-xi was still wriggling on the floor on his side, wailing in pain, while Chang-en was simply lying on his back stock-still, staring up at the ceiling in a daze.

"You know how they say your entire life and all your past incarnations will flash past your eyes just before you die?" Chang-en murmured. He turned toward Ying. "Turns out I was a prince in a past life, with a literal mountain of gold and a palace carved out of white marble, camouflaged within a snowy mountain valley." A wistful smile crossed his face. "Why don't I have that in this life?"

"How about I send you into the next life right now so that you can try your luck again?" An-xi screamed, kicking a loose head of cabbage at Chang-en's head. The distressed apprentice rolled over to a stack of crates, using them to help prop himself up. He tipped his head back and let out a loud cry. "We're going to die! They're going to use us as shark bait, or roast us for dinner, or do whatever barbaric things these pirates do."

Ying couldn't help but smile. If those two could still find it in them to say this much nonsense, then it meant that they were both fine. As for Ye-yang . . . She studied him carefully from head to toe. There was a gash running from his left ear to his cheek, ending just above his dimple. Other than that, she couldn't tell if he had any injuries.

"Does it hurt?" she asked quietly.

He shook his head. "I'm fine, but we should try to get your arm looked at, in case the wound festers." He looked around the store, scrutinizing every detail. "If they have some use for us, then we should be safe for the time being. Hopefully this will buy us enough time to figure a way to get out of here. I'll have to send a message back to High Command."

"How?" Hope flickered inside her like the glowing embers of a sandalwood incense tip. If Ye-yang had means of communicating with Fei, then there was yet a chance that they might get out of here alive.

Something clicked in Ying's mind. Lowering her voice, she whispered, "Through your spy?" Was that where Ye-yang's confidence came from? Why he hadn't seemed afraid when they were being forced to walk the plank?

"No. We haven't heard from them in a long while, long enough for us to believe that they are already dead. Even if that person was still on board, it would be too risky to try to uncover them and make contact. The identities of the Order's spies are known only to their original recruiters. Once they join the ranks, they only go by their codes."

"What was the code of the spy who was sent here?" Ying asked out of curiosity. It seemed almost pitiful, to have to give up their name and forever be known by a mere symbol. As if the person became secondary to the mission. As if they no longer existed.

"Black—"

The hatch leading to the main deck was abruptly flung open again, cutting their conversation short. A lithe figure slid down the ladder, the thick soles of her black leather boots landing with a resounding thump.

Wenjun.

Ying only recognized her because of the pearlescent sheen of her skin, which was unusual for someone who sailed the seas. She had large, walnut-shaped eyes and a slightly flat nose, and her pale lips curved downward in a judgmental pout. The girl had since changed into a fresh set of clothes and had her hair tied in a messy bun, fastened with . . . an ink brush.

Squatting down, Wenjun scuttled sideways like a crab, examining each one of them in turn with a circular glass eyepiece.

"Hmm."

She lowered her eyeglass and straightened herself up, regarding them with an air of quiet condescension.

"A-a-are you here to kill us?" An-xi stammered, inching closer to Chang-en for safety.

Wenjun rolled her eyes. She picked up a piece of dried cuttlefish from one of the baskets and smacked An-xi across the head. "If I wanted to kill you, then I would have let you walk the plank earlier, am I right?" she said.

"What do you want with us, then?" Ying asked cautiously. She didn't believe that Wenjun had saved them out of the goodness of her heart. There had to be a catch. Whatever Wenjun had up her sleeve could well be a worse fate than jostling with sharks, else Li-na would not have agreed so easily.

A crafty smile curled upon the girl's thin lips, sending goose bumps rising up Ying's arms. She walked up to Ying. "I thought that stuffy guild didn't take in girls? You must be quite something." Swinging herself onto a crate, she sat herself down with one leg propped up. "The annual Tournament of the Seas is happening in less than a week's time, and I've been having a little trouble with some of the modifications that I'm making to our boat," she said. "You're going to help me solve my problems."

"The Tournament . . . of the Seas?" Ying had never heard of such a thing before.

"A boat race?" Chang-en quipped, raising one skeptical brow.

"It's not *just* a boat race. It's the biggest event on the straits, and the only one where every single pirate fleet is represented," Wenjun said, sounding a little miffed at the lackluster response. "The winning fleet gets the Dunzhu Pearl, the mark of the pirate king, and no other fleet is allowed to challenge their claim to territory or loot for the rest of the year, until the next race. It's written into the pirate code. You should consider it an honor to be part of this."

Chang-en let out a hoot of disdain. "A *pearl*? Look, how about you let us go and I'll give you *ten* pearls that are even bigger and more expensive than that. I can even throw in a trunk of gold taels! That's all you pirates care about, isn't it? Gold?"

Wenjun's eyes narrowed, darkening with the cold glint of a sharpened blade. She flicked her wrist. A flash of silver skimmed the light.

Thud!

Chang-en swallowed hard, eyes slanting toward the dart that had impaled itself into the wooden crate he was leaning on. It was a mere hair's breadth from his left temple, its red silk tassel tickling the shell of his ear. A shocked silence simmered within the room.

"Hmm, I missed," Wenjun remarked, walking over and plucking the dart out. "It was supposed to go"—she pointed the silver tip right at Chang-en's forehead—"here." She pushed the point forward a notch, drawing out a single droplet of blood.

A trickle of cold sweat dribbled along the side of Chang-en's cheek, landing desolately on the floorboards. The lump in his throat bobbed, muscles tense along the sides of his neck. Chang-en had always been a patchwork of chaotic emotions, but fear was not one of them. Until now. If the fleet engineer were to stab him there and then . . .

Wenjun threw her head back, bursting out in peals of delighted laughter. "You look like you're about to piss yourself!" she howled.

She retracted her hand, sliding the dart back up her sleeve. "For the record—I never miss."

Ying didn't doubt that. Maybe it was the seasoned way in which Wenjun had sent that dart from sleeve to hand, hand to target, or maybe it was the brief glimpse of ferality that had appeared in the girl's eyes when she made the decision to strike. Behind the veneer of eccentricity lay something more dangerous, something that they couldn't take for granted.

"You're not wrong to think that a pearl is worthless. It is. In the past, the tournament was only a petty battle of unruly egos," Wenjun continued, as if that brief interlude had never happened, "but recently it's become much more than that. Besides the Dunzhu Pearl, there is one other prize that the winner will receive. Something that's actually valuable. Something that your wealthy Antaran clans can never provide." Her voice brimmed with eagerness, stirring up an inexplicable ripple of anticipation inside Ying. Wenjun's razor-sharp gaze swept the room, the right corner of her lips crooking upward once she saw that she had everyone's attention.

"A Blade."

A . . . Blade?

This new piece of information was a singular drop of ink falling upon clear waters, clashing fiercely with what Ying had previously known about the legendary vessels, about the pirates and how they functioned. Didn't the records say that Li-na and the Blood Phoenix controlled the Blades? But if that were true, then why would they care about winning one? And if this was a prize to be offered—who was offering it? The fine line between truth and myth blurred, forming a murky pool that clouded Ying's mind.

"Don't you already have the *Diamond*?" she ventured.

She caught the crease of disapproval forming between Ye-yang's brows, and the subtle shake of his head, but it was too little too late. The question had already spilled out, her curiosity getting the better of her.

"Yes, from last year's race, but it wouldn't hurt to have another one, would it?" Wenjun replied. Her tone turned somber. "A pearl is only a symbol, but a Blade is so much more. It's both weapon and shield, and gods know how important that is out here in these blood-sucking waters."

"And if we help you win this race, you'll let us go?" Ying asked.

Wenjun shrugged. "Maybe."

"Only maybe?" An-xi yelped.

"It's Da-dangjia's decision whether or not to release you, but I daresay your chances will be far better if we do win."

"What happens if we lose?" Ye-yang said, voicing the singular worry that was lurking at the back of their minds.

The grin reappeared on Wenjun's face, tugging higher with glee.

"If you lose—you die."

CHAPTER 14

THE FULL MOON HUNG LOW ABOVE THE treetops of Wu Lin, its warm, golden glow casting soft illumination upon the festivities at the hunting grounds. The rich fragrances of roasted meats and well-aged wines suffused the air, accompanied by the lively drumming of mechanical musicians and the tinkling bells hanging from the ankles of the capital's most skillful dancers. There was laughter. Chatter. But there was also something else—a quiet tension simmering beneath the surface of all this gaiety.

On a low dais set up at the head of the banquet stood an empty chair carved from ebony, the ends of its armrests curving upward to reveal the hissing faces of menacing cobras.

The first solstice hunt since the Order's seal of authority changed hands—yet the High Commander was absent.

Nian sat to the right of that empty chair, taking on the prime role as host of the banquet. She picked up the bronze cup that her attendant had just filled with wine, then quickly put it down again. The quiver in her fingers was too obvious.

Calm, Nian. You mustn't fluster.

Still, it was difficult not to, even as she knew that none of the attention was on her. Everyone's focus rested upon the jade seal that sat on the fourteenth beile's table, and everyone was waiting for someone else to ask the questions that circled in all their minds.

It was the second beile, Erden, who eventually broke the silence.

"Funny how Number Eight chose to hand the imperial seal to a kid like you, huh, Fourteen? When the three of us"—he gestured to himself and the two other beiles—"are sitting right here."

Nian knew that Erden was the most outwardly aggressive of the four lords—Ye-yang had mentioned this before in one of their lessons—but she had not expected such blatant belligerence and insubordination in front of the clan chiefs.

"Erden, are you intending to go against the High Commander's orders?" Ye-kan demanded. His fingers tightened around his wine cup. "That would be *treason*."

The second beile straightened his back and instantly grew a few inches, his bulky stature reminding Nian of a large bear. "Treason? If you ask me, you're the one committing treason. Why should we believe that the decree is real? You have the High Commander's seal," he said, pointing at the slab of jade, "so you could have forged the decree to usurp command! How do we know that you're not lying?"

Nian spied the slight tremble in Ye-kan's shoulders, and she prayed that he would be able to hold his ground in the face of Erden's fierce accusations.

Ye-han, the third beile, reached out and placed one fleshy hand on Erden's shoulder. He shook his head, hinting for the latter to back down. His narrow eyes creased into crescents upon his flushed, chubby face.

"There's no need to get so serious. Treason is not a charge that should be flung about so carelessly," he said. "I'm sure Erden is only

surprised, as we all are, about the High Commander's temporary—
and rather sudden—departure. It is not that we doubt the authenti-
city of the decree, but you cannot blame us for raising questions about
this rather bizarre circumstance. Where exactly has the High Commander gone, and when is he expected to return? If His Excellency
entrusted you with the imperial seal, surely you must know these
details."

Nian frowned. Unlike Erden, who behaved like a rabid dog and
could easily be subdued with force, Ye-han would be far more tricky
to deal with. The third beile was a seasoned politician and the richest
of the beiles, having amassed a sizable following and immense wealth
through the use of his glib tongue and shrewd socializing skills. If he
were to make a challenge for the imperial seal, then Ye-kan might
not be able to defend it.

While the third beile appeared to be defusing tension with his
intervention, his few simple remarks had cast more aspersions toward Ye-kan and lent weight to Erden's assertions. Several clan
chieftains were already murmuring in agreement.

"It is not up to any of us to question the High Commander's
decisions. I'm simply following the orders I've received. His Excellency will explain things himself when he returns," Ye-kan retorted.
"If you choose to defy the edict, then you'd best be prepared to face
the consequences when the time comes."

If *the High Commander returns.*

There was still no news of Ying's or Ye-yang's whereabouts, and
with each passing day Nian's fears and anxieties continued to grow.

"Number Fourteen, you're putting us in a spot," the third beile said, still wearing that innocuous yet strangely intimidating smile on his face. He clasped his hands together, the thick golden bangles that lined his thick wrists jangling noisily as he moved. "As much as I would like to trust you, this is command of the nine isles and the Order that we are discussing. You cannot expect everyone here to rely on your word and—forgive me for saying this—a rather dubious decree, am I right, little brother?"

"I agree with the third beile!"

"We cannot abide by a forged decree. We demand to know where His Excellency is!"

Once the first shout of protest rang out, others followed like a torrential flood. At Ye-han's behest, the tide had turned against Ye-kan. Erden's lips twisted in a contemptuous smile, pleased with the response. The first beile, Ye-lu, remained reticent, turning to ask his attendant for a top-up of wine, as if none of this furor concerned him.

"That's enough!" Nian said, her voice piercing through the rumble of objections. All eyes shifted toward her. Beneath the table, her fingers clenched around the silk fabric of her robes. "I'm sure everyone here is aware of the importance of the solstice hunt, and what its significance is for the unity and prosperity of the nine isles. That is why the High Commander instructed that the hunt *must* go on, even in his absence. We have no shortage of external threats, from the pirates, from the Empire. This is the time for every clan and every banner to stand in solidarity, not to tear ourselves apart from within."

An uncomfortable silence set in.

Ye-han's jovial façade faltered, the muscles in his cheeks stiffening. His gaze sharpened. "Lady Nian, perhaps you have forgotten who you are speaking to. This is Fei, not Huarin. I suggest you learn your rightful place, and when you should be seen and not heard," he said.

"Beile-ye, if my sister is in no position to speak, then what about me?"

Wen.

Her brother stood up from his assigned seat, beside the chieftain of the Ula clan, Ye-kan's maternal uncle. Two years of war had hardened the skin on Wen's back and left battle-weary creases upon his once youthful face. Under his leadership, the Aihui clan had flourished and grown in influence, but it was not without cost. A cost that Wen had chosen to shoulder by himself, while protecting their family in his own way.

The third beile folded his arms, saying nothing.

"Everyone is understandably concerned about the High Commander's absence, but as Nian quite rightly pointed out, the solstice hunt has always been of great importance to our people. I'm sure none of us would like to be responsible for incurring the wrath of Abka Han, in a time when we are in much need of his blessing." Wen paused, taking in the thoughtful nods from some of his peers. "I say we let the hunt proceed, and discuss the issue of the High Commander's whereabouts and the guardianship of the imperial seal at a later time, *if* His Excellency still has yet to return. In the meantime, since all the clan leaders and the commanders of the Eight Banners are gathered here, we can all help to keep an eye on things, am I right?"

"I agree with the Aihui chieftain. There's no harm in having some patience," said Ula Temuu, stroking the tip of his snow-white beard. He was the most senior of the chieftains, and the Ula clan was one of the most powerful in the Antaran isles, with roots running as deep as the ruling Aogiyas. A few simple words from him was enough to put an end to the argument.

Nian exchanged a glance with her brother, quietly heaving a sigh of relief.

Knowing that the fight was over, Erden's face twisted with fury. He snatched a jar of wine from the hands of his steward, taking a large swig to drown his frustration. Ye-han was far better at controlling his emotions, still smiling as he turned to engage in casual conversation with the other guests, as if the tense moment had never happened. As for the first beile, his surly, hawklike mien remained inscrutable, which could well make him the most dangerous of them all.

"Thank you," she caught Ye-kan mouthing to her, and she gave him an encouraging smile in return.

He had done much better tonight than either of them had expected, even if he still lacked political acumen when compared with the older beiles. When he had held his own against Erden, Nian saw the same aura of regality and assertiveness that she recognized in Ye-yang—a reminder that despite his everyday brashness and occasional immaturity, the same Aogiya blood ran through his veins.

Nian spent the rest of the banquet carefully observing the interactions between the invited guests, corroborating what she saw with what Ye-yang had taught her. For the first time, she was able to see the fault lines within the High Command with her own eyes.

"*The Antaran clans are like a pan of loose sand,*" Ye-yang had said, "*more inclined to scatter than to stay united. If we are not careful, our differences will divide us from within, faster than the external forces from without.*"

Each of the beiles maintained their own alliances, and then there were the larger clans, whose chieftains wielded considerable influence and power. What she had seen tonight was merely the tip of the iceberg, a glimpse into the fractious nature of the nine isles.

She let out a slow breath, trying to tame the apprehension that entangled her mind.

Wen had bought them some time, but if the High Commander still did not return, then a bloody storm lay waiting on the horizon. There was a delicate balance they needed to maintain—and she wasn't sure if they could.

CHAPTER 15

THE HORNS SOUNDED AT DAWN, SIGNALING THE start of the solstice hunt.

Icy-cold mist swirled around Nian's ankles, ghostly fingers extending themselves over her shoulders. Shadows flitted between the trees, and there was a constant prickling at the back of her neck, as if pairs of eyes watched her every move.

Today, Wu Lin thrummed with an air of danger. Foreboding.

"You really don't have to stay with me. I can look after myself," she said to Ye-kan, who was riding ahead and clearing a path by hacking at the bushes in the way. She had traded in her palace robes for a sharp set of riding gear today—fiery red robes with white fur trim, paired with a pair of loose-fitting trousers and leather boots. Her long black hair was fastened in a high ponytail around the back of her head, giving her a debonair appearance.

Traditionally, the High Commander's wife would also participate in the hunt, if only as a token show of support. Even though she had yet to marry into the Aogiya clan, Nian had volunteered to join. There was already plenty of speculation surrounding her engagement to Ye-yang, with several offhand comments passed at last night's banquet about a potential annulment.

If she was to stay on in Fei, to establish her foothold within the palace so that she could actually be of help to Ye-yang and Ye-kan in this tangled political cesspool, then there were some appearances that she had to keep up.

Like going hunting.

"I still don't understand why you insist on participating. Who cares what the other beiles say? I don't, and I'm pretty sure Number Eight wouldn't give a damn either. You could just get the attendants to hunt you two rabbits and call it a day. That was what E-niye used to do."

"I prefer to do things myself." Respect had to be earned, and she did not have the years of clout that Lady Odval had accumulated to be able to do the same. Nian brought her snow-white mare to a stop. "I'm serious—just go on ahead, else you'll lag too far behind the others."

Even though the hunt was meant to promote unity among the clans, it was still a competition. Every participant fought to return with the greatest number of prey, and bonus points were awarded to those who snagged rare catches. At the end of the three-day hunt, the rider who amassed the most points would receive a reward from the High Commander—and win the highest honor for his clan.

As childish as it might seem, succeeding in the hunt was a demonstration of strength and capability, something that Ye-kan desperately needed if he was to help stave off the offensives from the other beiles in Ye-yang's absence.

Ye-kan let out a derisive hoot. "Please, they won't beat me even if I give them half a day's head start," he said. "I'll help you catch some rabbits. Maybe even a mouse deer, if we're lucky."

They continued riding deeper into the woods, where the

vegetation grew denser and only sparse streams of light occasionally filtered through the thick canopy. A fur-lined cloak was placed upon Nian's shoulders.

"Keep that on so you don't catch a cold. Wu Lin's fog is absolutely miserable," Ye-kan said, his eyes still roving the forest floor in search of prey.

Ye-kan's warmth and clean musky scent lingered upon the fabric of his cloak, sending a flutter through Nian's heart. She tugged it closer around her frame, trying to focus on the path ahead instead of the rising heat up the sides of her neck.

"Rabbit!" Ye-kan breathed, pointing through a gap between the trees. Raising his bow and arrow, he quickly took aim and fired, then dashed ahead to collect his prey.

He returned moments later, carrying a gray rabbit by its ears. "I think I found a burrow. We can—"

A low rumbling interrupted Ye-kan—then the forest started to move.

"What's going on?" Nian asked, alarmed by the inexplicable shifting of the trees through the fog, leaves rustling in their wake. Rattled birds abandoned their nests and took to the safety of the skies, generating a cacophony with their flapping wings and cries of distress.

Ye-kan quickly moved alongside Nian, holding on to her reins. Their horses whinnied in protest, hooves frantically pounding the dirt.

"We must be at a plate junction," he said.

A plate junction. Qorchi had told her that Wu Lin was an artificial forest, built upon fragmented plates that could be repositioned at will using a set of controls. The unpredictability of the land coupled with its natural wall of fog made Wu Lin both an excellent protective barrier for the city of Fei and a tough training ground for the Order's soldiers.

But the plates weren't supposed to be moving during the hunt.

The vibrations of the ground stopped a short while later, returning the forest to its uneasy calm. Everything looked exactly as before, yet they knew they were no longer looking at the same patch of woods.

"Isn't it a coincidence?" a congenial voice called out. A small party of three emerged through the dense undergrowth, led by the first beile, Ye-lu. His gold ear cuffs gleamed in the dim lighting, well-oiled braids looping behind them. Nian did not recognize the other two barrel-chested men, but their clan pendants identified them as members of the powerful Tongiya clan, one of Ye-lu's closest allies. If her memory served her right, her sister's friend Chang-en also belonged to that clan.

"Don't you dare think of stealing my bounty," Ye-kan warned, shoving the rabbit he had caught earlier into the satchel hanging off the back of Nian's horse.

Ye-lu threw his head back and laughed, yet the keenness remained in his hawklike eyes. "Why would I do that? You know I've never paid much heed to the solstice hunt. No point in wasting energy on a game I know I can't win," he said.

And what of a game you think you can?

Nian had her reservations about the first beile. Out of the three older lords, he was the most reticent, displaying none of the second beile's aggression nor the third beile's ambition, yet the less he said, the more suspicious he seemed. Could he really be content with his lot, or did still waters run deep?

"I must say, I'm surprised, Lady Nian," the first beile continued, turning his attention to her instead. "Activating Wu Lin's subterranean plate mechanisms during the hunt? Quite ingenious."

"I'm sure everyone appreciates a good challenge," Nian replied, neither accepting nor denying responsibility. On the surface, she appeared unfazed; deep down, her apprehension grew.

If Ye-lu was giving her credit for putting the plates in motion, did that mean that he had nothing to do with it? Or was he lying to throw them off the trail?

Ye-kan suddenly pushed her from behind, pressing her down against the mane of her horse. An arrow sliced overhead, impaling itself in the trunk of an Antaran pine. Nian stared, aghast. Had Ye-kan been any slower, her head might have been pinned to that tree.

"Assassins!" the first beile shouted, cowering upon his steed with his hands shielding his head. His two companions switched out their bows for swords, deftly deflecting the flurry of arrows that came their way.

Ye-kan leapt onto Nian's horse, his arms circling around her to reach for the reins. Without waiting, he sent them racing through the woods, weaving between the maze of trees. Nian turned. Through the murky haze, she could see dark shadows gaining on them—shadows that resembled large, formless beasts. Behind them, the first beile's panicked screams faded into the distance.

A glint of metal caught her eye.

"Watch out!" Nian warned as the tip of an arrow came hurtling toward them.

Ye-kan's entire frame closed in more tightly around her like a shield. The arrow struck his left shoulder. He grimaced, clenching his jaw.

Then a second arrow flew out from the darkness, this time striking their horse on its hind leg. The mare bucked, and both Nian and Ye-kan went flying forward. They tumbled down a small slope, loose branches and stones jabbing painfully at their sides.

"Ahhh!"

The ground beneath them suddenly gave way, and they plunged downward through a narrow shaft, landing hard against rocky terrain. Every fiber of Nian's body was racked with pain. When the dust cleared, she slowly opened her eyes, meeting Ye-kan's clear, unblinking gaze.

"Ye-kan, are you all right?"

"I will be if you get off me . . ."

They were lying at the bottom of a man-made shaft, with smooth walls carefully hewn out of stone. And she was sprawled on top of him, her hands on his shoulders and his around her waist. The tips of their noses were almost touching, his warm breath tickling against her cheeks.

Nian gulped. Her mind went blank. She leapt up and stumbled backward, but a sharp pain shot through her right ankle, forcing her to sit back down again. She winced.

"What's wrong? Are you hurt?" Ye-kan asked anxiously. He picked himself off the ground and rushed to her side. Bending over, he gently lifted her trouser hem and peeled aside the cotton fabric of her sock, frowning when he saw the slight reddening at her ankle. "Might be a sprain," he said.

"It's nothing." Nothing compared to his injury.

Raising her fingers to the broken arrow shaft that still remained pierced through his shoulder, Nian hesitated. Guilt crept into her eyes. He could have dodged it if he weren't protecting her.

"No need to worry," Ye-kan said, sensing her distress. "It's only a small injury. Once we get out of here, the physicians can sort it out." He looked up. "I think we fell through one of the guild's old maintenance shafts. There's a whole network of tunnels and stores under Wu Lin, from when they first built the plate mechanisms, although most of them aren't used anymore."

He stood up, switching on one of the old kaen-gas lamps hanging from the rock wall. Warm light flooded the small cave.

"What do you think happened back there? Who sent those assassins? And who exactly were they after?" Nian asked.

Everything had happened in a blur, and various pieces of the puzzle were still floating haphazardly in her mind. First there had been the mystery of the shifting plates, then the "coincidental" encounter with Ye-lu. After that, assassins had appeared out of nowhere—assassins that none of them had actually seen, save for some vague silhouettes camouflaged against the shadows of the leaves.

The fear that she had seen in the first beile's eyes when the arrows started flying at them seemed genuine, yet she couldn't rule out the possibility that it was all an act.

"Someone who mistook us for a rare white tiger, maybe," Ye-kan joked.

She smacked him across the head. "Be serious!" she scolded. Trust him to be able to make light of a situation that could have killed them both.

Turning around, Ye-kan pointed toward his back. "Hop on."

"Excuse me?"

"Get on my back, unless you want to be stuck down here forever?"

Nian's tongue tangled itself in knots. Ye-kan was right, of course, because it would take too long for her to hobble out on her own. Even if he did give her a piggyback all the way out, it was for a perfectly good reason. All of this would be absolutely aboveboard, and—

The prince reached backward and grabbed her by the arms, pulling her onto his shoulders. He stood up, carefully adjusting her position upon his back so that she wouldn't be resting against the stump of an arrow that was still embedded in his flesh. If he sensed her discomfort, or detected her quickening heartbeat, he pretended not to notice.

They made their way through a narrow archway to a fork in the path that led to two separate tunnels. Ye-kan pulled out a silver circular pendant that had been tucked at his waistband, holding it on his palm.

"What's that?" Nian asked, peering curiously at the single needle attached to the face of the pendant. It oscillated back and forth, as if controlled by some unseen force, until it finally came to a stop pointing toward the left.

"A lodestone needle," Ye-kan replied. "Interacts with the natural properties of the earth to tell direction."

"Did you make that yourself?"

The prince nodded. "It's just a toy. Useless most of the time, unless you're lost in the forest. Like now." He pointed toward the tunnel on their right. "If we go that way, it should take us closer toward the city walls. We might be able to find an exit along the way."

"Mmm," Nian hummed. She took the lodestone needle from him, studying it more closely. No matter which direction she turned to, the needle pivoted back the same way. It was ingenious, really, making use of the natural properties of the stone to create this simple but effective device.

"Can I ask you something?" she said.

"Hmm?"

"Why did you give up engineering to join the military?"

She had always wondered why Ye-kan had given up his pursuit of engineering, after all the effort he went through to earn a place in the apprenticeship trial of the Engineers Guild. Occasionally, when he spoke of airship mechanics or weapon designs, his eyes would shine with enthusiasm—the same light that she recognized in her father's and sister's eyes.

He shrugged. "I wouldn't have made a very good engineer anyway. I don't have the sort of talent Ying has, so it's just as well that I gave it up."

"But the Order needs its engineers as much as it needs its soldiers."

"The Order *has* its engineers. It doesn't need me to be one." Ye-kan paused, a melancholy hanging upon his brows. "E-niye used to say that everyone has their own specific roles. Specific responsibilities. I'm an Aogiya, she said, and the people have placed their trust in us to lead, to secure the future of the nine isles. I've wasted enough time running away from my responsibilities. I only wish I hadn't realized that so late." His shoulder slumped. "I miss her, Nian. So much."

Nian could feel the sorrow radiating off him, footsteps heavy as he walked. She sighed. Ye-kan had never spoken of his mother's death so candidly before, always hiding his true feelings behind that devil-may-care attitude. Only now did she realize how deep that scar was.

"I'm sure Lady Odval is still watching over you from wherever she is," she said quietly. "Just like how I know that my a-ma and e-niye are watching over me."

"I know. I just wish I did more for her when she was here."

They continued plodding along in silence, lost in their own thoughts. The path meandered on, until suddenly—Ye-kan stopped.

"What's the matter?"

"Shh." He pressed an index finger to his lips.

There was a dim light glowing ahead, coming from a collapsed section of the tunnel wall. Muffled voices drifted in the stale air.

Ye-kan set her back down on the ground. They crept over, peering through the hole and into the immense chamber on the other side. It was an old, abandoned guild storeroom, with rotting shelves and leftover supplies strewn around—but it had been given a new lease on life. Several men were in the midst of stacking large wooden crates at the far end of the cavern, grumbling to one another as they worked.

"Are they from the Engineers Guild? Or the Order?" Nian whispered.

"I don't recognize any of them, and there hasn't been any instruction about repurposing any of these old stores."

Choosing to err on the side of caution, they waited until the men finished and left through a separate passageway. Ye-kan quickly clambered through the hole and into the cave before helping Nian over. They made their way to the small mountain of crates—at least thirty in total, she counted. At one corner of each crate was a small symbol stamped in red ink. A creature baring its sharp teeth, mane flaring and antlers extending regally upon its head.

A qilin.

One of the many mythical beasts from the Empire, and the namesake of the Qirin people.

Picking up a rusty metal bar that was lying on the ground, Ye-kan pried open the lid of one of the cases.

"Rice?" Nian puzzled, peering in at the pearl-white grains that filled the crate.

Ye-kan moved on to another crate, pushing aside the layer of straw within. This time, there were at least two dozen crossbows packed inside, along with bundles of gleaming new arrows. He flipped over one of the crossbows, revealing the symbol of a cobra branded into the wood. Nian swallowed hard, exchanging a troubled glance with him.

Someone was smuggling weapons. Not just any weapons— weapons that belonged to the Cobra's Order.

CHAPTER 16

"WHAT IN THE HEAVENS IS THIS?"

Hidden within the hull of one of the Blood Phoenix's ships was a bizarre-looking vessel that reminded Ying of a folktale she had heard from a Qirin merchant during one of Larut's colorful bonfire storytelling nights, where heroes were crafted from smoke and monsters formed from shadows. According to Qirin legend, there existed a venomous beast with nine heads and a coiled, serpentine body, its silver scales tainted by a carpet of repugnant mold. When the gods wished to punish humankind for their crimes, they would unleash it to flood the lands with poisonous water, turning fields barren and lakes foul, death and destruction trailing in its wake. The creature's name was Xiangliu—and she was staring at its many heads right now.

It had to be a boat of sorts, because that was the entire point of the Tournament of the Seas, but *how*? Half of it looked like a regular fishing boat—wooden hull, single mast, with a bamboo-battened sail neatly rolled up—but the other half was Xiangliu reincarnate. Attached to the bow of the boat via long metal chains were nine fearsome "heads" molded from iron, resembling sharks—streamlined bodies and singular dorsal fins gleaming menacingly under the lamplight. There was also a tiny bronze propeller fastened where a tail might have been.

"She's a beauty, isn't she?" Wenjun declared, running her fingers along the boat's freshly whitewashed rail.

"I'm not sure I know what exactly she is," Chang-en said. He circled the vessel curiously, the thick iron cuffs and chains at his ankles clanging noisily as he moved.

While all four of them, Ying, Ye-yang, Chang-en, and An-xi, had been allowed to leave the flagship and follow Wenjun here, their ankles had been chained to prevent them from escaping.

"Each one of these"—Wenjun squatted down beside the metallic heads—"is supposed to be an extra engine that will give us a speed boost." She pulled on the contraption's fin and flipped open a hatch, revealing the intricate mechanics within. A latticework of interlocking gears and shafts connected to a kaen-gas burner on one end and the propeller on the other. "Instead of one engine, I have ten," she said, beaming with pride.

"What seems to be the problem, then?" Ying asked, intrigued by what they were being shown. All ships and airships had a single engine—that was a fact that everyone had come to take for granted—but why did there need to be just one? The concept of having external engines was fascinating, assuming they worked.

Wenjun wrinkled her nose, rolling up her sleeves to reveal a pair of spindly arms. Her left forearm bore a tattoo of a rising phoenix in fiery ink, balancing a black lotus upon its upturned beak. It was a strange combination, Ying thought. As if the bird and the flower had been forcibly meshed together.

"Watch," Wenjun said.

She detached one of her engines and hauled it up on a wooden stand before flicking a switch that started the kaen gas burning within. The engine's propeller started spinning, generating a noisy whir that rang in their ears—before spluttering to a stop.

An-xi's hand shot into the air. "There's not enough kaen gas stored inside that thing," he said, looking smug at being the first to come up with the answer. Some habits from their early guild days had clearly not faded.

"Correct," Wenjun replied. "I've tested several permutations of this external engine model, and this is the largest size it can reach. Anything larger and they become too heavy, sinking the boat instead of helping it go faster. The current record time for the tournament is slightly over one stick of incense, so I need these engines to run for quite a bit longer if we want to win." A sly grin stretched across her pale face. "To put it more accurately, *you* need them to last longer if you want to reach the finish line without getting—" She did a swift slice across her neck with the spanner in her hand.

Because the Tournament of the Seas was a race to the death.

According to Wenjun, this contest was no holds barred, and competitors were allowed to use *any* means to win. Including sinking enemy boats—and their crews. In past cycles of the tournament, the boundless ocean became a cold, desolate grave for many participants.

With that out in the open, it became clear why Wenjun had suggested for them to participate—and why Li-na agreed. If sacrificial lambs were a necessity in this bloodbath, then it might as well be them instead of anyone from the Blood Phoenix's crew.

Ying took a closer look at the makeup of the engine, feeling her way around each connecting part.

It was a very similar problem to what she had faced with the Octopus—the need to increase speed while factoring in all these physical limitations. Wenjun had already streamlined the shape of these external engines as best she could. Their pointed heads would easily slice through the water like arrow tips, and the rush of the current would slide across the curved lines of their bodies with little resistance. In that case, there was only one thing worth a try.

Perhaps the trick was not to extend the lifespan of the kaen-gas burner, but to introduce an additional mechanism to complement it.

Water propulsion.

"I have an idea that might work," she said.

"You do?" both Chang-en and An-xi echoed in unison, the former looking delighted and the latter unconvinced.

As for Ye-yang, he simply stood quietly by the side, giving her a slight nod of encouragement. He had barely said a word ever since Wenjun showed up, but Ying was certain that his mind had not slackened for a single moment since they woke up on one of the Blood Phoenix's ships.

Except she would never know what he was truly thinking about.

"If this works, then maybe we'll really be able to go home!" Chang-en added, his lanky shoulders lifting, anticipation sparkling in his eyes. "I've never been away for this long. My e-niye will be worried sick."

"I wonder how things are back home," An-xi murmured. "The solstice hunt will be starting anytime now. A-ma must be up to his neck with the preparations. He'll be getting those migraines again . . ."

The thought of home brought an aching grip to her heart. Thoughts of Nian, their siblings, the Huarin grasslands. Would she survive to see all of them again?

She picked up a writing brush, quickly putting a list of materials on parchment. "I'll need the following items for the modifications. If my estimations are correct, this should be able to give the engines the boost they require."

The fleet engineer folded her arms across her chest and tipped her chin up, regarding Ying with great interest. "For your own sakes, I hope you're right."

Later that night, Ying lay awake on the hard, threadbare bed that she had been given, her unblinking gaze tracing the movements of the tiny spider scuttling across the ceiling beam. From the floor, Chang-en's loud, thunderous snores punctuated the stillness, occasionally joined by unintelligible cries from An-xi. The latter was tossing and turning, brows pinched and cold sweat drenching his forehead, the nightmare of being captured by pirates bleeding into his dreams.

They had been moved into this cramped cabin on board the ship that *Xiangliu* was kept in, to make it easier for them to work on the vessel. Still uncomfortable, but a significant upgrade from the flagship's pungent food store. Through the small porthole, a slant of moonlight cast a dim glow upon her face.

She placed a hand on her chest, feeling for the anxious rhythm of her own heartbeat.

"Be calm, my child, like the star that sparkles in the midnight sky. Or the blade of grass that sways with the summer's breeze."

"Or the little rock in the middle of the flowing river?"

"Yes, like the little rock. Because only when you are still can you clearly see how everything is moving around you."

That was her mother. Always calm, the beacon of tranquility amid frenetic disorderliness, the antidote to her and her father's poorly considered spontaneity. Nian had inherited a similar disposition, but she had not. As she lay here, her haphazard thoughts continued to push sleep further from reach.

How was Nian? Would her sister be worried about her disappearance? Or would Nian believe her dead?

"Something bothering you?" a voice called out in the darkness.

Ying flipped herself on her side. In the shadows, she could only make out Ye-yang's silhouette beside the other two boys, his hands propped behind his head to cushion it against the cold, damp floorboards. Her eyes traced the gentle slope of his forehead down to his sharp nose bridge, then farther to the soft curves of his lips and the harsh angle of his chin. The formidable High Commander, sleeping on rotting, fungal-infested planks with chains upon his ankles. Imagine what everyone back in Fei would say if they knew.

"We're going to be racing in a tournament where only five out of ten survive. I would be lying if I said I wasn't bothered."

"You're not going to die, Ying."

"What makes you so sure?"

"Because I won't let you."

Her heart pinched, aching at the sentiment—and at the reminder of how nothing had changed. Ye-yang was still as confident and assured as he had been before, staunchly believing that he had everything under control. Perhaps he believed that he could defy fate. That he could even dictate life and death. But how could anyone foretell the future? That was sheer arrogance, and such arrogance would not go unpunished. The former High Commander had made that mistake, and now Ye-yang was following in his footsteps.

"I don't think that's going to be up to you," she said, so quietly that she could barely hear her own words. A brief moment of silence passed, the ghosts of their past surging through the space between them, once again erecting an unsurmountable barrier that they could not cross. A reminder of their differences—and why she had chosen to leave.

"Should we not try to escape before the tournament?" she asked. There was still a week before the competition, and many things could happen in a week. The thought of being trapped here, prisoners to these murderous pirates, left her nauseated.

Ye-yang let out a low, thoughtful hum. Then he said, "We could try, but chances are that we'll fail. We're deep within the enemy fleet, surrounded by their ships, and we have no sense of our location within the straits."

"So there's nothing we can do. We have to race, whether we like it or not."

Her words came out flat. Despondent.

She knew they were already surviving on borrowed time. They could have died in the storm, joining the ranks of the drowned souls who haunted these seas. They could have been made to walk the plank, or been slaughtered under Li-na's blade—the same way Feng-kai and the sailors of Larut had been mercilessly killed.

Their luck would run out eventually, regardless of what Ye-yang believed.

"Racing might not be a bad thing," Ye-yang said. "This tournament could be a breakthrough for us. The key to winning this war."

"What do you mean?" Ying sat up, crossing her legs beneath her.

"You realized the discrepancy earlier, didn't you? Between what Wenjun told us and what the High Command's records say about the Blades. That's why you asked the question about the *Diamond*. The Blood Phoenix only has control of *one* Blade, contrary to what we believed."

"So the records were wrong."

"The records were wrong because someone *intentionally* made them so." He paused, tilting his head toward her. Even though his features remained cloaked in shadows, she could sense his keen gaze meeting her own. "Pirates have plied these straits for dozens of years, causing no shortage of trouble to the Order, but it's only in the past two years that there's been . . . a change. The movements of the various fleets have become more coordinated. More purposeful. As if there's someone pulling the strings in the background."

A puppet master controlling his pawns.

Ying's breath hitched in her throat. Two years. That was when Aogiya Lianzhe passed on and Ye-yang inherited control of the High Command. A dark, insidious web unfurled in her mind, stretching all the way from the emerald-gabled roofs of Fei to the blood-washed shores of Larut, across the mercurial waters of the Dunzhu Straits, and to the mysterious lands of the Qirin empire.

"That is roughly around the same time when the Blood Phoenix fleet rose to prominence, and when the first reports of the Blades were made."

Ying lowered her lids, letting each piece of information sediment in her mind. The fog began to clear, parting to reveal the truth with startling clarity. The Blood Phoenix, as notorious as it might be, was far from the endgame. Even if they sank this fleet, there would be another one groomed to take its place. Another Li-na. A different sword wielded by the same hand.

And what did this mastermind have to do with the attack on Larut? With the death of Feng-kai and so many other innocent people? She clenched her fists, nails digging into the flesh of her palms, uncertainty pulsing through her veins.

"You want to identify the mastermind through the tournament," she said.

This was the reason why Ye-yang had never broached the topic of escape, why he seemed so nonchalant about the tournament, even though they were constantly reminded that it was no different from an executioner's stand.

He had a bigger plan. He always did.

"There can be opportunity in adversity," he replied, confirming what she already knew. "I don't expect him to appear at the tournament itself, because he has proven to be extremely cautious, but if the Blood Phoenix wins a second time—"

"He might come speak to Li-na personally," Ying finished.

The Tournament of the Seas was no longer just a platform for scrappy, egotistical pirate captains to battle for territory and spoils; it was an evaluation ground for a commander to assess his generals, to decide which blade would help him cut the deepest.

"But what if we lose?" she asked. "We are engineers, not seafarers. Just because we can fix a ship doesn't mean we can steer it. And if we lose . . ."

We die.

Her gaze shifted past Ye-yang toward her two friends, still sound asleep, rocked by the gentle sway of the waves beneath. Chang-en had lobbed an arm and leg over An-xi, cradling him like a cushion. It was almost as if they were back in the guild, squeezed onto a single sweat-laden platform, slumbering through the exhaustion that had been baked into their bones after a long day of tedious lessons.

Ye-yang might be confident of their chances, but she wasn't. Even if this was the only chance they had to weed out the mastermind behind the pirates, she wasn't sure it was worth risking their lives for. She didn't want this. An-xi and Chang-en didn't want this. The only one who wanted it was Ye-yang, and they were given no choice but to follow along.

It was often too easy for her to forget that Ye-yang—no, Aogiya Ye-yang, High Commander of the Antaran isles—was also a skilled puppet master. This was a game of weiqi between him and the enemy, and the rest of them were only pieces on the board.

"We won't lose, Ying. This race. This war. I'm not losing any of it." Ye-yang sat up, looking as if he might get up and walk over to her.

Ying quickly flipped herself around, turning her back toward him instead. "I'm tired," she said. "You should try to get some sleep too. We'll have plenty to do when morning comes." She held her breath and waited, only exhaling when she heard the creak of the floorboards as Ye-yang lay back down. She didn't know what more to say to him, how else to tell him that she was tired of this tangled political game. Tired of being a puppet dangled on strings.

Raising her gaze to the porthole, she counted the dozens of stars that hung amid the dark drapes of midnight, pinpricks of silver that blinked and beckoned to her. She had once done the same, lying upon the fine, velvet sand of Larut's glistening beach while Feng-kai sat beside her skipping seashells across the water's surface. They had spoken of the future then, of what they would do when they were free of all the responsibilities that shackled them down, when they could spread their wings and fly wherever the wind might lead.

Closing her eyes, Ying let herself be drawn back into that beautiful tapestry that she had woven back then. A dream of better days. A dream that they had taken for granted.

CHAPTER 17

A WEEK WITH THE BLOOD PHOENIX FELT as fleeting as a summer's breeze, and also as arduous as the bitterest of winters. Ying would wake up before dawn each day, just to stand on deck to watch the sun rise above the horizon, to appreciate its warmth against her skin as it bathed her in its comforting amber glow. It brought a brief moment of calm, when she could allow herself to forget about the invisible guillotine hanging above her head, its ice-tinged blade waiting to fall.

Today was a little different, because today's sunrise could well be her last.

She leaned against the ship's rail, inhaling the salt-licked air as she waited for the first hints of gold to bleed from the edge of the sea.

"Here again?" a voice called out from behind. Wenjun strolled over, hugging a bamboo steamer basket with five buns piled within. She tossed one over to Ying, then picked one up for herself and tore out a huge bite. "Missing home? Or contemplating death?"

"Maybe a bit of both." The sweetness of lotus paste burst inside her mouth when she sank her teeth into the fluffy white bun.

Death was no stranger to her, not after all she had been through in her quest to seek justice for her father's murder, but never before had she been given so much time to actually process her own impending demise.

In the past few days, she had thought about home a lot. Of the ger she shared with Nian, half-decorated with her sister's tapestries and half with her messy engineering sketches. Of her father's workshop, where she had spent countless hours poring over his journals and fiddling with his tools. Of chasing sheep across the grasslands while riding Ayanga, her beloved mare. She wondered how Nian was coping with her disappearance, and whether Wen would even realize that she was gone. There were so many things she wanted to say to them—to apologize for her recklessness, to confess her lies, to tell them that she had never meant to hurt or abandon any of them.

But perhaps she might no longer have that chance.

Wenjun shrugged. "It's normal. Everyone who's new to the crew does that for at least an entire month. Some take even longer. When Yunshang first joined us, the silly girl would curl up there"—she pointed up at the crow's nest towering upon its mast—"and cry for hours every day. Er-dangjia had to climb up personally to persuade her to come down for meals, else she might have starved herself to death."

Ying blinked back her surprise. Yunshang was easily one of the most vivacious members of the crew, with energy like a firecracker, so boundless that it inadvertently ended up draining everyone else around her. It was hard to imagine her ever having a down moment, much less hours of crying in solitude.

"How did she end up here?" she ventured hesitantly.

How did all of you end up here?

It was a question that had been sitting in her mind for a while, but she never found the right opportunity to broach the topic. It was so incomprehensible—this crew of women from all walks of life, Qirin and Antaran alike, an assortment of different personalities that clashed like exploding fireworks, coming together to choose a life of piracy upon these temperamental seas.

"Yunshang? Mmm." Wenjun chewed on her second bun, searching through her memories for the answer. "I think she joined us almost a year ago. Her family's from Wei Zhou, not far from the northwestern coast of the Empire. There was a terrible drought that struck the mainland last year, and the harvests were exceptionally poor, so many people started to flee toward the coastal regions, hoping to make a better living there with the sea being so 'plentiful' and all, y'know. Long story short, things didn't pan out the way they imagined." She snorted. "The Empire is run by an infestation of swollen leeches, while the ordinary folk are skin and bones."

Wenjun's blunt description of the Empire was not unfamiliar to Ying. She had heard the same story from Ye-yang, from Wei Ru-er, and seen it with her own eyes in the desperate faces of all the Qirin refugees who had crossed her path. Once upon a time, she had believed that the Empire was akin to paradise, a land draped in verdant green, with rooftops lined with jade and streets paved with gold, and coffers filled to the brim with jewels and trinkets that sparkled like starlight. The Qirin people were wealthy merchants and traders, politicians and scholars, engineers with knowledge beyond the comprehension of the Antaran guild masters, with access to libraries of rare, mythical texts piled to the high heavens. It was a land of plenty, a land of enough. That fantasy of her childhood had long been shattered, replaced by a grim picture of reality.

Would it be that bad if the Antaran High Command were to seize control of the Empire from the hands of its incompetent, self-serving rulers?

"What happened to her family?"

"They were swindled by cheats who promised them passage to some safe haven for a small fee. A whole silver tael—and for what? To be sold as slaves to barbarians in a foreign land. Trust me, those bastards are going to rot in hell." Wenjun leaned over the taffrail and spat into the sea. "Anyway, the ship that they were on met with a storm, not much different from what we plucked you out from. Niangniang has fickle tendencies, and the goddess punishes more than she blesses. Yunshang was the only one who survived. I suppose that's why she was so adamant about rescuing you."

"Wait, was she really the one who pulled us out of the water?"

Yunshang had told her that, but she had assumed that the girl hadn't meant it literally.

Wenjun nodded, starting on her third bun. With a full mouth, she said, "She lives on the crow's nest most of the time, so she was the first one who spotted the bunch of you floating on driftwood. Er-dangjia didn't want to pull you up, because she's not keen on gaining dead weight, but Yunshang threw an absolute fit. It was the first time I've ever seen her so hysterical. She actually dove into the water to get you, and that was what made Er-dangjia change her mind. She's always had a soft spot for Yunshang."

Ying tilted her gaze up toward the crow's nest, and a pang of sympathy struck her when she spotted the small head with two pigtails peeking out.

"Everyone on board has a similar sob story. Lost their husbands, lost their parents, lost their children, lost their homes—so Dadangjia took them all in and gave them a new home. This one," Wenjun said in a strangely cavalier tone.

"Them? What about you?"

Ying could have sworn she saw the engineer flinch, a dark look flashing across the girl's raven eyes. But then it was gone, and she wasn't sure if it had really been there at all.

Wenjun grinned, flashing bits of yellowish paste stuck between her teeth. "Me? Good question"—she shrugged—"but I'm afraid I can't give you an answer." She tapped her head with a finger. "Remembered all my engineering but forgot everything else. Wenjun might not even be my real name, actually."

"You . . . lost your memory?"

"No need to feel sorry for me. Sometimes if you don't let go of the past, you can't embrace the future."

There it was again, the nonchalant, devil-may-care attitude that seemed almost too practiced to be real. Like a carefully painted opera mask, concealing the true expression of the actor below.

"Don't you ever wonder about it? What your life used to be like? If you have any family left behind?" Ying asked.

The muscles of Wenjun's jaw tightened, the tips of her fingers digging a little harder into the bun she was holding. "Why would I?" she said. "Look at the state of the world. Everything's in shambles, all fire and brimstone. If I did leave anything behind, it must have been hell." The last of the buns went into Wenjun's mouth, bobbing down her throat. "Enough chitchat for the morning. It's tournament day! Plenty that needs doing before we set off." With her usual care-free swagger, the girl headed toward the cabins and disappeared down the stairs.

Ying lingered on deck for a while longer, taking some time to observe the various faces that appeared as the ship stirred to life. For the first time, she noticed the invisible baggage that each one seemed to carry. It was in the slight dragging of the feet, or the slouch in the shoulders, or even in the occasional glazing over of the eyes when they thought no one was looking.

Wheels creaked against the wooden floorboards, as a solitary figure made her way over to the wheel at the ship's stern. The woman rested a hand lightly upon the polished walnut of the wheel, the silver streaks in her hair glistening under the rays of dawn. Bathed in the warm light, the harsh angles of her face softened, and the perpetual frown between her brows seemed to fade.

An illusion, Ying reminded herself.

What is your *story, Li-na?*

And can any story, no matter how tragic, possibly exonerate you from the crimes that you have committed?

CHAPTER 18

THE ANNUAL TOURNAMENT OF THE SEAS WAS a spectacle unlike anything Ying had ever witnessed before, even in her many years of tagging along with her father when he shuttled between the different isles. Each pirate fleet had only sent one or two ships, yet there were still vessels of all manners parked beyond where the eye could see. Colorful barges painted like the tail feathers of a peacock, adorned with handmade bunting of dangling seashells that jingled with the wind; sleek, streamlined vessels with metal hulls that gleamed under the sun's rays, wide propellers fanning backward like an impressive tail; even lumbering behemoths that looked like entire floating villages hastily cobbled together with scraps of wood. Drumming and singing filled the air, and whistles and catcalls came from every direction, creating a festive cacophony that overwhelmed the senses.

"I think I'm about to be sick," An-xi said, clutching tightly on to the taffrail with his shaky hands. He was green in the face, having already thrown up twice on the way here. Out of seasickness and fear. His hair had gone wiry in the salt-laden air, loose strands dangling across his pallid face. This was surely the most disheveled a son of the illustrious Niohuru clan had ever been.

Chang-en took him by the shoulders, giving him a good shake. "Pull yourself together. You don't want to vomit to death before the race has even started."

"Maybe that's the better way to die." An-xi sank down onto the floor in despair. "We're surrounded. Every gods-damned pirate fleet in the straits is here. We're going to be shredded and fed to the sharks."

"Don't be so pessimistic!" Chang-en said, giving his friend a light kick. "We're going to win this race, and then we'll use it to barter our way home."

But even as he tried to sound upbeat, there was a stiffness in Chang-en's tone, a tremble in his fingers that betrayed his true feelings about all this.

Apprehension lingered at the back of Ying's mind, her own nerves tangling in knots. An-xi was verbalizing the shared fear that was running through all of them—fear that they might lose, that their luck would finally run out.

"Are you that naive? These are *pirates*. They're never going to let us go! They just want to make use of us to win the race, and then they'll slit our throats regardless."

"How about I slit your throat now?" Yunshang bounded over, pointing the tip of a bamboo stick at An-xi's jugular.

An-xi leapt up with a yelp, jumping behind Chang-en. "You stay away from me!" he shouted, suddenly coming back to life.

"Coward! You're only pretending to be sick, aren't you? You just haven't got the guts to race because you're scared of losing."

"I'm not scared of losing. I'm scared of having one of those moon blades rip my guts out! Is that a problem?"

"No. Come here, and I'll show you what it feels like!"

The duo dashed around the deck, one fleeing, one chasing. With the ankle chains slowing him down, it wasn't long before Yunshang caught up with An-xi and had him in a headlock, using her stick to tickle him in the ribs. The boy erupted in fits of uncontrollable giggles. These squabbles between An-xi and Yunshang had become increasingly common as the week passed, and Ying had a niggling feeling that despite their outward animosity toward each other, they actually enjoyed it. Like now, where An-xi could probably wriggle himself free if he wanted to, yet didn't.

She wondered if Yunshang might want to leave with them when they did—*if* they did.

A shrill hissing came from above, drawing her attention toward the clear skies. A pair of condors were circling overhead, like a pair of sentries watching over bustling activity below.

Strange.

Condors made their nests upon rocky cliffs, so to see not one but two of them so far from shore was unusual.

Suddenly, one of the condors dropped into a steep dive, skimming the surface of the ocean right alongside their ship and picking out a fish with its sharp beak. As it veered back up toward its companion, Ying thought she saw an odd, silvery sheen lining its wings—and the glint of something shiny between its claws.

She squinted to get a better look at what it was holding on to— but the sun got in her eyes, and soon it had already climbed too high. The two birds made a few more circles in the air before flying away and disappearing into the distance.

Was this a bad omen? Or were her own fears making her see omens where there were none?

Something about those condors left her unsettled. As though someone had been watching her through their eyes, leaving a prickling sensation crawling up the back of her neck.

Swallowing her unease, Ying walked up to Ye-yang. He was standing alone near the bow, surveying the various ships surrounding them with a keen eye. Waiting—searching—for any sign of the one they were seeking. The invisible hand in the shadows.

"I never imagined there'd be so many," she said, gesturing at the mosaic of ships, a splendid collection of chaos.

Unlike her, Ye-yang had had his fair share of engaging with pirates. Even before they met, he had already been leading the bannermen in battles against them, with the singular goal of ridding the straits of these pests.

And yet despite the Order's best efforts, this was the result. Dozens of pirate fleets thriving upon these seas, waving their flags proudly above the watery graves of fallen Antaran soldiers and civilians.

This tournament was a triumph for the pirates but a reflection of the Order's failure.

A thoughtful glaze clouded Ye-yang's eyes. "I recognize some of these flags, but to see them all gathered . . . It's interesting how there's unity in the disorder, while in the Order, there's disorder in the unity."

"If we find out who's behind all this, what happens then? Can we truly win?"

If there was one thing that struck Ying about this magnificent, larger-than-life display of revelry, it was how much it pulsed with *life*. Given a choice, who would choose to live upon these perilous waters, subject to the temperamental elements? These were people with a will to survive, who were determined to defy the fates forced upon them by fickle gods. Such resilience was not so easily defeated. *Should* it even be defeated—or celebrated? What did winning even mean?

In her mind's eye, she saw the air fleet of the Cobra's Order, dozens of airships shrouding the sky with grim black, harbingers of a deadly storm. The cannons would fire—cannons she had once worked on—and ear-shattering blasts would ring out, entwining with terrified cries and the crash of waves to form a discordant symphony. Blood would seep across the decks and into the waters, painting the sea a harrowing red, bodies cold and bloated as they floated in slumber.

She blinked, and the nightmare vanished. The sun still shone. Buoyant voices still sang in jubilation. Smiles still hung on every face, anticipation etched in their eyes. Her heart clenched, guilt seeping into the crevices inside her head. She had almost forgotten the injustice that so many Antarans had suffered at the hands of these pirates. These murderers. If she pitied them, then who would pity the ones whose lives had been ended in their hands?

"Once we find the mastermind, the Order can focus our efforts where it matters. There's no point in weeding out one pirate fleet at a time." Ye-yang's jaw hardened, his lips setting in a somber line. "We've been going down the wrong path, exactly the way they want us to. Spreading ourselves thin. Wasting resources. We don't have many more chances to make mistakes." His eyes darkened, flecks of silver dancing dangerously upon the gray. "This might be the last shot we have, Ying."

Ye-yang had told her countless times that the Antaran isles were running out of time, that their people's only hope for survival was to cross the Dunzhu Straits and conquer the lands of the Qirin. Their land was barren. They were starving. Dying. The noose around their neck was slowly tightening, strangling what little air they struggled to breathe.

She had never believed him before. To her, there was always time. Time to find another solution. Time for the waters to chart their own course.

But what if she was wrong? Could she still walk away, pretending that all of this was none of her concern?

Ye-yang turned toward her, placing his hands on her shoulders. Her skin prickled at his touch, a strange mix of yearning and repulsion, of wanting to move closer yet also desperate to run away. "Are you afraid?" he asked.

"Who wouldn't be?"

There were many different emotions running amok inside her, and fear was most certainly one of them.

Ye-yang gave her a gentle squeeze. "I'll get you home, Ying. I promise."

Except she wasn't sure if those promises meant anything anymore.

A low horn sounded thrice, resonating across the sea of ships.

"Let the race begin!" Wenjun declared, strolling out onto the main deck from the inner cabins. She was accompanying the fleet's second-in-command, Keyan, who looked resplendent in her fiery vermilion outfit, much like a phoenix reincarnate. Respectful greetings of "Er-dangjia" rang out across deck. Li-na, however, was nowhere to be seen. According to Yunshang, the captain had "business to deal with," and presumably remained behind with the flagship instead of coming to watch the tournament. Still, the flag of the Blood Phoenix flew high, billowing proudly in the wind.

Ying's stomach did a cartwheel, anticipation and anxiety bubbling up from the pit of her gut. It was too premature to think about going home, or going anywhere else for that matter. That was a question for tomorrow. *If* there was a tomorrow.

Let the race begin.

The competing boats lined up between two floating buoys, in actuality just rusty oil barrels with small yellow flags lashed onto them. *Xiangliu*—their nine-headed sea monstrosity—was one of them, with its stand-in crew of four waiting on board, decked out in matching tunics of black with maroon trimmings.

"Good luck! You'll need it!" Wenjun hollered, waving at them from the Blood Phoenix's ship.

And so they would, judging from the menacing and downright threatening attitudes coming from some of their competition. An-xi was kneeling down with his forehead pressed against the deck, saying his last prayers to Abka Han, and even the typically upbeat Chang-en couldn't stop fiddling with his earlobes, a telltale sign that he was nervous.

"All challengers stand by!" a strident voice announced.

It belonged to one of the race overseers, a tall, strapping man who curiously had his hair braided backward in an Antaran style, even as he wore a plain gray Qirin tunic with neat knotted buttons down the front. The casual juxtaposition of Antaran and Qirin was so common among these pirates, perhaps a sign that Ye-yang's vision of assimilation was not as absurd as many might believe.

The overseer balanced upon the taffrail at the bow of a towering ship that bore no identifying flag. Large bronze propellers extended on both sides like majestic fins, and the cabins on the main deck were topped with elegant tiles of jade green and sloping eaves lined with gold. A ship fit for a king. Ying traced the direction of Ye-yang's gaze to the wooden pendant that was hanging from the man's waistband— one that resembled the clan pendants that each Antaran child was gifted at birth. From this distance though, it was impossible to tell what was engraved in the wood.

The starting horn blared—and they were off.

Ying pulled the lever to trigger the starting of the kaen-gas burners in their external engines, and *Xiangliu* rumbled to life. They shot away from the starting line, a gleaming chariot pulled by nine monstrous sharks, slicing through the rough waters.

"Get as far away from the other boats as possible," Wenjun had warned them countless times while lecturing them on the game plan.

Now that the race was actually underway, they could see why.

Boats that were slow off the mark already had holes harpooned into their hulls, ending their race before it even began. Those were the lucky ones. Others were overwhelmed by a flurry of arrows, turning their unfortunate crew into porcupines that would bleed to a slow death.

Thankfully, the harsh training they had gone through in the Engineers Guild kept them moving even in the face of imminent death. Dread painted An-xi's and Chang-en's faces a ghastly shade of white as they frantically continued to unfurl their sail.

At the wheel, Ye-yang expertly steered their boat far left, veering a safe distance away from their nearest competitor—a boat painted entirely in black, with sails extending from both sides of its hull like the wings of a manta ray. Its crew all wore the same sleeveless black tunics, with snaking tattoos of eels crawling over their bulging biceps and up the sides of their tawny necks.

"The Midnight Eels—bunch of ruthless, sadistic bastards. If you see them, just run. Unless you fancy being butchered and fed to the sharks, piece by piece, while you're still alive," Wenjun had said when giving them the rundown on their biggest competitors. The Eels were supposedly a newer fleet, with an ambitious zealot for a leader, eager to rise in the pirate ranks.

One of them flung a grappling hook toward a nearby boat, then simply *walked across* to the opposite deck by treading on the hook's thick metal chain. The curved moon blade in his hand glinted menacingly under the sunlight. Anguished cries ripped through the air—and then silence as the entire crew of the unfortunate vessel crumpled to the ground in pools of their own blood, entrails spilling over the deck.

An-xi stifled a scream, using Chang-en's tall frame to block his field of view. Ying stared, unable to tear her eyes away from this gruesome sight. The man turned in their direction, his thin lips curling in a cruel smile. He pointed his blade in her direction, as if to say, "You're next."

Ye-yang took her by the shoulders and spun her around. "Don't look," he said, his voice a steady anchor. "Focus."

She looked up, meeting his gaze briefly, then she quickly turned her attention back toward the sea. She exhaled, shoving the wretched sense of dread to the back of her mind. The course they had to complete was fairly straightforward—a race to a designated buoy and back to where they'd started, albeit with plenty of flotsam in the way and bloodthirsty pirates on their tail. With the boost from the external engines, they were temporarily in the lead, but there were still several boats within close range, including the murderous Midnight Eels. Based on their calculations, the amount of kaen gas stored in those engines would only be able to last them at most halfway, when they reached the turning point—after that, the water propulsion mechanisms would have to kick in for the return leg of the race.

"Come on! Can't this go any faster?"

Ying jerked her neck around, staring incredulously at the petite girl who was crawling out from under the large hemp sheet that had been covering a pile of rope.

"Yunshang? What in the heavens are you doing here?"

The girl clucked her tongue. "What does it look like I'm doing? Focus!" she scolded, parroting Ye-yang's earlier words. "We need to widen our lead, else those stinky Eels will catch up."

"Do they know that you snuck on board?" An-xi hollered from his position near the mast, beady eyes near bulging from their sockets.

"What do you think, smart-ass?" Yunshang snapped back. "If Da-dangjia and Er-dangjia knew, then I wouldn't still be here, would I?"

Ying sighed. There were very good reasons why the captains would not have wanted Yunshang to be here. Heck, they hadn't even wanted *any* of their own crew to be part of this brutal race, which was why she and the boys had been forced to participate instead. They were inconsequential pawns. Winning was a bonus, and even if they lost—or died—that was of no concern to Li-na and the Blood Phoenix. Yunshang was different.

"Just sit by the side and don't move," Ying said sternly. If anything happened to the girl during the race, then all their heads would surely roll, regardless of whether they won or not.

The gap between them and the competing crews was still shrinking, with the Eels trailing only about two boat lengths behind.

"There's the buoy," she said to Ye-yang, pointing at a small, bobbing flag some distance ahead, exactly the same as the ones at the starting line. They had reached the halfway mark. Squinting through the sun's glare, she thought she could see a hazy shoreline beyond the buoy, and even mountains towering on the horizon. A pair of twin peaks, stretching to the heavens. One of the nine isles? Impossible. They couldn't be so close to Antaran territory without being detected by the Order's patrols. But there was no time for a closer look. It was likely only a mirage, tempting her with the promise of land.

Turning to An-xi and Chang-en, she shouted, "Ready the sail!"

Her two friends nodded, trembling hands clutching tightly to the ropes.

They were almost at the buoy, still maintaining a tenuous lead over the pack.

Suddenly, a metal dart flew across the top of Ying's head, missing her by a finger's breadth. She threw herself down against the deck, glancing back at the attackers. An-xi and Chang-en clambered behind a large barrel, horrified by the onslaught. It was those Eels again, rapidly gaining on them. Two were holding crossbows aimed in their direction.

Ye-yang plucked out one of the darts that had embedded itself in the ship's wheel. With the flick of his wrist, he sent it flying back toward the assailants. A howl erupted.

"Now!" Ye-yang ordered.

The two boys pulled down hard, using their entire weight to shift the direction of the sail so that it would catch the wind at the correct angle. Ying jammed the rudder, and the entire boat heaved, groaning as it made a sharp pivot around the buoy. The deck tilted sharply, almost sending them sliding into the water. Right on cue, the nine external engines spluttered as they burned through their final remnants of kaen gas.

"What's happening? Why are we slowing down?" Yunshang asked. She got up from where she had been seated and leaned over the rail to check on the engines.

Ying reached for the lever to activate the water propulsion mechanisms—then a glint of metal caught her eye.

"Yunshang!"

She threw herself to the left, shoving Yunshang to the ground.

"Ah!"

A grappling hook caught her around the right shoulder, its sharp claw piercing through her skin. Ying winced, biting down hard on her lower lip. The rusty, metallic taste of blood burst between her teeth. She reached out for Ye-yang, but her fingers barely grazed the fabric of his robes. She flew backward.

"Ying!" her friends shouted.

Her back struck the side of the boat with a harsh thud, then she was wrenched overboard. The seawater was freezing against her skin, rushing into her nose and mouth, choking her like glacial blades. She was dragged toward the Eels' boat like a limp straw doll. The more she tugged at the metal claw, the deeper it sank itself into her flesh. Fear coursed through her veins, the icy touch of death caressing her skin. In the brief moments when she managed to lift her head out of the water, she glimpsed the vicious glee on the faces of the Eels as they overtook *Xiangliu*, the chain of the grappling hook sitting in the hand of the man who had taunted her earlier.

A flash of silver shot overhead—the tip of an arrow, striking the man in the chest. He roared, dropping the chain. The tension that kept her tethered to their boat disappeared. Ying quickly wrenched the hook out of her shoulder, ignoring the agonizing pain that ripped through her body. She surfaced, gulping in a breath of air. Chaos had erupted on the Eels' boat, thanks to the crossbow that was sitting in Ye-yang's hands. It had to be from Yunshang, since the rest of them hadn't been given any weapons. Within moments, he'd dispatched every single member of that crew, leaving a ghost boat drifting with the waves.

"Ying, catch the rope!" An-xi was shouting at her.

She struggled against the intense current to reach for the rope that had been flung to her. Taking three painful strokes forward, she finally grabbed hold of it with what little strength she could muster in her numb fingers.

"Activate the propulsion mechanism," she croaked, but no one could hear her.

If they dallied any longer, then the heat that had been generated from the burning of kaen gas would dissipate, and they would no longer be able to use it to trigger the water propulsion. Their boat came to a standstill. Behind them, other competitors were beginning to catch up.

An-xi and Chang-en reeled her in as quickly as they could, while Ye-yang continued to shield them from any incoming attacks. Once she had been hauled back on board, Ying wasted no time. Dragging her soaking, shivering self across the deck, with a trail of bloody water in her wake, she pulled the propulsion lever and prayed that it was not too late.

Time seemed to freeze over for a long, painful moment.

And nothing happened.

"What's wrong?" Chang-en asked, panic etched across his face. "Why aren't the engines starting? If we don't move, we're going to die!" He shoved Ying aside, desperately tugging at the lever, as if brute strength would force it to work.

Pain from her wounds shot up her spine as Ying struck the wooden wall of the boat, but it was overshadowed by the alarm and despair that flooded through her mind. Had she been too slow? She stared at the nine lifeless engines, bobbing aimlessly along with the ebb and flow of the waves. Hope of winning—and surviving— flickered like the dying embers of a fire. Not just for them, but for the rest of the nine isles. If the journey ended here, they would never know who the puppeteer was, not until his victory was complete and their bodies were cold and forgotten, drowned within these wintry depths.

Then she saw it—the broken link. When the lever was pulled, it would create tension in a singular chain that then branched out into nine separate chains, each connected to one external engine. This would bring down a metal plate inside the engines, allowing water to rush into the pipes to trigger the propulsion.

In the scuffle, one of the links of the central chain had come loose.

"Tie the rope around my waist. I'll climb out there and tighten the link," she said, picking up a pair of bronze pliers from the boat's toolbox.

"Are you out of your mind?" Chang-en exclaimed. "You can barely stand up as it is!"

"I'll do it," Ye-yang said.

Ying shook her head. "You can't. You don't know how." These were no ordinary chains. In order to provide sufficient tension, the chain links had been woven in a complex, tri-helical pattern that they had been taught by Master Kyzo in airship repair class. Unfortunately, the strength of this design was also its weakness, as one displaced link would cause the entire chain to fail—as it had.

"I can't swim," Chang-en said immediately, taking a step back.

An-xi chewed on his lip, his bony fingers clenching and un-clenching by his sides. "I'll go," he shouted.

Snatching the rope and pliers from Ying, he secured one end around his own waist, then placed the other end in Chang-en's hand. "Don't you dare let go, understood?" he warned. Swallowing hard, he climbed out and dropped into the water.

They watched as he swam out to the broken section of the chain and proceeded to mend the linkage.

"Hurry up, An-xi," Ying murmured, keeping an eye on the other boats closing in.

An-xi's shivering fingers pried open one of the chain links and hooked it back where it belonged. He gave it a tug, making sure that everything was secure.

"I'm done! Pull me back up!"

While An-xi made his way back to the boat, Ying tried the lever again. This time, the nine sharklike heads of *Xiangliu* rumbled to life. Their boat began to accelerate once again, allowing them to pull farther ahead just before their closest competitor could come within firing range. An-xi collapsed back on deck with a wide grin of relief on his face.

With the Eels out of the running, none of the other boats were fast enough to catch up. The propulsion mechanism worked exactly as it should, helping them maintain the lead all the way to the finish line. The horn sounded once again to signal the end of the tournament.

"I declare the winner of this year's Tournament of the Seas—the Blood Phoenix!" the overseer announced.

A thunderous roar went up around all the ships that were gathered, congratulating the crowning of a new pirate champion. Fireworks exploded in celebration, and a bitter coldness ran through Ying's veins down to her bones as the familiar silhouette of a flaming phoenix once again extended itself upon the dusky sky.

CHAPTER 19

THE GAS LAMPS AT THE CAMPING GROUND of Wu Lin burned bright even though it was the wee hours of the morning. Nian and Ye-kan hobbled out of the woods, exhausted and relieved. Much of the campsite was quiet, save for the heated voices that could be heard clamoring from within the main ger, no doubt debating the unfortunate events of the afternoon.

"Beile-ye?" Nergui exclaimed when he saw them enter. "Thank goodness you're all right! Where have you been? And Lady Nian!"

There were several people gathered in the tent. The second and third beiles, a few of the more senior clan leaders, and Ye-yang's chief steward Nergui. Wen was also present, standing beside the chieftain of the Ula clan. The two beiles were seated near the front, with Erden, the second beile, glaringly occupying the central position rightfully meant for the High Commander.

Her brother walked over immediately, inserting himself between her and Ye-kan. Frowning, he said, "Everyone's been looking all over for you. What happened?"

"We met with assassins, then fell into one of the old tunnels beneath Wu Lin while trying to escape," she explained.

"Nergui, get a physician to check on Lady Nian. Her ankle might be sprained," Ye-kan ordered gruffly. Turning to the others, he asked, "Did you manage to catch them? And where's Ye-lu? He was with us when the assassins appeared, but we were separated soon after. Has he not returned?"

The atmosphere in the ger tensed at the mention of the first beile, with grim expressions cast over the faces of the clan chiefs.

Nergui glanced worriedly at Ye-kan. "Beile-ye, the first beile . . . is dead," he said in a hushed voice, gesturing toward one corner of the ger. It was then that Nian noticed three bodies lying there, covered with sheets of white cloth. She stifled a gasp.

Ye-kan blanched. He walked over to the bodies, gingerly lifting the cloth to reveal the faces of the three men.

It was indeed Ye-lu and the two Tongiyas they had met in the forest earlier, their faces pale and covered with splatters of blood.

"What happened?" Ye-kan asked.

"Erden and a few others found them with numerous arrow wounds. By then, Ye-lu was already dead," the third beile explained.

"Shouldn't you know what happened far better than any of us, hmm, Number Fourteen?" Erden scoffed.

"What are you trying to say, Erden?" Ye-kan's fists clenched, an angry flush rising up the sides of his neck.

"Exactly what you think I'm trying to say. Ye-lu so coincidentally bumps into you during the hunt, and then he winds up dead, while you end up missing for a good part of the day, returning with some story about getting stuck in tunnels. Oh, and it just so happens that Number Eight has also disappeared while the imperial seal is somehow in your hands."

"Beile-ye, please be mindful of your words," the Ula chieftain interjected, displeasure etched across his graying brows.

The Ula clan was Ye-kan's maternal clan, so she'd expected Ula Temuu to speak in Ye-kan's defense. However, something still struck Nian as unusual. Why was Ula Temuu not saying *more*? That, coupled with the suspiciously nonchalant manner in which the third beile was sipping tea by the side, left her nerves crawling with unease.

"How dare you!" Ye-kan burst out, incensed by the accusation. He marched over to Erden. Nian's heart leapt up to her throat, fearing that Ye-kan would do something rash like throw a punch at the second beile's face.

But he didn't.

Instead, he stopped one step away.

"I didn't do anything to Ye-lu," he said, nostrils flaring. "These are all baseless accusations." The muscles lining his neck strained with tension, as if it was taking him great effort to hold back.

But he did.

"Baseless?" Erden chuckled. "When we arrived at the scene, Tongiya Tulishen was still alive. He was the one who told us that you attacked them and killed Ye-lu. Poor fellow clung on to that last breath just to make sure he wouldn't die in vain. If you don't believe me, ask your uncle."

The furrows upon the Ula chieftain's forehead deepened, his bony shoulders visibly stiffening at the second beile's words. He remained silent—yet his silence was as good as acknowledgment.

Why would the Tongiya clansman lie?

Unless he was already bought off by the true culprit?

Nian carefully studied the expressions of everyone in the tent, particularly the two beiles. Erden had one leg propped upon the chair, arms folded smugly across his chest; Ye-han remained relaxed and detached, setting down his teacup and casually popping some melon seeds into his mouth. One of them was likely the mastermind behind all this, or perhaps the both of them were in cahoots. Either way, things did not bode well for Ye-kan.

"That's impossible!" Ye-kan said. "That man was lying. I didn't kill any of them."

"Can you prove it?" the third beile asked.

Nian stepped forward. "I was there," she said. "The fourteenth beile is telling the truth."

Erden threw her a supercilious glance. "Aihui Nian," he said, not even bothering to address her with any sort of formality, "everyone knows that you are on *close* terms with Number Fourteen. Why? Have you decided to switch allegiances and climb into someone else's bed because Number Eight refuses to touch you?"

"I—"

"Nian," Wen interrupted, his tone reproachful, "the beiles are in the middle of a serious discussion. This is not your place to say anything."

The second beile's brazen remarks left Nian reeling, and her brother's reprimand left her ashamed, even as she knew that he was only trying to protect her. Her cheeks flushed with embarrassment.

"Erden!" Ye-kan bellowed, fire spitting from his eyes. He raised his fist into the air.

A sinking feeling took hold inside Nian.

She stepped forward. "That's enough," she called, her voice ringing strong. Her heart pounded nervously within. To her relief,

Ye-kan held back. His arm slid down, though the artery at his right temple continued to throb. "The High Commander charged me with overseeing all matters of the solstice hunt, so it *is* my place to speak," she said. "The first beile's death happened on my watch, so I have a responsibility to answer for this. A proper investigation needs to be made, instead of jumping to conclusions based on one or two pieces of contradicting evidence."

She could sense the judgment placed upon her, disapproving eyebrows raised in response to her uninvited comments. But there was also a thoughtfulness that set in. Hesitation.

The third beile cleared his throat. "Of course a proper investigation should take place, but in light of the suspicions that have been surfaced, it might be unsuitable for Number Fourteen to continue wielding the imperial seal on behalf of the High Commander. Perhaps it might be more appropriate for one of us"—he gestured to himself and Erden—"to help out for the time being?"

The clan leaders present nodded in agreement.

"But, Beile-ye," Nergui said, "that would be directly disregarding the High Commander's decree. The imperial seal cannot change hands without the High Commander's personal instruction."

"These are exceptional circumstances," Erden snapped. "Besides, the legitimacy of those instructions is still questionable. None of us know where the High Commander really is. What makes you think he hasn't ended up the same way as Ye-lu?" He swung his head toward the corpses, a sneer twisting upon his lips.

A hushed silence fell.

Then a condor's cries ripped through the air.

Two monstrous birds came swooping in through the entrance, their beating wings sending a gust of wind rushing over everyone's faces. Nian balked at the sight of the two majestic condors, now perching with their hooked talons upon the backrest of the High Commander's chair.

Chimeras.

Their silver wings gleamed, each feather a metallic blade. One of the condors even had a glass eye, giving it an even more menacing appearance.

"Batu! Boda!" Nergui exclaimed. The steward rushed over, catching a dull gray message tube that was released from the claw of one condor. He quickly pulled out the small scrap of rolled-up parchment within. Excitement flared in his eyes. "It's from the High Commander!" He skimmed through its contents. "His Excellency says that he will return in at most a week's time, and that all Eight Banners are to begin preparations for active battle immediately," the steward recited.

Erden marched over, snatching the message out of Nergui's hands. "Let me see that. Is this another forgery, hmm?"

"It is in His Excellency's own writing, and carries the stamp from his ring seal."

He's alive.

Relief washed over Nian before worry seeped in again. Even if Ye-yang was well, what about Ying? Was her sister also alive? And where were they?

"But why is His Excellency ordering us to stand by for active

eyes—"I would also insist that Number Fourteen relinquish command of his banner until investigations are complete, to avoid any complications."

Ye-kan opened his mouth to protest, but a steely stare from his uncle silenced him.

This was already the best compromise that they could get, given the damning testimony that Tongiya Tulishen had given before he died. It would be a blow to Ye-kan's pride, but it was only temporary. Once the High Commander returned, things would be restored to the way they were.

With the unexpected interruption by the two condors, the decision was settled. The small crowd soon dispersed, returning to their accommodations within the city. With the first beile's unexpected demise, there was no way that the solstice hunt could continue. Everything hinged on the High Commander's return.

Nian was one of the last to exit the ger, as decorum and her throbbing ankle would dictate. She followed behind her brother, looking around for any sign of Ye-kan, who had left a few steps earlier in the company of the chief steward. Although their crisis was temporarily averted, there were still many things they needed to discuss—like who might have been responsible for the first beile's murder and how that could relate to the weapons smuggling they'd discovered. She caught sight of him standing by a horse carriage. He waved, beckoning for her to come over.

"Nian," Wen called out, stopping her in her tracks.

"Yes, A-ge?"

Wen glanced at the fourteenth beile, then turned his attention back to her. "You will be marrying the High Commander very soon. I don't think I need to remind you about what boundaries you need to keep," he said, the muscles in his square jaw terse with disapproval. "People are watching, Nian, and they are waiting for you—for us—to fail."

Her brother's words came like a cold shower, dragging her back to the reality she lived in, reminding her of the expectations resting on her shoulders. What Erden had said earlier was a harsh reminder that her actions were in full view of everyone and she would be judged for them, whether she liked it or not.

"I'm sorry, A-ge," she said. "The fourteenth beile and I are only friends, nothing more. He has been very kind to watch over me while I'm in Fei, but that's because A-jie asked him to."

At the mention of Ying, Wen huffed in exasperation. "Does that girl even consider herself a part of this family anymore?" he said. "She didn't even bother writing to tell me what happened with the Jangmu clan! It's a pity Shi-ye couldn't attend the hunt this time. I shall have to pay him a visit after this and ask to bring Ying back to Huarin. No reason why she should be a widow for a man she had yet to marry."

Wen still doesn't know that Ying's already come to Fei . . .

Her mind did a quick turn, landing on the decision to keep the truth from him for now. If Wen found out that Ying had not only returned to the guild but also gone missing at sea, then there would only be more trouble to deal with.

"Also, it was highly inappropriate for you to have spoken against the beiles back there. You should know better, Nian. I don't wish to see that sort of behavior again, understood?" her brother said sharply.

"I understand," she replied, lowering her head.

But she did not regret what she had done, what she had said.

She was not some ignorant girl from the backwaters. There was weight to her opinions. Her thoughts mattered. Even as her nerves unraveled inside her, tonight she'd finally had the courage to take a stand.

"Go back to the palace and recuperate," Wen continued, gesturing at her injured ankle. "If you need anything, have someone send a message to me. I expect we shall all have to remain in Fei until investigations into the first beile's death are complete and the High Commander returns."

Even though the greatest suspicion rested upon Ye-kan's head, everyone else present at the hunt was not absolved from the crime. No one would be leaving Fei until the culprit was brought to light.

"A-ge, there's something I want to ask you. Have you ever seen a red symbol that resembles the face of a qilin before? Does that mean anything to you?"

"A qilin? No, not that I know of. It's rare for such Qirin symbols to be seen on the nine isles. Why do you ask?"

Nian leaned over and whispered into her brother's ear, telling him about the crates of weaponry that they had discovered in the Wu Lin tunnels.

"Are you absolutely certain about this?" Wen asked with a frown.

"I saw it with my own eyes. I don't know if any of this is related to the first beile's death, but regardless, smuggling weapons from the Order is treason."

Her brother rubbed his chin in quiet contemplation. Then he said, "I'll look into it and let you know if anything comes up. But in the meantime"—he wagged a finger at her—"don't go looking for trouble, is that clear? Our clan doesn't need a second—"

"A second Aihui Ying, yes, I understand."

CHAPTER 20

THREE DAYS AFTER THE INCIDENT AT THE hunting grounds, Wen came back with a lead.

Clutching her brother's letter in her hand, Nian rushed from her palace quarters to Chongzheng Hall. It was already close to midnight, but still the lamps within the High Commander's study burned bright. Qorchi dutifully stood guard by the side of the doors.

"Is the fourteenth beile still here?" she asked. "I have something urgent to speak to him about."

"Yes, he is," the chief steward replied. He wrung his hands together, fleshy lips tugging downward in concern. "Maybe you can try talking some sense into him, Lady Nian. He's been studying the military reports since dawn, refusing to take any breaks. If he carries on like this, I fear he'll collapse before the High Commander returns."

Nian sighed, nodding her head. Pushing open the doors, she walked in.

Ye-kan was standing behind the High Commander's long huanghuali desk, staring up at the enormous map that hung from the wall.

"The map isn't going to miraculously provide any answers to our problems, even if you keep staring at it all night," she said.

Our problems.

The words had tumbled out too easily, before she could catch herself.

Ye-kan turned.

"Nian!" His tired eyes lit up with a glimmer of delight. Then he gave a self-deprecating shrug. "I know. It's just . . . I don't know what else I can do that'll be useful. Number Eight entrusted me with command, but I've done nothing except become the biggest suspect in Ye-lu's murder." He gestured at the parchments that lay unfurled upon the table—reports that had come in from the various military camps. "Figured I might as well keep an eye on the Order's preparations, in case war is really coming for us."

Nian's heart clenched at the sight of the dark shadows underlining his eyes, of the weariness in the slouch of his broad shoulders. The recent events had taken a toll on him, leaving him disheartened. Doubtful of himself.

She had the impulse to run over and envelop him in a warm hug, to pat him on the back and tell him that none of this was his fault, that he was already doing much better than anyone could have expected.

But she held back.

Her brother's warning echoed in her mind, reminding her of the line between her and Ye-kan—a line that she should not cross.

"It's late," Ye-kan continued, glancing out at the orange hues of the moon hanging up high. "What brings you here at this hour?"

Shoving those messy thoughts to the back of her mind, Nian placed her brother's letter on the table. "Wen sent this over. It's about the qilin symbol that we found," she explained.

Her brother had traced the symbol to a mysterious underground triad that ran illegal gambling dens in the unsavory underbelly of the capital city. However, there was nothing else he could uncover about the organization, except the location of one of their regular haunts.

A temple in the western quarter of Fei.

While waiting for Ye-kan to finish reading the letter, Nian's gaze drifted across the length of the table, landing upon the octagonal lamp that still sat upon the corner. The lamp that she had seen Ye-yang staring at with a wistful fondness in his steel-gray eyes.

Curiosity reared its tiny head.

Nian picked up the lamp to take a closer look at the scene that had been carved onto one of the panels. It was of a girl riding a horse, perched upon a cliffside with the wind dancing through her hair. The carved lines were rough and jagged, certainly not the work of a seasoned artisan, yet she could sense the love and care that had gone into each painstaking cut. Had Ye-yang made this himself? And who was this girl who had been preserved in the wood?

Then something struck her.

A familiar palm-shaped silhouette that had been etched into the background, its gentle curves framing the girl in the picture.

The mountainscape of her home isle, Huarin.

A-jie . . .

The girl was Ying.

She turned the lamp, staring at every single image carved into each panel.

A girl sprawled on the ground, looking up at a boy with an umbrella, the shadow of a nine-tailed fox lurking in the background.

Them perched on a rooftop, jars of wine sitting by their sides. Them on a boat, setting lotus lanterns afloat upon the water's surface.

Ying hadn't told her much about what happened in Fei, but she *had* spoken of the chimeras built by the guild, of being chased by a fox with nine silver tails that fanned out in grotesque beauty.

These were all memories. Memories between Ye-yang and Ying. Memories that they had kept from her.

Hot tears pooled along the rims of her eyes, disbelief and disappointment seizing her by the heart. Her fingers slipped, the lamp falling onto the floor with a noisy crash.

"Nian?" Ye-kan looked up. "What's the matter?" He set the letter down and came to her side, bending to pick up the fallen lantern. He took one glance at it and froze, grip tightening around its wooden frame. Traces of guilt filtered through his shifting gaze.

"Did you know about this?" Nian whispered.

"Nian, I can explain—"

That was a yes.

Ye-kan had been with Ying through the guild's apprenticeship trial. How could he not have known?

"I don't want your explanation," she said. Her voice was quiet, slicing through the air like a knife's edge.

A memory floated to the forefront of her mind. Back at the celebratory banquet two years ago, when her betrothal to Ye-yang was first announced, Ying had pulled her aside and asked her to reconsider. She remembered the exact words that her sister had said then, when she did not convey any reluctance toward the engagement. "*You want to marry him?*" Ying had asked. She should have noticed the crestfallen expression on her sister's face then, or the hurt in her eyes—but she had been too caught up in her own excitement to realize.

Their story had already begun back then.

I was the one who tore them apart.

"Nian, we didn't mean to keep anything from you. Ying and Ye-yang—that chapter ended a long time ago! We never meant to hurt you, believe me," Ye-kan pleaded. "We were only trying to protect you."

But that was precisely what hurt the most—that Ying and Ye-yang had chosen to protect her happiness at the expense of their own. What else had her sister done behind her back that she wasn't aware of?

A-jie's engagement to Jangmu Feng-kai. She had found it odd that her sister would have agreed to such an engagement so willingly. Now she finally understood why.

A-jie was running away from Ye-yang.

And from me.

She stood up, the sudden onslaught of emotions—anger, sadness, guilt—manifesting in the tears that trickled from her eyes.

"Nian . . . are you okay?"

"No, no I'm not," she replied, wiping the tears off her cheeks. She took a deep breath, and then another, forcing her rational side to regain control. "But I'll settle this score with my a-jie when she returns."

And you had better return, Aihui Ying. Otherwise I'll never forgive you.

Later that night, while the rest of the city slumbered uneasily in their beds, two figures wound their way down the dimly lit streets of Fei's western quarter.

"Nian, I know you're upset, but I still don't think it's a good idea to be—"

Nian spun around, shooting Ye-kan a deathly glare. He shut his mouth, lowering his head like a guilty child.

The fire inside her was still smoldering, so she'd decided to channel that energy into something more productive instead. Like tracking down the qilin triad that her brother had discovered.

Ye-kan had not been thrilled with the idea, but his protests came up against a brick wall, and his guilt made him more obliging toward anything she suggested—including sneaking out of the palace disguised in the drab brown robes of vegetable deliverymen. He had been groveling the entire way, and she had been treating him like empty air. He deserved it, for hiding so much from her. The thought of it made her want to kick him in the shin.

They stopped in front of small temple dedicated to the goddess Niangniang, the deity responsible for protecting seafarers from the dangers of the tumultuous seas. The worship of Niangniang had originated on Qirin shores and had been adopted by the Antarans when trade began to flourish between the isles and the Empire over a century ago.

The entrance to the temple was a mere hole in the wall, a plain archway sandwiched between an herbalist's and an ink shop, both of which were already shuttered for the night. Inside, the cramped space housed a stone statue of the goddess, with two oil lamps and a few plates of fruit and steamed cakes on the offering table in front of it. Tendrils of smoke rose from the sticks of incense left in the large bronze tripod in the center of the room, suffusing the air with the overpowering scent of sandalwood.

"There's no one here," Ye-kan said. "Maybe your brother got it wrong."

Nian took another look around, trying to stem her disappointment about how incredibly ordinary the place was.

Or maybe not.

She walked up to the bronze tripod and bent over, studying the handles protruding from its sides. They had been carved as a pair of sea serpents, backs arched and forked tongues spitting from their open maws. But what was odd was that one side was covered with a thin layer of dust, as was the rest of the tripod, but the other was not.

Nian reached out and wrapped her fingers around the slender curve of the snake. The metal shifted under her touch. She pulled harder—and the handle rotated toward her, pivoting on its lower end.

Gears ground against each other somewhere within the walls.

"What was that?" Ye-kan spun around, startled by the sound.

Behind the statue of Niangniang, a section of the wall had slid aside, revealing a hidden passageway that led to a flight of steps heading downward. Voices drifted from below, punctuated by the rattling of dice.

Wen had been right after all.

She moved toward the steps, but Ye-kan reached out and took her by the arm. "Wait," he said. He fished out a thick silver bracelet from between the folds of his robes, then carefully clasped it around her wrist.

"What's this?" Nian held it up to the light, rotating the bracelet about her wrist. Elegant camellias had been engraved into the silver—her favorite flower.

Upon a closer look, there were also tiny pin-sized holes all around the circumference of the bracelet.

"Just a precaution, in case of trouble." Ye-kan tapped lightly at the cobra emblem carved into the silver. "If you press this, it'll fire needles that are dipped in numbing poison. I meant to give it to you before the solstice hunt, but then the news about Number Eight and the storm happened, and it sort of slipped my mind." His fingers lingered upon her wrist, and her skin burned hot under his touch.

She kept her eyes trained upon the bracelet, hoping that he couldn't see the flush of pink across her cheeks.

"Look," he said, running his thumb across the silver, "I know that nothing I say can make things right, but I still want you to know that I'm truly sorry. If we make it through all this and you never want to see me again, I'd completely understand. I won't bother you again."

Nian's chest constricted. When had she said that she never wanted to see him again? And why did that thought feel like someone had taken a dagger to her heart?

Ye-kan released her hand. "I'll go first," he said. He slowly descended the stone stairs, keeping her shielded one step behind.

When they reached the landing, Nian and Ye-kan peeped hesitantly around the corner.

The hideaway was packed to the brim with eager customers

surrounding the few gambling tables that had been set up. Wooden arms of mechanical dealers rose and fell as they shook bamboo canisters containing pairs of dice, accompanied by shouts of disappointment or jubilation that erupted every other minute as betting proceeded in fervor. No one even noticed the two figures who had slipped in through the secret entrance.

Nian and Ye-kan wound their way around the room, sieving through the sea of faces, unsure of what exactly they were looking for. Some sign of that red qilin symbol, perhaps, or maybe one of the men they had seen moving crates in the Wu Lin tunnels.

Just then, a small commotion broke out at one of the tables.

"You're cheating!" a bearded man was shouting, face purple with rage. "Those dice are weighted, aren't they? Give me back all my money, you swindlers!"

Two of the gambling den's crew members marched over, wielding thick wooden rods in their hands. "Old Dou, you can't make those claims just because you're losing. You know the rules!" one said.

"Fine, give me twenty coins on credit. Twenty coins, and I'll shut up and leave."

"Winning and losing is part of the game. You're already ten silver taels in debt, and you want to borrow some more? If you can pay what you owe, then we can talk. If not, then you're going to have to leave behind some other form of collateral. How about a finger? One finger for ten taels, that's a good deal for you." The men pinned Old Dou onto the table with a crash, gambling chips scattering all over the floor.

Fear flashed across Old Dou's hooded eyes. "C'mon, I'm a regular here. Don't do this to me. Give me another chance!" he begged.

But the argument wasn't what caught Nian's attention. Her focus was on the tattoos that covered the backs of the two ruffians' hands—the snarling mien of qilins inked in blood.

"I thought Old Dou made a windfall from a recent job that he took up? You mean he squandered it all away already?" Nian heard someone whisper.

"Beats me, but he must be a fool for thinking he can wriggle his way out of a debt owed to the Qilin triad. One finger *is* a good deal. If he's not careful, he'll lose both his hands."

The Qilin triad.

She exchanged a glance with Ye-kan. It seemed that the goddess Niangniang had chosen to bless them with a helping hand. They were in the correct place after all.

If they continued following this trail, it would hopefully lead them to whoever was behind the weapons smuggling—and possibly even Ye-lu's murder.

Just then, Nian spotted a cloaked figure lurking near the entryway of the den, speaking furtively to another triad member. She nudged Ye-kan with her elbow. "Is that Fucha Arban?" she whispered, trying to get a better glimpse of the features beneath the hood. She'd only seen Arban once before, but his squarish shoulders and tall, bulky frame were etched in her mind after that alarming encounter at the Engineers Guild.

The man he was speaking to had an unfamiliar face—thick brows and deep-set eyes that looked at odds with the shallowness of his other features. There was something about him that left a nig-gling unease in Nian's mind. Maybe it was the way the muscles in his cheeks barely moved when he spoke, almost like his face were sculpted from rock.

"Arban? What would he be doing here?" Ye-kan turned, squint-ing through the crowd to get a better look.

An envelope passed between the two, and the man resembling Fucha Arban quickly tucked it between the folds of his robes. They split ways—Arban slipping back up the stairway and the triad mem-ber vanishing into the crowd.

"Quick, we can't let him get away." If this den belonged to the Qilin triad, then Arban's presence here could not be a coincidence. Grabbing Ye-kan by the wrist, Nian pulled him toward the exit.

They dashed out of the temple and back onto the street, the rush of the cool night air providing welcome relief after the suffocating at-mosphere down in the den. Nian's eyes scoured the surroundings for any sign of Arban.

"There!"

She pointed at the shadowy figure some distance ahead, making his way hurriedly away from the temple. The man turned at the sound of her voice, the incandescence from the nearby streetlamps casting some light upon his face.

Slanted brows framed a pair of mean-looking eyes, with hollow cheeks sitting upon a boxy jaw.

There was no mistake. It *was* Arban.

His eyes widened, recognition dawning upon him. Panic drew

his face tight—then he whirled back around and took off running. *Escaping.* Once he turned the street corner a few steps ahead, they would lose sight of him.

They couldn't afford to let him get away.

He was guilty of something, and they had to know what.

The gears in Nian's mind flew into swift motion. She held out her right arm, wrist tipping downward to point her silver bracelet in Arban's direction. She jabbed at the cobra chiseled into the metal like Ye-kan had taught her, sending several fine-tipped needles flying out.

"Ah!" a cry rang out.

Arban continued running for a short while, but before he made it around the corner, his entire body lurched forward. He collapsed heavily to the ground. When they caught up with him, he was curled on the cobbles in a trembling heap, the effects of the numbing poison leaving his limbs weak and eyes dazed.

Ye-kan pinned him down with one foot, lips curling in contempt. "Well, if it isn't an old friend," he said.

CHAPTER 21

As NIAN FOLLOWED YE-KAN DOWN THE DAMP, dismal corridors of the Order's dungeons, buried far beneath the glittering capital city, her only thought was that this place was the manifestation of hell on earth. An overpowering stench of sweat and congealed blood permeated the air, making it difficult to even breathe. As they passed by each cell, its occupants would stare at her through the bars of their iron cages, some with feral hostility, others with vacant gazes—as if there was no soul within those shells.

They arrived at a cavernous space that still seemed ironically suffocating, with the amber glow from the gas lamps casting eerie, flickering shadows across the walls. A man was hanging from a wooden frame, arms lashed to a horizontal plank. His head hung limply to one side, long, grimy strands of hair strewn across his face, looking nothing like the proud, conceited young man that she had first seen in the Engineers Guild.

The Order's guards who were watching over him stepped aside.

"Beile-ye," they greeted, bringing their fists up in salute.

A scornful huff escaped from the prisoner's lips. He raised his head, regarding Ye-kan and Nian with contempt. Despite his dire circumstances, his spirit was not yet broken.

"Aogiya Ye-kan, what's the meaning of this? You have no reason to lock me here," he hissed.

"Is that so? Why were you so eager to run away, then?" Ye-kan asked. "Arban, I know what you've done. If you tell me everything you know, then I might be able to save you from a death sentence."

Arban laughed, slow and taunting. Then he spat at their feet. "What makes you think I'll tell you anything? Ye-kan, you're just a child. Without your mother to protect you, you're *nothing*." He yanked at the chains. "Let me go! My father won't let you get away with this!"

"Your father might not be able to save himself, never mind you. Stealing and smuggling weapons from the Order is treason. The lives of the entire Fucha clan are at stake."

Bewilderment flashed across Arban's eyes. "What do you mean? What weapons?"

"Over thirty crates of weapons across three military camps. What gave you the gall!" The fourteenth prince grabbed Arban by the neck, his nails digging into the man's skin.

"I don't know what you're talking about," Arban choked, his face reddening. "I never touched any weapons from the military camps."

Nian had been observing Arban carefully ever since they stepped in here, and the shock that appeared on his face when Ye-kan mentioned the smuggled weapons seemed genuine. Even so, Arban had to be involved in one way or the other, else he would not have had dealings with the Qilin triad, or tried to escape out of guilt.

She placed a hand on Ye-kan's arm, subtly shaking her head. It would do them no good if Ye-kan accidentally snapped Arban's neck.

Ye-kan let go.

Stepping forward, Nian asked, "If you didn't steal the weapons, then why did you run when you saw the fourteenth beile? Why did the Qilin triad pay you such a large sum of money?"

The envelope they had found on Arban contained a thick wad of monetary notes amounting to two hundred taels. That was more than Arban's own father, a high-ranking general in the Order, would have earned in an entire year.

Arban pursed his lips into a hard line, saying nothing.

"Let me put things plainly to you," Nian continued. "The Qilin triad are involved in the illegal smuggling of the Order's weapons, but they must be working with someone within the High Command, someone who has access to the camps. So far, you're the only suspect."

"I didn't do it! You can't accuse me of something I didn't do!" The thick metal chains binding his arms and legs jangled noisily as Arban tried to lunge toward Nian. The feral look in his eyes was now tinged with an equal portion of fear.

"It doesn't matter whether or not you actually did it. What matters is whether people believe you. Right now, the evidence is not in your favor. This is your only chance to redeem yourself. Tell us what you *did* do, if you didn't steal those weapons?"

Arban thought about the offer for a moment, then he lowered his head miserably. "I—I—was only trying to make some money. They told me there was a buyer interested in buying large quantities of rice and willing to pay a high price for any stock I could get my hands on. I only took a few sacks from the Shan-yi Halls, I swear!"

Stealing rice from the Shan-yi Halls . . .

So Arban was responsible for the rice that they had also found alongside the weapons in the Wu Lin tunnels.

The shortage of food supplies across the nine isles because of the blockade of the Dunzhu Straits meant that prices of rice and other staples had gone up tremendously. It would not be unthinkable for those like Arban to want to make a pot of gold off these developments.

"Do you know who that buyer is?" she asked.

"No. The Qilins would give me a location to drop off the goods, then they'd pick it up from there." He looked past Nian's shoulder toward the fourteenth beile. "Ye-kan—no, Beile-ye, you have to believe me! We were in the guild together. You know what I'm like. I would never dare do something like steal weapons! All I wanted was to earn more money. I thought that if I could show my a-ma that I was capable of doing something, *anything*, that he would stop treating me like I was worthless."

"Did it not occur to you that the Shan-yi Halls are run by the High Command? That it was the High Commander himself who set them up?"

Nian could sympathize with Arban's plight, understand his desperation to win approval from his father and clan, but she despised him for what he had chosen to do. Those sacks of rice were meant to feed the refugees, and Arban knew that. He had done what he did *precisely* because he was aware of that. In his mind, the lives of these refugees did not matter, and he had been counting on getting away with it because he knew that hardly anyone else in Fei cared about them either.

"Please, I'm begging you, give me a chance. I'll find a way to put back all the supplies that I took, I promise!"

"Then you should never have taken them in the first place," Nian said.

There were consequences to every action, and Arban would have to learn things the hard way.

CHAPTER 22

ON BOARD THE SHIPS OF THE BLOOD PHOENIX, a feast was underway. The crew set aside their duties and partook in joyous revelry, indulging in the best cured meats and rice wine that their stores had to offer. The fragrant aroma of bamboo-wrapped sea bass and chili-marinated squid wafted through the air, tantalizing taste buds. As the heroes of the day, Ying and the others were invited to join in the celebrations, albeit with the chains back on their ankles. By the end of the night, both An-xi and Chang-en were gloriously inebriated, An-xi in an attempt to drown his stress and Chang-en because he simply could.

It wasn't until the wee hours of the morning that things finally quieted down, with most of the pirates either retired to bed or collapsed somewhere on deck. The waning gibbous moon cast a delicate silver glow upon the ship's deck, the flag of the phoenix fluttering with the gentle breeze.

Leaning against the wooden rail at the ship's bow, Ying took a swig from the jar of wine that Yunshang had brought over earlier. The Qirin girl had fallen asleep on An-xi's shoulder not far from where she was, with Chang-en snoring on the floorboards beside them. Their half-finished game of four-colored cards still lay sprawled across the crate they had been playing on.

"You shouldn't be drinking." A hand reached over her shoulder, plucking the jar out of her hand. "It's not good for healing," Ye-yang said, gesturing at her injured shoulder. The grappling hook had left deep lacerations that cut all the way down to the bone. There would certainly be scars left behind, both inside and out, even after the wounds healed.

"But it helps to numb myself into believing that no healing is needed," she replied drily. Still, she didn't attempt to snatch the jar back. It would have been impossible with a healthy arm, never mind a badly injured one.

"Something on your mind?"

She shook her head first, then nodded.

After the initial euphoria of winning the race subsided, reality slowly began to set in. Surviving the tournament wasn't the end of it. She knew that. What would become of them from here on? Li-na never made any promises that she would set them free. And would they really be able to uncover the mastermind controlling these pirates, and make it back to tell the tale?

The way ahead was murky and uncertain.

Glancing over at the sleeping Yunshang, she sighed.

Yunshang reminded her a lot of a younger Nian, before life's responsibilities gradually smoothed down her sister's rough edges and transformed her into the poised, mellow version of her former self. Nian had been forced to mature before her time, and Ying knew that she'd had a role to play in that. If she hadn't shirked her own clan duties, Nian would not have had to fill those shoes. In Yunshang, she saw the reflection of what Nian could have been. Willful and carefree. Living for no one but herself. Perhaps that was why she had instinctively jumped in to protect the girl during the race.

"I miss Nian," she said. "Do you think she's okay, back in Fei?" It was unsettling, not knowing how the situation in Fei had evolved since their absence.

She bent over, picking up a short bamboo strip painted yellow— one of the stray cards from the game that Yunshang and the others had been playing.

"A-ma brought back a set of four-colored cards that he bought off a Qirin merchant once, but E-niye refused to let us play, insisting it was a form of gambling. Nian and I stole it out of A-ma's workshop and played in secret, hiding under the blankets in the middle of the night." The memory brought a wry smile to her face. "Nian was far better than me at it. The few times I won was because she let me, even though she thought I didn't know. She was always the better strategist—and the more considerate sister."

"Come." Ye-yang took her by the hand, leading her down the deck. His fingers intertwined with hers, sending a warm tingle up her spine. Her heart made an involuntary skip.

"Where are you taking me?"

"To get some air."

"It's fine, I don't need—ah!"

Ye-yang's arm circled around her waist, and then she was *flying*. Or at least it felt that way. A brief moment of weightlessness as her body lifted up into the air and the floorboards vanished beneath her feet. She could hear the light taps of his soles against wood, taking

them higher and higher until they landed upon the tiny circular platform located high above deck—the crow's nest.

"Why did you bring me up here? Someone could have seen us!"
she hissed. Wriggling out of his grasp, she immediately squatted
down, making sure she was well hidden from whoever might be
down below. A guild apprentice with qing-gong good enough to
carry a whole other person all the way up here in a mere three-step
leap, even while having his ankles chained, would make them *very*
suspicious.

They did not need a new reason to convince Li-na to make them
walk the plank.

Ye-yang chuckled, seemingly nonplussed about what he had
done. "Don't worry, no one's awake or sober enough to notice," he
replied. He leaned casually against the side and stretched his arms
out along the curved edge. "I can see why Yunshang likes to spend
her time up here. The view is quite magical. Are you sure you don't
want to take a look?"

Ying crossed her arms and huffed, slightly annoyed by his behavior. Overconfidence was a habit that would eventually come back
to haunt him, she was certain of it.

She straightened herself up, lifting her gaze out toward the
ocean. A gasp escaped from her lips.

They had been out at sea for over a week now, a pinprick bobbing
on the choppy waters of the vast Dunzhu Straits, but *this*—this was
the ocean like she had never seen it before. An endless blanket of
glittering darkness that stretched to the horizon in every possible
direction, the gentle sway of the waves reflecting the soft glow of

moonlight into her eyes. Above them, Abka Han had painted a river of stars that seemed to spill like a waterfall where the sky met the sea.

"*Every star is a soul that once walked this earth*," her e-niye once said, while the entire family was snuggled around a bonfire, "*watching over their loved ones even long after they have gone.*"

She believed what her mother said now, because she had to count herself infinitely lucky for having survived till this day.

Thank you for watching over me, A-ma, E-niye, she whispered inside her heart, hoping that her parents would be able to hear her from where they were, two stars hanging in the midnight sky. And if they were protecting her, then surely they would protect Nian and the rest of their family too.

The view from up here gave her a feeling of déjà vu, an inkling that she had been here once. Two years ago, she had stood upon the Fei city walls beside Ye-yang, with the hectic bustle of the city on one side and the tranquility of the ocean on the other. Shooting stars had soared across the sable sky, painting golden arcs with their fiery tails. She made a wish.

"*I wish for us to get our heart's desire.*"

A lifetime had passed since then, and nothing was the same.

They got what they wanted, didn't they? Revenge. Respect. Justice. Power. Yet she often wondered if they chose wrong. If what they'd achieved was not what they should have strived for.

"Nian will be fine," Ye-yang said. "As you said, she is a natural strategist. I fully expect her to be able to find her way out of any trouble. In some ways, I think she's made for the palace and the politics that comes along with it."

"That's why she's the one who will become the High Commander's wife," Ying said, the words spilling out too quickly for her to retract them. She hated it, the bitterness that lingered at the back of her throat. The jealousy. *Because Nian is more suitable than me.*

She thought she had already convinced herself to accept that, but maybe she hadn't after all—because it still hurt.

Ye-yang reached out a hand, placing it tenderly against her cheek. He didn't say sorry this time, perhaps because he had already apologized too many times before. Apologies were worthless. They could not rewind time and correct the mistakes that were made in the past. They would not change the fact that he had once deceived her, that he had once broken her heart, and that their fathers' deaths would continue to be a shadow that would haunt them for the rest of their lives.

"Yes, she will," he said quietly, "but that High Commander doesn't have to be me."

Ying blinked in confusion. Who else could the High Commander be except him? There was no two ways about it, unless . . . they never made it back to Fei.

"I told you my e-niye's story, didn't I? How she died with regrets, without being able to see her home one last time?" Ye-yang continued, turning his gaze back toward the open sea.

Ye-yang's mother had been a pitiful woman, forced to lead her entire life at the behest of the ambitions of the men around her. Even on her deathbed, her only wish of returning to her home isle of Yokre had been callously rejected because her husband and brother insisted on waging war against each other. Her tragic demise had left a scar upon her young son, a scar that eventually led to years of careful plotting, ending in the end of an era within the Antaran High Command.

"Do you know what her last words to me were?" he asked.

Ying waited. She could sense the deep sorrow running through him as he drew upon that memory, reflected through the melancholy in his eyes.

"She said she wished she'd never come to Fei. Lately I've been thinking that maybe she was right."

"Are you thinking of *leaving* the nine isles?" Ying asked hesitantly, trying to suppress the sliver of hope that had unwittingly sprung up inside her. If he was willing to leave, to let go, then maybe they could still find a way to mend what was broken?

But the question sounded incredulous, even as she was saying it.

"Why? Does that seem impossible?" Ye-yang replied with a chuckle. "Maybe I will, one day. After I've finished everything that I need to do."

"Which is never."

She should have known that he was only speaking in jest. Ye-yang would never leave Fei or the High Command, not with those lofty ambitions of his. He had fought too long and too hard to give it all up so easily.

"Did you ever consider that you don't have to be the one to carry this burden?" she said, the remnants of wine giving her a burst of boldness. "Two years. It's only been two years since you became

High Commander, and already it shows in the lines of your face, your eyes, in the way that you walk, in the tone of your voice. This position has a price, Ye-yang, and you're paying for it with *your life*."

He was staring quietly at her, the slant of moonlight softening the sunken angles of his cheeks, making his gray irises appear a lustrous silver. The creases and fine lines across his forehead and at the corners of his eyes seemed even more prominent in this light—and it made her heart ache.

Then he smiled.

"Am I right to think that you're feeling sorry for me?" he asked, taking a step closer. His voice carried a low, smoky timbre, beguiling against the soft echo of the waves. "That you're upset because you can't bear to see what I've been through?" Ying swallowed, regretting her outburst. She moved back, but ended up pressing against the side of the crow's nest. Heat rose up her neck.

"Take me back down, I—"

Ye-yang's lips crashed against her own, forcing her to swallow the rest of her demand. Ying startled. Her first instinct was to pull away, yet she didn't. Couldn't. There was an urgency in his kiss, a hunger that had been bottled up for all the years they had spent apart. She lowered her eyelids, letting herself indulge in the moment, in his touch. She'd never realized how much she missed it— the warmth and tenderness of his embrace, the familiar scent of orchids that somehow lingered upon his skin, the loving caress of his fingers upon her cheeks.

Yes, she was feeling sorry for him. Her heart bled for what he had to endure on his own, for the weight that he carried upon his shoulders. She should hate him, so much, for the selfish decisions that he made, for always forcing her to become a tiny cog in his big plans, but here she was admitting that she still loved him instead. She laced her fingers through his long strands of hair, deepening the kiss. Passion pulsed through her veins, heartbeat racing fervently within her chest. *Just once*, she told herself. After all, this one time could well be their last. Who knew what would become of them when the sun rose the next morning? She sighed softly against his lips, letting herself sink further into his touch.

Then something unusual appeared at the corner of her eye.

"Wait. Look." She tore herself away from him, pointing in the direction of the anomaly.

A haze of flickering lights was approaching from the distance, ghostly lanterns that marred the ethereal night sea.

"What's that? Another fleet?" she wondered.

A bell rang out, over and over, with discernible urgency in each toll.

"It's the Eels!" someone shouted from down below. "Everyone to battle stations!"

Ye-yang's lips hardened in a grim line. "We have to go," he said. Without waiting for her to reply, he took her by the waist once again. Ying wrapped her arms around his torso, allowing him to lift her out of the crow's nest and back down to the main deck.

Within seconds, dozens of crew members swarmed out from the cabins in various states of undress, many of them still groggy and dazed. They all rushed to man their assigned stations. Li-na and Keyan emerged as well, the captain still composed and unflappable, while her deputy wore a tenacious snarl upon her face. They headed for the command post at the ship's stern.

The fleet continued to sail toward them, now clearly visible as distinct ships arranged in the formation of an arrow's tip. Right in the middle, they spied the silhouette of its towering flagship, a behemoth that was possibly even larger than the Blood Phoenix's, deliberately painted entirely in forbidding black. Were it not for the glowing lanterns on board, they might not even have seen it coming, with the way it wore the night as a cloak.

Chang-en and An-xi, who had been rudely awoken, stumbled over to join them. "What's going on?" they asked, eyes still glazed and unfocused.

"It's the Midnight Eels," Yunshang answered. "The ones who attacked us during the race."

If not for them, the Eels might have won the Tournament of the Seas with their cruel, vicious tactics. By taking down every single member of their competing crew in order to rescue her, Ye-yang had ruined their chances completely.

"They're here for revenge," Ying whispered.

Gas burned brilliant in their glass receptacles, lighting up the sea as if it were day. In the night sky, the stars blinked into darkness, hiding because they could not bear to watch the bloodshed about to ensue.

Tension hung thick in the air, like a heavy, suffocating fog, as the two rival fleets faced each other head on, one flagship against the next.

"Zhong Kui, the tournament is over. Quit playing games and go back to sleep," Keyan hollered, her voice carrying loud and clear across the wind. The Blood Phoenix's second-in-command was standing by the ship's wheel, one hand resting casually behind her back, while the other rested a menacing crossbow upon her shoulder.

Although Ying could not see the er-dangjia's face from where she stood, she could tell from the sharp tone of the woman's voice that Keyan was in a foul mood.

In contrast, the silhouette seated in the wheelchair beside her remained still, watching silently as if none of this concerned her.

A piercing laugh rang out in response to Keyan's remark, its pitch so shrill that it made Ying's ears hurt.

"Ariha Keyan, even if I'm playing games, I'm certainly not playing with a child like you. Li-na, hand over your Blade, and maybe I'll let your crew of little girls go, how about that? You already have one, so what's the point of having another? Don't be greedy."

The voice that spoke was light and airy, drifting effortlessly across the water. It sounded almost ghostly, with a spectral, otherworldly quality that made the hairs on the back of Ying's neck stand. A slight figure perched upon the crow's nest of the enemy flagship, lounging with one leg propped up and the other dangling down precariously, clutching a jar of wine in his right hand. The burning lamps on board the ship lit his face with an eerie glow, making his complexion look an unnatural, pearlescent white.

"Is that even a human?" Chang-en quipped. "Looks more like a demon from hell."

"His name is Zhong Kui. Used to be a high-ranking eunuch from the Qirin royal court, but ended up a pirate after he was betrayed by his own," Yunshang said with a scowl. "He's been going around seizing some of the smaller fleets so that he can be 'emperor of the seas.' This isn't the first time he's tried to make a move on our Blade."

"I'm not going to waste time with a dog that can't stop barking. If you want the Blade, then come get it for yourself." Li-na spoke in a measured, almost nonchalant tone that was bound to enrage her enemy. From the way she behaved, it was clear that Li-na did not view Zhong Kui and his Eels as a threat at all. Ying itched to know where that confidence came from, and if any of it was misplaced.

Zhong Kui's disquieting laughter filled the air once more. He leapt from the crow's nest back down onto his ship's main deck. "I thought you'd care more about your crew's lives than that, but I guess I was wrong," he said. "In that case, don't blame me for this when you're rotting in hell. Blame your captain!" Raising his wine jar high in the air, he smashed it against the floor with a resounding crash.

The fighting began.

CHAPTER 23

THE NIGHT DESCENDED INTO CHAOS, THE BRINE-SOAKED
air soon overwhelmed by the grim odor of gunpowder and smoke.
Explosions erupted from all directions as cannonballs flew. The Eels
threw grappling hooks across to the Blood Phoenix ships, and men
came crossing over by the dozens. A flurry of arrows sent many of
them falling through the gaps and into the freezing waters below,
but still they came like a never-ending torrent. Fighting broke out on
deck. Blades clashed. Blood flowed.

Ye-yang immediately stepped in front of Ying, shielding her
from the onslaught. He pulled her behind a stack of crates, safe from
the splintering wood and flying debris. Chang-en and An-xi scurried
over as well, huddling against each other. In the melee, Ying tried to
grab hold of Yunshang, but the girl had already dashed off to man
one of the fixed crossbow stations on deck.

The battle intensified, with almost every ship in the fleet engaged in some manner of fighting. Two of their peripheral ships had
gone up in flames. The crew desperately tried to put out the fires
while guarding their own backs.

Zhong Kui lingered behind on his own flagship, a mocking
smile slowly spreading across his pale face. Like a reaper, here to collect his due of souls.

"Li-na, all you have to do is surrender the Blade. It's that simple," he shouted.

"I thought I made it quite clear the first time," Li-na replied. "The answer—is no."

"Then don't blame me for this."

Raising his voice in a bloodcurdling battle cry, Zhong Kui grabbed hold of a rope and swung himself onto the Phoenix's flagship, brandishing a moon blade in his free hand.

"We need to go," Ye-yang said. Snatching a sword off a fallen Eel, he swiftly severed the chains binding each of their ankles. Then he guided Ying in the direction of the ship's bow. If they lingered any longer, they would soon be tangled in the violence whether they liked it or not.

"Go where? The ship is only this big!" An-xi squealed, quickly following behind.

"Go . . . home?" Chang-en's eyes suddenly lit up. "We can go home! This is our chance!"

Chang-en was right. This mayhem created the perfect opportunity for them to escape. If they missed this chance, they might never be able to leave these seas alive, regardless of which side won. Li-na had never made any promises about letting them go, while Zhong Kui would only be too eager to skewer them to appease the souls of his crew members they had killed.

As they ran, Ying's eyes raked across the gleaming metallic top of the *Diamond*, still parked silently beside the flagship, indifferent to the commotion going on around it.

Wait—

There was something different about the Blade.

The glass walls of the vehicle had vanished, shielded entirely by an impervious casing of gleaming metal. A cannonball ripped through the air, hurtling straight toward the head of the *Diamond*.

Ying stopped, her breath catching in her throat.

The cannonball struck the metal shell, then slid all the way down the curved side of the vessel until it fell into the water with a dull splash. The surface of the *Diamond* remained unblemished, without even the slightest visible dent.

It was no wonder the Cobra's Order was having such a difficult time trying to destroy a Blade. How could they, when it was indestructible?

Truly a feat of engineering, she marveled.

This was a part of the puzzle they never even knew was missing. The records that Ye-yang had shown her, the information that the spy had provided—those were incomplete. A Blade was not only a house of glass. With such a shield, there was no way Master Lianshu's explosives would work.

"Are you done gaping?" Yunshang's voice came yelling. She had one hand busy firing arrows from a crossbow while the other gestured wildly at Ying to get away. "Go belowdecks now! I didn't save your life for you to be slaughtered by Zhong Kui's stooges!"

"Yunshang, watch out!" Ying sprinted toward the girl. Leaping forward, she pushed Yunshang over in the nick of time. A moon blade sliced above their heads, barely missing them by an inch. They tumbled to the ground in a heap.

Ying looked past Yunshang's shoulder, eyes widening when she caught the assailant raising his blade for another attempt. He bared his yellow teeth in frustration, a bloodthirsty glint in his narrow eyes. This time, Ye-yang intervened. With a bamboo pole he had picked up from the deck, he deftly deflected the pirate's attack, then swung the stick hard against the man's torso, sending him crashing against the ship's rail.

"That's the second time you've saved my life. Now *I'm* the one who owes you," Yunshang griped.

Ying quickly helped the girl back up to her feet. "Come with us," she said, taking Yunshang by the hand. Even though Yunshang seemed to know how to work a crossbow, her movements had been slow and clumsy, betraying a lack of familiarity with the weapon. It was too dangerous for her here.

Yunshang shook her head vigorously. "No, I'm staying. This is my home. My family. I'm not going anywhere," she said. Her gaze swept across Ying and the rest, landing upon An-xi. A cheeky smile quirked upon her lips. "We haven't finished that game of four-colored cards. After this is all over, I'm going to finish whipping your ass!" Shoving Ying aside, she turned and ran toward the ship's stern, straight into the midst of the fighting.

"Yunshang! Come back!" An-xi shouted. He moved to chase after her, but Chang-en clung to his arm like a leech.

"We *have* to go," Chang-en said, his voice bleeding with urgency. "This is our only chance."

Ying hesitated, staring into the pandemonium through which Yunshang had disappeared, a disarray of clashing swords and broken bones. An arrow came hurtling in their direction. They ducked, watching it sail past and fall into the bottomless waters of the sea.

"Ying," Ye-yang called, taking her by the wrist. "There are some small sampans suspended near the bow of the ship. Chang-en is right, we must leave now." He paused. "Don't forget which side we're on." His incisive gaze bored right through her, and she knew then that he could tell exactly what was running through her mind. He could tell that she was wavering.

"I'm sorry, Ye-yang, but I can't."

Yunshang might have written off her life debt, but she had not.

She wondered if Ye-yang would be upset, or disappointed, and he had every reason to be, but she found none of that in his eyes. Only a hint of resignation, like he had already seen it coming. His grip on her wrist loosened.

"I'll come with you," he said.

"You don't have to. This is my decision." Ye-yang was the High Commander of the Antaran isles—he had a duty to his people, and rescuing the enemy was tantamount to treason.

"But I want to. I'm not leaving you behind a second time."

A ripple ran through Ying's heart, a familiar ache from when she had said goodbye to him upon the Huarin cliffs two years back. They were never supposed to have met again. They were never supposed to have a second chance. Yet here they were—his words like a promise that seared itself into her soul.

"If we're going to help, then we have to move quickly," he

continued. "There are too many of the Eels on board the flagship now. Li-na's side will not be able to hold on for much longer."

"Are the both of you out of your minds? Who cares about these pirates!" Chang-en exclaimed, staring at them incredulously. He turned to An-xi. "You agree with me, right? Tell them!"

To their surprise, An-xi, the most timid of them, didn't give an immediate reply. His terrified eyes darted in the direction that Yun-shang had disappeared.

"Hurry up!" Sidestepping to avoid another arrow that came out of nowhere, Chang-en tugged at An-xi's arm, attempting to drag him toward the sampans. Billowing smoke was drifting across the deck, coming from the flaming remains of a neighboring ship.

"No."

"No? What do you mean, no?" Chang-en gawked at An-xi in disbelief.

Turning to Ying, An-xi said, "I'll help."

Gratitude and guilt entwined themselves within Ying's heart, creating a discordant note that she had to forcibly suppress. There was no time for that. She nodded, then quickly surveyed the situation. Even as they continued defending the ship with sheer dogged-ness, the crew of the Blood Phoenix was increasingly overwhelmed.

An idea struck. A recollection of the subtle, stinging odor she had picked up amid the pungent aromas of cured meat and salted vegetables in the ship's store.

"There's shar powder being kept belowdecks, in the storerooms," she said. It was likely for warding away unwanted pests from the crew's meager food supplies, but to an engineer, it could do far more. "Follow me."

Sucking in a breath, Ying turned and took off running in the direction of the stores, Ye-yang and An-xi following behind. Chang-en lingered for a moment, then he threw his hands up in exasperation and hastened to join them. "You're going to regret this! All of you!" he shouted.

Moments later, they returned to the main deck carrying small bundles, each the size of a fist, wrapped in scraps of hemp cloth. As they ran, sprinklings of acrid-smelling yellow powder spilled from their loads, leaving a trail of dust upon the floorboards. Shar powder—one of the ingredients of gunpowder.

Ye-yang disarmed an Eel and took his moon blade, helping to clear the way for Ying and the others. "Stay behind me," he said, leading them through the fracas toward the nearest crossbow station. The wooden platform was smeared with dark maroon, the lifeless body of the crossbow's last operator lying still beside it. A large gash ran down her back, from shoulder to waist, staining her cream-colored tunic with the shade of death. Ying stepped up to the weapon, her fingers pausing for a moment in front of the bloody fingerprints that had been left behind upon the chestnut.

She had known that woman. They called her Hua-yi, one of the matrons who worked in the kitchens. She only spoke in a lesser-known Qirin dialect, so most of the crew could barely understand her, but her cooking said everything. A bowl of warm ginger soup for rainy days, a tiny packet of dragon beard candy for the younger ones, a freshly caught pomfret—roasted on an open fire, not steamed—because she knew that was the taste that Antarans associated with home.

You fought well, Hua-yi. May you find peace now.

Ying let out a long, slow breath, then she sprang into action. An-xi had loaded an arrow onto the crossbow, its pointed head gleaming with the layer of rapeseed oil that it had been dipped into. She quickly lashed one bundle of shar powder to the arrow's shaft, only two fingers away from the tip. They aimed it in the direction of the nearest group of Eels, then tilted it a notch upward. At the space above their heads, Ying lit the arrowhead with the open flame from a gas lamp.

She pulled the trigger. The arrow flew.

Right as it soared above the pirates, drawing a fiery arc through the air, the sack of shar powder exploded. Flaming droplets rained down upon the Eels, as if the heavens had unleashed hell upon them. Screams and cries rang out. Men leapt overboard, desperate for the freezing seawater to douse the fires that burned through their flesh.

"She's over there! Yunshang!" An-xi shouted. He pointed toward the stern, where the petite girl had been cornered by three Eels. Her back was pressed up against the taffrail, a broken arrow clutched in her right hand. She turned to look at the blackened waters below, the strong winds whipping her long hair wildly across her face.

Ying swiveled their crossbow in that direction, but An-xi clapped a hand over its stock.

"No," he said. "If we fire, we'll strike her too." Their shar powder explosives were too blunt, too imprecise. While it worked beautifully to dispatch several targets at a time, there would inevitably be casualties incurred on their side as well.

Instead, An-xi picked up a stray moon blade lying on the floor. His sweaty fingers gripped its hilt, fear reflecting through the whites of his knuckles. He ran, charging toward Yunshang and her assailants.

"Ye-yang, Chang-en, quick! Help An-xi!" Ying called. The two boys had been stationed around the crossbow platform, defending against any enemies who dared approach. Blood was splattered across their faces, the blades in their hands already dripping red.

Chang-en took one look in An-xi's direction. "That fool!" he roared, giving chase. "Does he even know how to use a moon blade?"

Ye-yang hung behind.

"Go, please," Ying begged. An-xi needed the support more than she did, and Yunshang's life was teetering on the line. They had already cleared out their vicinity, bodies littered all around the crossbow platform. She was in no immediate danger—unlike the others.

He nodded, though a reluctance still flickered in his gray eyes. He ran off to An-xi's aid.

Nervous breathing rattling in her chest, Ying did another sweep of the main deck.

Up front, Keyan was going head-on with Zhong Kui. The second-in-command had swapped out her crossbow for a pair of twin daggers for close-range combat. Her cheeks were flushed, features pinched from the exertion. With each deflection, she was forced back a step, Zhong Kui bearing down with his merciless reclining moon blade.

Not far from them, Li-na remained perfectly still in her wheelchair, a strange juxtaposition to the havoc unraveling around her. Occasionally, she would glance down at something in the palm of her hand—the pocket watch—as if she were waiting for something to happen.

It was as if she was shrouded in a protective bubble that no one dared approach. Or that no one *could*. Hidden within concealed compartments along the frame of Li-na's wheelchair were rotating metal blades that could be extended and retracted on command, spinning at a speed so high that they became a blur, easily missed in the shadows of night. Any Eel that came within three steps of the captain would crumple to the ground within seconds, not realizing what had hit them until it was too late. Their bloodcurdling screams were the last note that would ever leave their lips, reverberating in the cold sea breeze.

Ying's pulse quickened, horrified by the deadly elegance with which Li-na was cutting down her attackers. The captain was barely lifting a finger. There was no need for that.

Then a wink of light was reflected into her eyes. An arrowhead, aimed right at Li-na's back. An Eel had seized one of the ship's crossbow stations, his dark eyes glinting manically as his trembling fingers fumbled for the trigger.

She reacted on instinct, sending her next shar powder projectile hurtling out. The arrow struck the Eel in the chest, detonating in a mess of flames and seared flesh. Ying stared, the air forced out from her lungs. A flashback struck. She was back in Qianlei Palace, in the

High Commander's study, staring at Aogiya Lianzhe in a pool of his own blood. Back in a nightmare.

Li-na turned her head, her steely gaze meeting Ying's. Her eyes narrowed briefly, the only acknowledgment that Ying received before the captain turned her attention back toward the bronze pocket watch in her hand.

Boom!

A thunderous explosion went off.

Not the same as a cannonball striking its target, or even a flare being fired.

The sea rumbled, sending vibrations rippling across the flagship's hull. Everyone froze, alarmed by the sudden motion. In that instant, Ying wondered if another storm was about to ensue, as the memories from the previous one sent a jolt of fear down her spine.

"Our ship!" a gruff voice yelled. One of the Eels, a burly man with stubble covering his lower jaw, pointed one shaky finger across the waters at their fleet.

Except there was no ship—or at least not anymore.

The explosion had completely ripped the ship apart, leaving behind nothing but piles of floating driftwood, the ship's flags floating limply in the water. Embers flickered upon the surface of the sea, licking hungrily at the remains.

What happened next was nothing short of horrific.

One by one the ships in the Eels' fleet lit up like firecrackers, accompanied by the same earsplitting explosions over and over. There had to be at least twelve ships in the fleet—and then there was only one.

Only the flagship remained, a lonely silhouette amid a sea of flames.

"W-w-what did you do?" Zhong Kui stammered. Gone was his earlier arrogance, and fear and disbelief were written all over his narrow face. Abandoning his fight with Keyan, he backed away toward the rail, pointing his blade at Li-na. "What did you do!"

Ying thought that the better question was: *how* did she do it?

The answer came to her almost immediately, in the form of monsters rising from the deep. In the distance, the ink-black waters glowed with an eerie, silver light belonging to the goliaths buried beneath. A pod of whales, with dramatic, metallic tails that undulated below the surface of the thrashing waves.

They're here. The Blades.

This was what Li-na had been waiting for. Reinforcements.

Zhong Kui turned toward his flagship just as the last explosion rang out. The final vestiges of hope in his eyes faded away as he watched the flagship disintegrate into pieces.

"Ahhh!"

The agony and rage in Zhong Kui's cry ripped through the air. Spinning around, he suddenly charged toward Li-na, his expression bloodthirsty and feral, swinging his moon blade erratically. Keyan stepped forward to parry his blows, but Li-na held her back.

The captain swung her arm, and a long, silver chain came snaking out from within her arrow sleeve. It reminded Ying of her own flying guillotine, except what was attached to the end of Li-na's chain was a metal dart the length of a palm. Its sharpened tip pierced straight through Zhong Kui's left shoulder. With a firm tug on her end of the chain, Li-na brought the man crashing to the floor before her feet.

Glancing down imperiously at her enemy, she said, "Zhong Kui, your problem is that you keep trying to take what doesn't belong to you, to pretend to be what you're not. There is a price to pay for that."

The man lifted his head from the floorboards, strands of long hair hanging disheveled across his face. He spat on Li-na's shoe, his thin lips curling in a contemptuous sneer.

"Li-na, you think you've won? You're exactly the same as I was, groveling in front of a master who sees you as nothing but a tool. Once you've outlived your worth, you'll be thrown away. Fed to the wolves."

"You would know, wouldn't you?" Rolling her wheelchair backward, the captain of the Blood Phoenix turned and headed back toward the cabins. "I thank you for your wisdom, Zhong Kui, but I don't think it'll be necessary. We are *not* the same, and your mistakes will not be mine. Keyan, you know what to do," her voice echoed.

The er-dangjia flipped Zhong Kui over, pinning him down with one boot upon his torso. She positioned the tip of one of her twin daggers at his throat.

Ying flinched.

A warm, steady hand tilted her face away from the grim scene, and she was enveloped by the familiar subtle scent of tie guan yin that always seemed to stay with Ye-yang. She stared up into his eyes, a disquiet churning within her gut.

"He's here," she whispered.

The one they'd been waiting for.

CHAPTER 24

YING STARED OUT AT THE OPEN SEA, her gaze transfixed upon the flotsam left behind by last night's hostilities. Pieces of debris remained floating on the surface. The occasional piece of fabric—someone's undergarment, a cook's dishcloths—lay snagged between splintered wood. A few barrels bobbed up and down with the waves.

Yet that was all that remained of a fleet of a dozen.

It was almost terrifying to imagine what the sea had swallowed in the span of a single night.

Ye-yang came up to her side. They stood there quietly for the longest time, neither saying a word.

"I asked Yunshang. There were twenty-two bodies offloaded from this ship, and scores more that would have died on board their own ships during the explosions. Over there"—she pointed at the empty space where the Eels' fleet used to be—"is a mass grave."

Yet no one cares.

On board the Blood Phoenix's flagship, life had returned to normal. After sending off their dead in a fiery salute, the blood had swiftly been scrubbed off the deck. Everything that had been broken in the chaos was in the process of being repaired. The crew bustled about, resuming their daily routines and chirpy banter. Perhaps it was their way of coping with grief, but it was not one that Ying was used to.

"Zhong Kui and his men were not innocent either. It was a fight to the death. They all knew the consequence," Ye-yang replied kindly. He placed a hand on her shoulder and gave it a pat. "Ying, I know how you must feel, but none of this is your fault. There's no need for you to bear this burden."

"But it *is* my fault. I chose to turn around to help, and I even dragged all of you with me." She tilted her head up toward the crowded skies, the roiling gray clouds heavy with sorrow. The first few drops of rain fell upon her cheeks. Tears of mourning for those who were lost. "Do you think Feng-kai will blame me? For not avenging him?"

If she had stood by and done nothing, if she had escaped like Chang-en had wanted instead, then perhaps the Blood Phoenix would have lost. Li-na's ashes would be the ones scattered upon these seas, not Zhong Kui's. If she hadn't intervened, Feng-kai's death, and the deaths of all those innocent people of Larut, would have been paid for.

"Because that is who you are, Ying. You are different from us. You have always believed in hope, in finding a new way of doing things that doesn't require bloodshed."

"And that is my curse."

"It is your gift."

"Sure doesn't feel that way," she scoffed. "Do you know what I'm most upset about? That if I had to make that choice again, I would have done the same. I would still have gone back. I'm supposed to hate them, Ye-yang. Aren't I?"

"It's much easier to hate a faceless enemy than people who you've come to know."

At the bow of the ship, Yunshang had started a round of rowdy singing and dancing, clapping and stomping around the deck to the tune of an upbeat Qirin folk song being played on the ocarina. Even her own friends, Chang-en and An-xi, wore relaxed expressions on their faces, tapping their fingers along to the beat. The bright smiles on everyone's faces and the laughter that filled the air created an atmosphere of warmth and genuine camaraderie that felt so familiar yet so foreign to her.

"Celebrations on Huarin were like this too," she said, reminiscing on those exuberant festivities that would light up the plains bordering their village, when she was surrounded by family.

That was it, she realized. Family. That was what the morning's scene reminded her of. That was what this entire fleet reminded her of.

Even though these women had suffered various tragedies and setbacks in their lives, they had found a home on board these ships, and a family in one another. Over the days she had spent here, she had truly felt the love and care that everyone showered upon their peers—even on her, a newcomer who they barely knew anything about.

Her mind told her that it was wrong for her to feel this way, but her heart told a different story, and that dissonance was tearing her asunder.

Were they truly criminals? Or were they merely victims of their circumstances?

Those questions once again stirred up splinters of guilt inside her. Guilt for doubting whether or not avenging the Larut tragedy was the right decision. Guilt for considering that maybe the better choice was to forget—to let go. After all, how many cycles of bloodshed would it take before vengeance could be satiated?

The only comfort she could give herself was the knowledge that at least they were one step closer to a different goal. A bigger goal— to secure the future of those who lived, so that the sacrifices of those who died would not be in vain.

"Will he really appear?" she asked.

After the heinous end to last night's battle, the ghostly underwater ships responsible for the carnage had vanished as stealthily as they had appeared. He must have been the one who sent them—the engineer in the shadows—but till now, there was no sign of any other ship approaching.

"He will," Ye-yang replied, his cool gaze sweeping the horizon.

"Do you already have someone in mind?"

"Unfortunately, I do, although I still hope that I'm wrong."

"Who is it?"

Ye-yang fell silent for a beat, the lines of his face stiffening. "The only other person who broke my mother's heart."

"Your . . . uncle?"

When Aogiya Lianzhe had sought to unite the Antaran isles all those years back, the Monggu clan of Yokre, Ye-yang's maternal clan, had been the only one to resist. Despite his sister's pleas, Monggu Yutai refused to concede, choosing instead to betray the Antarans and swear fealty to the Qirin empire. The ambitious feud between two men had fractured a people—and a family.

Ever since the Monggu clan officially severed all ties with the

Aogiya High Command, it was forbidden for anyone to speak of these traitors. Soon, many even forgot that a tenth isle existed.

"He's little more than a stranger to me. The last I saw of him was when I was four. I barely remember what he looks like anymore," Ye-yang replied. "But I remember Yokre and the curves of its land." Raising his index finger, he drew the shape of a crescent in the air. "My e-niye used to call it her isle of the moon, but to me, it resembled more of a demon's horns. There are two mountains, one at each end of the arc, separated by a narrow harbor that opens to the cove. The people of Yokre call them the Cursed Lovers Peaks, because they bend ever so slightly toward each other, yet are eternally separated by the sea."

Ying blinked, surprised at how easily those invisible brushstrokes had formed a painting in her mind. She had seen those mountains before, even though they had been draped in fog, like an image from a hazy dream.

"The Tournament of the Seas . . ." The sighting of land on the horizon was not a mirage. It was the tenth isle.

"You saw it too?" A bitter smile curled upon Ye-yang's lips. "I did think of returning to Yokre one day, to install my e-niye's remembrance tablet back in her village, where she would have wanted it to be. Never expected to be seeing the isle again in this manner."

He was trying his best to disguise it, the hurt of an old scar newly formed, but Ying could see the echoes of those painful memories reflected in the still pools of his eyes. She reached out a hand toward him, wanting to smooth away the creases between his brows. But then she let it fall back to her side instead.

"I'm sorry," she said.

"What for?"

"We should have left the Blood Phoenix. It was my mistake."

Ye-yang had figured out who the mastermind was during the tournament. If they had escaped last night, then that information would already be on its way back to the High Command. Her moment of selfishness, her need to defend her own principles, could have cost them everything. She chose to protect Yunshang, to rescue Li-na, but what if the price of that was the lives of hundreds of other Antarans? Suddenly, the true weight of Ye-yang's burden became clear to her, the difficult choices that he had to make.

"I already said, it's not your fault. Staying behind was my decision as much as it was yours." He patted the back of her hand. "Don't worry. We'll be leaving this ship very soon."

"How?"

Ye-yang opened his mouth to answer, but then his gaze drifted past her shoulder. Footsteps approached. Ying turned to find the fleet engineer striding across the deck toward them, a basket of steamed buns in her arms as always. She had not seen any sign of Wenjun the entire night, throughout the battle against the Eels. Perhaps the girl had been hiding on board the *Diamond*. Someone had to have brought the shields down.

Wenjun tossed a bun into Ying's hands. "Da-dangjia is looking for you. She's in her cabin," she said.

"She is? What for?"

Wenjun shrugged. "How would I know? I'm only the messenger. Hurry up. She doesn't like to be kept waiting," she said.

Ying exchanged a glance with Ye-yang, hesitant to go alone. This was the first time she would be speaking to the captain since the first day she had arrived on this ship, and after seeing what the woman was capable of, she wasn't sure if she dared face Li-na on her own. Ye-yang gave her a reassuring squeeze of her hand, mouthing the word "Go."

Everything will be all right, his eyes seemed to say, yet there was something else in there that she could not decipher. It was that haze that clouded his clear irises each time he had unspoken thoughts hidden in his mind. Thoughts that he intentionally kept from her, that left her unsettled.

Picking herself off the deck, Ying followed Wenjun toward the inner cabins. The captain's room was situated at the stern of the ship, and when the door swung open, Ying was greeted by glass windows stretching from floor to ceiling, providing an unblocked view of the sea. The cabin was sparsely furnished, with only a bed, a square wooden table with four stools, and a single watercolor painting of a young man hanging from the wall.

Wenjun announced her arrival, then promptly shoved her in and shut the door behind her.

Li-na was seated in front of the windows, staring thoughtfully into the distance. She did not turn when Ying entered, the fingers of her right hand drumming against the armrest of her wheelchair.

"Have a seat," the captain said, in her usual forbidding manner.

Ying slid herself silently onto a wooden stool. Her gaze lingered upon the painting in the room. The subject of it looked like he was in his early thirties, standing tall and proud with one hand resting on the wheel of a ship, his long hair blowing with the sea breeze. What struck her most about the man in the painting was the buoyancy and unbridled confidence that radiated from his dark, narrow eyes—as if this entire world was his to explore and conquer.

"That's my husband, Zhenlong," Li-na said. She turned her wheelchair and joined Ying at the table. "He died three years ago."

"I'm sorry to hear that."

"No need to be. I'd think he's probably happier now, to be free to travel with the wind like he's always wanted to, without having to bear the burden of worldly responsibilities." The captain picked up the clay teapot from its brazier and poured out two cups of tea. A heady fragrance wafted into the air—of fruit and spring blossoms—but it was one that Ying did not recognize. "Biluochun," Li-na said. "The best tea leaves come from Xishan, at the mountains at the western border of the Empire. This can hardly compare."

Ying hummed an acknowledgment, watching the emerald tea leaves unfurl in tiny, mesmerizing swirls within her cup. Then she looked up and found herself staring at the painting once again.

She had read a line about Li-na's deceased husband in the record books. Zhao Zhenlong had been a pirate as well, but his fleet had been destroyed in a skirmish with the Cobra's Order. He had died then. Not long after, Li-na had established her own pirate fleet—and here they were, one of the most feared contingents on the Dunzhu Straits.

Would things have been different if Zhao Zhenlong had not died?

"You must be wondering why I've summoned you." Li-na raised

her cup to her lips, taking a small sip. "I believe I owe you a debt, for what you did last night."

Ying blinked, taking a moment to register what the captain was referring to.

She frantically shook her head, bowing her head a notch lower so that she would not have to face the captain's incisive stare. "It was nothing, Da-dangjia," she mumbled.

"No. I don't like to leave debts unpaid. In exchange for what you've done for me, I'm going to grant you a favor. Anything that is within my means."

"Anything?"

Li-na nodded.

Ying could hardly believe the offer that was being placed on the table. Why would Li-na be so generous? Was there a catch? A trap waiting in the wings? Biting hard on her lower lip, she let the thoughts and suspicions steep in her mind for a little longer, before she said, "I would like to go home."

"Home? To Fei?"

"Yes, Da-dangjia. I've never been out at sea for such a long time before. I miss my family." That much was true. In her bouts of fitful sleep, she often dreamed of Nian, Wen, and their younger siblings. She would jolt awake with sweat lining her forehead and trepidation coursing through her blood, fearing for the safety of her siblings wherever they might be. She missed them, so much.

Li-na set her cup back down, interlocking her fingers in contemplation. Her straight brows dipped in a slight frown. After a short pause, one that felt excruciatingly long to Ying, she said, "Fine. As you wish."

"You're willing to let us go?"

A flash of irritation appeared in Li-na's eyes. Raising her teacup once again, she said, "We can drink to it, using tea in place of wine." With her other hand, she pushed Ying's cup toward her.

Doubts continued to circle inside Ying's mind as her fingers gripped tightly around the curved clay. She brought the rim up to her lips, tipping the warm liquid down her throat. The mellow, sweet aroma of the biluochun lingered in her mouth, together with a hint of astringency that stung her tongue.

When she lowered the cup back down, she realized that Li-na had taken out her bronze pocket watch and flipped it open, resting it on the palm of her hand. The soft ticking coming from the hands on the watch face was disconcerting, as if it were counting down to something—the same way it had counted down to Zhong Kui's demise.

"But," the captain started. There was a but. There had to be. "There is something I want you to do for me, before I let you go."

"What do you want, Da-dangjia?" she asked.

"No need to look so terrified. It's not as difficult as you might imagine. As you know, Wenjun has had some difficulty repairing the pumps on the *Diamond*, and we've already been anchored here for too long. I want you to help her fix it."

"I-i-is that all?"

Li-na nodded. "Only you, not any of those boys that you've got tagging along. I doubt they'll be very useful anyhow." She took a sip of her tea. "And if you do manage to repair the ship—I'll give you what you want. I'll let you go home. All of you."

Ying regarded the captain cautiously, trying to figure out what Li-na was playing at. Was she lying? Would she renege on her promise after the Blade was repaired?

"Aren't you afraid that I'll take the information about the *Diamond* back to the guild?"

"So that those guild masters of yours can finally figure out a way to destroy us?" A sardonic smile curved upon Li-na's face. "They can try, and I'll be waiting. Although I daresay they won't be able to get much out of what you bring back." She turned away, moving back toward the windows. "I'm not the most patient of people. I'll give you three days to repair the *Diamond*. After three days, the offer is off, understood?"

"Yes, Da-dangjia." Ying stood up hastily, the legs of her stool creaking against the floorboards. Li-na waved her hand, and she quickly hurried to the door, eager to leave this unsettling atmosphere behind.

CHAPTER 25

AFTER SPENDING THE AFTERNOON LISTENING TO WEN-
jun explain the nuts and bolts of how the Blade's air-pump mechanism functioned, Ying realized where Li-na's confidence came from.
The design of a Blade was far more complex than what she had
imagined. Despite all she had learned, she had barely scraped the tip
of the iceberg. Understanding the parts did not paint a clear picture
of the whole.

Like an airship, the *Diamond* ran on a kaen-gas engine, and the
engine powered a set of four massive propellers that extended near
the rear of the vessel, fanning out in a manner reminiscent of a
whale's dramatic tail. However, instead of generating lift via the in-
flation of the ballonet, the *Diamond*'s engine had a different secondary purpose—to power the ship's ventilation pumps and underwater
cannons. In order to do that, the engine, the air pumps, the weapons
mechanisms, all wove to form a delicate map, with components
housed across several different cabins. Most of these were out of
bounds, giving Ying a glimpse of only a tiny piece of the puzzle, useless on its own.

The blockage in one of the pipes channeling kaen gas had resulted in a buildup of pressure that caused the explosion. An entire
section of the pump mechanism had been blown apart and needed
replacing.

"Did you say that there were supposed to be two large pistons over here, connected to these pipes that lead to the kaen-gas storage tanks down below?" Ying asked, busy making annotations on the sketch that she had put together on a scrap of parchment.

"Yes." The engineer peered over Ying's shoulder, humming as she studied the drawing. "Not bad, you've got pretty much every detail down correctly." She stretched her arms out and yawned. "I think we should call it a day, though. I'm beat. Last night took far too much out of me."

"It's not even sundown!" Ying complained. "And you weren't even anywhere on board the ship while the fighting was going on." Wenjun had all the time in the world, but she didn't. Three days would go by in a flash.

"Everyone in the fleet has their own duties, and mine is to protect the *Diamond*. Seeing as we're standing here"—Wenjun gestured around the pump room—"it seems I've done spectacularly well. I think I've earned my sleep."

"So you were the one who brought down the shields."

Wenjun strolled across the room to the wooden board fixed upon the steel wall, filled with a haphazard array of bronze knobs and semicircular meters. A control panel that reminded Ying of the ones they had in the captain's cabin of the airships.

"Want to see how it's done?" Wenjun asked, giving Ying a mischievous wink. She twisted one of the knobs, and a loud screech suddenly pierced the air. "Sorry about that," she apologized, shouting over the din. "Haven't oiled the shields in a long while, so they scream when they slide over one another."

In the same amount of time that Wenjun took to explain the noise, the pump room was plunged into darkness. The glass windows were now entirely covered by the metal plates that had descended from the exterior. A gas lamp was switched on, and light flickered back into Ying's eyes once more.

"I hate bringing the shields down, to be honest," Wenjun said. "It's what I imagine being buried alive feels like."

Ying could understand the sentiment. With all the windows blocked, the space around them seemed to shrink dramatically, even though nothing about it had changed at all.

"What's it made of? And how does it work?" she asked, curiosity piqued.

There had been no shortage of cannonballs directed toward the *Diamond* last night, and yet they had left only minor dents and scratches on the vessel. She should have guessed that such a defensive mechanism existed, given how fragile the glass hull seemed to be.

A strange look appeared in Wenjun's eyes, one that Ying could not decipher. A glint of amusement? Glee? Almost like she had been waiting for this question to crop up.

"The shield is made from steel, exactly six hundred and eighty-eight plates of it. They're kept within some concealed brackets and can be extended or retracted by turning that knob I just used. Impenetrable to any standard-issue weapon—arrows, blades, cannonballs, catapult projectiles—you name it, we've got it covered. The *Diamond* is invincible." A pause. "Unless, of course, the damage is . . . self-inflicted."

Like a suit of brigandine armor, Ying thought. Simple yet incredibly effective.

Wenjun turned the knob counterclockwise, and the metal plates immediately began retracting back up. Sunlight flooded into the pump room once more.

"Don't tell anyone I told you all that, understood?" Wenjun quipped, although she didn't sound the least bit concerned about being found out. It was almost suspicious, the way the fleet engineer had revealed all that so casually. "It's so hard to find someone who appreciates all this, y'know? I'm the only one in the fleet who understands how all this magnificence works, what makes it tick! If only Master Cixin didn't insist on being so hard to find. I have some new questions that I want to consult her about . . ."

"Who is Master Cixin?"

"Only the best engineer across the land—or more accurately, across the sea. She's the one who built this beauty," Wenjun answered. There was a reverence that shone through in her eyes and tone that made Ying even more curious about this elusive master.

But if she's the one who built the Blades, then she must work for Monggu Yutai.

Still, she would like to meet this woman one day, to judge for herself what sort of a character Master Cixin actually was, and whether or not she could indeed compare to—or surpass—the skill of the guild masters. And of Ying's father.

∽

Three days was hardly any time, but thankfully for Ying, it was enough time. Everyone was gathered up on deck today, all eager to

witness whether or not the repairs on the *Diamond* proved successful. Staying locked in this position was not only dangerous for the
fleet, as the attack by the Eels had shown, it was also an unscratch-
able itch on the backs of its crew, all of whom carried a tiny explorer
within them who yearned to set sail in search of new adventures.

Still, the mastermind had not appeared. Neither had the new
Blade that the tournament promised.

"We're all counting on you, Ying," Chang-en said, clapping a
hand upon her shoulder. He was grinning, but with a slight tremble
to his lips, as if it took great effort to keep them up. "If this doesn't
work, then . . . it was nice knowing you. All of you."

Beside them, An-xi wrung his hands anxiously, too nervous to
speak.

"What if it doesn't work?" Ying murmured.

"Even if it doesn't work, we're still leaving," Ye-yang answered, a
quiet confidence in his hushed voice.

Ying turned toward him. "What's your plan?" She was certain
he had one, but he still hadn't told her what it was.

"Trust me," he replied. "I'll get us out of here."

If I trust you, will you trust me?

A little twinge of disappointment took root inside Ying's heart.
Perhaps she had been hoping for a different answer. She didn't want
him to ask her to trust him to help them escape if her attempt at repairing the *Diamond* failed—she wanted him to trust *her* to succeed
so that they could be allowed to leave after that.

"Da-dangjia," the crew greeted as Li-na emerged from her cabin.
She wheeled herself over to the starboard side, coming up alongside

Ying. Once again her pocket watch lay open in her palm, its silver hands sweeping across the circular face.

"Let's begin," she said.

Someone raised a yellow flag, and through the glass windows of the *Diamond*, Wenjun flashed a thumbs-up from within the vessel's engine room. There was a low rumble as the *Diamond*'s engines stirred to life.

The challenge with repairing the *Diamond*'s pump mechanism was finding the appropriate substitute parts, because they couldn't get the original parts reforged by a metalsmith while they were out at sea. In the end, Ying had rebuilt the section using a design modified off an airship's lift apparatus, which could be done using parts repurposed from a regular engine.

The entire gargantuan body of the *Diamond* sank into the murky waters of the deep, disappearing in a gurgling of sea-foam. Moments later, it resurfaced again with a dramatic splash. Wenjun opened a window hatch. "All good! Everything's working fine!" she shouted.

Cheers rang out across the flagship deck.

"It's working?" An-xi exclaimed.

"It's working!" Chang-en grabbed his friend by the waist and swung him up into the air, whooping loudly. "It's working! We're going home!"

"A-jie, you did it," Yunshang said, bouncing over to Ying's side and taking her by the hand.

Li-na turned to her, giving a slight nod by way of acknowledgment. "You have fulfilled your end of the bargain," she said. She signaled to Keyan, and the second-in-command proceeded to hand out ceramic bowls to everyone. A jar of rice wine was opened, its pungent aroma wafting into their nostrils as the clear liquid sloshed into each bowl.

"A parting toast," the captain said, "to unexpected acquaintances."

Ying and the others hesitated, exchanging wary glances with one another. Only when the other crew members had gulped down their wine did they dare follow suit. The atmosphere was effervescent, people laughing and joking as they passed out freshly steamed buns—no doubt a special request made by Wenjun to the kitchens.

Maybe I've been overthinking.

Maybe Li-na would keep her word after all and let them go.

The thought had only just precipitated in her mind when An-xi went down. He wobbled, striking the floorboards with a dull thud as he collapsed in front of a startled Yunshang.

Before Ying could react, her own knees buckled. Ye-yang caught her by the shoulders, but then he lurched forward and fell unconscious to the ground himself.

Pushing her palm against the ship's wall, Ying struggled to keep herself upright, the strength mysteriously draining from her legs. Her vision began to cloud over, dark specks floating across her field of view. She gasped as her airways narrowed.

Li-na was still watching her impassively, although Ying could have sworn that she caught a flicker of sympathy in the captain's eyes. Her gaze drifted toward the wine bowl that had fallen to the ground and splintered into a dozen pieces.

"What did you do?" Her voice emerged as a bare whisper.

Li-na turned, retreating back toward her cabin. "Don't worry. I always keep my word," she said.

In her dream, she was back in Fei, back in Qianlei Palace, running down the long corridors that snaked between the buildings in the deepest night. She couldn't see them, but she knew they were there. They were the shadows that lurked in the gloom, spectral forms that twisted and contorted into monstrous shapes. Their sharp, metallic teeth ground against one another, their foul breath grazing against her heels.

The chimeric hellhounds.

But why were they after her? What had she done wrong?

She emerged out in the open, greeted by a fountain with a towering stone dragon in the center, its serpentine body curving toward the obsidian sky.

Why am I back here?

Back at the courtyard in front of the Aogiya ancestral hall—a place that still sparked fear and apprehension in her heart. This was where she had first found out about the dragon's association with the High Command, where her reality began to unspool with the truth behind her beloved father's death. This place, that night, was the beginning of her losing everything.

Her family, the boy she loved, what she believed in.

A phantasmal figure hovered near the fountain, flitting in and out of existence.

"Feng-kai," she gasped, calling out after her lost friend.

He simply smiled, but did not reply.

Beside him, a few more ghosts appeared—ghosts that belonged to her past.

Her a-ma and e-niye. Aogiya Lianzhe, the former High Commander. Lady Odval, Ye-kan's mother. Zhong Kui.

Then they began to multiply. Faceless souls took shape, first a dozen, then a hundred, forming a legion of specters that curved around and surrounded her, trapping her within.

Were these all the spirits that had been condemned to an eternity upon the seas?

"What do you want?" she cried. "There's nothing I can do for you! Nothing!" She couldn't even protect herself, much less anyone else.

"Ying." It was her a-ma, his voice soft but urgent. "Remember who you are, my lamb. Remember that you are strong, and there is much you are capable of. A single ember can raze the entire plains."

Tears streamed down her face. She reached out for her parents, desperate for a sliver of warmth in this cold, icy dungeon, but her fingers slipped right through his outstretched hand. The ghosts slowly faded away, until there was nothing left but emptiness.

"Ying, wake up."

Something jabbed her in the ribs, forcing her to jolt out of the nightmare.

Her eyelids fluttered open, but a deep weariness continued to linger in her bones. She was seated on the floor, leaning against a stack of hemp sacks on the side. Her arms and legs had been bound with rope.

"Ying, are you all right? How are you feeling?"

It was Ye-yang, his back pressing against hers.

"What happened?" she mumbled, trying to piece together the jumbled fragments of her memory. They had been celebrating the successful repair of the *Diamond* with the rest of the crew. Li-na had offered them wine as a farewell toast, before they would finally be allowed to go home. "She drugged the wine." Or more precisely, the bowls.

She studied the dim surroundings. They were in one of the ship's many stores, cramped full of sacks and crates. A musty odor tickled her nose, the air still and stale. Light filtered in through a slim gap between the double doors.

Someone was sniffling. An-xi—who was seated across from her, similarly bound, trying to hide his face against some sacks so no one would see him crying.

"My head hurts," Chang-en groaned from somewhere else within the store.

"They were never going to let us go, were they?" An-xi murmured. "It was too good to be true."

The doors swung open, and in walked Wenjun. Ying's eyes lit up, a flicker of optimism sparking inside her. Then she noticed that there was something different about the girl. Gone was her typical lackadaisical, devil-may-care demeanor, replaced instead by a mask of careful guardedness. She flipped the latch, locking the doors behind her.

"The cobra never sleeps," Wenjun said in fluent Antaran.

"Until the dragon falls," Ye-yang replied. "It's been a long time, Black Lotus."

The engineer narrowed her eyes. "You were the one who sent me that message," she said, holding out a scrap of parchment. Whipping out a dagger from her waistband, she went straight for Ye-yang's throat. Ying gasped.

The tip of Wenjun's blade stopped right before it pierced through his skin. Precise. Purposeful. With the skill of a seasoned fighter. It was as if she had been possessed by a different person, one Ying did not recognize.

Realization washed upon her like a tidal wave.

Wenjun was the spy that the Order had sent to infiltrate the Blood Phoenix. The spy that they had believed to be dead.

Wenjun wasn't dead. She had defected to the other side.

"What do you want from me?"

"I want you to help us get back to Fei."

"Or I could slit your throat right here and now."

"I wouldn't have contacted you if I hadn't already taken the necessary precautions." Ye-yang let out a low whistle—two long, three short—that echoed across the storeroom.

There came a different whistle in reply, followed by the loud flapping of sturdy wings. A proud face appeared at the store's porthole, sharp beak tapping at the window's glass. The metallic sheen of the bird's wings gleamed under the moonlight, shaped from feathers of silver.

The condors.

"I've already sent word back to the High Command. If anything happens to us, and we fail to make it back to Fei, then your entire clan will pay the price for your crime of colluding with the enemy."

Wenjun scoffed. "What makes you think I care about them? I was never planning on returning to Fei. Ever."

"If you truly don't care, then why did you bother going through the trouble of convincing us that you were dead? Are you willing to let a hundred people die in exchange for your freedom?"

Wenjun glared at Ye-yang, her dark eyes blazing like hot coals. "I don't believe you. What's stopping you from killing them anyway, even if I do exactly as you say? Since when has the Order cared about our lives?"

"You don't have to believe me." Ye-yang arched his neck forward, letting the blade prick the surface of his skin. A drop of blood oozed out. "It's your choice."

Wenjun's stare remained fixed upon Ye-yang, as if trying to peel him apart layer by layer to figure out whether or not he was speaking the truth.

"Does Li-na know that you belonged to the Order?" Ye-yang suddenly asked.

The fleet engineer swallowed hard, immediately averting her gaze.

"I thought so. I can tell that you value this new life that you've built, that you care for this crew as if they were your real family, maybe even more so than those so-called blood relations that you have back in Fei. You can keep all that. Li-na never needs to find out. All you have to do is help us leave this ship, and I'll take it that we never met. Your name will be formally removed from the Order's register for good."

Wenjun remained silent for a long while, but Ying could tell that Ye-yang had succeeded in rattling the girl and breaking through her defenses. He had picked out what she cared about most—and then used it as leverage against her.

"I'll do what I can," Wenjun finally said, her dagger falling to her side. "But if they move you off the ship before I can put things in place, then it's out of my hands." Slipping her dagger back into its scabbard, she swiftly left the storeroom.

Move us off the ship? What does that mean?

"So," Chang-en started, "Wenjun is a spy? Who would have thought that? The Order truly has its claws everywhere."

"Can't you keep your mouth shut?" An-xi scolded, watching carefully for Ye-yang's reaction. Even though these were extraordinary circumstances, it was still inappropriate for Chang-en to be shooting his mouth off in front of the High Commander, commenting on the Order's business so casually.

Ye-yang paid no heed to either of them, focusing his attention on Ying instead. He said nothing, waiting patiently for her to speak first.

"I thought you said you didn't know who the spy was," Ying said.

"I didn't. If not for the tattoo of the black lotus that's still on her arm, I would never have found out."

The tattoo . . . She remembered seeing the tattoo, back when they had been working on *Xiangliu* and its nine-headed engines. Compared to the flamboyant phoenix that covered the girl's upper arm, the black lotus had been almost unnoticeable.

"Yet you said nothing." A familiar bitterness welled up inside her. "And what about those condors? You've been sending messages back to the High Command all this while?"

The condors belonged to Ye-yang. That's why she kept seeing them loitering in the vicinity, circling high above the skies. They were waiting for instructions. Waiting for the messages that Ye-yang needed them to carry.

He had never once lost contact with the High Command, contrary to what he had allowed them to believe.

Her fingers clenched tightly by her sides, knuckles straining against her skin. "They could have come for us. We could have gone home."

"Ying, our situation was—and *still is*—too precarious. Even if I could send word back to Fei, I had no means of relaying our location to them. If I had told you about this earlier, it would only have placed you at greater risk."

"More risk than participating in the Tournament of the Seas? Or facing Zhong Kui and his Eels?"

As usual, Ye-yang had been moving according to his own plans. To him, these were all "calculated risks." Remaining with the Blood Phoenix. Taking part in the tournament. Waiting for the mastermind. He was playing his own game of weiqi, and she was but one seed on the board. An important seed, a precious seed, but a mere seed nonetheless.

It was her fault for believing she might be more.

"I . . ." His voice trailed off, gaze shifting toward the doors.

Voices were approaching.

CHAPTER 26

THE DOORS OF THE SHIP'S STORE CREAKED open, and two silhouettes appeared at the doorway. Li-na, and a man Ying did not recognize. He was of a stocky build, with sloping shoulders upon which a cloak lined with rust-brown fox fur was draped. His angular jaw was covered with rough stubble, and his graying hair pulled back into two sets of looping braids, parted at the middle. Stepping in, the man took one glance at her, then at Ye-yang. His thin lips curled in a mocking smile.

"It's been a long time, Yang-er," he said, his voice deep and resonant, but with a gravelly quality that added a menacing touch.

"E-qike."

Uncle.

This was Monggu Yutai, chieftain of the exiled Monggu clan. He was the answer they were looking for, the one pulling the strings behind the pirates, using them as decoys to tear the Order asunder. Ye-yang had been right.

Monggu Yutai threw his head back and chortled, seeming pleased with his nephew's greeting. "I would have preferred for us to be meeting in more pleasant circumstances, but unfortunately I couldn't take any chances." He turned to Li-na. "Captain, you've done well. Your loyalty shall be duly rewarded." His tone was supercilious and patronizing, as if he were speaking to an inferior.

Li-na bowed her head in deference, saying nothing.

Whatever little sympathy and respect Ying had garnered for the pirate captain quickly evaporated. Anger churned inside her, twisting up in furious knots. She regretted giving Li-na the benefit of the doubt, wanting to let go of the debt of blood that the Blood Phoenix owed to Feng-kai and Larut.

Li-na had sold them out.

"Since when have you known?" Ying asked, glaring at the captain with cold fury.

Li-na shifted her gaze toward Ying, a tinge of pity filtering through. "Since the day we rescued you from that storm. I've crossed paths with the former High Commander before, so it wasn't too difficult to recognize his son, not when the apple has fallen so near the tree."

So they had been the gullible ones after all, believing that they had successfully hoodwinked the notorious pirate captain. It had been an act all along. Letting them participate in the tournament, giving her the chance to repair the *Diamond* in exchange for their freedom. It was only a trap to buy time until the Monggu chieftain could arrive to claim his bounty.

"I'm not going to hurt you, Ye-yang. After all, Monggu blood runs in your veins, even if it's been tainted by your despicable father," the Monggu chieftain said, squatting down in front of them. "That is, however, assuming that you cooperate. If not, then don't blame me for what I might do."

"If you want me to commit treason against our people the same way you have, then the answer is no," Ye-yang replied.

Monggu Yutai scoffed. "It is not treason to be unwilling to sub-mit to Aogiya rule."

"But it is to be colluding with the Qirins and the pirates to slaughter your own people. I was hoping to be wrong, for my e-niye's sake, but sadly you've proven to be as selfish and reprehensible as you always were."

"Aogiya Ye-yang! How dare you speak to me like that?" the Monggu chieftain hollered, rage palpable in every word he spat. He grabbed Ye-yang by the neck.

"I will speak to a criminal however I like." Ye-yang's voice strained under the pressure from Monggu Yutai's viselike grip, gaze sharp as a whetted knife.

"Stop! Let him go!" Ying shouted. She tried to turn her head toward them, but with her limbs bound, all she could manage was a sideways glance. Ye-yang's face was slowly turning a frightening shade of purplish-red from the strangulation, Monggu Yutai's long nails digging into his flesh. "Li-na, you promised! You said you would keep your word!"

The pirate captain did not respond, her expression inscrutable. Instead, she turned her wheelchair around and headed out of the storeroom. Her voice drifted back. "Monggu Yutai, we still have loose ends to tie up. If you want to kill the boy, then that's your pre-rogative, but don't do it on my ship. I'd hate to dirty my floorboards."

A pause, then Ye-yang gasped for air as he was finally released.

Monggu Yutai straightened himself back up, saying, "Take some time to think through your position carefully and correct that arro-gant attitude of yours. You are your father's son through and through, and that disgusts me. It's a good thing your e-niye left us early, so she doesn't have to witness what a disappointment you've become. We'll continue this later." He swiveled on his heel and stormed out of the room, slamming the doors behind him.

Silence steeped in every crevice as the captives processed what had taken place. Ying leaned back, allowing the warmth from her shoulder to press against Ye-yang, to let him know that she was still here.

Monggu Yutai's parting words had been cutting and cruel.

The tragic loss of his mother was the singular turning point in Ye-yang's life that had led him to where he was today. Years of careful plotting, of never stepping a foot wrong—all to avenge his mother's death, to do her proud. For his uncle to suggest that he was nothing more than a shameful shadow of his father, the man who he blamed for his mother's demise, was the worst insult that he could suffer.

"You're not like him," she said.

"There are many who would disagree, perhaps myself included," he replied softly. "But thank you. It means a lot to me."

The former High Commander's voice echoed from the depths of Ying's memories, the last thing she ever heard him say. *"Out of all my sons, you are most like me, Ye-yang."*

She had been unsure before, but she knew now that he wasn't. Yes, he still kept his secrets and lies, still insisted on doing things that he unilaterally believed to be correct, but he was in no way like his father, Aogiya Lianzhe.

Despite his somewhat heavy-handed methods, she had seen

what he had done for the Antaran people, for the Qirin refugees—and for her. As ruthless and calculating as he could be, he was not heartless. Even as she disagreed with his choices, she could understand why he had charted this course for the nine isles.

"Seems the Monggu clan is behind all this," Chang-en piped up. "Was anyone planning to tell us? Or were we meant to go to the grave none the wiser?"

An-xi stretched out a leg and kicked him in the shin. "Stop it," he hissed. "You're not helping."

"*I'm* not helping? If I recall, I was the only one who wanted to leave this gods-damned ship while we could!" Chang-en snapped, his neck flushing red. "If we had escaped that night, then none of this would be happening. But no, the bunch of you had to run off to play hero, and for what? To rescue a bunch of pirates who just sold us out!" His voice crescendoed until he was practically shouting, the veins at his temples throbbing violently.

Ying had never seen Chang-en so furious before. He was always the merry, happy-go-lucky one among them, the one who dished out the candied fruits when she was down or when An-xi was about to have an aneurysm. Guilt clawed inside her as she stared into her friend's bloodshot eyes. Who could blame him? Chang-en was not wrong.

She was the one who had made the choice to stay, giving up the best chance they had to leave—now they were all suffering those consequences.

"Maybe things won't be that bad. Didn't Wenjun say that she would try to get us out of here?" An-xi offered hesitantly.

Right on cue, a concealed trapdoor popped open, and a head full of frizzy hair appeared from beneath the floorboards. Then another appeared.

"Wenjun? Yunshang?"

Ying had not expected her to return so soon, and for Yunshang to have tagged along.

"Wenjun a-jie is terrible at sneaking around," Yunshang said with a cheeky grin. "This entire escape plan is *my* idea."

The girls climbed out and rushed over, fingers moving deftly to undo the knots that bound all their hands and feet. Ying rotated her sore wrists, looking down at the red chafe marks that marred her skin.

"Aren't you afraid you'll get into trouble for letting us go?" Ying asked, directing her question at Yunshang. Wenjun had no choice, because Ye-yang had practically put a knife to her and forced her to comply, but Yunshang had no need to get involved.

The girl shrugged. "I owe you, don't I?" she quipped. "Don't worry, Da-dangjia won't do anything to me even if she finds out. Maybe I'll get a few strokes of the cane, but it's nothing I haven't dealt with before." She stole a glance in Ye-yang's direction. "Are you really the High Commander of the nine isles?"

Everyone stared, astonished by the sudden question.

"What? I happened to overhear Da-dangjia talking to the Monggu chieftain about it while we were crawling here, that's all. So is it true or not?"

"That's enough. There's no time," Wenjun said, cutting off the chatter. A slight crease marred the space between her brows. "Follow me."

"Are you sure this is going to work?" Chang-en asked, sounding skeptical. "Or are you just marching us into another trap?"

Wenjun turned and flashed the boy a look of disdain, bringing back a semblance of her usual attitude. "If you ask any more questions, then no one is escaping, got it?" Beckoning to them, she hopped back down through the hole in the floor.

The rest of them quickly followed along. The trapdoor led to a narrow passageway that was only large enough for them to crawl through in a single line. Ying's heart almost stopped when she suddenly heard Monggu Yutai's and Li-na's voices floating overhead, accompanied by the shadows cast by footsteps upon the floorboards above.

She bit her lower lip and scrambled on, fearful that even a single breath would give them away. Thankfully, they emerged at the end of the passage with no mishaps, but instead of the main deck, they found themselves peering out from the hull on the ship's starboard side.

A familiar vessel was waiting for them several feet down, its nine heads bobbing on the water's surface. *Xiangliu*. It was almost dawn, and a splinter of light had cracked upon the horizon, splitting the sea and the sky.

"Quick," Wenjun said, tossing out a rope. The girls plastered themselves against the side of the tiny passage so that Ying and the others could squeeze through, watching as they climbed down the rope and onto the little boat. Pointing in the opposite direction of the rising sun, the engineer said, "Go that way, and you'll eventually reach Muci. It's not the nearest isle, but that strip of sea is most frequently patrolled by the Order"—she wrinkled up her nose in contempt—"and if you take the obvious path, then Monggu Yutai will catch you in no time."

"There's some dry rations on board that I've packed," Yunshang added. "Should be enough to last you at least three days, by which time if you haven't reached land, then you probably never will."

"Thank you," Ye-yang replied. "I'll keep my word."

Ying caught a flash of relief dart across the engineer's eyes. The girl pursed her lips together briefly, then she said, in the most deferent tone that Ying had ever heard emerge from that mouth, "Your Excellency, may I ask for another favor?"

Ye-yang arched a brow. "What is it?"

"If we ever meet in battle, could you . . . could you let the Blood Phoenix go?"

Chang-en was the one who replied first, with an imperious snort. "After you practically kidnapped us, made us take part in some race to the death, and then tried to sell us to traitors? Oh, and that's not forgetting how you murdered all those innocent Larut seamen—including Ying's almost-husband."

Ying choked, and An-xi stabbed Chang-en in the foot with his heel. Chang-en howled in pain.

"We were the ones who fished you out from the sea," Yunshang retorted. "If it weren't for us, you'd already be dead, so you owe your lives to us anyway. Also, we weren't the ones behind the attack off Larut, so stop accusing us of something we didn't do!"

"What?" The message came like a bolt from the blue. Ying's heart was suspended in her throat, disbelief flooding through her veins. "But that's not possible. We saw the phoenix flare," she said, her voice dropping to a whisper.

She had seen it with her own eyes, the phoenix that had burst across the night sky, spreading its fiery wings in its grim glory. The exact same phoenix that blazed upon every flag on board this ship. Everyone said it was the Blood Phoenix. Wei Ru-er. Shi-ye. The survivors of the Larut attack. The guild. The Order. How could they all have been wrong?

Yunshang clucked her tongue in condescension. "Anyone can fire a flare. I thought your brains were sharper than that. Zhong Kui and his goons have been using those flares to mislead the patrol guards and throw them off their scent for the longest time. Assholes finally got their comeuppance."

Zhong Kui? The Eels . . .

She had been too careless. Too presumptuous. Looking back, the signs had been there all along, if only she cared to take notice. The Blood Phoenix was a fleet of women. That alone should have been enough to make people sit up and pay attention, yet no one had ever reported this in their encounters with the fleet. The accounts of the Blood Phoenix and its captain were always vague and entirely wrong. And the wounds suffered by those who survived the Larut attack—those were wounds caused by blades, moon blades, to be precise. The same weapon carried by every member of Zhong Kui's crew.

Ying shut her eyes, exhaling slowly.

All this while, she had been chasing after the wrong culprit, channeling her anger to the wrong hands. A part of her was relieved, because this meant that Feng-kai's death had been avenged, that she could finally put his soul to rest; the other part of her was filled with self-doubt, at what more she could have gotten wrong.

Ye-yang only took a moment to mull things over, then he said, "I'm afraid all I can promise you is to write off the wrongdoings that the Blood Phoenix may have committed in the past. If Li-na chooses to continue supporting the Monggu clan, then there is little I can do. The nine isles must defend themselves."

Wenjun nodded solemnly. "C'mon, Yunshang, let's go. We're done here." Turning around, the fleet engineer retreated back into the passage.

Yunshang, on the other hand, took her time to pull the rope back up. "All right, off you go. I hate to say this, but I'm going to miss you." Turning to An-xi, she added, "We never got to finish our game of four-colored cards. Maybe some other time?"

An-xi gulped, a faint strip of pink appearing across his pale cheeks. "Maybe," he mumbled. He sat himself down in the boat and hugged his knees to his chest awkwardly.

"May Niangniang protect you." Yunshang gave them a cheeky wink, then she slammed the hatch shut, disappearing into the ship.

As *Xiangliu* sailed away from the flagship under the cover of the receding shadow of night, Ying turned and took a final look at the Blood Phoenix, its numerous ships sitting stoically upon the waves. Then there was the *Diamond*, resembling its namesake as its gleaming surface sparkled under the early rays of the sun.

Who knew if she would ever see them again?

CHAPTER 27

"WHAT IS THE MEANING OF THIS, Number Fourteen?" the second beile demanded, gesturing at the rather dramatic scene that was on display in Qinzheng Hall. Erden was evidently in a foul mood, but he was not the only one.

Ye-kan had summoned all the clan chiefs, commanders, and officials of the High Command to the palace before the first crack of dawn that morning. When they rushed in, still bleary-eyed and with robes hastily thrown on, the first thing that greeted them was the sight of several familiar faces kneeling in front of the High Commander's dais, and dozens of foul-smelling hemp sacks piled high.

Nian sat within a hidden chamber behind the High Commander's throne, concealed from view by a carefully positioned ivory silk screen bearing an elaborately embroidered map of the nine isles. According to Qorchi, this room had been built by the previous High Commander specifically so that he could spy on conversations between his subordinates while they were waiting for court to begin.

Through a tiny peephole that the chief steward had pointed out to her when they first entered, she had a clear view of everyone in the hall and could listen in on all the proceedings taking place.

"Why don't you ask them?" Ye-kan replied, pointing at the cowering figures before him. In consideration of what happened at the solstice hunt and the consequent curtailment of his right to preside over the High Command, the fourteenth beile merely stood on the dais beside the High Commander's seat instead of occupying that position. No reason to give the other beiles an excuse to find fault with him on such an auspicious day.

He gestured to Nergui, who promptly went up to the sacks and opened the top one, spilling its contents all over the hardwood floor. The sour odor intensified, forcing several officials to back away in horror.

"Is that . . . rice?" Ula Temuu asked. The old chieftain stepped forward, the creases upon his forehead deepening as he studied the mess on the floor. "All of it has gone bad."

"Indeed, and do you know where all these sacks of rice came from?" Ye-kan asked, his steely gaze surveying the nervous crowd. "Nergui, read it to them."

Clearing his throat, the chief steward unfurled a sheet of parchment and read, "The Shan-yi Halls at the western quarter, southern quarter, and central quarter, the military warehouses belonging to the Plain Blue Banner, the Plain White Banner, and the Plain Red Banner."

Their investigation into the smuggling had unearthed a can of worms.

Based on Arban's testimony, they had initially thought that only the supplies from the Shan-yi Halls had been targeted, but an unexpected report of food poisoning coming from Ye-kan's own military camp had led them to realize that what they'd discovered was merely the tip of the iceberg.

Whoever was behind all this had cast a net far wider than they could have imagined.

A commotion immediately went up around the hall. The Shan-yi Halls were not of any concern, because no one here truly cared about the welfare of Qirin refugees, but the military warehouses were a different matter altogether. The three banners in question were commanded by the third beile, the fourteenth beile, and the deceased first beile respectively, which made the situation all the more prickly.

Nian carefully observed the reactions of everyone present. There were plenty of outraged faces and no shortage of confusion, but upon mention of the three banners, most of the attention in the hall immediately swiveled toward the second beile, Erden. Erden's own banner—the Bordered White Banner—had not been mentioned, which seemed far too convenient.

After giving them a brief moment to digest the news, Ye-kan said, "All these sacks had moldy rice mixed in, and this rice was meant to feed not only the refugees, but also our own soldiers. Stealing and smuggling supplies from the Order—do we all understand the extent of what we are dealing with?" He held up a stack of folded parchments. "These are the written confessions of all these men here. Fucha Arban, Niohuru Hongyan, Niohuru Songben, Bira Murhaci, Keyere Lirong—all admitting to being involved in this disgusting crime."

"Erden! Is this your doing?" Ye-han demanded, wagging a fleshy finger at his cousin. "Did you think that just because I don't handle military matters directly that you can stretch your grimy hands into my camps!"

"I don't know what you're talking about!"

"Everyone knows that the Fucha clan works for you, and Fucha Arban has been desperate to win your favor, hasn't he?"

"If we're going to argue on that count, then isn't the Niohuru clan *your* e-niye's clan, Ye-han? And there are *two* of them caught up in this!" the second beile retorted. "Surely that makes you even more suspect!"

Minister Niohuru fell to his knees, pressing his forehead to the ground in a kowtow. "Beile-ye, I have no idea how any of this happened. I swear I was entirely unaware!" he cried.

The Shan-yi Halls had been placed under administration of the Niohuru clan, led by Minister Niohuru—the father of Ying's close friend Niohuru An-xi. The man had then happily installed plenty of his own clan members in key positions governing different aspects of the Shan-yi Halls' operations. Now that two of them were implicated in this case, it would be difficult for him to extricate himself cleanly from this.

"Even if you were unaware, it is still your negligence and inappropriate delegation of duties that resulted in this," Ye-kan said sharply.

"Number Fourteen is right," the third beile said quickly. "To think the High Commander trusted you with such an important job, and this is what it has amounted to!"

Nian's lips curled in a mirthless smile. Trust the third beile to think so quickly on his feet, pushing out one of his own so easily as a scapegoat.

"I'm not done," Ye-kan announced. His expression darkened.

"Other than stealing rice from the Order and replacing it with inferior stock, someone has also been stealing *weapons* from our military stores."

The entire hall sank into a stunned silence. Even Erden and Yehan both shut their mouths in unison.

Their reactions seem genuine, Nian thought. *Could it be that neither of them were behind this?*

But if not them—then who?

"This is an extremely serious allegation, Beile-ye," the Ula chieftain said slowly, verbalizing the thought that was going through everyone's mind. "May I ask what evidence you have of this?"

Stealing rice and replacing it with moldy grain was no trivial matter, but if they were to continue debating about it, it could eventually still be watered down to a case of mere greed. A group of lowly officials wanting to strike it rich by taking advantage of the high rice prices caused by the trade blockage. Those involved would get several strokes of the paddle and a few years' imprisonment, but that would be it.

Stealing *weapons*, on the other hand, was a wholly different matter.

This—would be treason. And treason was punishable by death, not just to those implicated, but possibly their entire clan.

"During the solstice hunt, while running from those assassins, Lady Nian and I discovered a group of men shifting weapons crates into one of the Engineers Guild's abandoned underground warehouses. The weapons all carried the mark of the Order. I've since asked my men to investigate the various weapons storehouses across the city, and they've identified several locations where weaponry has gone missing. Missing—yet unreported." Ye-kan's steely gaze swept the hall. "I have sent some men to retrieve the weapons crates from Wu Lin. When they arrive, you may inspect them for yourselves," he added.

While they waited, no one dared to move. Silence hung heavily within the air, everyone fearing that a single wrong word could result in suspicion falling upon their backs. Anxious glances were tossed back and forth. Tension within the grand hall reached a peak.

In the hidden parlor, Nian continued to watch.

Surprisingly, the revelation about the weapons smuggling had not stirred up any further consternation from the second and third beiles. On the contrary, that piece of news seemed to have calmed them down and given them a dose of confidence. While they still wore surly expressions on their faces, their overall posture had relaxed somewhat.

Perhaps they believe that a crime far more serious will take some of the pressure off the rice theft.

But that would also suggest that they had nothing to do with the weapons smuggling, or at least they were confident of leaving no traces of their involvement.

Nergui came rushing into the parlor, a small sheet of folded parchment clenched in his right hand. He bowed hastily to Nian.

"Lady Nian, the men we sent to retrieve the crates from Wu Lin just sent word back." The chief steward's narrow mien clenched with distress. "They're all gone."

"What?" Nian frowned.

They had not removed the crates earlier because they hadn't wanted to alert the mastermind unnecessarily, but arrangements had been made for the High Commander's personal guard to keep watch over the cavern to prevent the culprit from having a chance to remove the stolen goods. Still, they had failed. Everything had somehow vanished, right under their noses.

She quickly skimmed the message that they'd received.

According to the report, the guards who were on duty claimed that several of the Order's soldiers had removed the crates late last night, and that they were holding Ye-kan's pendant as proof that they were under his orders.

Someone stole Ye-kan's pendant.

"What's taking so long, Number Fourteen?" Erden bellowed. "Is this some kind of joke? You can't just fling accusations of treason about when you have nothing to show for it!"

A murmur of agreement went around the hall, with several members of the court—mainly those belonging to Erden and Ye-han's factions—shooting hostile glances toward Ye-kan. Even Ula Temuu, his uncle, seemed mildly displeased by the delay.

The third beile let out a contemptuous chuckle. "Were those crates even there in the first place? Or are they an excuse to help cover up for what you truly did at Wu Lin that day, hmm?" he said. "Let's not forget that Ye-lu's death is still unresolved."

There had been no new discoveries with regard to the assassination of the first beile. Somehow, those assassins had vanished off the face of the earth, leaving not a single whiff of a clue to be traced.

Much like the crates of weapons.

If the older beiles had been hoping to prod Ye-kan into a tantrum with their taunts, they would be sorely disappointed. Instead of responding with anger, Ye-kan faced them with composure, giving them an incisive glare that reminded Nian of Ye-yang, or even the former High Commander, Aogiya Lianzhe.

"Even if there's been a delay in bringing the weapons back, these records of our warehouse inventories already prove that I'm telling the truth," Ye-kan said, pointing at the stack of record books sitting by the side. "I have abided by our agreement to relinquish command and not use the imperial seal in any way while investigations into Ye-lu's death are taking place, but I will not stand idly by while someone tries to bleed us dry from within. That is my duty as a beile of the High Command, and a son of the nine isles," Ye-kan said, his voice ringing confidently across the hall.

Nian's heart swelled with pride as she listened to his speech. Ye-kan had his heart in the right place, and given time, those strengths that went unnoticed would begin to show.

"If there is a traitor among us, then the High Command and the nine isles are in grave danger. I hereby seek the agreement of the clan chiefs and the commanders of the Order to place Fei under lockdown, where no one is to enter or leave the capital until the one responsible for all these crimes has been brought to justice."

The clan chieftains gathered around Ula Temuu, heads bowed in discussion. Likewise, the various commanders of the Cobra's Order debated their decision in hushed voices.

After some time, the Ula chieftain came forward, saying

solemnly, "On behalf of the clans of the nine isles, I accept the four-teenth beile's proposal to lock the isle of Fei until further notice."

"Are you certain about that, Ula Temuu?" Erden questioned. "That would mean that none of you will be allowed to return to your home isles as well. Are you not afraid that this is some plot to hold you hostage?"

Erden's words were not without effect. Some of the clan chiefs seemed to hesitate, swallowing anxiously.

"I thank you for your concern, Beile-ye, but there are more im-portant things at stake here than our lives. The nine isles are bound by oath and by blood. If we allow the High Command to fall, then we are all better off dead," Ula Temuu replied, holding his ground. He glanced sideways at the men who were still kneeling on the ground, their shoulders trembling with fear. "What we have now was not built by the Aogiya clan alone, but from the collective effort of all our clans across the years. We have the right to demand ac-countability from those whom we have pledged our allegiance to. We will stay, and we shall see to it that justice is served."

Before anyone could respond, a soldier decked in the Order's standard black brigandine came rushing in, sweat dripping off his brows. "Beile-ye," he said, kneeling in front of Ye-kan, "fighting has broken out within some of our military camps. Some strange rumors started circulating this morning, and now many soldiers are demanding to leave the camps to return home."

"What rumors?" Ye-kan demanded.

"A-a-about the High Commander being dead. Also, there are

claims that the Order's stores are almost empty, that's why we've been feeding moldy rice to the recruits."

Whoever was pulling the strings from behind the scenes had begun to make their moves. Fei was descending into chaos, and if they did not manage to nip this problem in the bud very soon, then they might not be able to salvage the situation before it was too late.

Nian got up from her seat and headed for the parlor doors.

"Lady Nian, where are you going?" Qorchi asked, perplexed by her sudden movement.

"Gather some of the High Commander's guards. I'm going to retrieve the missing supplies and weapons."

CHAPTER 28

THE ONLY SECTION OF FEI THAT STOOD outside the city walls was its main trading port, located at the mouth of the city's largest central canal, where two colossal obsidian stone serpents towered from either side to welcome guests—and deter troublemakers. Dozens of gigantic storehouses were cramped onto both banks, filled with all manner of produce and wares that were shipped in and out of the capital. With the dwindling of trade between the nine isles and the Empire, the typically bustling port had quieted significantly, with only a handful of trading warehouses still in operation.

Nian and the small crew of the High Commander's personal guards that she had brought with her stopped in front of one of these nondescript warehouses, its only identifying feature being the number "52" inscribed on a small wooden signboard that hung beside the double doors.

This was the address that Arban had given them during his interrogation. The meeting place where he would hand over the rice shipments to the triad's handlers. It was a travesty, for this to have happened right under the noses of the port's Order patrols, but as the saying went: the most dangerous place was often the safest.

"Break the locks and search the place," Nian ordered. She did not expect any of those shipments to still be here, but there might be clues left behind that would point them in the correct direction.

The thick iron padlock was promptly hacked in two by a sharpened blade and the doors kicked open. Nian followed the guards into the storehouse, taking a moment to let her vision acclimatize to the darkness while the men fumbled for the lamps. Hemp sacks were piled in mountains one above the other, and wooden shelves were stacked with countless crates. A musty odor wafted into her nostrils, bringing on a sneeze.

Nian raised her free hand defensively in front of her, in case of any unexpected ambush. The silver bracelet that Ye-kan had gifted her remained firmly clasped around her wrist, protecting her in his absence.

He would not have agreed to her coming here, although there really was no better person to follow up on this. She was the only other person with full knowledge of the situation with the Qilin triad. Besides, with the latest disturbances to the Order's camps, Ye-kan would have plenty of more pressing matters to attend to.

Nian had to find those shipments before they left Fei's shores and restore them to the Order's camps before the situation deteriorated any further.

Nian sucked in a breath, then released it slowly. *I cannot fail. If I fail, we lose.*

While the guards proceeded with their search of the warehouse, Nian also began sniffing around for the faintest signs of anything suspicious.

She walked toward the back of the building, where there was a small larder used to keep dry rations intended for the meals of wharf workers, with a single-burner stove that had a bronze kettle sitting on it. Smoked meats and circular grain cakes were arranged in straw baskets on a wooden shelf nailed into the wall. Nian waved the palm of her hand above the kettle's spout. A sensation of warmth rippled against her skin.

Her brows dipped.

Someone was here.

"Lady Nian, there's been some movement of goods out of here not long ago," one of the guards reported from the second floor. "The metal tracks are still warm." Those tracks had been installed all across the warehouse, coupled to flat wooden trolleys that could be easily wheeled around to facilitate the transport of wares.

"Search the place for ledgers or record books," she replied.

They had to move quickly. If they managed to figure out the destination that the supplies were heading to, then there was a good chance they could intercept the shipment before it was sent away. There had to be a secret docking location that the triad was using to conduct their illegal trades.

Nian turned to rejoin the others out front, but then she paused as a glimmer of green caught her eye. Lying on the floor beside the stove was a single peacock feather, the pearlescent sheen of its indigo eye making it seem like it was winking back at her. She instinctively bent over to pick it up.

The tip of the feather was stained black, as if someone had been dipping it into an ink pot.

She immediately began searching around the larder, moving aside pots of cutlery and stacks of clay crockery and tapping on every stone brick in the walls. Finally, she struck gold. One particular bowl sitting on the shelf could not be removed. She carefully rotated it clockwise. A soft whirring sound could be heard as gears shifted within the walls, followed by a single brick popping out from the wall near her right foot. Nian squatted down and removed the loose brick, pulling out two rolled-up books from the hidden compartment.

This is it, she realized as she flipped through the pages.

The accounts of all the illegal trades that the Qilin triad had conducted, complete with quantities, prices, and locations of where shipments were coming from and where they were headed. As expected, it was not only rice supplies from the Shan-yi Halls and the Order's camps, but goods that were of an even more alarming nature—like armor and weapons that came from workshops all across the nine isles.

Looking at all these items listed at a glance, Nian suddenly reached an epiphany.

These were records of everything that was needed to grow an army.

Her heart sank right down to the pit of her stomach as the full extent of what had transpired was slowly pieced together.

Her gaze shifted toward a set of coordinates that appeared repeatedly across the different records. In her mind's eye, she quickly mapped the coordinates to a rough location on the isle.

"I've got it!" she shouted.

Nian galloped down the city streets on the back of her white mare, ignoring the biting winds that lashed against her cheeks. She sped across half of Fei, riding out through the northern gates with her guards following close behind.

She guided her horse past the Order's expansive airship yard, its occupants sitting silently upon the sand like giant black sentries watching over the city, and then through a small patch of forest leading to the northernmost tip of the diamond-shaped isle. Hardly any boats sailed near this end of Fei because the sea north of here was filled with treacherous rock formations concealed beneath the choppy waves. Seafarers typically took the longer route around the southern coast, where the waters were calmer and more welcoming.

But today was an exception.

The moment Nian emerged out of the forest's shadows and onto the gravel beach, her horse reared up on its hind legs, whinnying in fear. She gripped tightly on to the reins, narrowly avoiding being flung off the saddle. Behind her, her companions' steeds also came to abrupt stops.

Two small sampans were moored by the beach, in the process of being loaded with numerous sacks of goods, with a larger ship anchored farther offshore. That was not what had spooked the horses.

Standing guard in front of the boats were three wolflike creatures, their bright yellow eyes gleaming as they reflected the waning daylight. Yet these were no wolves—they were *qilin*, the mythical beast that supposedly descended from the heavens at the beginning of time to protect the emperor of the Great Jade Empire. The people of the Empire had adopted the name Qirin as a mark of respect toward these noble creatures.

Qilins were beasts of legend. They did not actually exist—*unless someone created them.* Silver antlers fanned out from the tops of their heads like vicious blades, and their bodies were covered with bronze scales that formed an impenetrable suit of armor. Saliva dripped from their open maws as they bared their sharpened teeth at the newcomers, warning them to stay back.

These were wolves—modified to become monsters.

After the initial shock at encountering the chimeras had worn away, Nian took a quick moment to survey their surroundings. There were seven or eight men—laborers, judging from their worn cotton robes—who were still busy shifting goods onto the sampans, and five others armed with swords.

The one in charge was someone Nian recognized—the Qilin member who had been speaking with Arban at the gambling den that night. Yet again, a strange sense of suspicion crept up her spine. A triad member with robes spun from fine silk and embroidery that matched the quality of the capital's finest artisans? Something was amiss about this man, yet she couldn't pinpoint what it was.

He turned at the sound of their intrusion.

"You again?" he snarled, hand shifting to the hilt of his sheathed sword.

"You are under arrest for the theft and illegal trading of supplies belonging to the High Command," Nian said, trying her best to sound confident in the face of his blatant aggression. "If you cooperate and surrender everything that you have with you"—she pointed at the sacks and crates on the boats—"then you might be able to plead for a lesser sentence. Otherwise, the punishment for treason is death."

The man's eyes narrowed into menacing slits. "Treason?" he scoffed. "It's only treason if you get caught." His gaze flickered toward the chimeras. He brought an ivory whistle to his lips, sending a series of shrill notes vibrating into the air.

The three beasts immediately pounced at Nian and her guards, raising their metallic claws to strike. Nian's horse was struck across the neck, forcing it to rear back once again, braying in anguish. This time, Nian was flung off and sent tumbling across the gravel. The tiny stones that littered the beach scraped against her arms and legs.

Wincing, Nian found herself staring at one of the qilins, who was slowly making its way toward her, dragging each paw in an intentionally taunting manner. Behind it, all her guards were engaged in a fierce battle against the other two beasts, who had already mauled three of their horses while sending the rest fleeing into the forest in terror. Their leader wore a mocking smile on his lips as he watched the bloodbath unfold with chilling nonchalance. Already they were down to the final few sacks that needed to be loaded onto the sampans, and soon the boats would be ready to leave.

Nian gritted her teeth and dragged herself back up to her feet, pointing her wrist toward the qilin. She might not be well-versed in martial arts, but she was certainly not going down without a fight. A low rumble was emitting from the beast's throat, as if daring her to make her move.

Its entire body was shielded with those scales—with the exception of its wolfish head.

The eyes.

Nian knew that she only had one chance. If she missed, then the qilin would be upon her in a flash, ripping her apart with its razor-sharp claws and teeth. Holding her breath, she focused on the creature's glowing amber eyes. Then, with only the briefest of hesitations, she fired her weapon in rapid succession, sending a flurry of poison-laced needles flying toward their target.

The qilin howled.

Everything became a blur.

Without waiting to see whether or not her darts had met their mark, Nian immediately turned and sprang toward the ringleader, just as the man was about to board the sampan to leave. She threw herself at his back, pulling him down to the ground.

A cry of annoyance left the man's lips as his face struck the gravel. He flung her off, dark eyes spitting venom.

"Why, you little wretch," he growled.

Nian stared, horrified by what she was seeing. A long, bloody gash had formed down the left side of the man's cheek—and his entire face was *peeling*. He reached up to the loose flap dangling from his left temple, ripping off the thin sheet of rubberlike film that covered his face.

Now she understood what was odd about his face, why his skin looked unnaturally stiff, like it never moved with his eyes or lips.

It was a mask all along.

How was this even possible? She had grown up in a family of engineers and seen her fair share of curious inventions, but never before had she encountered something like this. A mask that looked so much like real skin, hiding an entirely different countenance beneath.

Hiding the face of a man who was supposed *to be dead*.

"Tongiya Tulishen . . ."

His presence was nothing short of astonishing, because Tongiya Tulishen—along with another of his clansmen and the first beile, Ye-lu—was supposed to have died during the solstice hunt, a victim of unnamed assassins that they had yet to identify.

If he was still alive, then what about Ye-lu himself?

The gears shifted in her mind, puzzle pieces slotting into place to reveal a harrowing possibility.

"Don't waste your time," Tongiya Tulishen called out, lips twisting in a victorious smirk. "It's time for the High Command to change hands, so why bother clinging on to this sinking ship?" He stepped onto the boat, giving the command for them to set sail.

Nian clenched her fists, watching helplessly as the boats cast away, taking the much-needed supplies with them. Tongiya Tulishen's bodyguards brandished their bloodied swords in front of her, while the qilin she had wounded sealed off her escape route from behind. The poison on her needles was potent, but even as the chimera seemed to be struggling to keep on its feet, its eyes bled with savage determination. The rest of her guards were still wrestling with the other two chimeras, unable to extricate themselves to come to her aid.

Just as despair began to set in, the shrill cries of two condors circling in the skies caught everyone's attention. Nian's eyes lit up, a spark of hope springing up inside her.

The condors swooped down toward the three men who had cornered Nian, with such incredible speed that it left their victims no time to react. The men began swinging their blades wildly in the air, desperately trying to free themselves from the chaos of beating wings and ferocious claws.

Seizing the opportunity, Nian broke past the bodyguards and sprinted toward the sea—and the retreating boats. Water splashed around her ankles, soaking through the hem of her trousers.

I can't let them get away.

"Ah!" Metal claws dug into her shoulders, forcing her to fall forward. Her face struck the water's surface. She went under, swallowing mouthfuls of swirling sand and salt water. Nian struggled to right herself, but the qilin continued to press down upon her torso, determined to drown her in these shallow waters.

Her entire life flashed past her in those moments. Her family on Huarin. Her sister. The High Commander. All the little memories from her childhood. All the dreams that she had not yet achieved— and might now never be able to.

And then Ye-kan's face floated to the surface of her mind, that impish grin that he liked to wear, and the careless tone with which he spoke. She hadn't even had the time to figure out her own feelings toward him, feelings that she knew were there and yet she was still afraid to confront. But perhaps it was too late.

Her lungs constricted as air was slowly replaced with water. She closed her eyes, waiting for when her a-ma and e-niye would come and fetch her.

And then the weight suddenly lifted.

She was hauled out of the water and back onto shore. Still in a daze, Nian choked and spluttered, trying desperately to catch a breath. To her right, she glimpsed the qilin lying still on the gravel, a long spear pierced through its head.

"Nian! Nian, are you all right?" someone was calling out to her.

"A-jie?"

Shock intertwined with relief as Nian looked up at Ying's familiar face, staring down on her with grave concern.

"A-jie, what's going on? When did you return? How—"

"Shh, that's enough questions. We can talk about all that later. We need to get you back to the palace so that you can get your injuries treated."

"The supplies. We must get them back," Nian whispered, pointing a shaky finger in the direction of Tongiya Tulishen's departing boats.

"We will," another voice replied, stern and mellow, one that Nian had not heard in a long while. A long shadow was cast over her as a tall young man stepped into her field of view, the drab gray Qirin robes he was wearing doing nothing to disguise his authority. Reaching down, he picked up a stray sword that had been dropped by one of the bodyguards, then he simply flung it outward in the direction of the sea.

A scream of anguish ripped through the air as the blade impaled itself into Tongiya Tulishen's left shoulder.

Nian grimaced, turning away and curling herself more tightly against her sister.

It's over.

Ying was back, and so was the High Commander.

CHAPTER 29

A DARK CLOUD HUNG OVER YING'S HEAD as their carriage trundled through the city streets and toward Qianlei Palace. Nian lay cradled in her arms, face pale as a sheet and sweat beading upon her brow, her sky-blue robes stained with garish patches of blood.

This was not what she had expected to come back to.

Returning to Fei had not been an easy journey. As they sailed in the direction of Muci, they had crossed paths with one of the Order's airships, loudly blaring an announcement that the capital had been placed under lockdown and that no civilians were to attempt entry into Fei until further notice. Sensing that serious trouble had struck, they had then opted to take the shorter but more perilous route through the maze of partially submerged rock formations north of the capital, almost capsizing several times in the process because *Xiangliu*'s external engines kept getting entangled with the craggy rocks.

Ying never thought she would be so glad to see the familiar emerald rooftops of Fei's multilayered cityscape when she did, but that joy and relief was short-lived. They had been en route back to the city on foot when they sighted Nian riding toward the northern forest with a group of the High Commander's personal guards, yet another sign that things in Fei were not as they should be. The group had then separated, with Ying and Ye-yang heading to chase after Nian while Chang-en and An-xi were sent to seek reinforcements.

If I had been a moment later, I would have lost Nian.

She gently stroked the damp, salt-laced strands of her little sister's hair, guilt overflowing inside her heart.

From the bits and pieces of a conversation she had picked up between Ye-yang and one of the guards, it seemed that the capital was in chaos. The refugee situation was increasingly dire, and riots had broken out within the military camps because of the stolen shipments of supplies. Also, the first beile was dead. Dead! How in Abka Han's name had something like that even happened?

She thought back on the first time she had met Ye-lu back during the Engineers Guild's apprenticeship trial, with his stern, sober gaze and eagle-like mien that made her uncomfortable. Like he had many secrets to hide. It seemed wrong for someone like that to have died so easily.

"What have you been through since I left?" she murmured, staring down at Nian. Even in her unconscious state, the girl's brows were stitched in a frown, her cracked lips murmuring unintelligibly under her breath.

As reckless as Ye-kan could be, Ying knew that he would not send Nian on such a dangerous mission if the situation had not been dire. They must have had no other choice.

"We're here," Ye-yang's voice echoed from outside.

Ying lifted the curtain and peered out the carriage window. They were approaching the towering gates of the palace, its familiar gold-tiled roofs and sloping eaves looming beyond the stone walls. "It's His Excellency!" someone shouted. The gates immediately swung open to let them through.

The carriage came to a stop in front of Ye-yang's resting quarters, Qingning Hall, and Ying quickly alighted. "Where's the physician?" she asked.

"I've already sent for him. We should have your sister brought to—"

"Ying! Number Eight!"

"Your Excellency!"

Ye-kan emerged through the vermilion lattice doors accompanied by Nergui and Qorchi. His eyes lit up when he saw them, relief written all over his worn face. Then he caught sight of the wagons bearing the recovered supplies, as well as the guards who were escorting them. His smile faded.

"Where's Nian?" he asked, unable to hide the slight tremble in his voice.

"She's still in the carriage," Ying replied. "She's badly injured. We must let the physician take a look at her as soon as possible."

Ye-kan's shoulders tensed, then he swept past Ying and Ye-yang and climbed up the carriage. Moments later, he came back out with Nian carefully cradled in his arms, almost as if he was afraid that she would shatter at the slightest touch. Like porcelain. Ignoring everyone else, he marched her straight into the hall, disappearing through the open doorway. Ying blinked back her surprise, having not expected such a swift and frankly inappropriate reaction from the fourteenth prince.

"Come," Ye-yang said, placing a hand on Ying's shoulder. "Nian will need you by her side."

～⁓

The overpowering smell of medicinal herbs filled the room, the richness of ginseng and lingzhi suffusing every corner. Nian had suffered numerous lacerations to her back, courtesy of the qilin chimera, and remained unconscious even after the imperial physician had finished treating those wounds. Ye-kan remained by her bedside, silently holding her hand and staring at her sleeping countenance, as if doing so would make her wake sooner.

His actions were highly improper, given that Nian was a lady of the palace, but if the High Commander had yet to make any comment, then no one else dared breathe a word to the contrary.

Ying sat by, watching all of this, realizing that many things had changed since her disappearance.

Qingning Hall was divided into two main sections connected by a set of folding doors: the front half was a comfortable parlor where the High Commander could speak with guests, while the inner chambers served as his personal resting quarters. Through the translucent rice paper that covered the intricate diamond latticework, Ying would occasionally glimpse Ye-yang on the other side. He had been occupied with receiving updates about the current situation ever since their return, and a small group of commanders and clan chiefs had gathered within the hall—including her older brother, Wen.

Under different circumstances, Ying might have been bothered by Wen's presence, worried about what he would say if he discovered her here, but her concern for Nian's condition left no space in her mind for all that.

Ye-yang had already swapped out his tattered Qirin clothes for the Order's black brigandine armor, with gold trimmings and embroidery of a coiled cobra across the chest that set him apart from the others. Just like that, her Ye-yang was gone, replaced once again by the stoic High Commander of the nine isles. Suddenly, the days they had spent with the Blood Phoenix seemed like a lifetime ago.

A light cough distracted her from her thoughts.

"You're awake!" Ye-kan burst out.

Ying rushed to her sister's side. Nian had come to, and was staring up at them blankly, as if deeply confused by her circumstance. She opened her mouth to speak, but ended up bursting into another fit of coughs.

"No need to rush," Ying said. She gently helped Nian to sit upright, taking care not to touch any of her wounds. Then she poured her sister a cup of water. "The physician says that your injuries are only superficial, but they'll need at least a few weeks to heal. You're not to move about excessively in the meantime, do you understand?"

At the mention of the physician's diagnosis, Ye-kan's expression darkened. The physician had also said one other thing that Ying intentionally left out—that while Nian would make a complete recovery, some of these gashes were so deep that they would inevitably leave scars. Ying didn't know how Nian would react to that, but it was something that they could work through in time. For now, what her sister needed to focus on was recovering well.

Nian nodded, though anxiety still shone in her eyes. She reached out to Ye-kan, tugging his sleeve. "The supplies—did we manage to retrieve everything?" she asked.

"Does it matter? Why did you even go hunting for them on your own, without waiting for me! Don't you know how dangerous it was?" Ye-kan grumbled.

"We brought everything back, including what they had already sent over to the ship," Ying said.

The carcasses of the qilin chimeras had also been sent back to the Engineers Guild for further examination. She had once believed that all the chimeric abominations that walked the streets of Fei were born from the guild, but it appeared that she was mistaken. There was engineering genius hidden beyond the guild's reach, and much more that was out there for her to discover.

"What about Tongiya Tulishen?" Nian asked. "He's not dead. He didn't die in the solstice hunt. *He's* the one who's behind the smuggling. The one we saw talking to Arban at the gambling den."

Ye-kan's lips tipped into a glower. "He's been taken to the dungeons for interrogation. That bastard! How dare he betray the Order like this?" He slammed his palm against the wooden bedframe. "And Ye-lu . . . I'll bet he's hiding somewhere. Faking his own death to frame us for his crimes. I'm going to rip him to pieces when I find him."

Ying still didn't have the full picture of what had transpired in the capital in her absence, but the hazy pieces she had picked up were enough to leave her concerned. If their conjectures were correct, then the first beile had rebelled. The Tongiya clan had always been staunch supporters of Ye-lu, and with Tongiya Tulishen's involvement in this, it was unlikely that the clan would escape unscathed.

How would Chang-en react when he found out about this? And would he be implicated because of the crimes of his clansmen?

Nian took hold of her hands, shaking her out of her thoughts. "A-jie, where have you been all this while? What happened?" she asked.

"It's a long story," Ying murmured. She didn't know where to even begin telling the story. From the fortuitousness of their rescue by Yunshang and the Blood Phoenix fleet? Or when Wenjun blew up the *Diamond*'s air pumps and then forced them to participate in the Tournament of the Seas? Even though it had only been the span of a few weeks, so much had happened since then. Every memory of their time with the Blood Phoenix felt like a hazy dream, flitting in and out of reach.

Forcing out a smile, she said, "I'll tell you more about it another time, when you've had some time to rest and recover."

"She's awake?" Ye-yang's voice drifted over as he stepped through the doors and walked to the bedside. With him came Wen, who did a double take when he sighted both his sisters in the room. The Aihui chieftain looked like he hadn't slept well in days, with shadows hanging beneath his eyes and weariness etched across the lines of his tanned face.

"Your Excellency," Nian greeted, tipping her chin in an attempt at bowing. "A-ge."

"No need for the formalities," Ye-yang replied kindly. "You should avoid moving about unnecessarily, else your wounds will not heal well." His gaze instinctively shifted toward Ying, but the moment their eyes met, she turned her head in the other direction.

Now that they were back in Fei, everything had to go back to the way they had been. Nian was the one who belonged in Ye-yang's inner palace, while she was the one who was destined to leave. Her sister had already suffered too much because of her disappearance, and she could not bear to hurt Nian even more.

"A-ge," she mumbled, greeting her brother awkwardly. Things had been tense between her and Wen ever since what happened with the Engineers Guild two years back, and she realized she had no idea how to act around him anymore. A part of her missed him dearly, as she missed Nian, and she was grateful to have even made it back alive to be able to see them again—but she would never be able to find the right words to tell Wen that. They had grown up. Time had created a gulf between them that seemed too wide to cross, and the bond from their childhood had long faded into a fine, gossamer thread.

"How are you feeling?" he asked Nian. "What did I say about staying out of trouble?" Then he glanced up at Ying, a mix of exasperation and resignation in his warm brown eyes. "That applies to both of you."

There was no shortage of judgment and reprimand in his words, yet there was also concern in his voice. A pang of guilt wormed its way through Ying's heart. It hadn't been easy for Wen to shoulder the responsibilities of the entire clan after their father's demise, yet she hadn't been the least bit helpful, constantly grumbling about him being too controlling.

But maybe this was Wen's way of showing his care for them, in a way that she had never tried to understand.

"Sorry for making you worry, A-ge," Nian said, mustering a weak smile. "The physician has already treated my wounds. They'll heal."

Ye-kan walked over to the circular table in the center of the room, sitting down alongside Ye-yang. "How's the situation?" he asked hesitantly. He was sitting with his back stiff as a washboard, like a child waiting to be punished.

"Tongiya Tulishen refuses to talk. It might take some time before we get anything useful out of him," Ye-yang replied. "I've already issued the order to search the capital for any signs of Ye-lu. If he's alive, then he must still be in Fei."

"When I was searching the triad's warehouse, I found the coordinates of some of the locations that they were shipping supplies to," Nian said. "One of them came up several times. Using Larut as the starting point, three-mao, five-yin, five-ren."

Three-mao, five-yin, five-ren. Ying tried to trace the route that Nian had recited against the nautical star map in her mind.

"Yokre," the sisters said at the same time.

"The tenth isle? What have they got to do with anything?" Ye-kan asked.

Every trail led back to Monggu Yutai.

It was insidious and cunning, to siphon the Order's own supplies and weapons to wage war against them. How long had he been planning this? Since Aogiya Lianzhe's passing? Or since the tenth isle first broke away all those years ago?

After having met the Monggu chieftain in person, Ying had nothing but revulsion for the man, who had no qualms about betraying his family and people for the sake of his own selfish ambitions. That he had some hand in placing her younger sister in this precarious state made her loathe him even more.

"I'm not surprised. It tracks with what we already know," Ye-yang said. "We've also just received an update that the Monggu clan has launched a full offensive against the High Command. Their fleet is sailing toward Fei as we speak. They'll reach us in about ten days." He glanced in Ying's direction, and she understood.

Their escape from the Blood Phoenix had inevitably triggered the start of war, with Monggu Yutai knowing that he no longer held the element of surprise.

"But that's impossible. The strength of the Monggu clan isn't anywhere near enough to challenge the Order," Ye-kan protested, his eyes still clouded with disbelief.

"It is if they're sailing with pirates."

"Pirates?" Ye-kan's hand slipped, knocking over the cup of water he had in front of him. "He's colluding with the pirates?"

"*Controlling* the pirates," Ye-yang corrected. "Monggu Yutai has been using the pirates like a noose around our necks, to weaken us until we are unable to resist. He will not succeed." He reached over and picked up the porcelain cup that had toppled, setting it upright again. "Fourteen, if we hope to win a difficult battle, then the most important thing is not to lose confidence in ourselves. You have done well during my absence—do not let all this shake your faith in what you are capable of."

There was a flicker in Ye-kan's eyes. He opened his mouth, then shut it again, as if uncertain about how he was supposed to receive this unexpected sliver of praise.

Ye-yang glanced at Ye-kan, then tossed the bronze command seal of the Plain White Banner over to him—the seal that Ye-kan had given up as part of the agreement he struck with the two older beiles.

Ye-kan stared at the seal in his hand, the fanged cobra's maw snarling back at him through the lines cut in bronze. "This . . ."

"You should thank Nian. If not for her recovering the stolen weapons and capturing Tongiya Tulishen, you wouldn't be getting this back so soon." Ye-yang stood up. "Come, Fourteen, Aihui Wen, there are other matters we need to discuss." He looked across at Ying, gaze lingering on her for a moment longer, then he turned and left.

"I'll come back later," Ye-kan said to Nian, oblivious to the disapproving aura emanating from Wen.

Once they were alone, Ying sat back down by Nian's bedside, taking her sister's hand in hers. Nian's fingers felt ever so fragile, her skin cold to the touch. Her eyes glossed over with the sheen of tears.

"A-jie, I'm okay," Nian said, flipping her hand around and patting it comfortingly.

This was how Nian always was. Consistent and steadfast—a safe harbor in the face of any impending storm. Like their mother had been, when she was alive.

"I'm sorry," she whispered. "I should have been here with you. Then maybe you wouldn't have had to go through any of this." The thought of what Nian had to endure while she and Ye-yang had been lost at sea weighed heavily upon her heart, the taste of guilt sitting bitter at the back of her throat. If she hadn't returned to Fei, hadn't boarded the *North Wind* . . .

"It's not your fault. I'm thankful enough that Abka Han brought you home. I was the one who volunteered to help, because Ye-kan—" At the mention of the fourteenth beile, Nian hesitated, a faint dusting of pink spreading across her pale cheeks. "It hasn't been easy for him, having to hold his own against the other beiles."

"I can imagine. The older beiles are a pack of wolves. Compared to them, Ye-kan is far too wet behind the ears. When this is all over, I'm going to give him a good whipping for landing you in such danger."

"No, don't!" Nian burst out. "This has nothing to do with him. It was entirely my decision. If Ye-kan knew what I was going to do, he wouldn't have let me go either. I know he's inexperienced, but he's already doing his best. He didn't falter in the slightest even when the other beiles were pressuring him to relinquish the High Commander's seal."

"Because he's stubborn."

"Because he's steadfast."

Ying pursed her lips together, observing her sister curiously. "Nian, you and Ye-kan . . . Do you have feelings for him?" Ye-kan was certainly *very* concerned about Nian, and it seemed the sentiment was not unreciprocated.

The blush on Nian's face deepened. "I don't know what you're talking about, A-jie," she denied.

Ying placed an affectionate hand on Nian's head, like how she always did when they were growing up. *Take your time*, it meant. *I'll wait.* A moment passed in quiet contemplation, the space of years shrinking to the way it used to be, when they were still little girls snuggled beside each other inside their cozy ger on Huarin. The rich, buttery fragrance of warm yak's milk would fill the air as it bubbled cheerily inside its bronze pot, hanging above the glowing coals of their tiny hearth.

Nian sighed. She raised a hand to her heart, wistfulness brimming in her large eyes. "I honestly don't know, A-jie. And I'm not sure it even matters, because Ye-kan and I . . . we're not possible."

"You silly child." Ying wrapped her arms around her sister's frame, enveloping her in a warm hug. "Of course it matters. *You* matter. There's nothing wrong with loving someone."

"Then why did you run away from it?"

Ying stiffened. Holding Nian by the shoulders, she slowly pulled back, eyeing her sister warily. "What do you mean?" she asked.

"Ye-kan and I, you and Ye-yang—how did we end up this way?"

"H-h-how did you know?" Her heart leapt up her throat, pounding in alarm.

"There's a lamp that sits on his desk that looks very much like the ones that A-ma used to make. I only noticed it because it looked so incongruous with the rest of the furnishings, like it didn't quite fit in. While you were away, Ye-kan used that study from time to time, and that was when I finally managed to take a closer look at the lamp. At what was carved into each panel."

Ying shifted in her seat, her mouth becoming uncomfortably dry.

It was the octagonal lamp that Ye-yang had made for her, half-finished when they parted ways upon the Huarin cliffside. Had he kept it after all this time? And now that sentimentality had exposed the secret that she had been hoping to bring with her to the grave.

"Nian, it's not what you think. Ye-yang and I, we—"

"It doesn't matter, A-jie. I'm not upset anymore. I *was*, but only because I wish you'd told me about all this earlier. Why did you have to lie?"

"I didn't mean to. It's just . . . you were so hopeful. So happy. I didn't want to hurt you . . ." Her voice choked up, the weight of her guilt pressing down upon her.

"Do you know how angry I was when I found out about all this—that my sister thought to throw away her own happiness for the sake of mine? Did you think that I would truly be happy that way? Do I not deserve to find someone who loves *me*, the same way Ye-yang loves you?" A hint of offense lingered in Nian's voice, reminding Ying of how wrong she had been.

"I'm so sorry, Nian," she whispered. "It's my mistake."

Her sister sighed, her gaze softening. "If there's one mistake you made, it's going against your own heart. You should never have let go of the High Commander because of me, because the heavens know that he never let go of you." Nian smiled, and that smile pierced right through Ying's heart, prickling like a dozen needles. "Maybe you're right. I shouldn't avoid things. After all this, what I've learned is that I don't want to die with regrets. Maybe I should be brave enough to face my own feelings, even if nothing ever comes out of it."

Ying swallowed, choking up with pride as she placed one hand upon her sister's cheek. "You've always been the more sensible one between us," she said. "And the braver one."

"Haven't we known that all along?"

They shared a laugh, foreheads pressed against each other like they had done many a time throughout their childhood, as if they had never left the grasslands of Huarin.

CHAPTER 30

YING STAYED THE NIGHT IN THE PALACE with Nian, leaving only at daybreak while her sister was still in deep slumber. Before she left, she gave Nian a gentle peck on the forehead. It was Nian's turn to rest—and time for Ying's work to begin.

Rushing back to the Engineers Guild, she headed straight for the guild archives—the three-story pagoda that also served as Master Lianshu's hideout. If they were to face the pirates and the Monggu fleet, then the guild had a pivotal role to play.

Wenjun, the enigmatic Master Cixin, the prowess of the Monggu clan—her time with the Blood Phoenix had taught her that the world of engineering extended far beyond the meager confines of the guild's stone-cold walls, beyond even the precipitous cliffs and pebble-lined shores of the nine isles. As much as she despised Lianshu and her Bladebreakers, she needed Lianshu's expertise to compensate for her own lack of experience.

According to Nian, Master Lianshu had been effectively imprisoned in her own workshop after returning from the storm, in order to prevent her from revealing the High Commander's disappearance to the other beiles. The guild master would not have been pleased about that.

Bracing herself for the outburst, Ying pushed open the lattice doors to the guild master's workshop.

"Oh look, if it isn't another one who's risen from the dead," Lianshu quipped, her voice dripping with disdain.

Ying paused. The guild master was not alone. Ye-yang was already there, sitting across the circular table from his aunt. The atmosphere in the room hung thick and viscous, the tension between its two occupants like a taut zither string on the verge of snapping.

She stepped gingerly across the threshold and entered Lianshu's quarters. The loss of freedom had taken its toll on the haughty guild master, leaving dark circles around her eyes and loose strands of hair sticking out like stray twigs, her natural curls taking on a life of their own. There was still a fresh pot of jasmine tea on the burner, but the floral fragrance was tainted with a sourness that smelled as if she had not washed in days.

Lianshu waved a hand impatiently, gesturing for her to sit down. "Ye-yang here was just telling me how his dearest uncle is apparently sailing to Fei with an army of pirates, determined to destroy the Aogiya High Command at long last," she said. Picking up her glass teapot, she poured herself a cup of tea, offering neither of them any. "I still fail to see how that is any of my business, though."

"They're bringing their Blades," Ye-yang said. "We don't know exactly how many they have, but if our past estimates are correct, then there'll be no less than six."

Something shifted in Lianshu's eyes. A flicker of anticipation.

"That wily old fox," the guild master mused, rubbing her chin thoughtfully—almost gleefully. "A-ma always did say that Yutai had a good eye for both engineering and politics. Destined for great things. Too bad he wasn't born an Aogiya."

"The plans we had to disable and destroy the Blades will have to resume. Given the current state of our fleet, direct confrontation will put us at a severe disadvantage," Ye-yang said.

Lianshu cracked her knuckles with a fervent glint in her eyes that reminded Ying of the former High Commander. There was a callousness that was etched into their bones, an indifference to the world beyond themselves.

"Just as well that he's coming to us, so we can test our explosives without having to go searching for those Blades."

"They won't work," Ying interjected.

"Excuse me?"

"The Blades are not merely shells of glass. Each one is protected by an impenetrable shield that can be activated in the time it would take you to walk from one end of this workshop to the other. By the time we get close enough to deal any damage, the shields will already be down."

"And how do you know all this?" Lianshu raised her eyebrows skeptically.

"I've seen it with my own eyes."

Memories of flames and smoke were seared into her mind, the acridity of burning charcoal stinging her nose. Zhong Kui's ships— ripped apart in violent explosions, painting the midnight skies in harrowing shades of orange and gold.

But still the *Diamond* remained, invincible in perpetuity. Like a god, gazing upon the vulnerability of humans with quiet contempt.

The guild master's eyes bulged, amazement reflecting in her dark irises like flecks of starlight. "You *what*?" She grabbed Ying by the shoulders and gave her a hard shake. "How!"

Ying sucked in a breath, then she briefly relayed an account of what had happened after they had fallen overboard during the storm. By the end of it, Lianshu was all fired up with zeal and vigor, energy restored and resentment forgotten.

"If I had known, I would have jumped into the sea with you!" the master lamented, bemoaning the lost opportunity. "A diamond in the ocean with shields of steel—how majestic that must be. A pity . . ."

A pity that they had to destroy them.

They both fell silent for a moment, mourning the impending loss of these magnificent creations.

"We only have about ten days before Monggu Yutai's fleet sails within range of Fei," Ye-yang said.

Lianshu slapped her own thigh and bounced up from her seat. "Right, no time to waste, then! What's the plan? What do you need from me?"

"I . . . I have an idea, but I'm not sure if it'll work," Ying said. It was an idea she had been toying with since she learned of the Blades' shields, but the sight of those qilin chimeras had further solidified the concept in her mind. "The dragon automaton that you were prototyping before, the one that was used during the final test of the guild's apprenticeship trial—can I see the design plans for that?"

Chimeras were incredibly difficult to build—an entire automaton was even harder. But Aogiya Lianshu was the expert in this area. The master had a whole assortment of insect automatons at her disposal, but those were not going to be enough. They needed something far larger, far more powerful, far more maleficent.

Not a dragon of the skies. A dragon of the seas.

~⌒)

They were running on borrowed time. There was a growing tension that suffocated the capital, a coarse noose slowly tightening around the neck. The nine isles held their breaths in disquietude, waiting for the enemy fleet to appear on the horizon, for the battle drums to rise in crescendo, thundering toward the end of days. Airships of the Order patrolled the skies, warning civilians to stay indoors. Soldiers decked in their somber black armor pounded the streets, rushing to transport supplies and weaponry from storehouses to military camps.

Back at the guild, the mood was equally grim.

Within the underground workshop of the guild's Black Ops division, gas lamps burned night after night as they toiled relentlessly over the new prototypes—prototypes that they would not have the luxury of testing.

When Monggu Yutai and his pirates arrived, they would only have one chance for victory, else all was lost.

"Absolutely glorious," Chang-en quipped, circling around the snaking form of their suspended creation as the other apprentices put the finishing touches to the welding of its tail. He ran his fingers along the cold, dark steel plates that made up its grotesque yet beautiful body. "I have the perfect nickname for it. *Gonggong*—the Qirin water god of chaos and destruction. Part human, part sea snake, all powerful."

"What kind of a traitor are you, naming our weapon after a Qirin god?" An-xi scolded, throwing a dirty rag at Chang-en's face.

Chang-en tossed the rag aside. "Traitor?" He laughed, though his smile hung a little stiff at the corners. "The same traitor that worked on *Xiangliu* for the pirate tournament, which, in case you forgot, is *also* from Qirin folklore."

An-xi pursed his lips together, a distant look clouding his eyes. As if he had retreated into his own memories.

Ever since they returned from the seas, neither of them had spoken about the Blood Phoenix beyond what was necessary for the project to continue. The words that left their lips were only "the Blade," never "the *Diamond*"; only "those pirates," never "Yunshang" or "Wenjun."

If they didn't speak of it, then they could pretend like it never happened. That they never sang and danced on board a certain flagship, playing four-colored cards and getting drunk on wine under a blanket of glittering stars together with these friends—no, *enemies*.

Ying lifted her visor and tossed the welding torch onto the workbench, stealing a glance at Chang-en.

The Tongiya clan was still oblivious to Tongiya Tulishen's arrest, since Ye-yang had decided to keep things under wraps until the first beile's whereabouts had been found. Morale in the Order was already low enough with the recent riots, without more spanners being thrown into the works.

She sighed. Hopefully the rest of his clan would be spared. It didn't seem fair for Chang-en and his other family members to be punished for a crime they didn't commit.

She took a step back and studied the completed prototype. A silent beast, ready to strike.

Thankfully, Master Lianshu had not ceased work on improving

her dragon automaton ever since she first demonstrated it during the guild's apprenticeship trial, so their starting point was already fairly close to what they needed the end product to be.

All Ying had to do was modify the creature using some features inspired by the very vessels it was built to destroy, such as a series of protruding fins that functioned as propellers, much like a scaled-down version of the Blades' propellers. Inspired by the external engines that they had created for *Xiangliu*, she also fitted the Bladebreaker with a similar kaen-gas engine coupled with a water propulsion mechanism, to be attached to the beast's dramatic flame-shaped tail.

When finished, the Bladebreaker would transform into a spear, slicing gracefully through the water and splitting the seas—then piercing through the supposedly invincible shield of the Blade until it shattered the glass windows hidden beneath. A mosaic of fault lines would extend across the walls of the giant, all crooked angles and jagged edges, until the yawning pressure from the waters forced it to collapse upon itself in a myriad of splintered fragments.

That was how it would work. *If* it worked.

"Do you think we can really win?" An-xi asked, having moved quietly to her side. He handed her a waterskin.

"Either that, or we'll die trying."

The Monggu fleet was already pressing closer to the shores of Fei, and the latest estimates placed them at a mere four to five days away from where the Order's ships had set up their defensive line. Before that day came, the Bladebreakers would have to undergo their first—and final—test.

"If the Bladebreakers succeed, though, that would be a great achievement, wouldn't it?" An-xi pressed, a hint of expectation simmering in his tone. "The guild will be rewarded handsomely for it, and so will the pilots."

"Sure, if they succeed and we win this war, you could probably ask the High Command for anything, and they might just give it to you," she replied casually, taking a swig of water. "Thanks for this," she said, handing the waterskin back to him. "And don't worry yourself too much. We really don't have time to be stressing over the what-ifs right now."

A slim chance of success was better than no chance at all.

Master Lianshu was screeching instructions to run final checks on the metallic sea serpent. The kaen-gas engine was ignited, and propellers spun in a blur, the dragon's body straining under the thick leather straps that were used to pin it down. In the water, the automaton's serpentine body would swim in an undulating motion, accelerating until its sharp, arrow-like head met its target.

It has to work. It will.

Ying caught Lianshu's gaze and gave a slight nod to signal that everything was in order. The engine was extinguished. Apprentices moved to remove the monster from its harnesses and to replace it with another. Besides the original dragon that Lianshu had created, the remaining five had been hastily put together over the past few days, rallying the might of almost the entire guild.

Once they completed inspection of all six automatons, these creatures would be sent to slumber within large bronze shells—modeled after the Octopus submersibles that she had built before—only to be released when it was time for them to meet the enemy.

The doors to the workshop swung open, and the accompanying gust of icy night wind sent a depressing chill down everyone's spines.

"Your Excellency," the engineers greeted, fists raised across their chest.

Ye-yang stepped in, the gold metal trimmings of his brigandine armor clinking softly as he moved. His steady gaze surveyed the anxious faces that stared back at him and swept across the curled body of the black serpent that was now lying coiled upon the floor before finally coming to rest upon Ying's face.

"How's the progress with the Bladebreakers?" he asked.

Although he still maintained his usual commanding presence, Ye-yang looked worn, fatigue beginning to slip through the cracks of his steely façade. There were shadows beneath his eyes, telltale signs of having not slept in days, and flecks of dirt clung to the sable plates that lined his arms.

"We've just finished the final inspection on this one, so it's on its way to be sent for sealing," Ying replied. A pang of fear struck her. "Is something the matter? Have there been updates on the movements of the Monggu fleet?"

Since news of the impending attack reached their shores, a state of emergency had been declared across the nine isles. The Engineers Guild had been receiving daily reports from the High Command, informing them of the latest developments at the front line so that the guild could deploy their engineers and equipment to support the war effort as required. However, this was the first time the High Commander himself had come down to the guild to ask after their progress.

Ye-yang shook his head, lips curving in a tired smile. "No, nothing of that sort. Can I borrow you for a while?" he asked.

Ying blinked, then a hard shove to her right shoulder sent her hurtling toward Ye-yang. Her face crashed against the cold leather of his chest armor, and his arm instinctively circled around her waist. Chang-en gave them a knowing wink before turning back to his task of pumping kaen gas into the engine.

"Go, stop wasting time," Master Lianshu barked, rolling her eyes dramatically at them. "It's already too crowded here without the two of you lovelorn children getting in my way." As the last surviving member of the previous generation of Aogiyas, the guild master was possibly the only person in the nine isles who would dare speak to the High Commander in this manner and not have to suffer any consequences for it.

A rush of blood shot up to Ying's head, her cheeks flaming. Chang-en and An-xi sniggered to each other, and the other senior apprentices were quietly exchanging suggestive glances, greatly amplifying her embarrassment.

"All right, we've got a long day tomorrow," Lianshu said, clapping her hands together. "Once we've sealed the final Bladebreaker, run one final check on our inventory and call it a night. I don't want anyone to be late tomorrow."

Chang-en rushed forward, taking the workshop keys out of the guild master's hand. "I'll do the locking up, Master Lianshu," he said in a rare moment of diligence. He stared down at the bronze keys in his hands, then closed his fingers tightly around them. Turning to Ying, he patted himself on the chest as if to say that he would help keep an eye on things over here. "Don't worry," he mouthed, lips twitching in a cheeky grin.

Bristling with irritation, Ying turned and fled.

CHAPTER 31

THIS WAS THE SECOND TIME THAT YING was standing upon Fei's city walls, but there were whispers in the wind tonight, telling her that it might also be her last.

Although the walls themselves were exactly as she remembered, their slabs of gray stone imposing and unwavering, the sense of peace she had once felt had crumbled to dust. At the watchtowers located at regular intervals, kaen-gas flames burned an intense blue, war beacons blazing brightly in the night. If she squinted into the distance, she could make out the faint, fiery glow from the beacons on Muci, and somewhere far away, a similar flame would light up the cliffs of Huarin.

War is upon us, they warned. *Beware. Beware.*

Staring out toward the open sea, Ying's gaze settled upon the rows of warships floating upon the dark waters, the flags of the Cobra's Order flying high upon their masts. They looked like hazy shadows, ink-black sails upon midnight hulls, with only the silver insignia of the spitting cobra gleaming like ghosts against the moonlight. Her own brother would be on one of them, along with other Aihui clan members who served in the Order. Sleep would be elusive across the nine isles tonight, as every Antaran huddled beneath their blankets, cloaked in the uncertainty of tomorrow.

This was the calm before the storm.

"Why did you bring me here?"

Ye-yang came up alongside her, stretching his arms out along the parapet. "If our calculations are correct, then the Monggu fleet is less than four days away. The Bladebreakers will need to leave the capital first thing tomorrow morning if we hope to intercept the fleet before they reach our main defensive line."

"Tomorrow morning," she murmured, gripping tightly on to the sides of her guild robes. She had already known that it was coming, yet it still felt too soon. Turning her head, she glimpsed the glittering lights of Fei through the gaps in the battlements, illuminating the gracefully sloping eaves of the jade-green rooftops and the elegant arches of the many bridges stretching across the city's waterways. Red lanterns hung outside every home, and lotus lamps floated down the snaking canals, carrying the prayers of the Antaran people to the silent gods above.

"I saw from the guild's report that you'll be piloting one of the Bladebreaker submersibles."

Ying stiffened. So this was the reason Ye-yang had come looking for her.

They had no time to figure out how to place the submersibles on autopilot, so the vessels would still need to be controlled manually. One of the Order's ships would escort the six submersibles to the vicinity of the Monggu fleet, after which individual pilots would have to take their craft underwater in search of the elusive Blades. Once sighted, the pilot would then release the Bladebreaker from its hold, sending the serpent careening toward its target.

Six guild engineers had volunteered for this, because they knew best how to operate both the submersible and the Bladebreaker. Ying was one of them.

She had not told anyone outside the guild of this decision. Not Nian, not Ye-kan, and most of all, not Ye-yang.

"I know what you're going to say, but it's not going to change my mind. I'm the one who built these, so it's my responsibility to see things through till the end."

The risk involved in this mission was tremendously high. Coming within close radius of the Blades and the Monggu fleet meant that they would be within firing range of the underwater cannons. Speed was everything. If they could not deploy their Bladebreaker and steer their vessel away in time, then they would not be returning home.

If she could save one person from that fate by volunteering to go, then it was a choice she was willing to make. If they could save the lives of hundreds of Antarans by going, then the sacrifice would be worthwhile.

There was a sadness and resignation threading through Ye-yang's gray irises that she could not bear to look at. This was exactly why she didn't want him to know—because she didn't know how she was supposed to face him after.

Ye-yang slipped his free hand under his suit of armor and pulled out a pair of red knots of shimmering crimson string, each woven into a pattern resembling a blooming flower. He held them up against the moonlight.

"It's called a lover's knot. A Qirin tradition. One of the kitchen matrons from the Blood Phoenix taught me how to make one."

Ying reached out and ran a finger across the interlocking loops that formed the clover-shaped knot. It was clumsy. Uneven. Made from fumbling fingers on inexperienced hands. "Who would ever have imagined that the almighty High Commander might one day be fiddling with string by the kitchen hearth?" she joked.

"According to folklore, a lover's knot ties the hearts of two lovers together, so that they may always be with each other." He pressed one into her palm, closing her fingers over it.

A lump caught in her throat, warm tears threatening to spill out from her eyes. She clutched the knot tightly in her hand, as tightly as she clung to every word that he had said. Her lips trembled as she looked up at the soft smile on his face, at the sincerity reflecting in the pools of his eyes.

"Maybe one day, we can leave all this behind. Go somewhere where there's no High Command, no Engineers Guild, no pirates, no wars. I'll just be Ye-yang, and you'll be Ying, and we'll sail the seas and explore the world there is out there."

A light laugh escaped from Ying's lips, wistful like the last falling leaf on an autumn's day. She stretched a hand out, trailing her fingers along the side of his face, down the sharp line of his jaw. Then she reached around the back of his neck, pulling him close and placing her lips upon his. His arms wrapped themselves around her waist, cradling her against him as he slowly deepened their kiss, soothing away the apprehension that plagued her heart.

His touch remained gentle, familiar, yet there was bitterness lingering at the tips of their tongues, like a cup of tie guan yin that had been left to steep for too long. The fragrance remained, reminiscent of orchids in bloom; the taste—sorrowful, in anticipation of the withering.

When they parted, Ye-yang leaned forward and touched his forehead to hers. In the silence, a thousand words passed between them unspoken.

Tomorrow, the battle drums would sound out across the isles, and they would both have to lead their individual fights for the same cause.

"Ying, I'm sorry."

"What for?"

Ye-yang's silver-tinged gaze bored straight through hers, leaving her with a dreadful sense of foreboding. Something wasn't right. There was something he wasn't telling her, something—

A dull thud struck her at the base of her neck.

Her world went dark.

Ying awoke with a splitting headache. She touched her fingers gingerly to the back of her head, wincing at the soreness.

What happened?

She took in her surroundings—the dark sheen of the rosewood furniture, ink paintings of bamboo groves and winter blossoms hanging from the walls, and the subtle floral scent of tea floating in the air.

Qingning Hall.

Her mind desperately grasped at the loose fragments of

memories she could gather, piecing them together to form a coherent recollection. She had been up on the city walls with Ye-yang, and then—

By her bedside, someone startled.

"You're awake." Ye-yang's worried face appeared before her, creases lining his tired eyes. He sat along the edge of the bed and reached for her hand.

She pulled away. "What did you do?" she whispered, each word lancing toward him with the bitterest frost.

"I know you're upset, but I had no choice. I couldn't let you go diving headfirst into danger, Ying. I've already come close to losing you too many times."

The first rays of dawn were filtering in through the open windows, leaves of the elegant willow tree in the garden casting dancing shadows upon the floorboards.

It's already daybreak.

The Bladebreaker mission was due to depart at first light, which meant that they could already be gone. The realization of what Ye-yang had done rattled Ying to the core. Anger and disbelief intertwined and festered at the base of her gut like monstrous vines twisting inside her. She stared at him, her gaze a pair of keen blades.

"How could you? I was supposed to go! I *have* to go!"

Ye-yang took her by the shoulders. "No, you don't. There are plenty of others who can do this, Ying. It doesn't have to be you."

But this was her project. This was her idea. She was the one who convinced the guild and the High Command that this could work.

And if it didn't—she should bear the responsibility, not send someone else as her scapegoat.

"Yes it does." She pushed his hands away, climbing out of the bed and pulling her boots back on. If she hurried, she might still be able to catch them.

"Ying! This is not the time to be foolhardy. What is the point of jumping into a mission that may or may not succeed? Do you realize what the implications are? This is not a guild trial. There will be no safety nets waiting in the wings to rescue you. You could *die* out there!" He caught her by the wrist, his grip like an iron cuff upon her skin.

Ying spun around, her eyes livid with rage. "Is this what it is to you? Foolhardiness?" she scoffed. "Ye-yang, let me tell you what's really going through your mind. Deep down, you've never trusted me. Never believed in me. In your eyes, I'm someone who needs to be protected, someone who needs shielding from danger, because I'm not capable of doing that myself." As the words spilled out, so did the tears, flooding down her cheeks in a wild torrent. "To you, I'm only worthy enough to stay one step *behind* you—not beside you."

She could see it clearly now. She finally understood why there had always been a gap between them that they could never seem to bridge, even after everything they had been through since the first time they met on that rainy day in Muci. It wasn't because he was an Aogiya and she was an Aihui, or that he was the High Commander and she a regular engineer, or that there was their fathers' blood-stained past lying between them.

It was because he had never viewed them as equals, and so she would never be able to walk this path with him, even if she wanted to.

Disillusionment set in. Disappointment—at him, and at herself. After all they had been through, she had allowed herself to believe that there was still hope for them. Allowed herself to fall for him all over again.

Now this.

Ye-yang's gaze faltered, the storm-like quality of his irises misting over with a layer of quiet sorrow. Something inside him was breaking, crumbling, his defensive façade cracking to reveal a vulnerability that he always kept so carefully concealed. His grip on her loosened, hand falling weakly back to his side.

"That's not true," he said, knuckles whitening upon clenched fists. "It's not. I'm doing this because I *love* you, because I can't lose you the way I lost my e-niye . . ." His voice trailed off, trembled, as if he were trying to convince himself of his own justifications.

"No." Ying closed her eyes, willing the raging tempest inside her to calm, allowing it to form into one final teardrop that fell upon the hardwood floor. "Because you've never truly understood what love is."

~⁓⁓

Ying raced all the way to the Order's docks, where the Bladebreaker mission was to have departed from. She pushed her steed as fast as she could, blistering through the city's cobbled streets and past the sandy grounds of the airship yards until the glittering blue ocean came into view.

Still, she was too late.

Leaping off her horse, Ying ran all the way to the edge of the pier, but there was nothing there except the gently lapping waves, kicking sea-foam over the barnacle-encrusted legs of the boardwalk.

They were already gone.

"Got cold feet?" Master Lianshu's voice hollered from behind.

The guild master and some of the apprentices were shifting equipment into the makeshift tents that had been set up beside the docks, preparing to begin their long wait to find out whether or not the mission would succeed.

Ying rushed over, ignoring the critical, disdainful looks coming from the other apprentices. "How long have they been gone?" she asked.

Lianshu gestured at the huge sticks of incense sitting in the nearby bronze tripod. The first stick had only shortened by about two fingers' worth, releasing a mild fragrance of sandalwood as it continued to burn with its amber glow.

"Good thing someone volunteered to take your place, otherwise your punishment for dereliction of duty would be far heavier, I expect," the guild master said, her tone scathing.

"Who took my place?"

"Niohuru An-xi."

"What?"

That was impossible. How could it have been An-xi? An-xi, who was afraid of everything and valued his own life above all else, who went queasy at the sight of blood and constantly fretted about being eaten by sharks—that An-xi couldn't possibly have volunteered to pilot a Bladebreaker.

"I know what you're thinking, but if you think a little deeper, maybe it's not that surprising after all," Lianshu replied. "Aren't the Niohurus in a spot of hot water after what happened with the smuggling of the rice, or was it flour? Whatever—"

Ying thought back to the cryptic, pessimistic things that An-xi had been saying yesterday, finally realizing what he had meant by all that. He must have wanted to earn credit from this mission to plead for leniency against his father's sentence. But why hadn't he told her? There had to be another way to help his family without volunteering for something so dangerous. Even though An-xi was familiar with the workings of the Bladebreaker, his penchant for caution and over-thinking made him unsuitable for such a mission, where adaptability and quick reactions could make the difference between life and death.

Worry began to gnaw its way inside her mind, guilt curdling into a distorted mess at the base of her churning gut.

She had to do something. Even if she couldn't pilot a Blade-breaker, at least she could communicate with the rest of the pilots and help cue them when necessary. After all, she was the only one who had ever seen an actual Blade before.

Looking around, she spied something golden peeking out from beneath a large hemp sheet. "Is that my old prototype?" she asked.

Lianshu nodded. "I may have overpacked," she said with a sardonic laugh. "Didn't know what might come in handy, so I had them shift half our workshop over here, just in case we needed to extract any spare parts at the last minute."

Ying made her way over, pausing when she noticed a familiar figure sitting against the side of a tree. His gangly legs were bent at a stiff angle, knees hugged to his chest as he stared blankly ahead at the open sea.

"Chang-en? Are you all right?" she asked.

He startled, snapping his neck around to face her. "Oh, Ying. When did you get here? I'm fine. Why wouldn't I be?" he said quickly. "What's going on? Are you going somewhere?"

Chang-en didn't seem as fine as he proclaimed himself to be, not with that dazed aura about him and the slight tremor in his usually chirpy voice. He averted his gaze, refusing to meet hers. Instead, he began plucking at blades of grass and then tossing them aimlessly to the side.

Maybe he's worried about An-xi too, she thought, dismissing the grain of suspicion that floated across her mind.

"I'm going after An-xi and the others, to see if I can help. I should have been the one to go, not An-xi," Ying said, the guilt stirring deep within her. She gave Chang-en a squeeze on the shoulder. "Don't worry. I'll bring him back safely."

"You . . . will?" Chang-en looked up, a sliver of hope threading through the slant of his eyes.

"I promise."

There was no time to waste. Ying spun on her heel and went on her way. Her original Octopus prototype was far smaller and had a much lighter frame than the new Bladebreakers, so if she moved quickly, then there was still a good chance she might be able to catch up.

"Ying," Chang-en called after her.

She turned.

"You come back safely too."

CHAPTER 32

THE ATMOSPHERE IN THE PALACE WAS DENSE and suffocating, with an air of pessimism that had crept into every nook and cranny. The stewards and maidservants walked with their heads bowed, single-mindedly heading for their destinations. Gone was the idle chatter and occasional melodies of the zither that used to drift above the gilded rooftops, replaced instead by the silence of a people in wait—waiting for the blade to fall.

Even though Nian was under strict orders to do nothing but rest, her mind had done everything but. The Monggu clan, the first beile, the pirates—all these thoughts kept circling inside her. *What about me? What can I do to help?* she kept wanting to ask.

Finally, her chance had come.

"Your Excellency, is there something you wish to speak to me about?"

Nian was standing in the front parlor of Qingning Hall, after having been summoned by Ye-yang out of the blue. A tiny trace of anticipation wormed its way inside her, amplified by the days of boredom she had spent recovering from her injuries. The wounds on her back had already started to close, the burning pain from the raw, bleeding claw marks slowly transiting to an irksome itch as the scar tissue formed.

Ye-yang looked up from the map that he was studying and smiled. "The physicians tell me that you're recovering well," he remarked. "I should probably let you rest, but these are . . . difficult times, and I'm afraid I shall once again need to add to your burden."

There was a tiredness reflecting through the creases at the corners of his eyes, and through the visible tension in the muscles of his neck.

"Follow me," he said, turning to head for the inner chambers. "There's something I want to show you."

Nian trailed along, her mind curiously cycling through the various possibilities of what he could ask of her. A bookcase in the High Commander's sleeping quarters hiding a secret passage was not part of any such equation that she had come up with.

A nondescript bronze paperweight that was cast in the mold of a dragon sat on the shelf, and Ye-yang had rotated it three notches clockwise and two notches counterclockwise. The sound of rotating gears echoed through the walls, followed by a soft click. The entire bookcase swung open.

"Come," Ye-yang said, leading the way down a flight of stone steps.

Nian found herself passing through a narrow passageway that was some distance underground, well-lit by a series of gas lamps hanging at regular intervals. The air in the tunnel was surprisingly warm, as were the blocks of stone that lined its walls. Hot water pipes were running behind them, perhaps, same as the heating systems that were embedded beneath the floorboards of every palace hall.

At the end of the short passage, they passed through an archway and emerged into a secret chamber—or a workshop. The air stilled, and the breath that Nian was about to release remained trapped down her throat.

This is . . . It's A-ma's workshop . . .

How was this possible?

Her gaze flitted back and forth and everywhere at once, yet every single detail pointed to the same conclusion. She was staring at a replica of her father's workshop. The placement of the shelves, the order of the tools—and even the octagonal lamp that had sat on the rightmost corner of the tabletop. She picked up the lantern, turning it slowly.

This was the same lamp that she had first seen in Ye-yang's study. The one that he had made for Ying.

"This workshop sits directly under Guanju Hall, and this is why the hall has been under construction for so long," Ye-yang explained.

"Guanju Hall . . ." Nian murmured, letting each character ruminate in her mind.

The name that had been given to the newly renovated palace hall originated from a fairly well-known Qirin poem, several dynasties past. Nian remembered reading the poem in a compendium that her father had bought from a Qirin merchant during one of his travels. It was a poem of love—two elegant sentences that spoke volumes about the feelings of one man for the girl of his dreams.

And Ye-yang had built all of this for Ying.

Even though she had already known about the relationship between Ye-yang and her sister for some time, the sight of this place still left her overwhelmed. How much did Ye-yang love Ying, to have gone to the extent of creating this little piece of home for her here within the palace?

"I owe you an apology, Nian. I should not have accepted the betrothal, knowing that it would very likely hurt you one day," Ye-yang said.

Nian shook her head. A slight sting prickled at the back of her throat, a reminder of how naive she had been before. "It wasn't your fault. At that time, no one could have said no," she replied. "You've already done more than enough for me."

During her time in Fei, Ye-yang had been nothing but gracious and kind toward her, even going to lengths to tutor her in the ways of governance and politics. He had seen value in her that she had not even seen in herself, and for that she would always be grateful.

Ye-yang picked up the octagonal lamp, staring at the images that it was casting upon the walls.

"I had hoped to be able to bring Ying here one day, and I even dared entertain the possibility that she would agree to stay." A rueful smile hung upon Ye-yang's lips. "But I don't think that day will ever come."

"Did something happen?" Nian asked.

"Is it wrong to want to protect the ones you love, Nian? To want to keep them out of harm's way?" He set the lamp back down. "I always believed that it was the right thing to do, but now . . . now I'm not so sure."

Nian had not seen Ying since her sister had returned to the guild to work on the Bladebreaker project, but the last she had heard from

Ye-kan was that Ying had volunteered to be one of the Bladebreaker pilots, to seek out and destroy Monggu Yutai's Blades.

"Ying is not the sort of girl who needs to be protected, Your Excellency. That has never been who she is," she answered. "What my a-jie yearns for, what she has dreamed of ever since we were children, is freedom. Freedom to make her own choices and to chart her own path, independent of what people tell her she should or should not do. Ying is the girl who leaps off cliffs and dives in freezing water, because her thirst for knowledge has always been greater than her fear of even death. Is that not why you love her?"

Ye-yang's lips curved wistfully, staring up at the silhouettes of him and Ying cast by the lamp, standing side by side atop the city walls, looking up at a meteor shower raining down from the skies.

"Yes, that's why I love her," he murmured. "Yet I tried too hard to clip her wings. To tie her to my side."

"It is not too late, Ye-yang a-ge," Nian said. It felt appropriate, addressing him this way, without the awkwardness and formality that had always lain between them. Like things were finally being restored to their rightful place. "Ying will come around, because she loves you just as much. I know that."

"I hope you're right." Ye-yang took a deep breath to adjust his state of mind, then he said, "But that's not why I've brought you here today. There is something very important that I am going to tell you, and that I need your help with."

He walked over to the left side of the workshop, where four large, cylindrical kaen-gas tanks sat against the wall. "Each one of these tanks contains up to three barrels of kaen gas. One of them alone is sufficient to trigger an explosion that can bring down an entire room. Four together—an entire building."

"Why are you telling me this?" Nian asked, a sense of dread rising up inside her.

"Once the war against the Monggu clan breaks out, Ye-lu will make his move. He will come for the palace, and he will come for the imperial seal. Why do you think this is so?"

"For legitimacy. Without the seal, he will always be a traitor. A rebel."

"Correct. Legitimacy may not matter to Monggu Yutai, because he has strayed off that path a long time ago, from the moment he chose to seek allyship with the Empire and turn his sword against those of his blood. Ye-lu is different. Ye-lu is an Aogiya, and if he wins, it is not entirely impossible for him to convince the clan chiefs that he deserves to be High Commander, despite his betrayal. After all, we Antarans have always valued strength in our leaders—that is why the clans swore fealty to my father in the first place.

"Very soon, I must head to the front line to lead the banners in our charge against the Monggu fleet. When that time comes, I shall leave the defense of Fei and Qianlei Palace in Ye-kan's hands."

Nian bit back her surprise. Qianlei Palace was the seat of the Aogiya High Command.

Leaving Ye-kan to defend the palace and city spoke volumes about the amount of trust that Ye-yang had placed in him.

"When Ye-lu marches upon Qianlei Palace, I want you to help Fourteen to lure him to Guanju Hall." Ye-yang rested a hand upon a kaen-gas tank, running his fingers across the metal until he came to a coarse bundle of hemp string hanging off the side of the tank. One end of the rope had been fed into the tank through the top, while the other extended back toward the passageway that they had come through.

Like the wick of a firework.

"You want to blow up this entire place," Nian whispered.

"It will be extremely dangerous, because you will not have much time to work with. When you reach Guanju Hall, you must come down here and light these to trigger the explosions, and then you can escape through the passageway that leads back to Qingning Hall." Ye-yang's gaze dimmed, his lips settling in a somber line. "You can, of course, choose not to do this. I would not force you to take on such risk if you are unwilling."

"Why me? Why are you not telling this to Ye-kan?"

"Number Fourteen is intelligent, but tends to be impulsive and is easily ruled by his emotions. Ye-lu may use this against him." He hesitated. "I am merely erring on the side of caution, because we cannot afford to fail. In the event that Ye-kan is unable to fulfill his mission of defending the palace, you are the only one who I can trust to step in."

Nian was deeply honored that Ye-yang would entrust her with such a critical task, yet there were still doubts that lingered at the back of her mind. It was the way he didn't look her in the eyes, like he was hiding something. But what?

She placed a hand on the cold, metal surface of the gas tank, imagining the earth-shattering impact that would rock the foundations of the palace once its contents were ignited. This entire workshop—and Guanju Hall above it—would collapse into nothing more than scorched rubble.

"I'll do it," she said, quiet resolve shining in her almond eyes.

After all, wasn't this what she had been waiting for? The chance to make a difference. The chance to do her part to defend her people, her home, against the multitude of dangers that threatened to sink them.

"Thank you," Ye-yang replied. He reached over and patted her on the shoulder, as affectionately as her own brother would. "You are just as brave as Ying, Nian, in your own way."

He led her out of the workshop and back into Qingning Hall, coming to a stop in front of the map that he had been perusing before she came in. The same map he had used to teach her about the various issues facing the nine isles.

"We've reached a turning point in Antaran history," Ye-yang said, fingers gliding across the map's surface. "If we lose this war, then the journey ends here, but if we win—" He moved his index finger across the Dunzhu Straits, tapping at the shores of the Empire. "I may not be around to witness the arrival of that day, when an Antaran sits upon the dragon throne—but perhaps you will."

CHAPTER 33

WHEN YING SET OFF, SWIRLING STORM CLOUDS had begun to gather above the Dunzhu Straits, casting a bleak shadow across the isles. Beneath the surface of the ocean, the turbulence of the waves was replaced by calm and serenity, as if the tempest brewing above did not exist at all. Ying sat alone in her little golden sphere, traversing across the seafloor.

According to the coordinates they had received from the Order's surveillance airships, the Monggu fleet had been sighted in this vicinity, so this should be where the other Bladebreakers would have been headed. Through the curved glass window, she surveyed the murky surroundings, searching for any sign of the Blades.

It didn't take long.

Ying had only steered her vessel a short distance forward when she spied the familiar gleam from the metallic roof of a Blade. From afar, they resembled giant whales, undulating fanlike tails sending bursts of foaming bubbles rising to the water's surface. There were two of them, she counted, gliding northwest of her current location.

Only two?

Something didn't feel right. An uneasiness that crawled inside her, whispering a grim warning to her subconscious.

The Order had clearly reported the sighting of at least six Blades, but where were the others? Had they not been deployed, or were they intentionally arranged in a sparse defensive formation, lurking where the light could not reach?

She held back, keeping a safe distance so that the Blades wouldn't spot her. Squinting through the darkness, she searched for An-xi and the others. Given the head start that they had, they should have reached here by now.

A glimmer of gold caught her eye in the westerly direction, on the opposite side of the Blades from where she was.

That had to be them.

Ying spent a moment trying to plot the shortest course it would take to get over there, then it suddenly struck her that something *else* was very wrong.

They're in range. Someone should have fired a Bladebreaker by now.

Yet nothing was happening. The sea remained an inky swathe of calm, save for the slow spin of the Blades' propellers and the yawning oscillations of their metallic tails. Through the misty glass panes, tiny figures scuttled along the corridors and cabins, carrying on with business as usual.

Why?

According to the plan, the pilots of the Bladebreakers were supposed to fire their weapons the moment they sighted a Blade. Within each vessel was a button that would open the back compartment of the submersible to unleash the weapon hidden within. Any nearer and they would be at risk of being spotted—and annihilated.

Ying swiftly spun her vessel around, steering away from the Blades in order to swing around them from the back. As she got closer, she noted the relative positions of all six Bladebreakers, their dull bronze shells bobbing silently in the water.

Still nothing.

No doors were opening, no silver serpents being fired toward their targets.

It had to be a malfunction, but how was that possible? How could all six Bladebreakers encounter the same fault, when they had checked the mechanisms on each vessel several times over the night before?

A flash lit up the darkness of the waters, snatching her attention away. Ying watched in abject horror as a projectile shot out from one of the Blade's underwater cannons, sluicing through the water and toward one of their submersibles.

"No!" she screamed into the abyss, pressing her palms against the frosty glass. "Get out of there!"

Time slowed.

The cannonball—a silver, shadowy globe drifting through the darkness like an eclipsed moon. Bad luck, the villagers back home would say, because nothing good could come when light had been swallowed by the heavens. An eclipse of light was an eclipse of hope.

It hit its mark, the force of the impact causing the vessel's glass window to shatter instantaneously. There was no explosion, no flames, but in that moment the silence seemed all the more terrifying. The water around the broken submersible was slowly stained with a darker shade of black—with the blood of its pilot.

"An-xi!" Ying cried, recognizing the familiar scrawny figure of her friend.

He lay unconscious, half of his torso dangling out through the circular hole where the window once was.

Two more flashes of light streaked through the water. Another submersible went down.

Instead of turning her vehicle around to escape like the others were, Ying grabbed the small emergency ventilation device that hung from the wall—a conical bronze mouthpiece connected to an oilskin breathing bag—and strapped it around her head. Then she pushed open the hatch and swam out, kicking her way toward An-xi. The icy-cold water prickled against her skin, punishing her with the sting of a thousand needles.

Please, An-xi, stay with me.

Struggling through the growing numbness in her limbs, Ying tried to pull An-xi free from his submersible before gravity pulled it into the depths and dragged them with it. An-xi's legs had been crushed by the vessel's collapsed control panel, and it took almost all her energy to extricate him from the deformed heap of metal. What little amount of air she had in her breathing device ran out, and quickly, the first traces of seawater seeped into her lungs. Looking up, the shimmer of the water's surface seemed like an impossible distance away.

Just as her final vestiges of hope seemed to fade, a silhouette emerged from one of the Blades, swimming toward her. As the person came closer, Ying wondered if the cold was conjuring hallucinations in her mind, because it almost seemed as if she recognized the face behind that ludicrous bowl-like helmet.

Wenjun?

Ying thought she would have been numb to grief by now, but no. It still hurt all the same. She had cried till her tears ran dry, railed at the heavens till her voice grew hoarse, and then despair finally set in—when she realized that nothing she did would be able to turn back time.

Even though she was wrapped in three layers of thick blankets and a lit burner sat by her side, Ying still couldn't dispel the cold and hopelessness from inside her. An everlasting winter had taken root inside her heart and would no longer leave. Curled up against the floor-to-ceiling glass windows of her cabin on board the *Diamond*, she stared out into the darkness of the waters, eyes open but not seeing.

"If the Bladebreakers succeed, though, that would be a great achievement, wouldn't it? The guild will be rewarded handsomely for it, and so will the pilots."

That was the last thing An-xi had said to her—would ever say to her.

And what had she said in reply?

She had been so casually dismissive, thinking that he was wasting her time with these pointless questions.

By the time Wenjun had pulled them into the *Diamond*, An-xi was already gone. She would never know if he had died from the lacerations to his torso, caused by the exploding shards of glass and metal, or from drowning, slowly suffocating as water filled his lungs. Or maybe even from the sheer excruciating cold. Either way, it must have hurt terribly. An-xi always had a ridiculously low tolerance for pain.

She closed her eyes, memories of the better times they had shared replaying over and over in her mind. It had been much simpler then, back during the days of the guild's apprenticeship trial. Boring lessons, airship duty, dormitory nights, all filled with echoes of An-xi's condescending, self-important jibes and Chang-en's witty, one-line retorts.

The corners of her lips inadvertently lifted.

How could someone be as insufferable as Niohuru An-xi? Always preaching one lesson or the other, as if he was smarter and better than any other guild apprentice? Yet somehow, along the way, they had squabbled themselves into a strong friendship, built upon their common love for engineering, their shared suffering within the guild, and an understanding that maybe tolerating each other was not so bad after all.

It's my fault. I should have been the one piloting the Bladebreaker. Not you.

If she had been there on time and gotten into that submersible like she was supposed to, then none of this would have happened. He had died because of her.

At the thought of what could have been, of the lofty dreams her friend used to have that would now go unfulfilled, the tears began to stream down her cheeks once again.

The door to the cabin creaked open, and Yunshang walked in, pigtails swaying as she balanced the clay teapot and two cups in her hands.

"How're you feeling?" the girl asked, settling down across from her. "I made some ginger tea. It'll help with expelling the cold."

Ying took one glance at the wisps of steam issuing from the mouth of the earthenware cup that Yunshang was holding up, then she turned silently back toward the window.

"I just went to say goodbye to An-xi." A pause. A light sniffle escaping. "He still owes me a game of four-colored cards, you know?"

Through the reflection in the glass, Ying saw Yunshang huddling with her knees drawn close to her chest, clutching the cup of tea tightly between her fingers.

"I should have known better than to trust an Antaran. Erdangjia says Antaran boys never keep their word, but I didn't believe her. I mean, how was I supposed to know? Look at him! He's just one of those pale-faced, harmless, scholarly types. He couldn't even beat me in an arm wrestling match!" She laughed, but it came out sounding choked up, like grief had buried itself down her throat. "He promised to show me around Fei one day, you know? Insisted that it was the most beautiful city I would ever lay eyes on, and that he was going to build the most magnificent tower that scraped the clouds, so tall that we could pluck the stars from the sky. What a liar."

Ying believed that. An-xi's ambition was to become an architect, the greatest one in the nine isles, if he could help it.

"When the Order conquers the Empire, I'll build us a new capital, even grander and more breathtaking than Fei. Wide paved roads for double-decker steam carriages and mechanical palanquins, multistory airship holding yards, bamboo tracks connecting every household so a freshly roasted goose can be delivered to your doorstep from the Silver Spoon. Oh, and right in the center of it all, a palace more majestic than Qianlei Palace. Pillars brushed with gold, pearl-white jade for roof tiles, murals on giant

rotating drums that paint the story of our heroic victory over the Qirin. It'll be called—the Forbidden City."

"*In your dreams, Niohuru,*" Chang-en had said.

Yes, only in their dreams.

Yunshang broke down into fits of sobs, her entire frame quivering violently.

"We never finished that game. We should have finished it," she cried.

Ying's eyes brimmed with tears once again, yet she could not muster a single comforting word to say to Yunshang.

The Blood Phoenix shouldn't have rescued her. They should have let her drown in that wretched watery grave, so that she wouldn't have to grit her teeth through the pain of losing one of her closest friends, and bear the guilt of being the one who survived.

The cabin door swung open again. Wheels creaked against the floorboards, and a familiar silhouette appeared at the doorway.

CHAPTER 34

"Yunshang, that's enough," a stern voice interrupted. "Go back to your cabin and wash your face. Don't let your tears cheapen the value of his death."

The Qirin girl hurriedly wiped away her tears, retreating obediently from the room. Li-na wheeled herself in, and the door shut behind her.

Ying didn't even bother turning to face the pirate captain, even as she knew that Li-na's glacial gaze was boring through the back of her head. Her heart was bleeding, raw from the overwhelming sorrow that continued to carve her apart bit by bit.

She did, however, have questions that she wanted answered.

"Why?" she asked.

"Why what?"

"Why did you bother to rescue me? Is it because you want to use me as a hostage? Because then you might as well throw me back out there."

"I don't need to resort to such despicable tactics," Li-na replied, sounding slightly offended by the insinuation. "I rescued you because I could. The same way I rescued all the girls in my fleet."

Ying scoffed, shooting Li-na a poisonous glare. She didn't believe any of that. "Don't make yourself sound so noble," she said. "And don't think I'll be grateful to you for what you did. You *killed my friend*, and if you choose to let me live, trust me when I say that you will come to regret it."

"I never claimed to be noble, child, because that is a luxury that I could never afford. I do whatever it takes to survive, even if it means I have to become a villain." Li-na came up to her side, staring out through the glass at the gloomy darkness. "We can't send you directly back to Fei, but we'll arrange for a small sampan that you can easily row back to shore."

"I'm not going back."

"No?"

"No."

Going back to Fei the first time had been a mistake. If she had never let Ye-yang coerce her into returning, then none of this would have happened. Her presence only caused more trouble, instead of providing respite. It always had. To Nian, to Wen, to her friends, and possibly even to Ye-yang.

Master Gerel had always insisted that she was too full of herself—and maybe he was right.

"You're running away," Li-na said, not disguising the reproach in her tone.

"So what if I am? It's none of your business. If you're not going to kill me, then it's up to me where I want to go next. I'm never going back to Fei."

To Ying's astonishment, Li-na took off the shawl that always kept her covered from the waist down and stood up from her wheelchair. Lifting the hem of her black trousers, she revealed a pair of silver calves peering out from above her leather boots.

Mechanical limbs, like the replacement arm worn by Master Kyzo, the guild's airship expert.

"I know what you must be thinking," Li-na continued. "Why do I choose to use the wheelchair, if these mechanical limbs allow me to walk?" She sat back down, letting the cotton fabric fall back down to her ankles. "I lost my legs in the same battle that cost me my husband, and I would have bled to death if Master Cixin hadn't found me off the shores of Yokre and welded these new limbs onto my body—without my consent."

Master Cixin is from the Monggu clan? That explained many things—like why Monggu Yutai had control over so many Blades, and why Li-na had entered into an alliance with the man, despite her blatant disdain for him. A life debt was not so easily repaid.

"I am grateful that she helped me survive, but I also came away with an important realization of what little agency I had over my own life. The Cobra's Order robbed me of my legs, and the Monggu clan insisted on forcing a new pair back on. I had no say in any of that." A hint of pain flashed across her eyes. "I thought of running away then too. Of hiding in the mountains where I would never have to see anyone again. In my mind, I was worthless. Life had no meaning, not when I was merely a puppet that could be manipulated according to the whims and fancies of others." She paused. "Do you know why I changed my mind?

"Because I found Keyan. That was three years ago, somewhere near the main pier of Yokre, when I was trying to get off the isle. She was begging for food by a street corner, all covered with dirt and baked in grime—and when she saw me she clung on to my wheelchair, refusing to let go. I bought her a meat bun, thinking that it would send her on her way, but she never left. One meat bun, and her tears melted into a smile—and it was that smile that taught me my purpose. I wasn't worthless. I hadn't lost all agency. I could still make choices, no matter how small, to take back control of my life. If I could buy a girl a meat bun and turn her life around—then surely I could do more.

"They can bind these metal legs to me, but they cannot force me to use them against my will. I may be a pirate, but I can abide by my own principles. For one, I do not kill indiscriminately. Your friend's blood is not on my hands, just as the attack off Larut was not of my doing."

Li-na turned to Ying, her gaze softening. In that moment, Ying saw the shadow of her e-niye reflecting in the captain's eyes. Warm, comforting, reassuring.

"I cannot stop you from running away. That is your prerogative. But I think it's worth spending some time to think about what your own purpose is, and what you want to make of your life. Niohuru An-xi didn't run away, and for that, he died with honor."

Ying's first instinct was to reject Li-na's suppositions. Li-na didn't know her, didn't understand what she had been through, so who was she to draw these conclusions based on her own experiences?

But what is *my purpose?*

She had once believed that her life goal was to become a great engineer, the same way her a-ma had been, but her journey through the guild had made her uncertain. What made a great engineer? Was it someone like A-ma, who chose to squirrel away his own talent because he was so averse to the idea of war and bloodshed? Or was it someone like Master Lianshu, who was willing to go to any extreme for the sake of her creations, who would willingly sacrifice her family and friends in that pursuit of knowledge? Or perhaps it was the mysterious Master Cixin, who was such a brilliant architect that she even dared attempt to engineer another person's life?

A great engineer protects.

That was what it meant to her. The desire to protect those she loved and cared about was what drove her decisions. It was the reason why she left the guild, and why she later returned; why she chose to shield Yunshang from the grappling hook during the Tournament of the Seas, and why she turned around to help the Blood Phoenix crew while they were battling the Eels; why she created the Bladebreakers, and why their failure had left her broken.

Conviction grew roots, once again anchoring itself inside her heart and mind.

She closed her eyes, exhaling slowly.

"I'll go back," she said, turning to face Li-na.

She would return to Fei, because her work there wasn't finished, because there were still people who were worth protecting. Her grief at An-xi's loss would need time to heal, even as those emotions were already beginning to sediment, the murky waters in her mind gradually turning clear once again.

The captain paused at the doorway. "I thought you might," she said. "We'll surface in a few hours, once we have the cover of nightfall."

"Wait," Ying called out. "I have one more question."

"Hmm?"

"Where are the other Blades?" she asked. This was what she had been grappling with before everything spiraled out of control, and she had an inkling that it was of critical importance to the larger scheme of things.

Li-na pursed her lips together, her eagle-like gaze taking on a sharp, deliberate edge. "They're sailing toward Larut, not Fei. Only two were deployed here to distract your Bladebreakers. Did you never consider why the pirate fleets have been particularly active in the vicinity of Larut recently?"

Larut.

They were headed for Larut.

That had been Monggu Yutai's plan all along, part of the intricate web that he had been carefully weaving, each thread gossamer thin, evading detection. His real point of entry into the nine isles had been Larut all along, not the capital, and preparations had begun long ago—as early as when the ominous Phoenix flare first blazed high in the night sky.

But there was one more thing that Li-na had revealed. Something that made the blood in her veins run ice-cold.

"How did you know we call them Bladebreakers?" she whispered.

The undisguised pity in Li-na's eyes felt like a dagger stabbing her through the heart. The captain sighed. "Surely you must have guessed by now?"

A spy. Within the guild.

That was why the Bladebreakers had failed.

They had been sabotaged.

"Why are you telling me all this? What's in it for you?" she asked. Li-na confused her. The pirate captain was working for Monggu Yutai; she had even tried to sell them out to the clan chieftain before, hadn't she? Yet at the same time, Li-na had rescued her from a certain death, talked her into returning to Fei, and revealed all Monggu Yutai's plans, despite knowing that they stood on opposing sides in this war.

Li-na's lips twisted in a sardonic smile. "Like I said, I don't claim to be a good person. I'm only someone who wants to survive—ideally on my own terms," she replied. "The Blood Phoenix cannot dream of defeating Monggu Yutai, but the same cannot be said of the Cobra's Order. Have you heard the saying: 'the enemy of my enemy is my friend'?" The captain held out her hand to Ying. "I would like to propose a partnership."

⁓

"Welcome to the engine room! The beating, breathing heart of a Blade," Wenjun announced, waving her hands melodramatically in the air.

A large kaen-gas furnace sat in silence at one end of the cabin they had entered. Steel pipes ran in all directions, forming a haphazard maze of arms that extended from the monstrous bronze body and led to other parts of the ship. This was the single most important room on board the *Diamond*, even more so than the pump room Ying had seen before. It was as Wenjun said—the vessel's heart.

This was the final leg of the tour that Li-na had instructed the fleet engineer to take her on. A lesson, really, on deconstructing the inner workings of a Blade.

On any other day, this knowledge would have lit a fire of enthusiasm within Ying. Yet as she followed Wenjun over to the engine map that was hanging across from the furnace—a long parchment that stretched from ceiling to floor, filled by a hand-drawn sketch labeling every single part of the engine and every outlet pipe leading away from here—the only thing she felt was emptiness and loss.

"This map is probably self-explanatory, so I won't go into the details. Feel free to ask if you've got any questions, though," Wenjun babbled. She patted the silver pipe leading in the eastward direction. "This is the one that goes to the air pumps. The one that we fixed."

Ying stared at the yellow parchment, saying nothing.

Although she still didn't know the purpose behind showing her all this, she could only trust that Li-na had good reason for it. Except she wasn't sure if she should trust Li-na at all.

"*If there's one thing I've learned from these years upon these seas,*" the captain had said before sending her to Wenjun, "*it's that all knowledge is useful knowledge. It's only a matter of time before it comes in handy.*"

"Is that all?" she asked.

"Just one final thing—my favorite part of the ship, if I'm being honest."

The fleet engineer lifted the engine map off its hook and dropped it to one side, revealing a concealed door. She grabbed a small handle and pulled it open, gesturing for Ying to take a look.

On the other side was a tiny space, only large enough for a single person, leading to another heavy metal door with a tiny porthole. A sturgeon floated past the circular pane of glass, oblivious to the two pairs of eyes watching its fluid movements.

"This little protrusion is the only section of the *Diamond* that isn't covered by a shield plate—and the only way to get in and out while the vessel is underwater," Wenjun declared with a flourish.

A buffer space to allow someone to leave the ship without flooding the engine room.

"I claim credit for this," the engineer added with a smug smile. "I was the one who suggested this extension to Master Cixin. In the event of an attack, protecting the engine room is top priority, failing which—a cowardly escape."

"Very useful . . ." Ying mused. So this was how Wenjun had gotten out to fetch her.

"Go inside and take a look for yourself!" Wenjun said. "I like to sit there and meditate sometimes, to get some peace and quiet."

Ying found herself jostled across, and then the door heaved shut behind her.

"Wenjun, what're you doing?" she asked, banging against the metal.

"Close your eyes and take a moment to listen to the sound—of nothing. Very calming! I highly recommend it!" the engineer's muffled voice replied.

Throwing her hands up in exasperation, Ying glanced around the tiny pod. She turned toward the porthole, staring into the solemn abyss of the deep ocean. The sturgeon had gone on its way, leaving only a few pathetic strands of brown seaweed drifting by.

Silence roared back at her. The sound of nothing, as Wenjun had put it.

Or the sound of death.

She sat down, leaning against the cold steel wall. After this, she would be boarding the sampan back to Fei, carrying with her a daring proposition from Li-na to the High Command—one that she was still apprehensive about.

"Hey, Wenjun," she said, "can I ask you something?"

"Hmm?" the other girl's voice vibrated through the door.

"Why did you choose the Blood Phoenix?"

In other words—why did you betray the Order? Why did you become a traitor?

It was a question almost too barefaced and brazen to be asked—but it tumbled out from her lips anyhow. Perhaps it was reassurance that she was seeking, affirmation that her choice to trust Li-na was the right one.

There was a long pause, almost long enough to make Ying wonder if Wenjun was still there. But then the engineer's voice wandered back, mellow and grave as it resonated through the walls, stripped of the insouciant façade she typically wore.

"Because they're my family, more than my actual family has ever been," she said. "I was sold to the Order when I was barely five, to help my useless father pay off his gambling debts. My grandmother cried, and my mother begged, but when push came to shove, they still let me go. 'This is for the best,' they said. 'You'll have a better life this way.' As if they weren't only trying to convince themselves of those excuses."

Ying listened quietly, shedding a silent tear for what Wenjun had been through. Not everyone had a life as blessed as her own, to have been able to grow up surrounded with the love and indulgence of family. She had taken it for granted before, but never again.

"To the Order, I was only ever a commodity. A tool that they bought for a fair price. They stripped me of my name, my identity, and trained me for ten years until I became the weapon that they needed me to be. Then they threw me into the sea and left me for dead." A bitter, self-deprecating laugh echoed from Wenjun's lips. "There were five of us, y'know, given this exact same mission. To infiltrate the Blood Phoenix. To spy on them. Burn them from within. I was the only one who clawed myself out of the Dunzhu Straits alive. If I hadn't, they'd simply throw in another five, and another, until one of us succeeded.

"Da-dangjia had no reason to take me in, but she did. No reason to trust me, a girl claiming to have lost her memory, but she did. She was the one who gave me back my name—Wenjun. A new name. A chance to start over. A chance to be *free*."

The sincerity and conviction in Wenjun's words tugged at Ying's heartstrings. It was an echo, a mirror of what she had heard many times before, from different mouths, in different forms, all converging on the same truth.

The Blood Phoenix was home. Family. Freedom and belonging.

And in return, its crew willingly dedicated their undying loyalty.

Ying's misgivings diminished, the resolve in her eyes crystallizing like a diamond under pressure. War was coming, brewing like a turbulent storm upon the horizon. Monggu Yutai would not rest until he had the nine isles within his despotic grasp, and the Order would have to fight the battle of their lives to stop him. Although she was only one girl—she was not powerless.

Like Li-na said, she could still make choices, no matter how small, to take control of her life and future.

To protect the right of her people to live in freedom.

To protect their tomorrow.

She had made her decision. Only time would tell whether it was the right one.

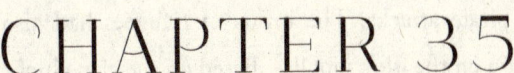

CHAPTER 35

THE FAILURE OF THE BLADEBREAKER MISSION CAST a grim shadow upon the fate of the nine isles. Only three out of the six submersibles had made it back to Fei, and the account relayed by the survivors had been harrowing.

The Bladebreakers had malfunctioned.

They had been discovered.

Cannons were fired—and blood stained the seas.

Nian sat quietly within the secret workshop beneath Guanju Hall, seeking solace in the familiarity of her surroundings. Looking around at the neat rows of tools hanging from their bamboo racks and the half-finished sketches lying on the workbenches, she could almost deceive herself into believing that Ying would burst in at any moment.

But she wouldn't, because according to the guild, Ying had gone after the Bladebreaker crew and had not returned. They could only presume her dead.

"How could you not even tell me that you were going?" Nian murmured. Some things would never change.

At the same time at which they learned of the failed attempt, the High Command had also received news that Larut was under attack. The Jangmu chieftain had sent an urgent missive to Fei, reporting an invading fleet that numbered over fifty ships—the flag of the

Monggu clan flying at its forefront. Larut had already been severely weakened in the past months, having been suffering the aftereffects of several vicious pirate attacks. The influx of refugees had also placed a severe strain on the isle's supplies. Based on the clan chief's estimates, Larut would not last even three days.

The report sent shock waves across the court.

Even if the High Command were to redeploy the banners to Larut now, it might still be too late.

Nian had not seen any sign of Ye-kan nor Ye-yang ever since those reports came in. Had she not managed to coerce Qorchi and Nergui into telling her all this by threatening to stop taking her medicine, she might never have learned of any of it.

She shut her eyes, taking a brief moment to calm her own nerves. There was still hope that Ying was out there somewhere, alive, just like how she had survived the storm and the pirates before. And even if she wasn't . . . there was no time for grief, not when the fate of the nine isles hung in a precarious balance.

Nian was still lost in her own thoughts when a sudden *crash!* shook her out of her daze. One of the shelves in the workshop had almost toppled over, and several bronze and clay receptacles had been knocked onto the floor. Qorchi wobbled as he tried to regain his balance after his collision with said shelf, then he frantically made his way over to her.

"Lady Nian, here you are! We've been looking all over for you. You must come with me now," the chief steward said, panting as he spoke.

"What's the matter? Did something happen?"

"We must leave right away. The palace is under siege!"

Nian's eyes widened with alarm.

"It's the first beile. The first beile is marching on Qianlei Palace," Qorchi replied, panic lacing his words. "The fourteenth beile has arranged for a carriage to take us to the nearest camp of the Plain White Banner. Come, we have no time to waste!" He grabbed Nian by the arm and began dragging her toward the exit.

The first beile? So soon?

Ye-yang had predicted this would happen, but she thought that they would still have a few more days. She chided herself for being careless. Those calculations were based on the assumption that Monggu Yutai would attack Fei directly, but those plans had changed, and the front line had shifted to Larut instead. Now that Ye-yang had left for Larut to lead the defense against the invading Monggu clan, it was also time for Ye-lu to make his move.

"Where's the fourteenth beile?" she asked, following the chief steward down the narrow passage back toward Qingning Hall.

"He's at the palace gates. The palace guards and part of the Plain White Banner are holding the line against the first beile."

"How many men does the first beile have?"

"I'm not sure, but he appears to be marching with his Plain Red Banner. Those traitors," the steward spat. "If the entire banner has defected, then that would be around . . . five thousand."

Nian stopped. That number was far higher than what she had expected. Upon the discovery of Ye-lu's betrayal, they had immediately locked down the military camps of the Plain Red Banner to guard against this exact scenario. It was still too little too late. They had underestimated the loyalty of the bannermen to their commander.

There were only three hundred guards stationed in and around the palace, along with a small section of Ye-kan's Plain White Banner. The rest of his banner and the bulk of the Ula clan's defenses had been deployed to other critical locations around Fei.

Their attempt at defending the palace—and Fei—against the first beile was nothing short of doomed.

Doubts began to claw their way into Nian's mind. She glanced back toward the hidden workshop where the four kaen-gas tanks sat silently in wait.

Can I do this? What if I fail?

"Lady Nian, what are you doing? We must hurry! The first beile's men have not yet surrounded the back gate, but we don't know when things will change. We have to leave while we still can!" Qorchi pleaded.

His voice broke through the fog that had started to form inside her head, and she hurriedly shoved those intrusive thoughts aside.

"I'm not leaving," she said.

Qorchi's face turned ashen. "Lady Nian, please don't do this. Don't you know how dangerous it will be once the first beile's men breach the palace walls? The fourteenth beile clearly instructed for us to get you away from here as quickly as possible!"

"No." Nian shook her head resolutely. "I'm not going. There is something that I must do." Instead of heading toward the back of the palace, she took off running in the direction of the main palace gates instead. "Go ahead and evacuate with the others," she shouted.

"Make sure that you get as many of the palace attendants out of here as possible, and keep everyone away from Guanju Hall, understood?"

~~~

Dressed in the gray uniform of an ordinary palace steward, her long hair tied in a single braid behind her back, Nian climbed up the stone steps of the barbican main gate of Qianlei Palace.

Ye-kan stood at the top in his black brigandine armor, staring over the parapet wall at the rebel forces on the outside with a fire blazing in his eyes. A row of archers flanked him on both sides, bows raised and arrows notched, waiting for the command to fire.

"Ye-lu! Stand your banner down and surrender, otherwise I will have no choice but to give the order. I don't wish to use Antaran weapons against Antaran men," the fourteenth prince shouted.

"Number Fourteen, that's quite enough bravado from you," Ye-lu's nonchalant voice echoed in reply.

Peering through the gaps in the merlons, Nian saw the first beile riding upon his white stallion, standing at the head of his banner. The triangular flags of the Plain Red Banner flew proudly, and the soldiers stood in strict, regimental formation, all looking confident and assured. A gold-embroidered cobra, only meant to be worn by the High Commander, was emblazoned across his armor.

"Let's not even discuss whether or not your pitiful defenses stand any chance of victory, which is already a foregone conclusion, but the fact that you're standing up there wielding a sword on behalf of *your enemy*." A scornful smile stretched across Ye-lu's thin lips. "And you don't even realize it, do you?"

Hesitation and uncertainty flashed across Ye-kan's eyes.

"How do you think Lady Odval died, Ye-kan? How she *really* died?" Ye-lu continued.

Ye-kan's mother?

Nian had heard that Ye-kan's mother, Lady Odval, had killed herself shortly after the former High Commander's death, choosing to follow her husband into the next life. Stories of her unfailing loyalty had spread far and wide across the nine isles, painting her as a faithful and devoted wife. In hindsight, the speed at which the story had traveled did seem a little unusual, perhaps even intentional.

She glanced worriedly at the fourteenth beile, whose jaw muscles were pulled tight, the veins throbbing at his temples. Ye-kan cared deeply about his mother, often bringing up the memories that they had shared. She knew that he missed her greatly. Her death was the reason why Ye-kan had chosen to give up his love for engineering and become the military commander she had always hoped for him to be. If there was more to her death than met the eye, then . . .

"Number Fourteen is intelligent, but tends to be impulsive and is easily ruled by his emotions. Ye-lu may use this against him."

Ye-yang's words to her floated back to mind, as did the trace of suspicion that he had been hiding something from her then.

No . . . It can't be.

"Think about it, Number Fourteen. Was Lady Odval the sort of woman who would end her own life because of one man, even if that man is as great as our a-ma?" Ye-lu asked. "She was killed by the very person you are so foolishly serving. How did you think he became High Commander, when everyone believed that you were A-ma's favored candidate? Ye-yang killed her, because he knew that she would not let him win."

The revelation left Nian aghast. Ye-lu could well be lying, but her instincts told her that he spoke the truth. And Ye-yang knew it. This was the real reason why he was worried Ye-kan might not be able to fulfill his duty of defending the palace.

Her gaze fixed upon Ye-kan, who was standing still as a statue, his face a blank parchment.

After a long pause, Ye-kan finally spoke. "You're lying," was all he said.

"If you want to continue deceiving yourself, then so be it. Just know that even if you fight to your death helping him defend his position, he will not thank you for it. Ye-yang is the most heartless one of us all."

Even though Ye-kan remained expressionless, Nian could see the tremble in his shoulders and the tension in his clenched fists. What was going through his mind? How much was he hurting?

She quickly made her way to his side, placing one hand upon his arm. The fourteenth prince flinched, instinctively pulling his sword out of its scabbard. When he saw that it was her, a momentary haze of confusion clouded his eyes.

"What are you doing here?" he demanded. "I thought I told Qorchi and Nergui to get you out of the palace."

Nian pulled him back, where Ye-lu would not be able to see. Taking hold of his hand, she said, "I'm not leaving you here alone. Don't listen to Ye-lu. He's only trying to make you surrender."

I'm sorry, Ye-kan. There will be a time and place for your grief, but it is not now. If we don't stop him, then there'll be thousands more who will have to mourn the loss of their mothers and fathers, daughters and sons.

"But . . ."

"There's no time for buts. Ye-lu has been colluding with Monggu Yutai all along. Faking his own death, smuggling food and weapons to the tenth isle—all of it to seize power for himself. If you give in, then all is lost. Fei and the High Command will fall, and the nine isles will be soaked in blood. Think about the people, Ye-kan. They need you. *I* need you."

Ye-kan's expression wavered with uncertainty and apprehension, and Nian knew that deep down inside, he had come undone. But then he lowered his eyelids and took a deep breath, and when he opened them again, a shield of steel had been erected within him, wiping away all hints of consternation.

"I know," he said. "Don't worry, I won't let him get to me." He surveyed the rows of rebel soldiers, creases deepening across his forehead. "I'm not sure we can hold them off for much longer, though. There are too many of them."

"We need to draw Ye-lu to Guanju Hall," Nian said.

"Why? What are you trying to do, Nian?"

"I . . . have a plan. I don't have time to explain everything, and I can't be sure that it'll work, but it's the best chance we've got. Can you trust me on this?" She met his gaze firmly, hoping that her word would be enough. If she told him the truth, if she told him that this plan came from Ye-yang, would he still follow through with it? She wasn't sure, just as Ye-yang hadn't been sure.

Ye-kan hesitated, the muscles of his jaw tightening. For a moment, she wondered if he would say no, but then he nodded. His lips curved in a tired smile. "Even if I can't trust anyone, I'd still trust you."

A sliver of guilt streaked across Nian's heart, but she held her silence.

She couldn't afford to risk it. Not now.

Now was not the time for personal grievances to stand in the way of protecting the future of an entire people. The stakes were too high. Whatever lay between Ye-kan and Ye-yang—injustice or misunderstanding—would have to be untangled another time.

Ye-kan walked up to the parapet, holding up the one thing that Ye-lu would need in order to legitimize his coup. The imperial seal of the High Command.

He was supposed to return the seal to Ye-yang upon the latter's return, but Ye-yang had asked for him to hold on to it, to lend him the authority to defend the capital in the High Commander's stead.

"If you want to become High Commander, then you'll need this," the fourteenth prince hollered. "But you'll have to step over my dead body to get it."

Once they were certain that Ye-lu had seen the seal, Ye-kan and Nian quickly retreated away from the palace gates, taking most of the palace guards with them. Behind them, Ye-lu's men began pounding their battering rams, and the thick, cast-iron hinges began to creak ominously under the strain. They did not stop to watch the drawbars break, nor Ye-lu's rebel army swarm into the palace grounds.

Nian paused in front of the entrance archway to Guanju Hall, taking a moment to steady herself as they waited for Ye-lu to arrive. It wouldn't be long; she could already hear the clangs of clashing swords and tortured battle cries fast approaching.

"When Ye-lu gets here, we need to lure him inside with us and seal the doors," she said.

"You want to trap him?" Ye-kan frowned. "Ye-lu is extremely cautious. He will not enter on his own."

"That will depend on exactly how much he wants the imperial seal, won't it?"

They barely had enough time to issue instructions to the palace guards before loud footsteps rounded the corner and Ye-lu and his men ran across the courtyard toward them, blades drawn and dripping with blood. Pointing his sword at his brother, the first beile said, "Ye-kan, hand over the imperial seal, and I'll pretend that this never happened. After I become High Commander, you can continue to be your fourteenth beile, living in your lap of luxury. I'll even deliver Ye-yang's head to you, to exact vengeance for what he did to your e-niye."

"If you can do that to Number Eight, then one day you can also do the same to me," Ye-kan replied coldly. He held up the jade seal on the palm of his right hand. "Even if I destroy this, I will never give it to you. If you want it, then you'll have to pry it from my dead fingers."

"Follow me," Nian whispered. She turned on her heel and ran into the hall, with Ye-kan trailing behind. Once they were gone, the palace guards stepped forward to form a barrier in front of the moon gate, each one prepared to defend the palace with their lives. The sounds of fighting resumed.

Nian led Ye-kan down the stairs and into the secret workshop, where the trap lay in wait.

"What is this place?" Ye-kan wondered out loud.

"Quick," she said, moving across the workshop. She followed the trail of the rope toward the passageway that led to the High Commander's quarters.

Ye-kan squatted down and picked up one of the hemp lines between his fingers. Grease came off the string.

"Wait, what exactly are you trying to do?" Ye-kan exclaimed. He marched over to Nian, grabbing hold of her wrist as she was reaching for a gas lamp from the wall. "Don't you know how dangerous that is? We can't predict the scale of the explosion! This entire place could come down on us!"

Turning to Ye-kan, she said, "Will you trust me?"

Their gazes locked, unspoken belief and conviction passing between them. Then Ye-kan suddenly wrapped one arm around her waist, pulling her close to him. He bent forward and pressed his lips against hers in a fierce, burning kiss. All the thoughts and meticulous plans were immediately wiped out of Nian's mind. He was the only thing she could see. His warmth and fervor enveloped her, threatening to swallow her whole.

When she had first stepped foot on Fei and into this palace, Nian had never imagined that the road would lead her here, fighting side by side and gambling her life together with this impetuous, brash, but also thoughtful and warm-hearted young man. In her mind, love was meant to be peaceful and tranquil, like how her a-ma and e-niye had been, and yet she had fallen so recklessly in love with someone who was like a fiery star, whom she yearned for even despite all the years of lessons in protocol and propriety telling her to turn the other way.

Their lips briefly parted, and she gasped to take in a breath.

"I love you," she whispered.

She had been meaning to tell him that ever since she clawed her life back from the iron grip of the qilin chimeras, but with the eruption of the war against the tenth isle, she had feared that she might never have the chance to.

As the words left her lips, a weight lifted itself off her shoulders.

A flicker of astonishment mixed with elation appeared in Ye-kan's eyes. "Nian, I—"

The words remained trapped down his throat as Nian reached out to place her hands upon the sides of his face, lifting herself on the tips of her toes to silence him with another kiss.

"Ye-kan, don't be foolish. You can't run away—the entire palace is surrounded!" Ye-lu's voice came booming from afar, echoing through the walls. Doors slammed shut. "What—"

It's time.

Stepping back, she spun around and ripped the gas lamp off its hook, smashing its glass casing against the wall to reveal the bare flame within. Pulling Ye-kan into the passageway, she lit the end of the hemp wick, watching as the wisps of black smoke began to rise and the rope rapidly char.

"Go!" she yelled, breaking into a run away from the workshop.

Hand in hand, they sprinted down the narrow passage, bracing themselves for what would happen next.

They had barely made it halfway up the flight of stairs to the High Commander's private quarters when the explosion rocked the entire palace. The force of the blast sent Nian and Ye-kan flying forward, landing heavily against the stone steps. Behind them, part of the passageway's ceiling was beginning to cave in, boulders falling one after the other, sending clouds of dust hurtling up into the air.

"Nian, quickly, the passage is going to collapse," Ye-kan shouted, scrambling to get back to his feet.

He reached his hand out toward her, but before she could take it, another quake sent her tipping backward, tumbling back toward the foot of the stairs. A hailstorm rained down upon her.

"Nian!"

CHAPTER 36

YING ARRIVED BACK TO A PALACE IN chaos. Terrified palace attendants were fleeing through the back gate, pushing and shoving at anyone who got in their way. A sinking feeling churned at the pit of her stomach.

"Have you seen Lady Nian? Or the fourteenth beile?" she asked, grabbing a steward by the arm.

The man swallowed hard, pointing one shaky finger in the northwest direction. "I—I—I don't know, but I saw the first beile leading his men toward Qingning Hall," he said.

Ying let go and ran, ignoring the painful blisters that laced her palms and feet, remnants from the arduous journey it had taken for her to get back to the capital. Just when she reached the High Commander's resting quarters, an ear-shattering blast shook the earth beneath her feet. Black smoke and dust clouds were billowing above the golden rooftops, accompanied by frantic shouting in the distance. Fear ripped through her heart, sparked by the thought that Nian could be caught in the cross-fire.

Please, don't let me be too late.

Qingning Hall was abandoned, its rooms shrouded in shadows. Ying rushed into the front parlor and then toward the inner quarters, searching for any sign of Nian or Ye-kan. Panic flooded her veins.

Then she heard voices echoing through the walls, voices that seemed to be getting closer to where she was.

There—

The violent quaking from moments ago had left a bookcase askew, revealing a hint of a hidden passageway peering out from behind. She dashed over and squeezed her hands through the gap. With a loud cry, she mustered all the strength she could, sending the entire shelf toppling to the ground. A flight of descending steps appeared before her eyes—and two figures scrambling up amid a flurry of dust and crumbling stone.

"Nian!"

She reached out her hand and grabbed hold of her sister, pulling the girl up to safety. The trio tumbled out of the doorway, landing in a heap on the wooden floor. Behind them, the ceiling of the passage collapsed, closing it off entirely. Ying clung on to Nian, half sobbing against her sister's shoulder.

She had barely made it. Any later and Nian would have been lost to her forever, the same way An-xi was.

Beside them, Ye-kan heaved a massive sigh of relief. Glancing her way, he said, "Thank the gods we're still alive."

∽

"A-jie, they said that you . . ."

"That I died? Wouldn't be the first time."

Ying patted her sister on the shoulder, returning her confused expression with a wry smile. They were sitting in the front parlor of Qingning Hall, together with Ye-kan, waiting for the update from the palace guards on the situation back at Guanju Hall. Flecks of dust and debris clung to their hair and faces, hints of blood seeping through the torn fabric of their robes.

According to a preliminary indication, the entire hall had collapsed from the explosion, burying the first beile and his men within. The remainder of Ye-lu's Plain Red Banner had thrown down their arms and surrendered once they learned of their commander's defeat. They would be temporarily incarcerated.

"How did you escape? Did you not reach the Bladebreaker contingent before the mishap?" Nian asked.

Ying winced, the mention of the Bladebreakers dredging up the agonizing memory of An-xi's death once again. She had meant to bring him home, so that he might have a proper burial, surrounded by family and friends, but she couldn't. It was already difficult enough for Li-na to smuggle her back to Fei without her dragging An-xi's remains with her. Wenjun and Yunshang had promised to give An-xi a respectable send-off, so she had no choice but to say her final goodbye to him on board the *Diamond*, leaving him in their hands.

She closed her eyes, breathed, shoving those intrusive thoughts back to the inner depths of her mind.

Honor his memory with your actions, Aihui Ying. Don't let him die in vain.

Her eyes flickered open, darkening with determination. "It's a long story. There's no time for that right now. After this, Fei should be secure. I must head to Larut immediately." As much as she hated having to face Ye-yang again, she had to convey Li-na's message to him.

Turning to Ye-kan, she said, "Monggu Yutai's main fleet is far larger than what we anticipated, and there are four Blades sailing with them. Can you afford to deploy more of your bannermen to Larut? Nian can stay in Fei to help manage the situation, but you should come along too. They'll need all the support they can get at the front line."

The fourteenth prince did not reply. Instead, he averted his gaze, jaw clenched. His fingers were clutching on to the mahogany arm-rests of his chair, nails almost digging into the wood.

"Ye-kan?"

"I'm not going. And I'm not sending any of my men to Larut."

"Excuse me?"

Ying stared at him in shocked silence, flabbergasted by his response. Had she heard him wrong? The nine isles were fighting for survival, yet he was refusing to send reinforcements? If she could set aside her personal feud with Ye-yang for the sake of this war, then what excuse did Ye-kan have to behave like a petulant child?

When Ye-kan turned back to face her, there was a cold, simmering rage in his eyes that left her nervous. Her righteous indignation wavered. A seed of doubt began to take root in her mind, dragging her back to one fateful day two years ago—a day that had changed many lives.

"Did Number Eight kill my e-niye?" he asked, each word layered thick with frost. It wasn't a question. It was an accusation.

Ying trembled, her clammy fingers gripping on to the sides of her robes. Some secrets were not meant to remain buried forever. Perhaps no secret ever could.

"Did he kill her!" Ye-kan shouted, even though they all knew that her silence was answer enough. The hurt and betrayal etched in the lines of his face made Ying want to shrivel in guilt. She had believed that keeping the truth from him was a way of protecting him, but in reality, it was only an excuse for her own cowardice.

"I'm sorry," was all that she could muster.

Ye-kan raised his fist in the air.

Nian leapt up and held him back. "What are you doing? This is exactly what Ye-lu wanted. He wanted to use this to turn us against one another, so that the Order will be weakened, so that our defenses will crumble! Can't you see that?"

"But he *wasn't lying*! Ye-lu didn't lie to me. *She did!*" Ye-kan swung his arm, causing Nian to lose her balance. She struck the side of the table, wincing at the impact. Ye-kan faltered, momentary remorse flashing across his eyes. Then he let out a loud roar. He picked up a vase from the shelf and flung it against the wall, splintering it into a dozen fragments of heartbreak.

Ying swallowed hard, her guilt and regret continuing to fester. "I know that nothing I say will change anything. I made a mistake. I betrayed your trust. Ye-yang . . ." She hesitated. It was not her place to apologize on Ye-yang's behalf. As someone who had also lost a parent to a wrongful death, she knew that forgiveness was far too much to ask. This was a debt that they could never repay. "Please, I'm not asking you to help me, or Ye-yang. The Antaran people need you."

"The Antaran people need their High Commander, and since Number Eight wanted that position so much, then he can shoulder this responsibility on his own. I owe you *nothing*," Ye-kan spat. He turned and stormed out of the chamber without looking back.

Ying crumpled against the back of her chair, but she knew that no amount of regret or despair would be able to turn back time. A mistake was a mistake, and some mistakes could not be repaired.

"A-jie . . ." Nian slowly lifted herself off the ground, walking back to Ying's side. "Why?"

"I was the one who killed the former High Commander, Nian," Ying said quietly. This was the first time she was revealing the truth to anyone, and the scar that she thought had healed was once again ripped apart, bloody and raw.

Nian's clamped a hand over her mouth, the shock in her eyes raw and undisguised.

"Ye-kan's mother, Lady Odval—she happened to bear witness to everything. Ye-yang did it to protect me."

Lady Odval's death might have been an inevitability, because the woman was a pebble in Ye-yang's path to consolidate power. But if not for her, perhaps Ye-kan's mother would not have died how and when she did. She had given Ye-yang the excuse to wield the sword.

She looked up at Nian, wondering if what her sister saw in return was a monster. A liar. A murderer.

"I'm so sorry, Nian. I just—"

"It was for A-ma, wasn't it? You killed the High Commander to seek revenge for A-ma."

Her lips trembled in a sigh. "Does the reason matter anymore?"

Vengeance was a vicious cycle to which there was no end. A lesson she had learned too late. She had sought her revenge, and now she owed Ye-kan his. Maybe the way of the Blood Phoenix was the wiser one—to let go of the past and focus on making the next day count. To find blessings in what they had instead of what they'd lost.

She lowered her gaze, waiting for the admonishment she deserved. But it never came.

Instead, Nian placed a hand upon her shoulder, saying, "You did what you did because none of us had the courage to. If I had been stronger, if Wen had been willing to listen, then things wouldn't have come to this." Her sister exhaled, long and slow, but there was no reproach in that breath. Only resignation. "What's done is done. Nothing we say or do will be able to bring A-ma back, or the High Commander, or Ye-kan's e-niye, but there are hundreds of Antaran lives that we can still save. Go to Larut, A-jie. Nergui and Qorchi can arrange for an airship to take you there. I'll try to convince Ye-kan to send the reinforcements. This—the war against Monggu Yutai and the pirates—this is far bigger than all of us."

Ying bit back her tears, gratitude flowing like a comforting waterfall inside her heart. In the darkest of times, she could always rely on Nian to be the voice of reason and comfort, like their a-ma and e-niye used to be.

"You know how we always say that Abka Han messed up our birth order?" she said.

Nian smiled through the sadness. "I know."

∽

As the airship approached the west coast of Larut, Ying could already see the dense defensive line of black ships sitting in formation along the opposite shore, facing off against the sizable Monggu fleet. The feeling of déjà vu sent a shiver up her spine, and fear tightened its grip over her heart.

Not so long ago, she had seen these same seas on fire, with the bodies of the dead littering the sand. Not so long ago, she had said goodbye to a dear friend, and set his ashes free upon these waters.

Now Larut was once again in flames.

Loud explosions ricocheted through the air as the airship made its descent, docking upon the grassland that had once been filled with laughter and revelry. Through the yun-mu windows of her cabin, Ying saw soldiers of the Order rushing about, the makeshift airship base in disarray as they struggled to handle the damaged airships and casualties being brought in.

The first person she saw when she stepped off the gangway and onto the grass was a familiar face. Master Kyzo, the guild master in charge of the Order's airship repair yard back in Fei, was standing with his back to her, scribbling down some instructions on a scrap piece of rice paper before shoving it at another engineer.

"Master Kyzo," she called.

Kyzo turned, his beady eyes lighting up when he saw her. "Aihui Ying?" He walked over, placing the cold fingers of his mechanical arm on her shoulder. A broad smile stretched across his fleshy face. "You're alive! Ha! I knew it. Never believed it when Lianshu said that you had died. What about the others? Niohuru and Emoto? Barra?"

Ying slowly shook her head. "They didn't make it. An-xi . . ." She choked up, tears threatening to spill out yet again.

Master Kyzo sighed, mumbling a prayer for their lost souls. "Take heart, young Aihui. They died in service of the nine isles and our people. Their sacrifice was not in vain."

But was that true?

Looking at the chaos around her—injured soldiers being stretchered from burning airships, engineers desperately trying to salvage the debris—she wondered if all their efforts had been futile. An-xi had died for nothing, because they were still going to lose.

"Did the entire guild get mobilized? Is Chang-en here too?"

The guild master's gaze shifted from side to side as he hemmed and hawed, unable to come up with a straight answer.

"What's the matter? Did something happen to him?" Ying asked hesitantly, unease rising up her gut.

Master Kyzo sucked in a long breath, then he said, "Ying, you have to promise me that you will stay calm after hearing this. Tongiya . . . he's alive, but he's been arrested by the High Commander's personal guard."

"What?"

"The entire Tongiya clan is facing charges of treason for aligning themselves with the first beile, including Chang-en. They'll face execution once the war has ended."

Treason.

Execution.

She had always known that the Tongiya clan served the first

beile. After all, Chang-en entered the guild's apprenticeship trial at Ye-lu's behest, the same way she had ridden on Ye-yang's nomination. But all that scheming and politicking belonged to their father's generation, belonged to the High Command and the court—not to them. They were only apprentices at the guild; what did treason have anything to do with—

Suddenly, a frightening possibility crossed her mind. She stared at Kyzo.

"The Bladebreakers . . . Chang-en couldn't have . . ."

Fragments of blurred memories cast shadows in her mind, hazy images and voices that slowly gained focus.

"*I'll do the locking up, Master Lianshu,*" he had said when he had taken the keys to the workshop on the eve of the Bladebreaker mission.

"*I'm fine. Why wouldn't I be?*" he had said when she found him sitting by the pier in a stupor after the Bladebreakers had already left.

"*Ying, you come back safely too,*" he had said when they waved goodbye. When she promised to bring An-xi home.

Ying staggered back, the weight of this striking her like a sledgehammer.

Chang-en was the spy. *Chang-en* was the one who had betrayed them. *Chang-en* was the reason why An-xi was dead.

But why?

Weren't they the best of friends? Or was she the only one who had been mistaken?

A smiling tiger. That was the nickname that An-xi had coined for Chang-en. To her, it had always been a joke. A nickname that Chang-en never denied, always shaking it off with another flippant gibe. But behind those easygoing smiles, those frivolous laughs, was someone Ying didn't recognize.

"Ying!"

She turned her head. Through the thin film misting her eyes, she saw Ye-yang marching toward her, his brigandine armor stained with blood and dirt. The black cloak pinned upon his shoulders billowed in the wind, framing him like the wings of a proud eagle. Relief at seeing him alive and well was mixed with the lingering resentment she still held over An-xi's death, forming a suffocating web inside her. She wanted to hate him, to rail at him once again for his role in all of this—yet at the same time, she couldn't deny that she didn't want to lose him either. She had already lost too many people who mattered.

Ying was swept up in a crushing embrace, his familiar scent of tie guan yin providing a shred of comfort to her bleeding heart.

"Thank goodness you're all right," he said, his warm breath tickling the side of her neck.

Ying didn't cry. Not this time.

She had already shed all the tears she could have shed. There was no purpose in that anymore.

She slowly pushed him away, taking a step back. Breathed in, then out. The surging waves inside her began to calm as she regained control of her own thoughts.

"There's something I need to speak to you about," she said, "but Chang-en—can I see him first?" she asked. She didn't think she would be able to move on with what she needed to do, not when her mind was in shambles.

Chang-en owed her an answer. He owed An-xi an answer. She wanted to hear what he had to say, how he would justify his actions, his betrayal.

Ye-yang moved forward, reaching out to her once again. Then he stopped. She caught the slight shiver in his steel-gray eyes, a hint of hurt threading through the silver flecks.

"He's being held in custody over in the southeast of the Jangmu village," Ye-yang said. "There's a temporary ceasefire, so I have some time to take you there."

Ying nodded, keeping her expression impassive, the muscles of her cheeks remaining still like the surface of a frozen lake. Whatever remained between her and Ye-yang was but a regretful echo of what could have been, of wasted opportunities swept away by the passage of time. There were only so many times a heart could break before there was nothing left but ash and dust.

Regardless, they had more important things to do now.

With the sweep of her sleeve, she turned and walked away.

The Order had converted several gers in the village into cells where they held the prisoners of war, kept under the watchful eye of the High Commander's guards. As they approached, Ying slowed her footsteps, preparing herself for what she was about to face. A sliver of fear crept up her spine. She had never been this scared, not even when they had been captured by the Blood Phoenix, or when she was close to asphyxiating in the deep ocean—yet the thought of having to confront one of her closest friends about his betrayal left her stricken.

Beads of cold sweat gathered upon her palms, her own frantic heartbeat ringing in her ears.

"He's inside," Ye-yang said, pointing at one of the white, dome-shaped gers, its entrance guarded by two stern soldiers. He nudged her forward. "You deserve to hear his side of the story for yourself. I'll be right here if you need me."

With a wave of his hand, the guards stepped aside, clearing the way for her to enter. Ying took a deep breath to steady herself, then she pushed the door and stepped in.

The inside of the ger was completely bare, with only a small bronze pot in a corner meant for the prisoner to relieve himself. A bowl of foul-smelling gruel lay untouched on the floor, the lumps of flour dumplings disintegrating in the brown mush.

Chang-en was curled in a corner, still wearing his maroon guild robes, albeit ripped in certain sections. His eyes were lightly shut, but when he heard her enter, his lids immediately flew open.

"Y-Y-Ying," he called. Shock flashed across his eyes, then relief, then guilt. He pressed his lips together, remaining silent.

Ying stared at her friend quietly for a moment, letting her own thoughts and emotions coalesce inside her.

"An-xi is dead."

"I know. I thought you had died too," he replied, staring down at his own knees.

"Did you want me to?"

"No! Of course not!" Chang-en leapt up, indignance flaring across his face. "I didn't want any of this to happen. An-xi . . . gods, I was the one who killed him." Squatting back down, he rocked back and forth on his heels, clutching his forehead with his hands. "I didn't want this. I had no choice. If I didn't do it, the first beile would have destroyed my family. My e-niye, my younger siblings, he had them all hostage. We had no choice." He looked up, anguish carved into his reddened eyes. "I figured the High Commander wouldn't let you go, so you'd be safe for sure. An-xi . . . I didn't expect him to volunteer. I tried to talk him out of it. I really did! But he wouldn't listen. He never listens!"

Did it matter? Even if it wasn't her, wasn't An-xi, there were others who would have died in their place. Their lives were not worth any less.

Ying shut her eyes, exhaling slowly. Maybe she could give Chang-en the benefit of the doubt, believe that he had been pushed down this path of destruction by external forces beyond his control, trust that he had tried his utmost to prevent this tragedy from happening.

But knowing this didn't make the betrayal hurt any less, didn't change the fact that they had lost a friend.

"If you had said something sooner, we could have helped," she said.

"How? Do you even know what the first beile is like? He doesn't accept any form of defiance. He will destroy anyone who goes against him. You left, Ying. If you hadn't returned, then none of this would have happened. I would never have been stuck on board that pirate ship. If we'd come home sooner, maybe I could have been around to help my family to escape. Maybe it wouldn't have come to this!" Chang-en protested.

Ying's blood ran cold. Was this still her friend? The same boy who had reached out to her on the first day at the guild with that cheeky smile and quirky attitude?

They had been through thick and thin together. They'd survived the Blood Phoenix together. Fragments of those memories flickered in her mind, of the days they had spent working on *Xiangliu*, and of the nights that were filled with wine, song, and noisy games of four-colored cards. When she closed her eyes, she could still see the picture of all three of them sitting on the ship's deck counting the stars in the night sky, wondering whether or not they would eventually make it back home.

She spun around, coming up against Ye-yang's chest.

"Tongiya Chang-en, that's enough. No amount of justification can absolve you from the consequences of your choices. There are no what-ifs. This is the outcome that you chose, that you will now have to live with. You can't blame anyone but yourself," the High Commander said.

Chang-en's bitter laughter rang out. "No one is to blame but me," he muttered, over and over.

"Come, we should go," Ye-yang said softly, taking Ying by the shoulder and steering her toward the exit.

Before she stepped out, Ying took another glance at her friend, now little more than a stranger. Chang-en was staring into space, his bloodshot eyes vacant, as if he was merely an empty shell.

How did we come to this?

Her, Chang-en, An-xi, Ye-kan. There was a time when they had learned and played side by side, laughing and quarreling with one another as they overcame challenge after challenge in the Engineers Guild. A lifetime seemed to have passed since then, and she began to doubt whether those memories she cherished were even real. This war had changed them all, forced them down different paths, broken them in different ways. Some for better, some for worse.

"Goodbye, Chang-en," she whispered.

CHAPTER 37

APPREHENSION HUNG THICK IN THE SALT-LICKED AIR as the banners tried to maintain some semblance of order upon the shores of Larut. While the fighting had thus far been confined to the seas, the sheer number of casualties that were continuously streaming in told a dire tale of the situation at the front line.

"How bad is it?" Ying asked as she followed Ye-yang across the beach.

"Three days. That's how long our warships will likely last before Monggu Yutai's fleet breaches our defenses and brings the war to land," Ye-yang replied, his lips pursed in a grim line. "His Blades have already shot down almost every single one of the Order's airships, but we still haven't sighted them. This was what we were afraid of—fighting an enemy that's hiding in the shadows."

"And if they do bring the fighting on land—what are our chances?"

Ye-yang stopped, turning to face her with firm insistence in his iron-tinted gaze. He placed both hands on her shoulders. "Ying, when that time comes, I want you to leave the isle. The Jangmu chieftain is already coordinating the evacuation of villagers to Muci. I want you to be on one of those boats, do you understand?"

"You think we'll lose."

"I . . . I cannot guarantee that we'll win." There was a sadness

etched in the lines of Ye-yang's face as he surveyed the chaos unfolding around them. Soldiers shouting instructions, physicians rushing
to treat the injured, screams of mothers who could not find their
sons, cries of wives who had lost their husbands.

"I'm not going anywhere," Ying declared.

"But, Ying—"

"I came here because there's something I need to discuss with
you," she said. Leaning over, she whispered Li-na's plan into his ear.

When she was done, Ye-yang stared at her doubtfully. He took
a moment to consider what he'd been told, which was already more
than what Ying had expected. He could have shut her down immediately, told her to stop being foolish. But he didn't.

"Are you sure that Li-na can really be trusted?" he asked. "She's
Monggu Yutai's right hand. One of his most trusted subordinates.
What makes you think this isn't another one of his traps?"

"I'm not asking you to trust her. I'm asking you to trust *me*," Ying
replied. She knew it would be difficult to convince Ye-yang to go
along with the plan, because it was incredibly risky. As the High
Commander, he was accountable to the whole of the nine isles, and
responsible for the lives of every soldier in the Order. He was right to
be cautious. "I can go alone. That way, if things don't work out, you
can still muster a response in time."

Ye-yang shook his head, his brows slanting into a deep furrow.
Then he said, "We'll do it, but I'll come with you. Monggu Yutai is a
shrewd and guarded man. If I'm not there, he'll suspect that something's amiss. To convince him that we are sincere, I must go. As for
the backup, Number Fourteen should be arriving soon. He can—"

"Ye-kan isn't coming."

"What?"

Ying bit down on her lower lip, grimacing at the memory of Ye-kan's unbridled rage. Would he ever forgive them for what they had done? She scoffed, ashamed of her own audacity, of even thinking that she deserved his forgiveness.

"The first beile told Ye-kan the truth behind his mother's death. Ye-kan refuses to deploy his banner to Larut."

Ye-yang fell briefly silent. "I didn't think we could keep it a secret forever. These things have a way of writhing their way into the light." His eyes dimmed with a haze of regret. "As the High Commander, I should punish him for insubordination, and for forsaking his people, but as his brother . . . I'm the one who let him down. He has every right to be angry. Every right to point his sword at me."

"Did you really have to do it?" Ying asked. It was a question that had been lingering in her mind, one that she should have asked a long time ago. "If Lady Odval hadn't been at the wrong place at the wrong time, would she still have to die?"

"You've seen for yourself what being an Aogiya means. If Odval lived, then the one to die would have been me."

"You don't know that."

"I know enough. Odval only ever had one goal, and that was to see Ye-kan sit on the High Commander's throne. She was no less cunning than the other beiles, perhaps even more so, and her love for her son meant that she would be willing to do anything to remove the obstacles in his way." He paused. "A mother's love knows no bounds."

"Yet you took away Ye-kan's right to it." Ying faltered, a memory of her own e-niye floating to mind. A memory that would always be filled with summer sunshine and winter lullabies, kind words and warm hugs.

"That will always be one of my greatest regrets. I never meant to hurt Fourteen, but I've done so anyway." Ye-yang took her hand and gave it a squeeze. "This isn't your fault, Ying. You don't have to take responsibility for my choices."

"No. I had a part to play as well. I chose to keep the truth from him too."

She could have tried to stop Ye-yang, but she hadn't. She had let her own selfish fears and misgivings stand in the way. Then, instead of owning up to what she had done, she had chosen to run away.

Li-na had been right to call her out for it, because it was true. She was always running away.

Not anymore.

Ying pulled her hand away from Ye-yang. The warmth of his fingers vanished, replaced by the prickling of the cold sea breeze against her palm. For that short moment, the distance between them had shrunk again, drawing them back in time when things were still possible, when they could still pull back the reins.

But then the illusion shattered.

They continued making their way along the shoreline, heading toward the few warships that were berthed a short distance away. Amid the disarray, Ying spotted a familiar face in the crowd, kneeling beside an injured man.

"Ru-er?" she called.

Wei Ru-er looked up, eyes creasing into smiling crescents when she realized who it was. "Ying! What are you doing here?" she asked. The tavern owner quickly finished tying up the bandage on the man's wounded arm, then she wiped her bloodstained hands against her apron and straightened herself up.

"I should be asking you the same question," Ying replied, rushing over to give her old friend a hug. "I heard that Shi-ye is evacuating the villagers on the opposite side of the isle. Why aren't you there?"

"Me? Evacuate? Look around you—does it look like many of us are leaving?"

Most of the villagers were bustling around and helping with whatever they could, from carrying supplies to treating the injured. Ying recognized several of them, the presence of familiar faces a comforting sight. There were even a sizable number of Qirin people milling around.

"Even the refugees are helping . . ."

"This is our home. We're not going anywhere," Ru-er replied.

Ying exchanged a glance with Ye-yang, who had been quietly listening to the exchange by the side. This was what he had been advocating all this while, for Antarans and Qirins to live together in harmony. What Ru-er was showing her was a glimpse into the possibilities of the future, a future that could be shared by both Antarans and Qirins alike.

They could not let a despot like Monggu Yutai tear down this dream before it even had the chance to become reality.

They had to win.

~⌒

Li-na had been correct in predicting Monggu Yutai's response to a call for truce negotiations. He agreed.

"Monggu Yutai is a practical man, and also a greedy one," Li-na had said. *"If he is able to achieve his goal while minimizing his own losses, he will. He is mentally prepared to raze the Order to the ground, but if he thinks he can win without doing that, he will try, because he still harbors hopes that the Order will serve him one day. That is why he was still keen on meeting with the High Commander on our ship. He believed that if he could get Aogiya Ye-yang to surrender, then he could take over without having to lift a finger. Unless absolutely necessary, Monggu Yutai will not annihilate what he believes is his."*

Ying stood on the deck of the small sampan, staring ahead as the gap closed between them and the enemy's flagship—a gleaming behemoth painted bronze with sails that were black as night, matching those of the many pirate ships accompanying it, and the red flag of the Monggu clan flying from its highest mast. The Blood Phoenix's ships were also amid the flotilla, and the *Diamond* had to be somewhere lurking in the waters below.

"Are you ready?" Ye-yang asked, coming up to her side.

He had changed into a fresh suit of armor, each black brigandine plate scrubbed clean. His long hair was braided back with not a single strand out of place, and the gold cuffs on his ears caught the sunlight. He was the High Commander of the nine isles, and it would not do to look any less, not on a day like this.

She nodded. "Can I not be?"

One of the conditions stipulated by Monggu Yutai was for the meeting to take place on board his own flagship, so they had to drop anchor a safe distance away and transfer to a smaller boat that would take them over. As expected, he was being extremely wary with this. It might have seemed suspicious for Ye-yang to agree to such a condition, because it would put him at the mercy of his enemy, so they had arranged for over a dozen of the Order's ships to stand by to create the impression that they, too, were being cautious.

"There's still time to change our minds," he said. "The Order is prepared to see through this battle till the very end, even if it means fighting to the very last man."

"But every life lost is one life too many. My a-ma taught me that."

She knew why Ye-yang was worried. This was not a mere small-time skirmish between pirates but a carefully coordinated plan that had been years in the making. It was impossibly risky to place their trust in the hands of Li-na, a pirate captain notorious for being ruthless and bloodthirsty, who had always been one of Monggu Yutai's sharpest claws.

"To yearn for great opportunity without the courage to accept great risk is naive," she murmured, reminding herself of the lesson she had learned from her father.

Shouts rang out as the sampan prepared for docking. A rope ladder was flung down from the main deck of the Monggu flagship, and stern soldiers peered down at them, wearing bronze lamellar armor that resembled that of the Qirin empire. Ying had to admit that Monggu Yutai was an extremely resourceful negotiator and politician, to have managed to wrangle support from the likes of their historical enemies—the Qirin royal court—and over a dozen fleets of mercenary pirates.

Ye-yang climbed up to the deck, and Ying followed behind. They had only been allowed to bring five guards with them, to ensure that they would not have the means to launch any sort of viable offensive while on board.

Monggu Yutai was already waiting for them, seated comfortably upon a high-backed ebony chair that looked exactly like the High Commander's seat in Qianlei Palace, complete with the cobra's head looming above. A thick cloak covered his broad shoulders, the shine of silver fox fur gleaming majestically under the sun's rays. If the first beile had known the extent of Monggu Yutai's ambitions, perhaps he would not have been so hasty to ally himself with such a man.

Ying's eyes scoured the deck, her gaze falling upon the subdued silhouette of Li-na, sitting on her wheelchair not far from the Monggu chieftain.

"In order to ensure that the pirate fleets do not double-cross him, Monggu Yutai has demanded for all of us to send a representative from our crews onto his ship, as 'guests.' Hostages, if you will. I will volunteer on behalf of the Blood Phoenix."

"But would he not be suspicious? Why would a captain volunteer themselves as a hostage?"

"No other captain would but me." Li-na had glanced down at her own legs, running her fingers along the handles of her wheelchair. *"I'm a Qirin woman, a widow, disabled, running a crew of women and orphans. To put things very bluntly, Monggu Yutai underestimates me, he always has. That is also why he trusts me more than any of the others,*

because he doesn't believe me capable of betraying him. He will come to regret this."

Her nerves settled somewhat. At least thus far, Li-na had not lied.

"Ah, Nephew!" Monggu Yutai exclaimed, beckoning to them with a casual wave. He wore a broad smile upon his fleshy lips, but there was something unnatural about it. Something wooden. "I must confess I was very surprised to receive your message. I was beginning to think you had the exact same stubborn streak as that father of yours, but it seems like Monggu blood still runs inside you after all."

"Being stubborn will not save the lives of my people," Ye-yang replied coolly. "Name your terms, so that we may consider if a permanent ceasefire is possible."

Monggu Yutai let loose a guffaw, with a laugh that did not reach his eyes. "Straight to the point. I like that," he said. "You are young and inexperienced, Ye-yang. If you agree to hand over the position of High Commander and control of the Cobra's Order, I will not only spare your life, I'll even let you retain your title as a beile. You can even keep control of Fei, if you wish, since I fully intend to shift the capital of the *ten* isles to Yokre."

"And what would you do with that position? Cede the Antaran isles to the Qirins? Become a vassal to the Empire?"

"Come to a mutually beneficial agreement, is a much better way of putting it."

"What if I say no?"

Ye-yang leveled his gaze at the Monggu chieftain with the intensity of cold steel. Monggu Yutai narrowed his eyes, and in that moment, Ying's instincts told her that something was off, even though she could not pinpoint what that was.

"Then you will not be leaving this ship today," the chieftain replied. He held up his right hand. Steel slid against steel as dozens of swords were drawn out of their scabbards, pointing toward the Aogiya contingent.

Ying kept a watchful eye on Li-na, who had quietly shifted closer to Monggu Yutai. The pirate captain concealed herself behind two of his personal bodyguards, remaining inconspicuous amid the fraying tensions.

"I'm afraid that's not for you to decide," Ye-yang replied. "Here is my formal response to you, as High Commander of the Antaran isles. We will *never* surrender to a traitor like you." Pulling out a flare from his sleeve, he fired it into the air. The face of a cobra, fangs bared, bled across the sky in strokes of smoke and flames.

Explosions went off in all directions, cannons firing on both sides. The stinging stench of gunpowder permeated the air. On deck, fighting broke out between the Monggu crew and Ye-yang's guards. Ying and Ye-yang moved in synchrony, backs against each other as they inched their way toward Monggu Yutai, who was still sitting calmly on his throne as if none of this fighting concerned him.

Or perhaps he was not as composed as he tried to seem, because there was a barely noticeable tremble to his hands as they clutched on to the near-black armrests of his chair.

"Ye-yang, to your left!" Ying shouted.

He immediately fired an arrow from his crossbow, striking one of the Monggu soldiers before the man could swing his curved blade.

At the same time, Ying threw out her right fist and stabbed another who had been closing in on them from behind, using the concealed blade in the jade ring that Ye-yang had slipped onto her finger before they set sail. The man fell lifeless to the ground. Ying stared at the blood staining her knuckles, a lump rising up her throat.

Monggu Yutai's bodyguards—four of them in total—moved toward them in a bid to protect their master.

Exactly as Ying and Li-na had intended.

Li-na blinked twice.

Ye-yang and Ying lunged forward, engaging the guards in a resounding clash of metal.

Behind Monggu Yutai, a flash of silver caught the light. A blade stabbed through his back—into his heart. It was not even a sword, but a mere long dagger that Li-na had kept hidden beneath her shawl, camouflaged between her metallic bones.

Monggu Yutai stared down at the bloody tip piercing out from his chest, then he turned.

And smiled.

"All of you are dead," he whispered, in a voice two tones higher than before. A voice that did not belong to Monggu Yutai.

Li-na immediately stretched her arm out toward Monggu Yutai's face, and in one swift ripping motion, she *pulled it off.*

"It's not him. It's a mask," the pirate captain said, throwing the sheet of rubberlike material onto the ground.

Ying stared at the translucent film that lay on the floor, with its grotesque contours and eerie eyeholes lying in a puddle of the impersonator's blood. Her heart thrummed at the implications.

The dead man was not the Monggu chieftain. Monggu Yutai had tricked them the same way Ye-lu had feigned his own death. They had tried to lay a trap for him, but now they had walked into one that he had set for them. It didn't matter that they had Li-na's help. He was still one step ahead.

She bent over and picked up the mask, feeling the almost gelatinous material between her fingers. It was a material unlike anything she had ever seen before, and when she laid it over her palm, it molded almost perfectly with the contours of her hand. Was this also the handiwork of Master Cixin? Materials development was often neglected in engineering, even at the guild, because it was deemed too basic and unglamorous—but the Monggu clan had just proven that all great inventions began from the most basic of building blocks.

This would be an expensive lesson. One that could cost them the war.

"We have to get off the ship immediately," Ye-yang said. He dispatched the final guard that remained and then threw his crossbow to the ground, grabbing Ying by the hand.

"There is a submersible docked at the starboard side of the ship, toward the stern. It can get you back across to Larut without being caught in the cross fire," Li-na said, addressing Ying. "I'm sorry. I didn't know that Monggu Yutai had this up his sleeve. He kept it a secret, even from me. If he isn't here, then he's likely hiding on one of the Blades. Look for the one with the Monggu clan symbol painted on its roof."

The ocean rumbled, sending a tremor across the entire deck.

One of the Order's ships suddenly began cracking from the base of its hull, as if a sledgehammer had struck it from below. The ship disintegrated before their eyes, its crew leaping overboard in a desperate attempt to save their own lives.

The Blades.

"Hurry, go," Li-na urged. "The Blades will not pay any attention to you, because they'll think you're part of the Monggu fleet. But the rest of your ships . . ." She glanced over at Ye-yang, with a hint of apology flashing across her eyes. It was unlikely that even a single of the Order's ships would be able to make it out of this battle, not with the Blades in motion.

"Wait—look over there," Ying interrupted, pointing toward the sky.

A dense storm cloud was floating in their direction, the whir of propellers getting louder as it approached. It obscured the sun, casting an ominous shadow across the seas like a flock of angry crows. Airships. At least a dozen of them, each one bearing the silver emblem of the Cobra's Order.

"Ye-kan . . . he came after all," she murmured.

Their reinforcements had arrived.

With the cover from above, there was a far better chance for them to retreat, to minimize the losses that this failed gamble would cost.

"You can come with us," Ying said, turning to Li-na.

The captain shook her head. "Don't worry. Keyan will come for me," she replied. "Now go." The crow's feet at her eyes deepened with the wry smile that crossed her face, then she simply turned her wheelchair around, disappearing through the doorway leading to the inner cabins.

"Come," Ye-yang said, pulling Ying away.

A small submersible the shade of copper was exactly where Li-na said it would be. It was slightly larger than Ying's own design, and its control panel resembled a simplified version of a Blade's. Recalling what Wenjun had taught her about the Blades' operating mechanisms, she hurriedly turned a few knobs and flipped some switches. The submersible detached from the ship and dropped into the sea, with its twin propellers, protruding from each side of the vessel, whirring into motion.

And then the entire flagship exploded in flames.

CHAPTER 38

Ying sat on the beach in silence, staring out at the inky sea as it blended with the night sky.

Three entire ships had been decimated by the Monggu clan's Blades, which was already the best possible outcome they could have bargained for. Without the timely arrival of Ye-kan's banner, their losses would have been far greater. Despite that, hundreds of Antaran soldiers were gone, their blood washed away by the ebbing of the tide.

When night fell, the sea regained its calm, gentle waves rushing upon the shore. As if none of that devastation had ever happened.

Ying could not feel any of that tranquility.

Closing her eyes, she let out a deep sigh. When the sun rose at dawn, the day of reckoning would be upon them. Even with the reinforcements, less than half of the Order's fleet was in functioning condition. They would not be able to withstand the onslaught for more than another day.

"A-ma, what would you do?" she asked, turning her gaze toward the blinking stars.

Her father had always emphasized that engineering was only a means to an end. What that end might be rested in the hands of the engineer—whether to use their creations for the greater good, or to harm others. She only had a vague understanding of the weight of his words before, but after today, this lesson was engraved into her bones.

There was nothing inherently evil about the Blades, the mechanical limbs worn by Li-na, or even that arcane human-skin mask, all of which had come from the hands of the elusive Master Cixin. Yet when they were wielded by the wrong people, those creations became abominations.

"Abka Han gave us the ability to create things so that we can make the world a better place for others, so never treat it lightly, little lamb. It is, unfortunately, as much a gift as it is a burden," her father's voice echoed in her mind.

She thought she knew her purpose. That she wanted to use her engineering skills to protect those in need, and those she loved.

But what if I can't make the world a better place? What if I'm just not good enough to protect anyone?

"Trying to figure out how to save the world?" a teasing voice echoed from behind.

Wei Ru-er appeared beside her, tucking her skirt beneath her as she sat down on the sand. Exhaustion was written in creases lining the woman's eyes, but still her mood was upbeat.

"That would be highly presumptuous of me," Ying replied with a dry chuckle. "In case you haven't heard, I didn't even manage to save my closest friends."

Ru-er wrapped an arm around her shoulders, giving her a comforting squeeze. "I know. It's hard when it seems like there's nothing you can do to change the outcome. We cannot turn back time, but that's not your fault."

"I'm not sure I can convince myself of that."

"Did you know that I set up an altar for my husband recently? Not long after you left for Fei."

Ying looked at the tavern owner in surprise. Ever since she arrived on Larut, Ru-er had made it clear that she was determined to wait for her husband to return, that she would not believe he was dead unless she saw his body in front of her.

"I guess I've known that he was gone for a long time, except I refused to accept it, because if I accepted that, then it would mean that I would need to take responsibility for his loss. For not having stopped him from going out to sea that day, for not setting off to search for him sooner, for searching the wrong sections of the straits. But after I started helping out with settling the influx of Qirin refugees and hearing more and more of their stories, I realized how foolish I was. I can't keep living in the past, and I shouldn't force myself to shoulder the blame for what was beyond my control. We only feel guilt because of hindsight, Ying. If we were to reverse time, we still wouldn't be able to predict the future."

Ying pondered quietly over Ru-er's words, letting the reasoning steep in her mind, entangling with that very guilt that her friend was describing. "Did he put you up to this?" she asked.

"The High Commander?" Ru-er laughed. "He did stop by to check on the refugee situation, and he might have mentioned that he was worried about you."

"There are far more important things he should be worrying about . . ."

Like reorganizing what remained of the Order's troops in

preparation for their final stand against the Monggu clan. In the distance, she could see the gas lamps burning brightly at the Order's temporary encampments, the thick leather soles of soldiers' boots pounding the dirt and sending vibrations through the earth. There would be no sleep for anyone tonight, not until this war was over.

"Then don't let him continue worrying about you!" Ru-er reached out and tapped her on the temple. "I thought there was a very sound head upon these shoulders. Don't tell me I was mistaken all this while?"

"Ru-er, please—"

"Uh-uh, enough excuses." The tavern owner wagged her finger at Ying. Standing back up, she dusted the sand off her skirt. "I'll be heading back to the refugee camp now. There's still plenty to be done. Instead of sitting here wallowing in self-pity, I suggest you start cranking those gears in your head, because I, for one, am absolutely confident that someone who managed to dream up those impossible little bronze bubbles—What did you call them? Octopuses?—will be able to dig herself out of this rut that she seems to have buried herself in."

"They changed their name to Bladebreakers," Ying replied, but Ru-er had already gone too far to hear. She watched as the tavern owner's silhouette retreated into the shadows, the woman casually throwing out a wave of her hand as she went.

Those impossible little bronze bubbles . . .

Those Bladebreakers.

~⁀つ

When the battle drums sounded at dawn, Ying stood by the docks with just one golden orb beside her—the single Bladebreaker that Master Lianshu had managed to salvage and restore. If she had repaired it correctly, then this lone submersible should be able to achieve its original objective.

Destroy a Blade.

She had not told Ye-yang of her plan, and she had beseeched Master Lianshu to help her keep this secret, at least until her mission was complete. He could not afford to have this distraction, not when today's battle would determine the fate of the nine isles.

Farther down the coast, dark masses of soldiers were gathering, like crawling ants in their black armor. They moved to board the warships, scores of them swarming up the gangways amid the roaring chant of a traditional Antaran rallying call. Above, the Order's airship fleet hovered against a backdrop of mournful clouds, the gaping maws of their silver air cannons protruding from their chambers, ready to rain fire.

"Ying."

She startled, glancing around in bewilderment. For a moment she wondered if she was hallucinating, because it looked as if Ye-yang was walking down the boardwalk toward her. He was in full brigandine armor, gilded helmet tucked beneath his left arm. The gold trim on his shoulder plates gleamed, giving him the intimidating aura of a god of war.

Maybe I miss him too much.

That would be pathetic, by her own standards. After what he had done, after how he had trampled over her trust, it hurt that she still cared.

She squeezed her eyes briefly shut, then opened them again. He was standing right in front of her now.

It was no illusion.

"What are you doing here? Shouldn't you be . . . somewhere else?" *Just not here.*

She instinctively took a step back, raising one hand to the back of her neck. Her other hand gripped tightly on to the spanner she had brought with her, in case she needed to adjust the mechanisms on the submersible. If he dared try to knock her out again, she wouldn't hesitate to use it on him first.

He smiled, a tinge of resignation tugging at the corners of his lips. "I'm not here to stop you," he said, reading her mind.

"You're not?" She eyed him with the slant of her eyes, suspicion in every wary angle of her body.

"I just wanted to say that I'm sorry, Ying. You were right. I thought that I was protecting you and keeping you safe, but that was never what you needed from me. I know that anything I say will just sound like an excuse, especially on the back of An-xi's death, but I hope you know that I never meant to hurt you. I . . . I always believed that if I was stronger, that I could have protected my e-niye better, and then she'd still be alive. But maybe that was never what she wanted either. She only wanted to be understood by the ones she loved, but my a-ma never tried to understand her, not even till her very last breath."

She could see the melancholy and regret reflecting in his clear gray irises, emotions that she was all too familiar with. He placed one hand on her shoulder, giving it a gentle pat.

"I'm done protecting you," he declared. "Now it's your turn to protect me."

He kept his smile up, intentionally maintaining some light-heartedness, but the stiffness in his jaw did not lie. The more cheerful he tried to seem, the more her heart broke. A sourness stung at her nose, tears trickling uncontrollably from the corners of her eyes.

"Why are you crying?" Ye-yang asked. He cradled her cheeks in the palms of his hands, the calluses of his fingers rough against her skin as he wiped the tears from her cheeks. A thin layer of mist formed across his eyes. "You know, even though I'm supposed to be the all-powerful High Commander, I never know what to do the moment I see you cry. I just want to give you everything, as long as it brings a smile back to your face."

Ying sniffled.

"You've already given me everything you can," she said. And she didn't begrudge him what he couldn't.

She still resented him, occasionally maybe even hated him, for always keeping secrets from her and for making her feel like nothing more than a tool, a stepping stone to help him achieve his grand ambitions.

But maybe he just didn't know.

He didn't know how to navigate this relationship—and neither did she.

They were both feeling their way in the dark, trying to do what they believed was right. Even if they had hurt each other in the process, that had never been their intention. After peeling away all the lies and misunderstandings and wiping away all the blood and tears, there was still something that lay between them at the core of it all. Something that she couldn't sweep away no matter how hard she tried.

Love.

He would always be the one who first stepped into her heart, and then never left.

She wrapped her arms around his neck, tipping her face upward. Ye-yang pressed a gentle, tender kiss upon her lips. In the distance, the drums continued to beat, a constant reminder that their time was running out, but in this moment they could hear nothing but the steady rhythm of each other's heartbeats. He pulled her close, crushing her against the metal plates of his armor. She sighed, lips parting ever so slightly. The tip of his tongue touched her own, both hesitant at first, then eager and desperate, intertwining in a dance that was filled with longing.

A horn rang out. Thrice.

The Monggu fleet was here.

Their time had run out.

"I must go, and so must you," she whispered, breathing her words against his cheek.

She planted one final kiss upon his lips, imprinting the memory deep within her mind. The tenderness. The warmth. The scent of orchids in bloom. Then she turned and headed for her submersible, climbing in through the open hatch.

"Wait! Wait for me!" a third voice called out.

Ying balked at the sight of Master Lianshu sprinting along the wooden planks, her frizzy ponytail bouncing behind her as she ran. The guild master arrived in front of them, panting to catch her breath.

"I'm coming with you."

"Excuse me?" Ying stared.

"You heard me."

Ignoring the barbs of confusion that she was being given, Lianshu shoved Ying's head down and climbed in after her. The hatch was shut, immediately dampening the sound of the battle drums.

"No time to waste," Lianshu said, moving straight to the control panel. Once the engine lever was pulled, the vessel would descend into the water—and there would be no turning back.

Ying lingered at the frosted glass window, gazing at Ye-yang's silhouette on the outside. A flash of red appeared in front of her eyes. Ye-yang was pressing his lover's knot to the glass.

She pulled out her own clover-shaped knot that she had kept carefully hidden between the folds of her guild robes, holding it up to his.

"Maybe one day, we can leave all this behind. Go somewhere where there's no High Command, no Engineers Guild, no pirates, no wars. I'll just be Ye-yang, and you'll be Ying, and we'll sail the seas and explore the world there is out there."

It was a beautiful dream, but there was no chance of it happening in this life.

"Goodbye, Ye-yang."

Lianshu pulled the lever, and the submersible began to sink beneath the water's surface, until she could no longer see his face before her. From here on, all she had were memories.

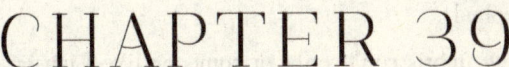

CHAPTER 39

THE SUBMERSIBLE GLIDED THROUGH AN UNDERWATER trench, the coarse rock walls of the watery chasm rising high on both sides, casting a sinister shadow that kept them well hidden.

"Why did you come?" Ying asked Lianshu, who was peering out through the periscope to survey their surroundings.

"Are you complaining about having an extra pair of helping hands?"

"No . . . but you really didn't have to."

This was a mission—more like a last-ditch attempt—that had a ridiculously low rate of success. They not only had to locate the correct Blade that Monggu Yutai was on, they also had to launch the Bladebreaker and destroy the Blade before they were detected and obliterated. They would only get one chance, and failure could well mean the end of the war for the Antarans.

Ying had never expected to return.

There was no need to drag someone else to hell with her.

"The Bladebreaker is my creation too," Lianshu huffed, sounding miffed that her presence was being questioned. She tore her gaze away from the periscope's rectangular window and turned toward Ying, eyes bulging through her bronze goggles. "I was the one who developed the dragon automaton. All you did was to fit in a bunch of bells and whistles. If anyone deserves to have their name logged in the history books as having created the weapon that won the war for the nine isles, it should be me, so don't think of stealing my credit."

"Sure," Ying replied.

Such astounding hubris could only fit someone like Lianshu. She wondered how Lianshu would react if she ever came head-to-head with the elusive Master Cixin one day. It seemed like they would either get along swimmingly, or end up ripping out each other's throats.

Lianshu took off her goggles, setting them down on the control panel. She plucked the submersible's breathing apparatus off its wall hook and threw it at Ying.

"Later on, when we find that bastard and his Blade, I want you to put this on and eject yourself from here, no matter whether or not we succeed in launching the Bladebreaker," the guild master said.

"Why?"

The woman shrugged. "Because I don't want you getting in my way."

Ying clutched on to the ventilation apparatus that she had been given, the gas bag hanging limply by the side of its bronze mouthpiece. Each vessel had only one, because it was only meant to have a single pilot.

Lianshu was trying to save her life.

That was the real reason why the guild master had insisted on coming along.

A warm stream rushed through Ying's heart, intertwined with a tinge of bitterness.

"Don't look at me like that," Lianshu said, shoulders sagging.

"This is just something that I owe Shan-jin, all right? I can't go back and change what happened, so the only thing I can do is to help him stop his foolhardy daughter from reuniting with him too early." She stared out through the glass window, expression softening. "As much as I hate to admit it, perhaps my time has passed. Now, when I look around, I realize I'm the only one left. My a-ge, Shan-jin, none of them are here anymore." She patted the cold, bronze wall of the vessel. "Only these dead, lifeless things are left."

For once, Ying felt a pang of sympathy for the guild master.

Maybe Lianshu wasn't entirely heartless after all. And maybe they weren't entirely different. Reckless dreams. Withered friendships. And here they were, sailing side by side toward an inevitable ending.

Lianshu picked up a stray screw and threw it at her. "Are you even listening to me? I said, get the heck out of here the moment we find the Blades, got it? Based on my calculations, we shouldn't be far from a collection of small atolls. If you surface, you can swim to one of them and wait to be rescued."

"Master Lianshu, I appreciate what you're trying to do, but . . . I don't need you to do this." She held out the breathing apparatus. "I've been sheltered and protected my entire life. Now it's my turn to do my part."

In the past, she had never realized how blessed she was, never appreciated the freedom that she had been given. She had naively gone about her life in her little bubble, burying herself in building sandcastles out of her own whims and fancies. This war, her time with the Blood Phoenix, the losses she had suffered—all of it had taught her a harsh lesson about who she wanted to be, what she needed to become.

The guild master pursed her lips together, displeased. "Don't be stubborn. This is—"

"Master Lianshu, look there," Ying interrupted, pointing through the window at the glimpse of silver that sliced through the darkness. She quickly peered through the periscope.

It was a Blade, floating about twenty ren below their current position. She squinted, trying to make out whether there was any insignia printed on its metallic roof, as Li-na had mentioned.

There was none.

She quickly diverted the submersible before the Blade's crew could detect her presence. "The Blade that we're looking for should have the Monggu clan's emblem etched on its roof," she said.

Once they had located the first Blade, it didn't take them long to find the second. This time, they could clearly see the outline of a wolf's head emblazoned upon its roof, the same wolf that adorned the flags flying from the Monggu ships.

We've found it.

Taking care to stay far enough within the shadows, she slowly brought the submersible lower, until it was level with the body of the Blade. The Blade's shields were not down, allowing her to see right through its glass hull. The crew of the vessel busied themselves with their respective duties—and there he was, Monggu Yutai, sitting in the captain's cabin, occupied in discussion with a few of his men.

"Go now. I can launch the Bladebreaker from here," Lianshu urged.

"Master Lianshu, I'm not going to repeat myself. I'm not leaving." Her voice was firm, her determination unwavering.

Turning around, Ying touched the bronze wall that kept them separated from their cargo—the slumbering sea dragon that they would soon unleash.

"An-xi, this is for you," she whispered.

Suddenly, a beam of light homed in on them, flooding the cabin with the glare of a dozen suns. In the space of a single breath, the steel scales of the Blade came cascading down, enveloping the vessel in its protective shell.

No.

Ying slammed her fist down on the button, triggering the release of the Bladebreaker. The hatch at the back of the submersible opened, and a long, serpentine body swam out, spiraling at high speed toward the Blade and kicking up a trail of sea-foam as it sliced through the water.

The razor-sharp head of the Bladebreaker made contact with the shield, piercing through the steel like they had intended.

Then—nothing.

Either the force of the impact hadn't been sufficient to penetrate entirely through the shield, or it had been unlucky enough to strike the Blade's metal frame instead of its glass windows.

Ying quickly strapped a small watertight barrel across her back and pulled the portable ventilation device across her nose and mouth.

"What do you think you're doing!" Lianshu exclaimed.

"Once I'm gone, shut the hatch and get out of here immediately," she replied.

Throwing open the submersible's hatch, Ying swam out into the freezing waters, making her way toward the Blade. Pins and needles pricked at her skin, her lungs struggling to expel the cold. Out of the corners of her eyes, she spied Lianshu swimming out after her.

What was that woman doing? She had no breathing apparatus, so she would end up drowning in no time, if hypothermia didn't get to her first.

A silver projectile flew out through one of the Blade's underwater cannons. It went right past them in a trail of effervescence, ripping into their submersible in a silent explosion. The darkness was lit by a ball of ghostly blue flames, shards of metal flying outward in slow motion. Then the light went out, extinguished by the overwhelming pressure of the deep waters. Her stomach did a somersault.

Maybe Lianshu was right to have followed her out after all.

Swimming as fast as she could, Ying eventually reached the single point of entry into the shielded Blade.

"*This little protrusion is the only section of the* Diamond *that isn't covered by a shield plate—and the only way to get in and out while the vessel is underwater,*" Wenjun had said.

She gestured to the guild master, guiding her over.

Grabbing hold of the silver bars on the door, she turned it clockwise with all the strength she could muster from her numb fingers. The circular hatch came ajar, like she knew it would. Once both of them were inside, she shut the door again, before draining out the seawater through the inbuilt pipe mechanism.

"Are you all right?" she asked the guild master.

Lianshu was shivering, her lips having gone a frightening shade of bluish-purple.

"Alive," the woman replied between chattering teeth. "Are we . . . *inside* the Blade?"

"Yes."

Ying reached for the handle of the second door, but Lianshu put out a hand and stopped her. "What are you doing?" Lianshu hissed. "This is Monggu Yutai's ship. If they find us here, they'll kill us."

"If we stay here, we're already dead."

Ying opened the door, letting them into the engine room. The interior of the Blade was shrouded in shadows, illuminated only by a few flickering gas lamps. Loud voices crisscrossed overhead as Monggu Yutai's crew scrambled to figure out what had struck them.

Ying quickly untied the barrel she was carrying and set it down on the ground. Footsteps were approaching, which meant that her time was running out. Lifting the lid of the barrel, she pulled out the bundle of explosives that she had prepared as a fail-safe, in case the Bladebreaker didn't manage to achieve what it was supposed to.

"Oh no, no you're not," Lianshu muttered, staring at the explosives in dismay. "Come, we should just try to find a way out of here. There'll be another opportunity to get to Monggu Yutai. We don't have to resort to this."

"Chances like this don't come twice."

If they escaped now, they might never have the opportunity to locate the Monggu chieftain again. This war had to end today, one way or the other.

"There's someone here!" a voice shouted.

A man had appeared at the doorway. He ran at her, brandishing a dagger in his hand. Ying dodged to one side, the explosives sliding out of her hand as she fell to the floor. The man's blade pierced her left thigh. Lianshu grabbed a welding iron that was hanging from the tool rack on one of the walls, slamming it across the man's head. He stumbled back, howling in pain.

Gritting her teeth, Ying lunged forward and grabbed her sticks of explosives once again. She quickly picked herself off the ground, backing to Lianshu's side.

"It's you?" Monggu Yutai's voice boomed across the engine room, having entered along with four other men. "That little scoundrel sent a girl to do his job for him?" He shifted his gaze toward Lianshu, then he threw his head back and laughed. "And Aogiya Lianshu? How long has it been?" He gestured toward her scraggly, wretched appearance. "Looks like the years haven't treated you well at all."

"Shut up," Lianshu scolded. "You're still the same pathetic bottom feeder that you've always been."

Monggu Yutai scoffed, bearing no heed to Lianshu's caustic remark. "Do you really still fancy yourself a princess? Your brother is dead, and your nephews are too busy fighting among themselves to care about governing the nine isles. I'm doing all of you a favor by volunteering to take over. This is the end of the Aogiyas, Lianshu."

While the Monggu chieftain was busy engaging with the guild master, Ying slowly inched her way over to the engine furnace. Inside, the kaen-gas flames roared against the metal.

She flung open the furnace door, biting down a cry as the scorching heat seared through the palm of her hand.

Everyone's attention shifted to her.

The Monggu chieftain's eyes widened. "Don't do that," he bellowed, moving forward to stop her. Ying extended her arm a little, bringing the bundle of explosives even closer to the furnace's open door. He froze. "Don't," he repeated. "You want to talk? Let's talk. Negotiate. We can sit down, have a proper discussion. Come up with terms that we're both happy with. I knew your father too, Aihui Ying. He was very talented, someone I admired greatly. He wouldn't want to see things come to this."

"You keep Shan-jin out of this," Lianshu hissed.

"I can give you what the Aogiyas can't. You're an engineer, aren't you? We have the most advanced engineering facilities across the isles, better than what those archaic fools at the guild can ever dream of. When Master Cixin returns, I'll ask her to take you under her wing, teach you everything she's capable of. You'll become an engineer greater than all those so-called guild masters. How does that sound?"

The Ying of the past might have been tempted by that offer, by the glittering dream of becoming the best engineer the Antaran isles had ever seen. Not the Ying who stood here now.

While they were here having this conversation, the fighting would be raging on above the waves. Ye-kan would be commanding his airships—that brash, impetuous kid who had grown into a strong, dependable young man. Her brother Wen—their father's "little ox"—would be leading their clansmen in battle, wielding his sword in defense of the nine isles, becoming the hero that he always wanted to be. Nian—clever, considerate Nian—would find a way to hold strong amid the chaos, to maintain order upon the shores of Larut.

And Ye-yang. Where would he be?

In her mind's eye, she saw him standing at the fore of the Order's flagship, his gray irises reflecting the ferocity of the storm that brewed in the skies. He was the High Commander, and with that power came duty, responsibility that she knew he did not take lightly. Today, he would live and die with that ship, to protect the dream that he had spun for the future of the Antaran people.

They all had their roles. And so did she.

"I'm done protecting you. Now it's your turn to protect me."

In her moment of hesitation, Monggu Yutai's eyes darted surreptitiously to the right, toward the crew member who had attacked her earlier. A glint of silver peeked out from beneath the man's sleeve.

Liar.

Steeling her heart, she threw the explosives into the flames.

"No!"

Ying grabbed Lianshu by the arm, flinging the both of them toward the Blade's emergency exit. The blast thundered around them, piercing through her eardrums. Flames and blood mingled into a garish shade of red that flooded her vision. Glass was shattering, shards cutting through her burning flesh. Through the excruciating pain, she imagined herself reaching for a door.

The door opened.

Someone pushed her out from behind, and a cold gush of water rushed over her.

Then there was emptiness.

And peace.

EPILOGUE

NIAN STOOD UPON THE GRASSY PLAIN OF Larut, gazing upon the celebrations taking place beneath the river of stars. The storm clouds had passed, leaving behind a perfectly clear night sky and the smell of raindrops that clung to the blades of green beneath her feet.

Hundreds of people were dancing around bonfires to celebratory drumbeats, voices raised in song. There were plenty of bannermen seated among them, engaged in relaxed conversation over jars of wine.

What a difference a day made.

"Here." Someone took her hand and placed a leather waterskin in it. "I'll bet you haven't had a drop all day because you were too busy tending to everyone else." Ye-kan stood beside her, folding his arms across the embroidered silver serpent that curled up the front of his brigandine armor. He wore a stony expression in spite of the buoyant atmosphere, the usual ebullient spark in his eyes replaced by a deep weariness.

Nian could understand. She hadn't stepped foot onto the front line, only helping to tend to the injured and to coordinate operations back on shore, yet she also felt the fatigue echoing through her bones, a biting cold flowing through her veins.

She took a sip of water. "At least our effort hasn't gone to waste," she said, the corners of her lips curving into a graceful smile. The

Monggu fleet had withdrawn earlier that afternoon, after one of their Blades was destroyed—with the Monggu chieftain on it. If only she had been able to witness this momentous victory for herself. "Look at them. You wouldn't think they'd just suffered through the weeks of violence and bloodshed."

The sovereignty of the nine isles had been balancing on a knife's edge for the longest time, this victory hard earned. It was no wonder the people were so jubilant.

She turned to Ye-kan. "You helped."

After much trying, Nian had finally scolded some sense into Ye-kan and convinced him to deploy his banner to Larut to support in the battle against the Monggu clan. They had rushed here as soon as they could, and thankfully it wasn't too late.

"I helped him to secure his empire," Ye-kan replied, the bitterness in his tone raw and undisguised. The muscles in his cheeks drew tense, his jaw set in stiff lines.

"You helped to protect your people," Nian corrected. Ye-kan had a caustic tongue but a soft heart. She sighed softly, placing a hand upon Ye-kan's arm. "I wish my parents were still around too, but the dead cannot be brought back to life, Ye-kan. Your e-niye loved you dearly. She would not want you to spend the rest of your life tormented by revenge because of her."

Ye-kan scoffed. "No. You didn't know my e-niye. She wouldn't want me to spend the rest of my life serving in the shadow of the person who killed her." He grabbed the nearest bannerman by the scruff of his neck, pulling him over. "Where's the High Commander?"

"B-b-beile-ye," the young man stammered, bringing his fist up in salute. "I'm not sure. No one has seen him ever since the fighting ended."

"What about Chief Stewards Nergui or Qorchi? Have you seen them?" Nian asked. In the hectic aftermath, she had not seen a single familiar face in the vicinity until Ye-kan appeared. Not the High Commander, not Wen, not Ying. A shred of unease stirred inside her gut.

"They're over by the main encampment along the northeastern shore." The soldier bowed and scampered off, only too eager to get himself away from the fourteenth beile.

Nian and Ye-kan turned to head in the direction that they had been given, but a voice called out to them, halting their steps. It came from a middle-aged woman in a wheelchair, being pushed over by a beautiful young lady with glowing bronze skin. Both of them wore Qirin attire, carrying with them the brine-soaked scent of the sea.

"You won't find them there," she said.

Ye-kan's brows dipped. "Who are you?" he demanded.

"Li-na, captain of the Blood Phoenix," the woman in the wheelchair replied. The other merely responded with a huff of disdain, her paper-thin lips tilting downward in a scowl.

Ye-kan immediately reached for the hilt of his sword, but Nian held on to his wrist, preventing him from making any rash moves.

She remembered what Ying had told her before leaving for Larut. Li-na was the one who had rescued her a-jie, not only once, but twice. There was more than met the eye behind the infamy of the Blood Phoenix, and her sister had not had the time to tell her everything. However, if Ying trusted this woman, then she would too.

"How do you know we won't find them there?" Nian asked. "Have you seen my sister?"

Li-na remained silent for a moment, looking at her with what felt like sympathy threading through her dark eyes. "Why don't you follow me?" she said.

~⌐

They followed Li-na to the beach, walking up to a broken metal shell, its window shattered and its wall heavily dented. Nian's heart sank when she laid eyes upon it. Grim realization washed over her as she stared into its interior, now filled with debris tangled with seaweed.

"This is a Bladebreaker, isn't it?"

Although she had never seen one before, she recognized its design from the sketches that Ying had showed her, and the prototypes she had seen in the guild's Black Ops workshop. This was the weapon that her a-jie had been working on, meant to destroy the impregnable Blades controlled by the Monggu clan.

The Order had successfully taken down a Blade, and Monggu Yutai with it.

Till now, Ying was nowhere to be seen.

Hot tears welled up in her eyes, cracks forming across the surface of her heart. She knelt in the sand, running her fingers along the smooth surface of the metal, tracing the jagged shards of the broken window.

"What's wrong?" Ye-kan asked, placing a hand on her shoulder. Turning to Li-na, he asked, "Why did you bring us here? I thought you were supposed to take us to where Ying is."

"Because this is where Ying is," Nian whispered in reply.

With a solemn expression on her face, Li-na began her account of what had happened. She told of how their trap had failed, and how almost half the Order's fleet had been wiped out. She spoke of the High Command's imminent defeat, how Ying had made the decision to pilot the sole functioning Bladebreaker in an attempt to hunt down Monggu Yutai and to strike the enemy where it would hurt most. And then she came to the end of her tale—of how they had all felt the seas tremble, and a thousand shards of broken glass floated upon the water's surface, catching the sunlight in the most dazzling way.

Even in death, a Blade was magnificent.

"Did you . . . find her?" Nian asked, turning toward Li-na with her tear-filled gaze.

The captain shook her head. "We only found the body of one of your guild masters," she said. "Not your sister."

"Th-th-that's impossible," Ye-kan muttered, collapsing beside Nian. "Ying can't be gone."

Picking herself back up to her feet, Nian wiped away the dampness from her cheeks. "What about the High Commander? Where is he?"

"After the Monggu clan's surrender, he left to search for your sister. I haven't seen him since," Li-na replied. "If you ask me, I don't think he's coming back."

"What do you mean, he's not coming back!" Ye-kan roared, rage filling his reddened eyes. "How could he have let Ying go off on her own like that? Why didn't he stop her!"

"Because she wouldn't have wanted him to," Nian replied softly. She bit down hard on her lip until she could taste the blood on the tip of her tongue.

No one could have stopped her.

As long as there was that one chance to help turn the war around, Ying would have taken it.

Something had changed in her sister when she returned from the first Bladebreaker mission. She had become more determined, more resolute—but she had also seemed more at peace with herself. This was what Ying wanted to do, even if it meant that she might never return.

"Beile-ye! Beile-ye!" Nergui interrupted. The High Commander's steward came running over, his robes a disheveled mess and strands of hair matted along the sides of his narrow face. He was clutching a gold-backed scroll in one hand and a folded sheet of parchment in the other. When he reached them, he panted several times to catch his breath, before saying, "I've been looking all over for you. The High Commander left you a decree . . . and a letter."

Ye-kan looked up, his expression glazed and unfocused. Seeing that he was in no condition to respond, Nian took the letter from out of Nergui's hand first, unfolding it gingerly. It had been written in Ye-yang's own hand, but there was a shakiness to his typically strong and confident strokes. Taking a deep breath, she began to read:

Fourteen, I do not expect you to forgive me for what I have done, but I must still apologize nonetheless. You and I were both born into a family where blood relations run thin, and even the ties between father and son can be sacrificed for the sake of power and ambition. I confess that I have always been somewhat jealous of you, because you grew up with the love and shelter of your e-niye, and had the privilege of being our a-ma's favorite son. That is, of course, through no fault of yours. Some of us are just luckier than others.

However, luck has also been showered upon me, because Abka Han chose to bring Ying to me. For the first time since my e-niye passed, there was once again a ray of sunshine in my life, but I feared that I would not be able to hold on to this beam of light. And so I told myself that this was not real, that I did not love her, that she was merely a tool that I needed in order to achieve my goals. I hurt her more terribly than anyone could, and when I finally realized how foolish I was, it was already too late. I made mistakes that could not be undone, and even though I gained the ultimate position of power, I lost what truly mattered to me. I lost Ying.

I will not make that same mistake again.

I know that I cannot reverse the wrongdoings that I have committed, and I cannot give your e-niye back to you, so the best I can do is to restore to you what is rightfully yours, and what she would have wanted for you. I trust that the nine isles will be well taken care of in your hands, and that Nian will serve as the loyal voice beside you when you are in need of guidance and comfort. Even though Monggu Yutai is gone, the dangers faced by the nine isles are not over. The Empire is decaying, but a decaying dragon is still a dragon none-theless. You must push on with our campaign against them, because that is the only way our people will be able to survive and prosper.

I wish the both of you the very best. May you lead the lives that Ying and I never could, and perhaps we may yet meet again one day, when you sit upon the dragon throne.

Your a-ge, Ye-yang

A single teardrop rolled down her cheek and onto the parchment, smudging the name that had been signed at the bottom. Li-na was right. The High Commander—or former High Commander—was not coming back.

How long had Ye-yang been planning this? From the moment they played their first game of weiqi, when he took her under his wing and began training her in the ways of politics and the court? Had he already been setting up the pieces then?

The letter was for Ye-kan, but it was also meant for her. Her heart trembled with the weight of the responsibility she had been given.

"'By decree of the High Commander,'" Nergui announced,

reciting from the unfurled scroll, "'the fourteenth beile, Aogiya Ye-kan, has proven himself to be a capable and worthy leader of the Eight Banners, having effectively served as regent in my absence, and later on successfully thwarting an attempted coup in Fei. This unprecedented war against the Monggu clan of Yokre could not have been won without his shrewd strategizing and decisive leadership, and through that, he has shown that he can be a dependable and committed caretaker of the Antaran isles and her people. With that, I formally hand over the position of High Commander and the imperial seal of the High Command to the fourteenth beile, who will henceforth succeed me as the leader of the Antaran people, to safeguard the peace across the nine isles.'"

Nian helped a thunderstruck Ye-kan back up, placing the decree firmly into his hand.

Staring down at it, the prince whispered, "Nian, what am I going to do?"

"Exactly what it says you have to."

Moonlight cast a shimmering hue of silver across the gardens of Qianlei Palace, complementing the warm light from the stone lantern holders that curved gracefully by the sides of the pebble-lined pathways. Upon a circular wooden platform that had been built in the middle of the garden, next to the gourd-shaped pond, a lithe figure spun in the air, the clean blade of her sword catching the light.

To be a lone rock in the middle of a flowing river.

To be that sharpened blade in the face of a thousand enemies.

To be the calm amid a raging storm.

Nian felt like she could better understand the meaning behind each line of that poem now, and translate that into each seamless movement of her body. Every stroke that she executed was smooth and confident, with a stability that might well rival a seasoned swordsman.

Another sword appeared in her field of vision, its tip pointing straight toward her head. She leaned backward, arching into a somersault. The blade went across her. Landing on the heel of her left qixie, she spun across the platform, her own sword twisting in a series of elegant curves. When she came to a stop, she pushed her weight forward. Her sword pierced through the air, coming to a stop barely a notch away from Ye-kan's throat.

The newly minted High Commander held his hands up in the air in surrender.

"Please have mercy on me, Lady Nian. It's all my fault," he begged.

Nian laughed, moving her sword away. She walked over to the stone table by the edge of the pond, pouring both of them a cup of wine from its jar.

"Your sword dance has improved tremendously," Ye-kan remarked. "You might even be able to defeat some of my junior commanders with those moves."

"When you've stared death in the face, suddenly wielding a sword isn't so difficult anymore." She raised her sleeve to her forehead, dabbing away the beads of sweat. "What brings you here at this hour?"

Ye-kan pouted. He sat down, resting his chin against the table.

"I just suffered through half a day of my uncle's lectures. Can't I come and seek some comfort from my wife?" he said.

"The wedding ceremony hasn't been conducted yet," Nian said, a blush dusting her cheeks, "and we're not supposed to see each other before that. It's bad luck."

"I don't believe in that superstitious nonsense. Besides, the date has already been fixed, and the invitations have been sent out. You can't back out now!"

Nian rolled her eyes. Even though he was now the High Commander, there was still a streak of childishness that he couldn't seem to get rid of. It was endearing, but sometimes she also wanted to smack it out of him.

It had been two months since the battle against the Monggu clan, and the nine isles were slowly beginning to rebuild themselves. With Ye-yang's decree, Ye-kan had officially succeeded the position of High Commander, but as expected, his rule was not yet stable. If it were not for Ula Temuu's continued presence in the capital in his new capacity as advisor to the High Commander, perhaps the second and third beiles might already have launched challenges against Ye-kan's command.

One of the more unexpected pieces of news that had emerged since then was her engagement to Ye-kan, which had stirred up quite a bit of debate within the court. There were many officials who disagreed with the decision, claiming that it was inappropriate given that Nian had previously been betrothed to Ye-yang. However, Ye-kan had been particularly belligerent about this, and surprisingly the Ula clan chieftain supported it. Nian suspected that a large part of it had to do with her brother's recent appointment as the new Minister for Trade, taking over from the disgraced Minister Tongiya.

"What did the Ula chieftain speak to you about this time?" she asked.

"He's worried about the refugee situation again. Says that resources in the nine isles are running low and that we cannot afford to feed any more mouths. What does he want me to do? Throw them back out to sea?"

"He's not wrong. I've seen the recent stocktake records from the Fei warehouses. The demand for food and basic necessities still far outstrips our supply. The situation might get dire in a few months." Nian rotated the cup between her fingers, pondering upon their predicament.

Although the pirate situation across the Dunzhu Straits had eased up now that they were no longer under the coordinated control of the Monggu clan, allowing for more trade ships to pass between the Antaran isles and the Empire, it still wasn't enough.

Maybe Ye-yang was right. A military campaign against the Empire is the only way.

But not now.

The Order had suffered heavy losses from the previous war, and they needed time to rest and regroup. Being hasty would only quicken their own demise.

"I have an idea," Ye-kan suddenly said, shooting upright. "How about you discuss these matters with my uncle on my behalf? Didn't Number Eight say that you had talent in strategy and politics?" He clapped his hands together. "It's a win-win situation. You're actually interested in all this, and my uncle will not be on the verge of getting an aneurysm every time he speaks to me."

"And you'll be running off to the Engineers Guild to tinker with their latest inventions again?" Nian arched a judgmental brow.

"Of course not! I shall be at the military camps training the men, and keeping an eye on Erden and Ye-han to make sure they've got nothing up their sleeves." He leaned over, resting his head on Nian's shoulder. "Being the High Commander is too tiring. Sometimes I wonder if that's the real reason why Number Eight left. He simply got tired of all this endless politicking, trying to please a bunch of people who will never be satisfied."

"Oh, did you only realize that now?"

"But at least I have you, my true advisor."

Nian flicked him across the forehead with her index finger. Turning her gaze up toward the clear night sky, she admired the tranquility of the blanket of stars that blinked back at her.

Are you out there, A-jie? Has he found you yet?

Two condors cried in reply, swooping across the moon with their giant wings of silver.

Somehow, Nian felt like they hadn't seen the last of Ye-yang, or of her sister, but that would be a story that would need to be left for another day. For now, peace had been restored across the nine isles, and the many souls whose blood had been spilled in exchange for this, whether rightfully or wrongfully, could finally be put to rest.

ACKNOWLEDGMENTS

The Fall of the Dragon duology has been several years in the making, and I'm so delighted to be able to say that it's finally finished! *Of Jade and Dragons* and *The Blood Phoenix* are the first two books that I've published, which makes them extremely special to me, and I'm thrilled to finally be able to share Ying's complete story with everyone.

Many thanks as always to my fabulous editors, Kelsey Murphy and Awo Ibrahim, for following through with this story from start to finish and helping to polish it into the beautiful final version that you're seeing now. A big thank-you as well to my agent, Laura Crockett, for all the enthusiasm and support you've shown for these books (and for *other* books too), and to Meg Davis, for helping to see this project through till the end. Thank you to the teams at Viking Children's and Penguin Random House UK for everything you've done for this book. To my cover illustrator and designers, Kelly Chong, Lily Qian, and Ellice Lee—I'm forever thankful and in awe for the gorgeous covers you've put together! To my publicity and marketing teams—Jenna Smith, Sarah Doyle, Chess Vincent, Ericka Serrano, Keri Horan, Jennifer Javier—thanks very much for all the support you've given to these books, and for helping to get these books in front of readers everywhere. To my audiobook team from Listening Library and narrator Jen Zhao—big thanks for creating such a gorgeous audio version of the story and for bringing these characters to life. Each and every one of you has played such a big role in helping me launch my writing career, and I'll forever be grateful.

To my family—thank you for being my biggest fans, enthusiastically reading my books and taking pictures of them in every bookstore.

To the Chillichurls—Jenny Pang, Amy Leow, Saika Tsai, Cindy Chen, and Trisa Leung—thanks for being my writing besties, and for all the banter about books, Seventeen, *Genshin*, and other random things under the sun. I shall always be here kicking all of you into finishing your manuscripts!

I would also like to take the opportunity to shout out to the teams from Illumicrate and Owlcrate who have put so much effort into creating the beautiful special editions of *Of Jade and Dragons*, and to the amazingly creative artists who have brought Ying, Ye-yang, and the nine isles to life. Thank you also to the editors and translators who have worked on the various translated editions of these books—I'm so excited to be able to share this story with more readers across the world!

To everyone who has picked up a copy of *Of Jade and Dragons* and *The Blood Phoenix*, I hope you've enjoyed the story and that some part of Ying, Ye-yang, Nian, and Ye-kan's journey has resonated with you. Thank you for joining me on this adventure, and for all the love and support you've shown to this baby author and her first books. I want you to know that I truly appreciate every comment, review, photo, like, and share that you've given to these books, and I hope you'll stick around for more stories to come!